Praise for Dee Henderson and her novels

"This poignant tale [is] sure to touch every reader's heart."
—*RT Book Reviews* on *The Marriage Wish*

"This touching story of faith and acceptance shows how trust in God can turn a difficult struggle into happiness."
—*RT Book Reviews* on *God's Gift*

"This is a great romance dealing with complex matters of faith."
—*RT Book Reviews* on *The Guardian*

"*The Negotiator* is sterling romantic suspense; lots of action, and plot twists tempered with the gentle intimacy of a sweet love story. Brava, Ms. Henderson."
—*RT Book Reviews*

DEE HENDERSON
The Marriage Wish

&

God's Gift

Love Inspired

Recycling programs
for this product may
not exist in your area.

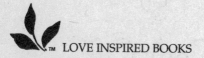

™ LOVE INSPIRED BOOKS

ISBN-13: 978-0-373-65151-1

THE MARRIAGE WISH AND GOD'S GIFT

THE MARRIAGE WISH
Copyright © 1998 by Dee Henderson

GOD'S GIFT
Copyright © 1998 by Dee Henderson

This edition published by arrangement with Love Inspired Books.

® and TM are trademarks of Love Inspired Books, used under license. Trademarks indicated with ® are registered in the United States Patent and Trademark Office, the Canadian Trade Marks Office and in other countries.

www.LoveInspiredBooks.com

Printed in U.S.A.

CONTENTS

Books by Dee Henderson

Love Inspired

The Marriage Wish
God's Gift

DEE HENDERSON

is the daughter of a minister, serves as church treasurer and is currently part of the launch team for a new church. She reads extensively, writes nonfiction, as well as fiction, and frequently can be found online. "Stories are my way of opening a dialog with people on how God has interacted in their lives."

THE MARRIAGE WISH

Thou hast turned for me
my mourning into dancing.
—*Psalms* 30:11

Chapter One

If Trish sat any closer to Brad, she would be in his lap.

Scott Williams watched his friend keep shifting closer to her husband on the couch and Brad keep trying to squeeze closer to the arm of the couch. Trish was doing it deliberately. Scott's parents, sitting at the other end of the long couch, had plenty of room, but Brad hadn't caught on to that fact yet. Scott wanted to laugh. The games newlyweds played.

No, he had to revise that, it wasn't just the newlyweds. His sister, Heather, was sitting in her husband Frank's lap, and they had been married ten years now. Heather was pregnant again and refused to sit down to rest so Frank had solved the problem. Heather didn't seem to mind. She was flirting with her husband, whispering things in his ear when she thought no one was watching. Frank was enjoying it, Scott noted. He suspected they would come up with an excuse not to linger after the party was over.

His birthday party. He was thirty-eight today. Scott looked at the coffee table and was grateful to see there were only two gifts left. He really appreciated his parents' efforts, and he was enjoying the night with his family and friends, but right at this moment he wished he had spent his birthday alone. He felt lonely, and being here just made the problem worse.

He sat in the winged-back chair, his long legs stretched out in front of him, a bowl of cashews at his elbow and his second diet cola beginning to sweat. His parents had cooked out for dinner, barbecued chicken with roasted potatoes and fresh ears of corn. It had been a fun dinner, it always was when all the family was together, but he hated feeling like a third wheel. It had never bothered him before that everyone but him had someone special, but it was bothering him tonight. For the first time in his life he felt envy and it was a disquieting sensation.

He should be married by now. For years his focus had been on building his career, serving in his church, being a loyal friend, being a much loved uncle to his niece and nephew. He had never thought he needed a wife to make his life complete. He had been wrong.

His gaze settled on Amy a couple steps away, holding his next-to-last gift. When he saw her, his face relaxed into the special smile he reserved just for his niece. She wore the dolphin shirt he had brought back from Florida for her. It was her "most favorite" shirt she had told him when he had arrived that night. Heather said she had trouble getting it off long enough to wash it. Scott grinned. He would buy this little lady the moon if she wanted it. She was four, and he adored her. Amy grinned and climbed into his lap. "Uncle Scott, this feels like a book," she told him importantly. He took the package and weighed it in his hands.

"I think you're right. Like to help?" He turned the

package to let her at the tape. With full concentration, Amy worked at ripping the paper.

"Thank you, Mom." Margaret had bought him a cookbook, this one on breakfast foods. She knew he loved to cook, had seriously considered becoming a professional chef back in his college days. He didn't have company for breakfast very often; he promised himself he'd rectify that problem.

"I think you'll like the muffin recipes," she said with a smile.

Scott added the book to the small stack of gifts on the floor beside his chair.

"Last one," Greg, his nephew, told him as he brought over a two-foot-long package. Greg was eight years old, further evidence of how time slipped by without Scott realizing it. Scott could remember the pleasure of holding him as an infant, could remember the way Greg at two and three had always found him at church on Sunday mornings, and Scott would pick him up and carry him and make him feel important.

"Thank you, Greg."

The gift was from his dad. Scott opened the package as Amy held it steady for him. His eyes lit up when he saw what it was. A new fishing rod. "This is great, Dad." The perfect gift for a man with a new boat.

Larry smiled. "You've about worn out the last one I gave you," he said. Scott had to agree. But that fishing pole was lucky. He had caught his biggest bass with that rod. Still, this one was a beauty. It would be a pleasure to break it in.

He had spent the morning out on the water doing what he did every year on his birthday, evaluating his past year and laying out his priorities for the coming year. It had been hard to face the truth. He was thirty-eight, alone, and even his mom no longer asked when he was going to get married and have a family. As good as his life had been to date, he had been wrong to assume he wanted to spend it alone. He wanted what his friends and family had. He wanted marriage and kids.

The cake was brought in from the kitchen and the candles lit. Scott looked around the group that gathered around the table, especially the kids, and he grinned and turned his attention to the candles. He paused to make a wish.

Lord, how did I ever think I could go through my entire life single? I've enjoyed the freedom and the success in my career, but I never intended it to become a permanent arrangement. There isn't someone to go home to tonight, and I'm feeling that sadness. I really miss not having a wife and having that close, intimate friendship I see in these couples around me. I want to change that, Lord. I want to get married. I want to have what the others around me have. I don't want to be alone anymore.

Scott blew out the candles.

It was a cold morning for late August. The darkness was giving way to the dawn, creating an early-morning twilight. Jennifer St. James pushed her hands deeper into the lined pockets of her windbreaker, trying to ward off the chill. The wind coming off the lake was sending shivers up her spine. The peaceful beauty of the deserted beach, however, more than made up for her discomfort. It had been a difficult night.

She walked along the water's edge, kicking up sand and watching the water smooth it back into place.

"Good morning."

Her older brother had drilled safety precautions into her for so long that she reacted by instinct, her feet breaking into the start of a sprint to ensure she wasn't pinned between water and a threat. No sane person was up at this time of morning.

"Easy!" the man walking a few feet over from her exclaimed, "I didn't mean to startle you."

Jennifer let her sprint fade away and came to a stop several feet up the beach, her heart racing. He had said good-morning. That was all. Good-morning. She'd made a fool of herself again. She felt the heat warm her face. Was she cursed to live her entire life starting at every surprise? She had badly overreacted. She rested her hands against her knees, ignoring the hair that blew around her face, trying to still her racing heart. She watched the man warily as he moved toward her. He was a tall man, reminding her somewhat of her brother's build, probably a basketball player with those long legs and upper-body muscle. As he drew nearer she could see dark brown hair, wavy in a way that made her envious, clear piercing blue eyes and strong features; he was probably in his mid thirties. She had never seen him before, he was the type of man she would have remembered. Not that she came to this stretch of beach very often anymore. Her gut clenched. She hadn't been back in precisely three years.

"Are you okay?" He had stopped about five feet away.

She nodded. Why did he have to be out taking a walk this morning of all mornings? The beach was supposed to be deserted at this hour. The last thing she wanted was conversation with a stranger. She looked and felt a mess. Normally she could care less what she looked like, but when it led to being embarrassed, she cared. Her jeans were the most ratty in her closet, and the jacket hid what had once been a paint sweatshirt of Jerry's.

"I didn't mean to frighten you." His voice was deep and full of concern.

"I didn't realize you were there."

"So I found out."

She straightened slowly, pushing her hands off her knees and forcing her legs to take her weight again, fighting the weakness and the light-headed sensation that hallmarked the exhaustion and dwindling adrenaline.

"You're not okay."

She shied away from the concern in his face, in his voice, instinctively took a step back as he took a step forward. "I had a long night. I'll be fine."

She looked down the beach to the distant grove of trees she had arbitrarily been walking toward. Awkwardly, because he was here and her solitude had been broken, Jennifer turned to resume her walk. The weariness was suddenly weighing heavily on her, and her desire to keep walking was fading, but her only choice was to go home, and that was not an option. She shoved her hair back from her face again and twisted the long hair once, in an old habit, to temporarily prevent it from blowing in her eyes.

"Would you mind if I walk with you?"

She was surprised at the question, surprised at the sudden tenseness in his voice, surprised at the rigidness she saw in his stance as if he had momentarily frozen. She couldn't understand the change. His hands had closed into fists at his sides, but as she watched, they opened and relaxed, almost as if he consciously willed them to do so. He had kept his distance after that one step forward and her one step back. She was not a very good judge of character, but she somehow knew he was not going to be a threat to her. She shrugged. It really didn't matter. "No." He fell into step beside her, slowing his pace to match her slow wander.

They walked along the beach in silence, a few feet apart, both with hands tucked in their jackets, the wind blowing their hair. Jennifer's thoughts drifted back to the night before, and she winced as she remembered, began to mentally draw big *X*s through each scene and force herself to deliberately try to discard the memories. It had worked in the past and it would work again. With time. When the memories faded to the point she could discard them. She sighed, haunted. These memories were not going to go away. Not for a very long time. There was a distraction at hand and she chose to ignore her own rule of respecting silence. "What's your name?" she asked, not looking at him, but knowing he was looking at her. He had been watching her since they started walking and it was a disconcerting sensation. Hers were the first words spoken in several minutes, and the sound of her voice was out of place in the quiet dawn.

"Scott Williams," he replied. "Yours?"

"Jennifer St. James."

She realized immediately her mistake. Questions prompted questions. On this particular morning, even a polite social exchange felt like an intrusion. She breathed a silent sigh of relief when he asked that one question and then went silent. She was grateful he was content with his own thoughts, but she wished he would move his gaze away from her.

"I haven't seen you walking on this beach before. Do you live around here?" he asked eventually.

She shook her head.

"My home is up ahead, off the point," he told her. Jennifer thought it must be nice to live on the lake, be able to enjoy this beach whenever the notion struck. It was expensive property. They walked in silence again and Jennifer hoped the next thing said was going to be goodbye.

"What happened last night, Jennifer?"

His voice was low and deep, the emotion carefully checked. He had stopped walking and was watching her closely, watching her reaction. "What?" Jennifer honestly didn't know how to answer the question.

"You're married. You have a beaut of a black eye. I want to know what happened, so I can decide what I should do," he elaborated patiently, but tensely. There was nothing idle about his body language or his focus on her.

She didn't answer him right away. What was she suppose to say? She already felt horrible. The last thing she wanted was someone treading in an area of her life where she herself was not yet able to cope. "They are not related."

He removed a hand from his jacket pocket and reached out slowly, clearly afraid he would startle her again, to gently touch the swelling that radiated around her right eye and down her cheek, and when he spoke, the emotion was no longer contained. "Jennifer, this is recent."

His touch burned and made her cringe inside over

everything she had lost. "I walked into a door," she said flatly.

He frowned. His entire face tightened at her non-answer and her rejection of his question. "Jennifer..."

He wanted to help and it was the last thing she wanted. "I don't want to talk about it." Her voice was firm, rigid and laden with warning. Scott wanted to protest. She could see that. All the signs where there. The clenched hand, the set jaw, the eyes that refused to yield the question. But something stopped him, and he pushed his hand back into the pocket of his jacket and nodded abruptly before looking away. Jennifer watched, grateful. He was angry and doing his best not to direct it toward her. She had left an awful dilemma for him, but she couldn't release him from it. She did look battered. She was bruised, tired, exhausted and jumpy. But for the life of her she simply couldn't explain the truth. She could barely cope with it herself. She simply couldn't deal with it this morning.

He started walking again, and she followed him. He deliberately shortened his steps so she would once again be walking across from him. They walked along in silence, and Jennifer could see Scott measuring every step she took, measuring the growing exhaustion, the heaviness of the fatigue that made her veer off center time and time again. She could do little about what he saw. She was exhausted and she knew it and she had no reserves left.

They'd gone more than a mile down the beach and were near a private boathouse and pier when he stopped. "This is my home." He said the words, and she heard that he hated saying them. He didn't want to go. He didn't want to leave his questions unanswered. He wanted to help. She read all of those desires as he stood and looked at her. She did her best to look directly back, even if the intensity of his gaze made her want to drop her eyes and look away. "Could I walk with you a while longer? Would you like some company?" he asked, and she could feel the tug to let him do so.

She shook her head. She suddenly realized what a mess she'd created, and the fact that she had no desire to fix it both amused her and made her sad. She smiled, and it was the first genuine smile she had formed in the past seventy-two hours. "No. I'll be just fine, Scott. Thank you for offering."

He didn't want to hear that answer. "You're sure?"

He was pressing her to change her mind, and her sense of fatigue grew all the greater. She needed to be alone now more than ever. There was no room in her life for company and conversation when there were memories demanding her attention.

Jennifer nodded. "Go on. I'm just going to walk for a while longer," she assured him.

He reluctantly did as she asked. Jennifer watched as he walked up the path to his back patio. She turned toward the grove of trees and began to walk again, determined to not return home until her body demanded sleep and the memories were banished. A few minutes later she was frowning, angry with the fact she now suddenly missed the company. No, not company, him. She missed him. The sun was barely up, and she was thinking about a stranger. She would never see him again, but he had entered her life briefly on one of the toughest mornings of her life, and she would probably always remember him because of that one fact.

Jennifer racked the balls, flipping them to solid, stripe, solid, the eight ball in the center, and sent the cue ball rolling to the far end of the table. The college kids at the next table to the right were laughing at rather crude jokes, and the group of six guys at the bar were boisterous and drunk. Jennifer ignored them with the ease of practice. The first two tables to her left were empty, but Randy and William were playing at the third, and she occasionally tuned in to their conversation, a rather fascinating discussion of a drug case that had been in the papers the past couple of days. The two cops were serious players, and she often played one or the other during the course of an evening. Tonight she preferred to play alone. She broke the rack of balls with a vicious stroke—short, explosive, centered.

She had killed Thomas Bradford tonight.

The chapter, written an hour ago, sat in her briefcase, scrawled by hand on a tablet of white paper while she sat at the back corner booth, shelling peanuts and nursing a diet cola.

The only thing she had left was her career and she had just hung it out to dry. Ann was going to kill her; her agent would not appreciate having the golden goose killed. Jennifer smiled tightly without it reaching her eyes and drilled the seven ball into the rail to send it the length of the table and into a corner pocket. He was quite dead, her detective, Thomas Bradford, the bullets having hit him in the middle of the back and ripped through his chest. He was now as dead as her parents, as dead as her husband, as dead as her three-month-old daughter. Dead.

Maybe she should sell the house.

She contemplated the idea as she moved around the table, laying out her next shot with the precision of someone who had learned to see the game as an interesting study in geometry.

"Jen, what the hell happened? Who hit you?!" The jacket dropped onto the stool next to her, the detective's shield flipping visible. Randy and William both looked over at Bob's words and immediately left their game, heading her way. Jennifer looked up at her friend, annoyed, and then looked back at the cue ball and laid her next shot with finesse, nudging the ten ball into the side pocket without disturbing the eight ball. She wasn't surprised to see him. It was midnight, and Bob Volishburg got off at eleven-thirty. He knew her car. This place was on his way home. He would come in to talk with the other guys from the force, maybe play her a game and then see that she got safely home. He had a mission in life to see that she always got home safely. Compliments of her brother, Jennifer was sure.

"I walked into a door," she replied flatly.

The honest answer went over about as well tonight with the three cops as it had done four days earlier with Scott.

"I was wondering if you would come back," Scott said, stopping a few feet away from her so as not to crowd her space and startle her. His voice was calm and steady while inside his reaction was one of elation. She was back. He had been praying and hoping and working toward this day. She was sitting out on the pier behind his house, dangling her feet over the edge, her hands tucked into the same windbreaker she had worn the last time he had seen her.

He had spent ten days trying to track her down. His conscience had given him no rest. He had finally decided she must have an unlisted phone number. He had tried every St. James in the phone books for the surrounding area. He had ended up calling every battered women's shelter in the surrounding county—not that they would tell him anything, but he had had to try. He had been ready to consider calling the police and the local hospitals, she continued to weigh so heavily on his mind. Then, three days ago, he had his first bit of what he knew had to be providential luck.

He had been browsing a local bookstore when he had chanced upon her picture. She was a writer. The author of a mystery series about a detective named Thomas Bradford. Scott had held the book in his hand and looked at the picture and been stunned at the change in her from the picture on the back of the paperback to the woman he had met on the beach. The book was the paperback release of a previous hardback so he figured the picture was about four years old. The difference was painful to see. Her face was gaunt now. The light in her eyes was gone. What had happened to her in the past few years? Calling her publisher had managed to get him the name of her agent, but there his luck had run out. Her agent—Ann something or other—had refused to give him any information about Jennifer. All he'd been able to hope for was that she would deliver a message.

Jennifer turned now on the pier, drew her knees up to drape her arms across them and quietly looked up at him as he stood at the top of the steps to the pier. "Hello, Scott. I understand you have been looking for me." Her voice was dry and her smile slightly amused.

She looked like hell. The black eye had faded to an ugly dark bruise that marred her cheek, and the tenseness in her body and in her face reminded him of a rubber band stretched to its limit for a very long time. "I was worried about you," he said simply.

She nodded and looked down to spin her wedding ring for a moment before looking back up. "Don't be. I'm fine."

Fine compared with what? Her black eye was now an ugly bruise, and she looked as brittle as toffee. She had been exhausted the last time he'd seen her, and the past ten days hadn't made much of an improvement. She looked well past worn out. He walked down and sat on the steps to the pier, close, but not so close as to crowd her. The last thing he wanted to do was give her reason to move. "Been taking another walk?"

"Sort of," she replied. She smiled, and it was a real smile. "I haven't gotten very far."

"Which message finally reached you?" he asked, interlacing his fingers and watching her.

"My agent called. Relayed your message. Really, Scott, 'Come stay with me' does raise a few eyebrows among my friends."

She was embarrassed now; he could see the blush. He knew that his message might cause her some embarrassment with her agent, but it was what needed to be said. He was serious. His home had plenty of guest rooms. He would prefer she accept a place with his sister and her husband, but he would make whatever arrangements she considered reasonable. The idea of someone, her husband, hitting her had haunted him. "I wanted to make sure you knew you had a safe place to stay."

She sighed and dropped her hand to rub it along a wooden beam of the pier. "Scott, I walked into a door."

"So you said," he agreed evenly, very aware of the

fact she was not looking at him again. She did it when she didn't want him to see the truth in her eyes.

She looked up. She didn't even look offended that he didn't believe her. She did look like she was in pain. She ran her hand through her hair. "Monday night before we met," she said abruptly, "the third anniversary of my husband's death. I got myself royally drunk. Finally went to bed about 3:00 a.m. When I woke up I headed for the bathroom. I was in a bit of a hurry. I ran right into the edge of the bedroom door." She didn't spare herself when it came to telling the story.

She was a widow. A chunk of his gut tightened. "Jen, I'm sorry. You're way too young to be widow." He put together what she had said, what he had seen, and he winced. "You must have had an awful night."

She grimaced. "That's one way to describe it." The memories of that night came rushing back, and she felt the tension radiate up through her shoulders and neck. She wanted so badly to forget that night. She had thought drinking would help her forget, but it hadn't. If anything, it had simply given her one more memory to regret.

She picked up a small twig the wind had blown down onto the pier and twirled it between her fingers. "How did you find out I was a writer?" she asked, changing the subject.

"I found *Dead Before Dawn* at the local bookstore."

"Honey, it's a perfect title. It's short. To the point. An attention grabber."

"Jerry, there isn't a single murder in the whole book."

"Then let's add one. It's a great title. Great titles are hard to come by."

The memories haunted her. Jennifer tossed the twig she held into the water and watched the waves push it around. Scott's answer surprised her. The paperback was out already? She had lost track of the publishing schedule. "Jerry liked the title," she told Scott.

Scott wasn't sure how to interpret Jennifer's expression, there was distance there and memories of the past. Did she not like to talk about her work? Jerry—was that her husband's name? "It was a very good book," he told her, trying to feel out what she would consider comfortable to talk about.

He thought she was a very good writer. He had bought *Dead Before Dawn* and read it in one evening, not finishing until well after midnight. He had searched bookstores during the past two days until he found all eight of her books. They were now piled on his nightstand in the order she had written them. He was almost done with the first book in her series, the book that introduced Thomas Bradford. Her series was great. The closest comparison he could draw was to Robert Parker's Spenser novels, and he loved those books.

"I'm glad you liked it." She shivered slightly as the breeze picked up.

"Would you like to join me for breakfast?" The question came out before he realized it was going to be asked. He instantly regretted it. Had he learned nothing about her so far? Give her an opportunity to leave and she was going to take it. She had accomplished what she had come here to do—acknowledge his message and set him straight as to what had actually happened. How many times in the past ten days had he told himself he would be careful not to make her shy away from him again?

He felt an enormous sense of relief when he saw her smile. "That depends. Are you a good cook?"

He laughed. "You'll have to decide that for yourself. I like to think I am."

She moved to stand up, and he offered her a hand, feeling delighted when she accepted the offer. Her hand was small and the fingers callused, and she would have a hard time tipping a scale past a hundred pounds. He lifted her easily to her feet. The top of her head came to just above his shoulder, a comfortable height for him, and her long auburn hair was clipped back this morning by a carved gold barrette. Up close, her brown eyes were captivating. He forced himself to release her hand and step away once she was on her feet. He wanted to reach out and touch her cheek, say he was glad to see her bruise beginning to heal. Instead, he shoved his hands into his pockets and gently smiled as he waited for her to precede him.

The back patio door was unlocked, and they entered into a large kitchen, adjacent to a formal dining room. The coffee was brewed, the aroma rich and strong. Scott placed his jacket and hers across one of the six kitchen chairs and held out a chair for her at the glass-topped table.

His kitchen was spotless, a matter of honor with him. He found that cooking relaxed him, so he spent a lot of time here unwinding after a day of work. "Do you have any preferences for what you would like?" he asked, mentally reviewing the contents of the refrigerator. He had been planning homemade muffins, peaches and cereal for his own breakfast this morning, but that was pretty routine. He wanted this breakfast to be special. Maybe eggs Benedict, or fresh blueberry waffles, he could even do a batch of breakfast crepes with fresh strawberries.

"Since breakfast is normally coffee and maybe toast or a bagel, I think I'll let you decide," she replied.

He turned from the open refrigerator to look at her, knowing immediately that what breakfast normally was, was skipped. The last thing this lady needed to be doing was skipping meals. "Breakfast is the most important meal of the day, you should at least try to have something like muffins and fruit," he told her firmly. "How about an omelet?" he offered. He did a great omelet.

"Sure." She spotted the bookcase he had in the kitchen for his cookbooks and got up to study them. "These are all yours?" she asked, surprised.

"Yes." He started pulling items from the refrigerator. Ham. Tomatoes. Green peppers. Cheese.

He watched as she randomly selected one of the cookbooks from the bookcase and opened it. "Why are the page corners turned down?" she asked.

"A favorite recipe," he replied. As the eggs cooked and he chopped the ham and tomatoes and green peppers, he reviewed the dishes he liked to cook, pointing out different cookbooks and which recipes were uniquely good in each one. It was a comfortable conversation. He liked to talk about his hobby, and she was more than casually interested. It was a comfortable conversation that continued as they ate. They split a western omelet between them and a half dozen warm, homemade blueberry muffins. It was not until they finished breakfast that the conversation turned back to personal subjects.

"How did Jerry die?" Scott asked quietly as he sat

watching her drink her second cup of coffee. He didn't want to ask, but he needed to know.

She looked out the large window and out over the lake. "He'd gone to the gym to play racquetball with my brother when he collapsed. He died of a massive heart attack."

How old would he have been? Thirty? Thirty-five? "It was unexpected," Scott said, stating the obvious.

"Very."

He looked at the wedding ring she wore. He had noticed it ten days ago, a small heart of diamonds, and it looked like it belonged. "Was there any warning? High blood pressure? A history in his family?"

She shook her head. "No. He had passed a complete physical not more than six months before."

"I'm sorry, Jennifer." It was such an inadequate response. Her life had been torn apart, and all he could convey was words. She would have felt the loss like a knife cutting into her, especially if they had been a close couple. "You loved him a great deal." Scott made the observation, more to himself than her, but she answered him, anyway.

"I still do," she replied calmly.

He heard her answer and was envious that love could be so enduring. Not many couples had that kind of closeness. No wonder the anniversary of his death had been so painful for her.

She set down her cup of coffee and changed the subject abruptly. "I've decided to end the series of books."

Scott didn't know what to think, both of the abrupt change of subject and the statement she had just made. She couldn't be serious. She had been writing the series for almost ten years. She wanted to end it? "Thomas Bradford is going to get killed?"

"Yes."

"Why?"

"Because it's not the same without Jerry."

"You wrote the books with your husband?"

She nodded.

Scott didn't say anything for some time. It wasn't wise to make such dramatic life changes when you were grieving. But the books had to be a continual reminder to her of what she had lost. "You've been writing the series for years. Are you sure, Jennifer?" he finally asked.

"I'm sure. I've known for months it's something I needed to do."

"What are you going to do once the series is finished?" he asked.

"I don't know."

He frowned, not liking one possibility that had come to mind. "You are still going to write, aren't you?"

"It is the only profession I know."

He leaned back in his chair, thinking, studying her. He had never known a writer before, and it was hard to make any sort of intelligent judgment about the decision she had to make. The sadness he saw in her expression made him frown. She needed some help. She needed to recover. She needed someone to ensure she ate. He forced himself not to follow that line of thinking any further.

"Do you know when you start how the book is going to end?" He had always wondered that. He assumed that knowing in advance would be helpful as far as clues and situations were concerned, but on the other hand, knowing the ending would make writing the book less interesting. Like seeing a movie for the second time.

Jennifer couldn't stop the memory from returning—

"Jerry, you can't kill the gardener. He's the man who stole the will to protect Nicole's inheritance. Kill the gardener and the will disappears forever." Jennifer didn't like the twist Jerry had added to the well constructed story. They had spent two months hammering out the details of a tight story plot and Jerry was changing the game plan a hundred pages into the book. They were out in the backyard, Jerry reclining in his hammock watching the 49ers and Rams game on his portable TV, Jennifer having come outside to find him. She dropped into the lawn chair beside him, retrieving the two pillows on the ground to use as a headrest. She was distracted momentarily as she realized she had missed the start of the game.

"Who said the gardener was dead?" Jerry asked, handing her a diet soda from the cooler beside him.

"Thanks," Jennifer said, accepting the cold drink. She flipped open the dog-eared manuscript. *"Page ninety-six, and I quote, 'The bullet entered the man's chest and did not exit. He fell forward into the cold waters of the lake without anyone seeing his departure from among the living.'"* She dropped the script on his chest. *"That sounds like dead to me."*

The 49ers threw a deep pass which was caught inside the twenty. The discussion paused while they both watched the replay.

"Did I ever say the man in the boat was the gardener?"

Jennifer thought about it carefully. "No. The killer assumed the man in the boat was the gardener."

Jerry grinned. "Exactly."

"Okay Jerry, what are you planning?"

"I don't know," he replied seriously.

Jennifer tossed one of the pillows at him. "Why do you always insist on adding wrinkles to our nicely planned books?" she demanded, amused.

Jerry smiled. "I have to keep you guessing somehow, don't I?"

Scott watched as Jennifer struggled to come back from somewhere in the past and answer the question he had asked. It was not the first time he had seen memories cross her eyes, and he wondered what memory had just made her smile. "Every book we wrote had at least one major change in the plot by the time we finished writing the story. We would construct an outline for the book, then take turns writing chapters. Invariably Jerry would create a few extra twists in the story."

Jennifer rested her hands loosely around the coffee mug and was amazed at how easy it was to talk to Scott about the past. Normally sharing about her life with Jerry brought back the pain, but not today. They were memories of good times, and she had thought they were gone forever.

She had been so embarrassed by her panicked flight, her reluctance to explain exactly how she had gotten the black eye. It had taken over a week to put the incident into the back of her mind, get past the embarrassment, and thankfully accept the fact she would never have to see Scott Williams again. The next morning her agent had called. Jennifer had wanted to crawl into a hole and die. Her one consolation had been the mistaken belief that Scott would have at least let the incident go. It had taken her forty-eight hours to work up the nerve to come back to this beach. She was glad now she had. Glad that now he knew the truth.

"You know what I do for a living, what about you, Scott?"

"I'm CEO of an electronics firm called Johnson Electronics."

"Really?" She had expected him to be high up in some corporate setting, but she had not expected this answer. "How long have you been CEO?"

"Three years. They've been good years for the industry, so I haven't had to weather my first downturn in the business. How well we do then will determine how good I am at this job."

Interesting answer. A man who considered his performance under adversity to be the true measure of this worth. "You've been at Johnson Electronics a long time?" He was young to be a CEO.

"Eighteen years. I started out as a draftsman during my junior college days. I worked as an electrical engineer, got an MBA and moved into management."

Jennifer asked him about every facet of the business she could think of—products, competitors, partners, financial numbers. She found the picture he presented of his company fascinating. He shared the smallest details, and she found his grasp of the business remarkable. It was obvious he loved his job. They talked for another thirty minutes before Jennifer rose to her feet and said it was time for her to be leaving.

"Jennifer, I've got tickets for the musical *Chess* next Saturday night. It's an old play, kind of dated, but it's a benefit performance and will be well attended. Would you like to join me?"

His offer caught her by surprise. She had to think about it for a few moments. She had not been on a date since Jerry died. She'd had no desire to. "Thank you Scott, I would like that," she finally replied. She was lonely. She knew it. And he was good no-pressure company. A night out would be a welcome diversion.

"The play starts at eight-thirty. I'll pick you up at seven and we can have dinner first?"

She smiled and wondered how far he would extend the invitation if she let him. Dinner before and coffee afterward? "Sure, we can do dinner first," she agreed.

He grinned and she liked the grin. "Good. I want an address and a phone number."

She laughed. "I like my privacy, hence the unlisted phone number." She wrote down the information on a piece of paper he pulled from a notepad beside the phone.

As he walked with her across the back patio and down to the beach, she slipped on her jacket and freed her long hair from the collar. "Thank you for breakfast, Scott."

"It was my pleasure, Jennifer. I'll pick you up at seven o'clock Saturday."

Chapter Two

She was late. Jennifer rushed up the front walk of her home, fumbling with her keys. Scott was going to arrive in less than an hour. Her detour to Rachel and Peter's to drop off a book had been a mistake. Her brother had wanted to debate the wisdom of her ending the Thomas Bradford mystery series and she hadn't been able to invent an adequate excuse to leave. She knew better than to mention Scott and a date. She would never have gotten out of there. Peter took the responsibility of being her older brother very seriously.

Jennifer pushed open the front door to be met with the fragrant smell of roses. The bouquet sitting in the center of her dining room table had arrived Wednesday. Three dozen red, white and peach roses. The card had simply said "Looking forward to Saturday—Scott." Jennifer had started crying. She couldn't help it. It had been a long time since anyone had sent her roses.

"Jerry, I got a special delivery today." Jennifer was curled up beside her husband on the couch, using his

shoulder as a pillow. The credits of the late, late movie were beginning to roll by.

"You did?" Jerry asked, feigning surprise. His finger gently traced the curve of her jaw.

She smiled. "I think it was a bribe."

"What was it?"

"Two dozen red roses."

"It was a bribe," Jerry agreed. "You know how much red roses cost these days?" he asked, amused.

She giggled.

"So what do you suppose this mystery person wants?"

Jerry leaned down to kiss her. "That's hard to say," he said softly. "I suppose you had better ask him."

Jennifer turned on the couch to face him. "So what do you think my husband would like in return for two dozen red roses?"

The memory stopped Jennifer in the doorway. She sighed. These memories were going to drive her crazy.

She dressed with care. She had shopped for a new outfit. Those in her closet held too many memories. She had found a light green, long-sleeved dress. It looked expensive, moved with grace, and it helped her badly shaking self-esteem. She had bought a purse and new shoes to go with the dress. The gold necklace and earrings she wore had been a gift from Jerry.

She was ready before Scott arrived. To keep from pacing back and forth Jennifer went into her office, picked up the black three-ring binder on her desk and the red pen beside it. She turned on the stereo, already tuned to a favorite jazz station. Finding the page marked with a paper clip, she picked up the work where she'd left off, soon forgetting the time.

The doorbell rang. Quickly slipping the paper clip

onto the top of the page she was on, she set the book back on the desk and went to answer the door.

He stood there, looking at the profusion of flowers growing around her porch, elegantly dressed in black slacks and an ivory dress shirt, contained, comfortable. A pleased smile lit his face as he turned and saw her. "Hello, Jennifer."

She smiled back. "Hello, Scott." She stepped back to let him enter her home. "Thank you for the flowers." She motioned to the arrangement, already nervous.

"You're welcome," Scott replied easily. "Did you have a good week?"

"Quiet," she replied. "Let me get my purse and jacket and I'll be ready to go."

She entered the living room, and he followed her. It was a simple room. A fireplace, couch, coffee table, easy chair, two end tables, display shelves. A prominent bookshelf held all the Thomas Bradford first editions.

The pictures caught Scott's attention. There were several on the fireplace mantel, one on the end table. Her wedding picture. Jerry. Scott looked at the picture for several moments. His competition. He was surprised at the feeling, but it could not be ignored. He was competing with Jennifer's memories of Jerry. Jennifer looked different in the pictures. She looked young. She looked happy. The past few years had taken a great toll.

"I'm ready," she said quietly.

He turned to find she had joined him again. He smiled. "Then let's go."

Scott held her jacket for her to slip on. "You look beautiful tonight," he said softly. The soft green dress had caught his attention the moment she'd opened the door, and he'd been watching it flair around her, wondering at the elegance she presented and how many more surprises she had in store for him. She was beautiful. Her face had healed, and while she still looked thin, there was color in her face and life in her eyes tonight.

She flushed. "Thank you."

He gently slipped her long hair free from the collar of the jacket.

After she locked the front door, Jennifer walked beside Scott to his car, an expensive sports car. He held the passenger door, and Jennifer slipped inside. Her car was comfortable and dependable. This car was pure luxury.

"How does Italian sound?" Scott asked, looking over at her inquiringly.

"I love it," Jennifer replied.

Scott nodded as he started the car. "I know a great place."

Jennifer began to relax. Scott drove well, and she found it was a relief to be able to sit back and let someone else manage the traffic. They shared a comfortable silence, rather than the strained one she had feared.

"I've been looking forward to this evening all week," Scott said, breaking the silence.

Jennifer looked over at him, and a chuckle escaped. "The week was that bad?"

Scott gave a slight smile. "I've had better," he admitted.

He reached down and turned on the radio, his eyes not leaving the road. Jazz. Jennifer grinned. Okay, at least they had music in common. He clicked the volume down low. She studied him as he drove and wondered what had made his week so rough. She would have to ask him later. She liked a great deal the fact he was not threatened by the silence between them. She wasn't one to chatter, and silence gave one time to think.

They arrived at the restaurant he had chosen, and the parking lot was crowded. Jennifer had heard of the place, but had never been here before. Scott found a place to park and clicked off the ignition. "Stay put," he told her with a smile. Jennifer took a deep breath as Scott came around the car to open the door for her. She forced herself to smile. It was not Scott's fault that her stomach was beginning to turn in knots again. This was a date, a real, honest to goodness, date. She had conveniently forgotten that fact. Scott offered her his hand to help her from the car, clicked a button on his key ring and all the car doors locked. He offered her his arm. Somewhat embarrassed, Jennifer accepted. He was picking up her nervousness and his smile was kind.

"Relax," he said gently.

"Sorry, Scott. I hate first dates," she admitted, then wished she hadn't.

They were almost across the parking lot. He squeezed her hand. "I know what you mean. Trouble is, you can't have a second one without it." As they reached the door, Scott's arm moved down to around her waist and Jennifer found the touch both disconcerting and comforting. He kept it there as they were escorted by a smiling maître d' to the table Scott had reserved. The restaurant was elegant, the tables spaced for privacy, the lights slightly subdued. Scott helped her slip off the jacket, held her chair for her. He took a seat across from her. Jennifer forced herself to meet his eyes. She knew she was flushed, her face felt hot. All he did was offer a soft reassuring smile. He handed her a menu. "The veal here is very good. As is the quail."

Jennifer nodded and gratefully dropped her eyes to the cloth-covered book that was the menu. She opened it. No prices.

"Jerry, there are no prices in this menu." Jennifer nearly giggled. *"Do you suppose everything is free?"*

Jerry just smiled and motioned the waiter over. "Could we have two coffees please?" He didn't need one. Jennifer did.

His wife had had too much champagne.

He wasn't annoyed. Far from it. She had been petrified of attending the party their publisher had hosted for several writers introducing new books for the Christmas season. She had gone despite the fear and done a magnificent job. When they left the party shortly after eleven, it was with the knowledge that several nationwide bookstore chains would be prominently displaying their seventh book. Their agent, Ann, had sent a bottle of champagne to their hotel room with her congratulations. Jennifer had drunk three glasses. Jerry, who knew Jennifer had been too nervous before the party to eat, had wisely escorted her to the hotel restaurant. She needed to unwind.

"Jerry, let's not do that again, okay?"

"You did a great job, honey."

"I have a headache."

"Too much champagne."

"Too many people," Jennifer replied. *"Did you see the lady with the diamond necklace, the one with six strands?"*

"Lisa Monet. Her last four books have been on the bestseller list," Jerry replied calmly.

"She was beautiful."

"She couldn't hold a candle to you."

Jennifer smiled. Her husband meant it. "Thanks."

"Sure, beautiful. Want to go dancing after we eat?"

"Could we? It's awful late."

"This from a lady who thinks three in the morning is a perfect time of day?" Jerry kidded gently.

"Only if Thomas decided he wanted to keep talking."

Jerry smiled.

The coffee arrived.

"Jen, have you decided, or would you like some more time?" With a start, Jennifer realized Scott was addressing her.

"The veal, please," she replied, trying to cover the lapse of concentration.

He signaled the waiter, gave their order, having chosen veal for himself. "What were you thinking about?" he asked.

Jennifer blushed. "Jerry and I were at a restaurant much like this in New York a few years ago. I had forgotten that memory."

"There's no need to apologize," Scott replied gently. "What took you to New York?"

"Our seventh book came out about Christmastime. The publishers held a party for all the authors with new books coming out. A way to generate some publicity."

"I seem to remember reading that that book was very popular."

Jennifer nodded. "It sold well." *That's why we decided we could start thinking about starting a family.*

She couldn't prevent the look of pain that fleetingly crossed her face.

The salads arrived before Scott could question that look.

They ate in comfortable silence.

"Tell me a little about your family, Jennifer. Do they live around here?"

Jennifer set down her crystal water glass. "My parents died a few years ago in a car crash. I have one brother, older than me. Peter is married, has three children. Alexander is nine, Tom is eleven, and Tiffany is twelve."

"You and Jerry never had children?" It was the wrong question to ask; Scott knew it as soon as he asked the question, but it was too late to take back the words.

"Jerry, can we get a Jenny Lynn crib?"

Her husband's arms around her waist gave her a gentle hug. "Sure. Next month as a seven month present?"

"You'll have the baby room painted by then?"

Jerry smiled. "Right down to the teddy bears around the door," he assured her.

Jennifer gave her husband a hug. "Wonderful. I've been thinking about names some more. What do you think about Colleen for a girl?"

"Colleen St. James. I like it. Have a middle name yet?"

"Not yet."

The raw pain Jennifer felt at the memory tore at her heart. Jerry had not lived long enough to see his daughter born. "No," she finally whispered. "No, we never had children."

Scott could see the pain in her eyes. "Jen, I'm sorry. I didn't think…"

She shook her head and forced a smile. "It's okay. I'm not normally so touchy. What about you? Is your family in the area?"

"My parents live in Burmingham, about forty minutes away. I have one younger sister, Heather. She's married and has two children, is expecting her third."

They talked about family for a while, Jennifer laughing at the stories he told of his and Heather's childhood.

"Would you like some coffee?"

"Please," Jennifer agreed.

"How is the book coming?"

"Not too bad. I've actually been working on it for some time. Another week of writing will finish the first draft."

"You are still planning to end the series?"

"Yes. It's best. The books are not the same without Jerry."

Scott looked at his watch and reluctantly said it was time to leave for the theater. Jennifer would have been content to stay and talk for the evening, miss the play.

Scott escorted her from the restaurant, across the parking lot. When he held the car door for her, she was expecting it. "Thank you," she murmured softly, slipping inside.

They were quiet during the few-minutes' ride to the theater. "Have you ever been here, Jennifer?"

She shook her head.

"The theater has seats that circle the entire stage. The stage is an octagon, different parts of which can be raised and lowered during the play. An orchestra will provide the music."

Jennifer smiled. "I'm going to love this, Scott."

Scott held the door for her. They stepped into a massive lobby. Scott, a hand at the small of Jennifer's back, led her into the crowd, angling them to the left. An usher accepted the tickets from Scott, handing back the seat assignment portion along with two programs. "You are in the fourth row in the blue section."

"Thank you."

The seats fanned out from the stage. Jennifer did not see what markers Scott was using until she realized the floor lights along each section were different colors. They were elegant theater seats of royal blue crushed velvet. Scott helped her slip off her jacket and laid it across the back of her chair. The program Jennifer opened was ten full pages of information about the play, the actors, the director, costumes and scenery.

The lights dimmed and the music swelled.

It was a fast-moving play. She hadn't realized it was based on political intrigue.

The intermission, an hour into the play, caught Jennifer by surprise. Scott had been enjoying the play, but he had also been enjoying watching Jennifer, leaning forward in her seat, being totally captivated by the presentation. "Like it so far?"

She leaned back in her seat with a big smile. "Oh, yes." She gave a soft laugh. "I'm exhausted. Too much intrigue."

He chuckled. "You must get tense writing your books."

"After writing a description of a crime scene, it may take me several hours to unwind."

"Jerry, this was a wonderful idea."

The hotel had a gorgeous indoor pool, softly lit and surrounded by tropical plants. They were the only guests taking advantage of it. The warm water was easing knots in her back that Jennifer had been afraid would be there permanently. Jerry gently moved his hand up to rub the back of Jennifer's neck where tense muscles were causing her a splitting headache. "I wish you would start taking more breaks, Jennifer. Get up and walk around the house if nothing else. These twelve-hour marathons of yours are deadly."

"Hmm." She leaned forward to give him better access to her shoulders.

"How did you manage to get us reservations on less than an hour's notice?"

"I made reservations three weeks ago."

Jennifer opened one eye. "You did?"

He smiled. "I'm not the one who forgets our anniversary."

She groaned. "Guilty. I will make up for the meat loaf dinner. I just got tied up with the story."

Jerry smiled. "Don't worry about it. I like your meat loaf." He gently kissed her. His arms folded across her waist, supporting her.

"We're almost done with this book," Jennifer said drowsily.

"Another week," Jerry agreed. He gently rubbed his hand across her midriff. "How's our baby coming?"

"She likes ice cream and chocolate and hates meat loaf," Jennifer replied. "And she hates getting up in the morning."

Jerry chuckled. "Nausea still bad?"

"No." Jennifer gently kissed the side of his neck. "It's hard to believe she's six months old," she said with a sigh.

Jerry stole a kiss. "A perfect six months."

"Scott, excuse me. I'll be right back," Jennifer said, her face pale, hands suddenly trembling. She got quickly to her feet. "The ladies' room is along the way we came in?"

Scott's hand steadied her. "Yes." He had seen the emotions rapidly crossing her face. Whatever memory he'd triggered had been a powerful one. He watched as she hurried toward the door.

The ladies' room was actually three rooms, a lounge with beautiful couches and antiques, a powder room and rest rooms. The rooms were crowded with guests. Jennifer moved directly to the lavatory and wet a paper towel. She avoided looking at herself in the mirror, she knew how pale she must look. She returned to the lounge and found a place to sit down.

The racing thoughts didn't settle. She finally forced herself to take a deep breath and get to her feet. She didn't know how long the intermission was, but it was probably no more than fifteen minutes. She had no idea what she was going to say to Scott.

He was standing across the hall from the ladies' room, waiting for her.

He moved to her side when he saw her.

"Sorry about that," Jennifer said quietly, apologetically.

He studied her face for a moment.

"I brought you a drink. It looks like you could use it," he said finally, handing her one of the glasses he carried.

It looked like liquor. "Scott, I don't drink. Except under extreme duress," she qualified, remembering the anniversary of her husband's death.

"Neither do I, actually. It's iced tea."

She blushed with embarrassment.

"Quit that, Jen. If you hadn't asked, I would have been upset."

Jennifer tilted her head to look at him. He was serious. She was never going to get used to this man. "Thank you."

She took a long drink of the iced tea.

"Are you okay?"

He wanted an honest answer. Jennifer didn't know what to tell him. She looked down at the wedding ring she wore. "I remembered forgetting our wedding anniversary the last year Jerry was alive." She forced back the tears, but her eyes were still shining with the moisture. "There are some memories that still wrench my heart, Scott. It's not fair to you. I'm sorry."

Scott slid his hand gently under her hair around the nape of her neck. His blue eyes held her brown ones. "It's okay, Jen," he said softly. "He was your husband. You don't have to forget him in order to go on with your life."

His hand slid down to grasp hers. "Finish your drink. Intermission is almost over."

Jennifer finished the iced tea. Scott took her glass and returned it to one of the waiters mingling through the crowd. He led them back to their seats.

The lights dimmed.

Scott reached over to calmly catch Jennifer's hand, hold it firmly. She squeezed his hand in reply, not looking over at him.

The final act was very moving. Jennifer was crying before the curtain dropped. Scott slipped her a handkerchief. Jennifer squeezed his hand in thanks.

"That was very good, Scott," Jennifer said when the play ended, drying her eyes. "Sad, but good."

"I'm glad you liked it." He intertwined their fingers. "Want to get a nightcap? Some coffee?"

"My place? I really need a couple of aspirins," she admitted.

"Sure." Scott picked up her jacket and their two programs.

"Scott, I *thought* that was you!" His hand stiffened. Jennifer looked up in surprise to see Scott looking back into the crowd.

"Hello Mrs. Richards," he said politely as a lady in her late fifties stopped at the end of the row of seats, effectively blocking their exit.

"Wasn't it just a divine play? My Susan does such a great job. She has such a natural talent for the part, don't you think?"

Jennifer choked, remembering that Susan Richards had been one of the actresses. She'd played a waitress, Jennifer recalled. A very attractive waitress. Scott squeezed Jennifer's hand in response. "Yes, Netta, Susan is becoming a very good actress," he agreed, easing them forward.

"We are having an informal party to celebrate her success. Please do say you will come."

Jennifer saw a beautiful lady in her early twenties wearing a white dress step up beside the older lady. "Mother, that is not necessary." She offered an apologetic smile. "Hi, Scott."

"Susan." He smiled. "Good job, as always. Congratulations on getting the lead for Towers."

She smiled. "Thanks. Jim told you?"

Scott nodded. "Excuse us, ladies, but we need to be going. Jennifer is not feeling well tonight." Before Jennifer realized what was happening, Scott had maneuvered them out into the lobby.

"Susan looks like a nice young woman."

"She is. She's engaged to one of my hardware designers, or will be once Jim gets the nerve to face Netta."

Jennifer had no trouble putting together the full picture. "Oh."

Scott smiled. "Exactly." He playfully squeezed her hand. "You're pretty good at this."

"Lots of practice," Jennifer replied, amused.

"Scott." It was a male voice calling his name this time.

Scott glanced around. "Jen, can you manage a few more minutes? I would like you to meet someone," he asked, looking at her carefully.

"I'll be fine," she insisted.

Scott, his arm around her waist, took them forward to meet the couple. An older gentleman in his late sixties, holding hands with the lady at his side.

"Scott, thanks for the tickets. We enjoyed the show."

Scott smiled broadly, shaking hands with the gentleman. "My pleasure Andrew." Scott leaned forward to kiss the cheek of the lady. "You look stunning, Maggie."

She blushed. "Thank you, Scott."

"Andrew, Maggie, I would like you to meet Jennifer St. James." Scott's hand around her waist felt very reassuring. Jennifer smiled at the couple as they all said hello. "Andrew is my executive vice president, Jennifer. He knows the business better than I do."

The older man smiled. "Don't believe everything he says, Jennifer. One of these days I may have to retire just to show him I'm not indispensable."

"The day you do, I may resign," Scott answered

with a laugh. "Maggie, how's your granddaughter? Still wrapping grandfather, here, around her little finger?"

The lady beamed. "In a big way." She smiled at Jennifer. "Andrew spent the weekend putting up a swing set. My granddaughter is only six months old, but Andrew wanted us to be prepared. In case we ever have to baby-sit," Maggie said, looking over with amusement at her husband.

He just grinned. "Scott, would you please tell Maggie you can never be too prepared?"

Scott, his attention caught by an emotion that had flickered across Jennifer's face, feeling her sudden tension, had to force himself back to the conversation. He offered a soft smile to Maggie. "Maggie, I think he's determined to always be prepared. You'll have to humor him, I'm afraid."

Lord, what's causing Jennifer this pain? I wanted her to have a relaxing night. I don't know what's wrong. Scott prayed the words silently as he shifted his arm to support more of Jennifer's weight. "I hate to say hi and run, but we need to be going," he said to his friends. "Maggie, it was a pleasure. Andrew." Jennifer softly echoed his goodbyes.

They walked together to the car. Scott looked at her closed expression, could see the tension in her and knew she needed some space. He gave it to her. He turned on the radio, found a station still playing soft jazz. "Are you going to be okay?"

Jennifer finally nodded.

"I'll have you home soon," Scott promised.

It was a thirty-minute drive. When they reached her home, Scott came around to open the passenger door and escort her up the walk. She unlocked the front door, then hesitated. "I need some coffee. Would you like to stay and join me?"

Scott knew she must want this evening to simply end. But she was trying to make amends. He silently nodded. Jennifer gestured him toward the living room. "I'll be back in a minute."

She was gone almost ten minutes. Scott didn't crowd her. He walked around the living room. There was a Bible on the end table. Jennifer's name was inscribed on the leather cover. He frowned briefly. What had Jennifer said? He had asked her over dinner where she attended church. "My husband was a very religious man. I haven't been to church much since he died."

Her home suggested that Christianity had not been just one-sided, at least not at some time in the past. There were Bible verses cross-stitched on the throw pillows, two of the pictures had verses of scripture stenciled in. Who knew where she stood now? Other than the clear fact that she was hurting, he did not have much to go on.

It bothered him to realize she had walked away from the one person who could help her heal. God. She had to have felt anger and shock when her husband died, the agony of why it had been allowed to happen would have naturally cut pretty deep. But after three years, there should not still be this distance from God. Was she simply stuck and didn't know how to return? He was going to have to find a way to fix this.

She came back in, carrying their coffee.

Scott accepted the cup she offered him with a quiet thanks. He watched her warily. He had never seen this expression before, the quiet intensity that said she had made a decision.

"I think you chose the wrong time to get to know me, Scott." She took a seat across from him when he sat down on the couch.

He tensed. He suspected this was heading somewhere he did not like. "Because of the memories?"

"Because I don't want to get involved," she replied. "Not now."

He sighed. "Jennifer, you're going to go through this, no matter how long you wait. The first time you venture out, the same set of circumstances is going to occur."

"The memories are too raw, Scott. I can't handle half a dozen flashbacks every day to a time when life was perfect. I'll shatter."

Scott winced at the image. "Was it perfect, Jen?" he asked carefully.

"For a time, yes, it was," she whispered.

"Do you want me to leave, Jen? Say goodbye for good?"

She leaned her head back and looked over at him. "I want the past back," she replied. She gave a half smile. "I sound like a spoiled child, wanting what I can't have." She sighed. "Scott, I don't think I can even be a good friend right now. I don't have the energy or the nerve to take a risk again."

"Jen, I can't take away the pain you are going through. But I can give you all the time you need, time without any strings attached."

"I get nasty when I'm hurting," Jennifer warned softly.

"I'll survive," he said firmly. "Just don't hide, Jennifer. I can't deal with something I don't know is there."

You don't know about Colleen. You don't know how she died.

She looked at his eyes. He wasn't ready to handle that level of her grief. Not yet. "Okay, Scott."

"Good."

Jennifer kicked off her shoes so she could tuck her feet beneath her.

"Would you like to try a simple dinner out this next week?"

She shook her head.

Scott looked disappointed. Before he could comment, Jennifer nodded toward her office. "I've got to get the first draft finished, or I'm going to lose my nerve to finish the series."

He grimaced. "Work. I have used that excuse more times than I care to admit myself. What about the week after?"

"Any night but Monday," Jennifer replied, giving him carte blanche to set her schedule. Monday nights her brother and his two boys came over to watch the football game.

"How about Thursday?"

"Sounds fine," Jennifer agreed.

Scott nodded. "Thursday it is." He couldn't prevent the yawn. It had nothing to do with the company, it had simply been a very long, heavy week.

"Like a refill?" Jennifer asked, gesturing to his coffee cup.

"Please," Scott replied.

Jennifer filled his cup then sat back down. "What other authors do you like to read?" she asked, then grinned. "Besides me?"

He laughed. They passed a pleasant hour, talking about books, authors they liked, then about movies they had seen. Jennifer happened to glance at her watch. "Scott, it's twelve forty-five."

He nodded. "You are right. I had better get going." He got to his feet. He smiled. "I enjoyed tonight."

"So did I," she admitted.

She turned on the porch light and watched him start his car. He lifted a hand. She waved back, then quietly closed the door.

"You look tired. Late night?"

Scott's sister, Heather, grinned as she asked the question, leaning over the back of the pew to get his attention. Busy cramming for the youth group lesson he had to give in twenty minutes, Scott just grinned and said, "Yes. Now go away, Twiggy. And don't tell Mom." The nickname she had picked up in high school had stuck. Scott ensured it got kept alive. She liked to protest, but he knew she would be hurt if he dropped his pet name for her. She had a green thumb and now owned a greenhouse, making her name even more fitting.

She squeezed his shoulders. "I knew it. Is she pretty?"

Scott stuck his finger on the text he was going to use and leaned his head back to smile at his sister. "She's beautiful," he replied gravely. He hadn't told her much when he had reneged on his offer to take her to see the play so he could take Jennifer instead, and her curiosity had to be killing her. Scott loved it. His grin told her he was holding out deliberately.

She swatted his shoulder. "Come on. Spill the beans. Or I will tell Mom you were on a date last night."

"I took Jennifer out to dinner, we went to the play, and then we sat and talked over coffee at her place. I didn't get home till 1:30 a.m. I had a nice time, and yes, I'll probably see her again. Sufficient?"

She grinned. "Not hardly. But you can tell me the rest over lunch. Frank's taking the kids roller skating. You're buying."

"It's your turn to buy," he protested.

"Then we'll go to Fred's," she replied, knowing how he hated the boring food served there.

Scott sighed. "If you're going to twist my arm like that, I'll buy. Why do I love you so much, anyway?"

"Because I've got two kids you adore so you have to be nice to me," she replied with a grin. "I'll find you after church. I'm on piano today."

"Break a finger."

She smiled, tugged his hair, and left him to finish preparing his lesson.

Chapter Three

The doorbell rang just as Jennifer finished turning the caramel popcorn out onto the wax paper. Setting down the wooden spoon, she went to answer the door.

"Hi, Tom." She held open the door for her nephew.

"Hi, Aunt Jen," he replied with a big grin. "Dad bought out almost the entire store." He was carrying a full grocery sack.

Jennifer smiled. "He hasn't changed." She could see the cookies and the bag of chips. "Take them straight to the living room, Tom. On the coffee table."

"Okay."

Peter was coming up the walk, carrying Alexander. Jennifer held the door for him. "Thanks." He stepped inside, carrying his sleeping son. "He fell asleep as soon as we got into the car," Peter said softly.

Jennifer nodded toward her bedroom. "Go ahead and put him down."

Her brother nodded and disappeared down the hall.

The roses. Jennifer hurried after Peter. She had moved the roses Scott had sent into her bedroom. Peter would ask too many questions if he saw them.

Peter didn't bother to turn on the bedroom light, and by chance, the door to the bathroom was open, partially hiding the flowers on the dresser. Jennifer helped slip off Alexander's tennis shoes. Peter pulled a light blanket over him.

"Okay." Peter nodded to the door. "I think he'll be fine."

They left the bedroom. Peter didn't notice the flowers.

"Aunt Jen, what channel is the game on?"

"Seventeen." Jennifer smiled at Tom's worried expression. "We're still early, Tom. It's on after this show," she reassured him. "I've got caramel popcorn made if you would like to help bring it out from the kitchen," she offered.

Tom was on his feet in an instant. "Sure."

Peter pulled out glasses, filled them with ice as Jennifer and Tom put the finishing touches on a huge bowl of caramel popcorn. Peter reached around them to sample the warm, slightly sticky caramel mixture. "Good job, Jen."

She grinned. "Thanks."

"Sticky, though."

Jennifer tossed him two clean towels from the bottom drawer by the stove. "For the living room."

He nodded and wisely got one of them damp. He added them both to the tray he was putting together. "Anything else we need?"

Jennifer added two large spoons to the tray. "That should be it."

As was tradition, Peter and Jennifer sat on the floor, using the couch as a backrest. Tom stretched out in front of the fireplace.

"Did Rachel and Tiffany go for their night out?"

Peter nodded. "They left about six-thirty." He opened the box of cookies and offered Jennifer one. She accepted. "They were going to get ice cream, Tiffany finally decided she wanted one of those two-scoop sundaes, then they were going to the show."

"Tom, how was your day?"

Her nephew had pulled out the sports page of the newspaper and was reading intently. "It was good," Tom replied absentmindedly.

Jennifer looked over at Peter and shared a smile. Tom was a reader. A very intense, careful reader. There was always one in the family. Jennifer had lightened up over the years, but she could also be like Tom, totally absorbed in something.

"Tom." Peter finally got his attention. "It's not polite to ignore your hostess."

"Sorry, Aunt Jen," he apologized.

"Look on page 26, there is an article about the state soccer finals," she said, apologizing as well for interrupting him.

"Really?" Tom turned the next few pages. "Thanks."

The show credits rolled by. Peter reached for the remote and adjusted the sound. Jennifer settled back, propped her knees against the coffee table, a cold glass of diet cola cradled in her hands, got comfortable. It was going to be a great game.

"Nice socks, Jen."

Jennifer admired the bright rainbow of colors on her feet. "I bought them for myself last Tuesday." *Right after I bought a very expensive dress to wear to a play you still don't know I went to see.*

The sports page landed back in the basket with the rest of the paper. "There's Grant," Tom said, excited.

They were playing in San Diego and it was a nice

night there, low seventies, no wind. Perfect game conditions.

It was a disappointing first quarter. The announcers explained away the repeated pass run, pass punt as the teams were feeling each other out. That was one way to describe it. Jennifer could think of a few others. If a receiver broke free and clear, the quarterback got sacked. If it was a good pass, the receiver dropped it. Punt returns consistently got stopped within five yards. The snacks started to disappear, but there was little excitement among the threesome watching the game.

Tom disappeared into the kitchen at the end of the quarter in search of some ice cream.

"Like a refill?" Peter gestured to the empty glass she was holding.

Jennifer handed it to him. "Thanks. Let's hope the second quarter is not quite so dead."

Peter smiled. "What is it they say about expectations? Low ones are the only kind that don't lead to disappointment?" He handed back her refilled soda.

"Very true," Jennifer admitted. Her right hand slid up the back of her neck and massaged the tight muscles, lessening the pain building inside her head.

"Here, Jennifer, give me back the glass and turn around." Peter had seen the gesture.

Jennifer handed him the glass and turned toward the fire. Peter gently massaged her shoulders. "You've been working too hard again."

"Hmm." The massage felt great. Peter still needed a little practice before he would be as good as Jerry had been, but he wasn't bad at all. "I completed twenty more pages today," Jennifer said, dropping her head forward so Peter could work on her neck.

"You are still planning to end the series?"

"Yes."

"When was the last time you saw your doctor, Jennifer? These headaches are getting more and more frequent."

"Last month. He said to quit crying so much," Jennifer replied, muffled.

Peter's hand worked along the vertebrae in her neck. "Still having bad nights?" he asked, concerned.

Jennifer nodded. "Not as frequently, but yes, I'm still having bad nights," she admitted. She gingerly rolled her head. "That's much better, Peter. Thanks."

"Sure."

"Aunt Jen, do you have any of those chocolate sprinkles left?"

"Try over the sink, Tom." She looked over at her brother. "How in the world can he eat all that stuff and never get sick?"

"I want to know how he can eat all the stuff and not gain weight," Peter replied. "He's a bottomless pit."

"I'm a what?" Tom had returned.

"A bottomless pit."

Tom grinned. "I'm a growing boy, Dad."

Peter gave him a playful swat. "You won't always have that hollow leg."

A sleepy boy appeared in the doorway. Jennifer saw him first. "Hi, Alexander. Come on in."

"Hi, Aunt Jenny. I fell asleep."

"Come sit beside me," Jennifer offered, hiding a grin. Alexander was so adorable when he was sleepy.

"Hi, champ." Peter gave him a hug, lifted his son over to sit between himself and Jennifer. She gently combed his hair with her fingers.

Alexander looked over the food with interest, starting to wake up. "What have I missed?"

"Nothing," Tom replied, somewhat disgusted with the performance of his favorite team.

Jennifer offered Alexander a cookie.

"Nice socks, Aunt Jen," Alexander said gravely.

"Thank you, Alex," Jennifer replied with a smile. His own socks were blue with lots of little brown footballs. It was tradition between the two of them to give each other socks for Christmas; Alex was almost as opposed to shoes as Jennifer.

The second quarter of the game started. The home team actually put together a decent drive before fumbling on the twenty yard line. The phone rang.

"I'll get it," Peter said, motioning his sister to stay put. "It's probably Rachel. She said she would call when they got home." He got to his feet to get the phone in the kitchen.

He was gone only a few minutes. He came back to lean against the doorjamb. "Jennifer, it's for you. He said his name was Scott?"

Jennifer's eyes closed briefly. "I'll take it in the bedroom," Jennifer replied, knowing that statement only dug her a deeper hole, but needing the privacy. She was going to get grilled as soon as she got off the phone. She shifted Alexander so she could get her legs clear of the coffee table. She passed her brother, choosing not to meet his eyes.

In the bedroom she turned on the lamp on the end table. Took a deep breath. Pulling together her nerve, she picked up the phone. "Hi, Scott."

"I'm sorry, Jennifer. I didn't mean to interrupt."

Jennifer cut him off. "My brother, Peter, and his

boys are over. We're just watching the Monday-night football game."

"Who's winning?" She could tell he was relieved.

"The San Diego Chargers. The 49ers can't execute even a simple screen pass tonight. It's awful."

Scott chuckled. "I didn't know you were a football fan."

"Monday-night football is something of a tradition at my place," Jennifer explained.

"I just wanted to call and say hi. I'm just leaving work."

"Problems?"

"Just a lot of paperwork to catch up on," Scott replied. "How's the book coming?"

Jennifer pulled her feet up on the bed to get comfortable. "Good. I wrote twenty pages today."

"You sound tired."

Jennifer smiled. Perceptive man. "I am." She propped the second pillow behind her back.

Scott, at his desk fifteen miles away, quietly tapped his pen against the pad of paper in front of him. He had been doodling her name along the edge of the pad of paper, then finally decided to call her. He swiveled his chair around to look out over the surrounding countryside. The city lights were hazy tonight.

"I've got a favor to ask," he said, having finally made up his mind how to handle the dilemma he found himself in. Having canceled out on taking Twiggy to see the play in order to take Jennifer, he was now on the hook to his sister.

"Name it, Scott."

"My sister, Heather, wants to meet you. Would you be game after dinner next week to stopping by her place for coffee?"

Jennifer's memory for certain things was very good. Scott's comment that Heather was pregnant was still clear in her mind. Could she handle meeting her? Jennifer simply did not know. But to say no would force her to talk about some things she simply was not ready to talk about. She forced a lightness in her voice that she was far from feeling. "That would be fine, Scott."

"We won't stay long." Her hesitancy had not escaped him. "Thanks, Jennifer." He glanced at his watch, realizing he'd keep her on the phone almost twenty minutes. "I had better let you get back to the game."

"Thanks for calling."

He smiled. "I'll talk to you later, Jennifer. Good night."

"Good night." Jennifer set down the phone quietly. It was several minutes more before she got the nerve to venture back to the living room.

Alexander had moved down to stretch out beside his brother.

"The 49ers scored just before the half ended. They are ahead seven to three," Tom informed her, his gaze never leaving the display of stats being shown during the halftime break.

Jennifer smiled. "Great. Let's hope they walk all over the Chargers in the second half." She took her seat again on the floor beside Peter. Peter handed her back her drink.

"Who is he?" Peter asked quietly.

Jennifer knew there was no way to duck the questions. Frankly, it was nice to know Peter was still there to run interference. Even if it was not needed in this case. "A friend. We went out to dinner and a play last Saturday night."

"Who is he?"

"His name is Scott Williams. He runs an electronics company."

"Where did you meet him?"

"On the beach when I was taking a walk." In for a penny, in for a pound. "He fixed me breakfast last time." It was clear she had thrown him a hard curveball. Jennifer reached over to put her hand on his arm. "Relax, Peter. You would like him. He's active in his church, single. He's a nice man. He's read all the Thomas Bradford books now. We're friends."

"You like him a lot?"

Jennifer nodded, surprised with how true the answer was. "Very much."

"Does he know about Jerry and Colleen?"

Jennifer looked away. "He knows about Jerry," she replied.

Peter's hand touched her arm. He offered an apologetic smile. "I'm sorry I'm prying, Jennifer."

"That's okay. I've been kind of ducking telling you about him."

"I noticed," Peter replied dryly. "That's why you couldn't stay for dinner Saturday?"

She nodded.

Peter gestured toward the other room. "Did he ask you out again?"

Jennifer chuckled. "We already have a date arranged, brother dear, that was a hi-how-are-you call."

"It takes half an hour to say hi? You who can't stand talking on the phone?"

Jennifer thumped him with a pillow pulled off the couch. "Yes. Now lay off," she ordered with a grin.

"I can't wait to tell Rachel."

Jennifer groaned. "Don't you dare elaborate, Peter. She already suspects something."

"Have you told Beth yet?"

"Are you kidding? She'd be buying a maid of honor dress within the hour."

"Face it, Jennifer. You're surrounded by serious matchmakers."

"Just don't you join their numbers," Jennifer warned.

Peter laughed. "When do I get to meet him?"

"Never," Jennifer muttered beneath her breath.

"What?"

"I don't know," she replied. The second half of the game began, buying her a reprieve. The 49ers finally won the game but it took them until the final few seconds, a field goal giving them a two-point lead.

Alexander was asleep again. Even Tom was nodding off. The caramel popcorn was three-quarters gone, Jennifer and Peter having both begun to work seriously on it during the fourth quarter of the game. Peter got slowly to his feet as the commentators gave the game wrap-up. Jennifer began packing up the remains of the chips and dip and the snack crackers. If they left it with her she would eat it. While her doctor would definitely like her to gain ten pounds, she didn't think this was what he had in mind. Tom held the sack for her. "Thanks, Tom."

"Alex, it's time to go home, son." Peter gently woke the boy. Alex reluctantly got to his feet. "Who won?"

"The 49ers," Peter replied. Alex could not keep his eyes open. Peter picked him up. "I'll be back in a minute, Jennifer. Let me get this one settled in the car."

Jennifer nodded. "Tom, can you reach the porch light for your father?"

The glasses back on the tray, it took only a couple minutes to put the room back in order. Jennifer carried the tray into the kitchen.

"Thanks for having us, Jennifer."

She smiled at her brother. "Same time next week?"

He smiled. "Deal. I'll get Tom to help me make some homemade ice cream."

Jennifer groaned. "I am so full that doesn't even sound good."

Peter looked at the bowl of caramel popcorn. "We did a pretty good job on that," he agreed. He smiled. "Let me know when you hear from Scott again."

She pushed him toward the door. "Go home, Peter."

The phone rang as she was getting ready for bed.

"What's this I hear about you having a date?"

Jennifer sat down on the bed. "And hello to you too, Rachel."

Rachel laughed. "Sorry. Who is he, Jennifer?"

Jennifer settled back against the headrest, using the pillows to get comfortable. It did feel nice to be able to talk to someone who she knew would adore the entire the story. "Do you want the short story or full tale?"

"Peter is putting the boys to bed. Give me the entire story."

"I was walking on the beach. He said hello. Scared the daylights out of me because I didn't realize he was there. You know how jumpy I am when I'm tired. This was the morning after I'd given myself that great shiner. He jumped to the conclusion that I was a battered wife or something, because he apparently tried to track me down afterward."

"Jennifer, you didn't explain?"

"I didn't think it was any of his business. I had just met the guy." She smiled. "The story gets better.

"He found out I was an author and somehow got in touch with Ann because I got this message from her saying that some guy was trying to get in touch with me. She relayed the message he had left and I about died. His message said 'Come stay with me.'"

"Oh, my."

Jennifer laughed. "I went back to the beach, figuring he probably walked there every morning about the same time. Sure enough, I met him again. After I explained the real circumstances, we ended up having breakfast together, and he invited me out to dinner and a play. I had a good time."

Rachel cut her off. "Hold it, Jennifer, I'm still trying to get beyond you had breakfast with him."

Jennifer chuckled. "I like this guy."

"I can tell. What's he look like?"

"Six foot two. Brown hair. Blue eyes. He's thirty-eight. Athletic. He has very expressive eyes."

"Are you going to see him again?"

"Dinner a week from Thursday," Jennifer replied.

"Well I'm glad you're dating again."

"We are becoming good friends, but that is as far as this will ever go, Rachel. Jerry and Colleen are still too big a part of my life to seriously make room for someone else right now. In a couple of years it will be different. Right now is just bad timing."

"Are you sure, Jennifer? He sounds perfect."

Jennifer chuckled. "Nobody is perfect. Not even Jerry," she admitted.

"Peter is telling me to get off the phone."

Jennifer laughed. "I told him not to tell you."

"As if your brother could ever keep a secret," Rachel replied. "Besides, I twisted his arm. He had orders to find out where you were Saturday night. I tried to call and you weren't home."

Jennifer laughed. "Thanks, friend. I'll talk to you later."

"Sweet dreams, Jennifer."

Jennifer leaned over to hang up the phone, still smiling.

Ann really was going to kill her. Jennifer dropped the three-ring binder onto the bed beside her and rolled onto her back, groaning as she rubbed bleary eyes. It was after 2:00 a.m. She had taken the printout of the story to bed with her so she could read the entire story and see what sections still needed work. The story was great, and Thomas Bradford was unmistakably dead. She had to warn Ann what was coming. Her publisher was already projecting that two more books would put the series on the bestseller list, and when that happened, demand for all of the books in the series would shoot through the roof. They were not going to be pleased when they got a book that ended the series.

They might not publish it.

It was a possibility she had to consider. But the books were getting strong sell-through numbers and even now they made a decent amount of money. If her publisher declined their contractual option and turned down the book, Jennifer knew Ann would have no trouble placing the book with another publisher. Money was money.

The ironic thing was, this book was by far the best in the series.

Jerry, why did you have to die? Our ten-year plan would have actually worked. Now, I'm going to be starting all over. I miss you, Jerry.

Chapter Four

Where was page 325? It was almost seven o'clock in the evening on Friday night. Jennifer had been editing the book since seven that morning. Her eyes burned, her throat hurt, she had been reading the pages aloud, and she was hungry. She was not in the mood to be looking for a missing page. She looked through the next dozen pages in the three-ring binder. Pages 326 on, no page 325. The top of her desk wasn't visible, but she'd been working there earlier in the morning. She lowered the leg rest of the recliner and went to search the desk. The phone rang, startling her, and she cracked her knee against the open desk drawer. Swearing under her breath, rubbing the throbbing bruise, she grabbed the phone. "Hello?" A thick binder threatened to slide off the back of the desk and she lunged for it.

"What's wrong?"

Scott. "I just cracked my knee against the drawer, I've lost page 325, and I think I'm seeing double I've been reading so long," she replied, pulling the binder back toward her and forcing it closed. It went back on the shelf.

"Ouch. Put ice on the bruise, try closing your eyes for a while, and can you reprint the page?"

Jennifer laughed. "The printer is somewhere under a stack of books," Jennifer replied wryly, "but I'm working in that direction. Where are you?"

"Still at the office. Have you eaten yet?"

"No, and I'm starved. I forgot lunch. I was on a roll until page 325 decided to disappear."

"Could I interest you in some Chinese food? We deliver."

"I would love some," Jennifer replied, touched by the offer.

"Good. I'll see you in about half an hour."

Jennifer cleared off the printer and reprinted the missing page, hesitated, knowing she should pick up at least some of the clutter since Scott was coming over, but didn't want to lose the time, either. She finally decided the book was more important. She was deeply involved in a chase scene when the doorbell rang. She marked in red where she was at and went to answer the door. "Where would you like this?" Scott asked with a smile. She smiled back, glad to see him.

"The round table in the office," she replied, pointing the way.

"It's getting cold out there," Scott remarked as he entered the office. He set down the two sacks on the table and looked around the room with interest. It was a large room. The walls were lined with bookshelves, the desk had a recent-model computer, and there were work tables at the end of the room spread with documents, newspapers, magazines and file folders. It was a comfortable room, a plush long couch and deep recliner, an open view of the large backyard. The binders on the shelf by her desk were three inches thick, and he recognized the handwritten names of each of her books across the spines, and there were even a few titles he didn't recognize. Future books?

Jennifer picked up her empty glass. "What can I get you to drink, Scott? I've got coffee made, or there is soda."

"Anything diet is fine."

Jennifer went through the house to the kitchen, refilled her glass from the open two liter of diet soda, found a glass for Scott.

"Where can I find forks, spoons and plates?" Scott asked, joining her.

"The top drawer by the stove is silverware. Directly above that is plates."

Jennifer carried both drinks, leading the way back to the office. "What did you bring?"

He began pulling containers out of the bags. "Sweet and sour pork. Fried rice. Hunan beef. Cashew chicken. You can take your pick or sample them all."

"Everything sounds wonderful." She carefully opened the container of rice. Scott handed her one of the spoons. "Thanks." They both filled their plates. "I didn't realize how hungry I was," Jennifer commented, sampling the Hunan beef.

"I had a meeting over lunch, ended up talking so much I didn't get a chance to eat," Scott admitted.

Jennifer pushed the soft sided package toward him. "Try a wonton. They are delicious."

When the edge of her hunger had been blunted, Jennifer leaned back in her chair. "I could get very used to this."

Scott smiled. "It sure beats eating alone."

"What kept you at work tonight?"

"Shipment problems. Anything that brings down a

production line, Peter usually brings me in to settle. Logic Partners has been a good customer for several years. They plan well, let us know far in advance if they are considering a large order. It's a big deal with them if they ever get into a position they have to ask for a fast turnaround of a part. The order we got today asked for a lead time to be reduced by ten weeks. And we had no notion that it was coming. Somebody didn't do their job. Peter thinks the sales manager for the account didn't follow up on some calls as he should have. It's going to be a mess to sort out."

"Not a good day."

He leaned back in the chair. "Today was a sinker, low and away, thrown in from left field."

Jennifer chuckled. "Find some music and take the couch, Scott. Relax." She picked up her drink, then moved back to the recliner.

"Sounds wonderful." He got up to turn on the stereo.

"If you search, you might find the Chicago Bulls game on. They are playing the Pistons tonight," Jennifer offered.

"And you are not listening to it?" Scott teased.

Jennifer held up her hand. "I'm football only. I can follow a baseball game on the radio, but basketball has forever eluded me."

Scott chuckled. He found her preset station playing jazz.

"Nice," Jennifer commented, already back at work.

Scott went to refill his soda. When he returned, he moved the four books from the couch to the floor and stretched out. "I needed this."

Jennifer smiled. "Are you implying you are tired?"

Scott already had his eyes closed. "*Exhausted* describes it better."

Jennifer smiled as she marked out another word. She was listening to the book as she read, fine-tuning the words, just as a master violinist would fine-tune the pitch of his instrument. She worked in silence for forty minutes, adding page after page to the edited pile. She chewed absentmindedly on the plastic cap of her pen as she reached a difficult section. "Scott, is the book on tropical islands over there?" She knew he was still awake, he had just shifted the two throw pillows.

He looked through the stack of books by the sofa. "Here it is." He slid it across the carpet to her.

"Thanks," she answered, her attention never totally shifting from the story. She found the page in the reference book she had paper clipped earlier that day. She frowned. She had got another fact wrong. Jennifer changed the description in the story. How many mistakes in this book had she missed? It was not a pleasant thought.

"What's the matter?"

"I'm rereading the chapters I've written so far. I've got some serious discrepancies. I need to take a class in geography," Jennifer replied abruptly, having just caught another error. With a muttered oath she got to her feet and crossed to her desk. She pulled up the entire manuscript and did a search for the word *island*. Thirty references. She rubbed the back of her neck where a tenseness was beginning to form. "This I did not need." With a sigh, she printed the list of pages she would have to check.

"Can I help?"

"Yes." Jennifer did not question the offer. She took

the list, retrieved the three-ring binder and quickly pulled out the specific pages. "Find where I describe the island and make sure I got the basic geography right. Mount Montgomery has now been both north and south of the capital city. Here—" she handed him her red pen "—you are going to need this."

Scott nodded. He watched her pace back to the chair, retrieve her glass. "I'll be right back."

She was annoyed with herself. Scott nearly chuckled as he watched her leave the room, but caught himself in time. It would seem all artists had that temperamental streak; his hardware designers acted the same way.

Jennifer returned in a few minutes to plop back in the easy chair. She picked up the binder, but thinking better of it, dropped it back on the floor. She was getting thoroughly fed up with this book. Too keyed up to sit, Jennifer got up, picked up the books beside her chair and started placing them back on the shelves with the rest of the reference books she had used during the day.

"Only three places need changing," Scott said several minutes later.

"That's all?" She turned to look at him, clearly relieved.

He smiled. "The top three pages."

Jennifer took the pile. She slipped paper clips on the pages, then opened the binder to file them.

"I like what I read, Jennifer." Scott didn't know what kind of comment would be acceptable. Jennifer and her writing was a difficult combination to figure out.

She dropped the binder in his lap. "A book doesn't mean much unless you start on page one."

Scott looked at the binder, back at Jennifer. Was she serious? He knew instinctively that not many people had this privilege.

She shrugged. "I'm beat. That means I'm through for the night. But if you read it, it's on the condition that no comments are allowed," she warned.

He smiled. "Even if I like it?"

"Not even if you like it. I might cut your favorite scene tomorrow because I don't like it," she replied with a smile.

"Okay." Scott settled back on the couch and opened the binder. Jennifer disappeared into the living room to return with her sewing basket. She was making a rose square quilt for Rachel's Christmas present.

Jennifer watched Scott slowly turn the pages of the book, trying to read from his expression what he was thinking. It was impossible. She concentrated on her embroidery.

Half an hour passed. Jennifer tied off the rose-colored embroidery thread. She stuck the fine needle into the pin cushion attached to the top of the sewing basket and sorted through the basket for the light forest green embroidery thread. The end of the thread was frayed. Jennifer licked it, then rolled it between her thumb and first finger to ensure the fibers were tightly coupled together. Retrieving the needle, Jennifer turned the needle carefully until she found the small thread hole. With a very steady hand, she threaded the needle on the first try.

She could hear pages turning.

She began making the stitches that would define the leaves.

Jennifer finished the current quilt square, carefully releasing it from the wooden hoop. She watched Scott for several minutes. She had never seen him look so serious before. His expression made her nervous. She reached down into the basket, retrieved a new square to work on and carefully framed the white square so that the rose pattern was centered in the hoop. She forced herself to concentrate on her work, not Scott.

The ten o'clock news came on the radio. Scott put his finger on the page to mark his place, then looked up briefly. "Am I keeping you up?"

"I'm a night owl, Scott, 1:00 a.m. is a normal night."

He nodded. He went back to reading.

As the evening wore on and Scott continued to read, Jennifer began to feel very guilty. She should not have given him the book so late in the evening. He was already tired. He would be very late getting home. He was reading it all because it was the polite thing to do. Guilt grew as the minutes passed.

"Scott, it's midnight."

He didn't look up. "I know."

What if he didn't like the book? The thought made her feel physically sick. He did look…grim. The book was very different from the other books in the series, and it was still rough even after the editing. He was almost done with the book. Jennifer dropped any pretext about not wanting to know what he thought. She wanted to know his reaction desperately. Setting down her embroidery, she got up and crossed the room. She sat down on the couch beside him.

He turned the last page she had written, closed the book slowly. He didn't look at her, didn't say anything.

Scott felt like his heart had just been wrenched out. There was a bit of the writer in every book. In this yet-untitled book, there was more Jennifer than Scott knew how to handle. The plot was basic. A murder.

The widow hired Thomas Bradford to find out who killed her husband and why. The mystery was intriguing, well written, believable, even humorous in places.

The widow in the story haunted him. She was a minor character. She introduced the mystery, providing Thomas Bradford a logical person with whom he could discuss the case. Her grief, her loneliness, her sense of drifting eloquently spoke for Jennifer herself. The critical need for the widow to understand why her husband had died wove like a tapestry thread through the entire book.

The story was so vivid in Scott's mind that emotionally he felt he had lived through the scenes personally.

"Scott? Was it that bad?" Jennifer finally whispered, afraid to know, but more afraid of not knowing.

Scott turned toward her. Jennifer didn't understand the emotions she saw.

"The story is the best you have ever written," he reassured softly.

"Really?"

"Yes." He reached for her hands. "Come here." He gently pulled her over to him, brought her to rest against his chest. Her hands settled of their own accord against his powerful upper arms.

"I was afraid you didn't like it."

"I like it." Jennifer, her head resting against his chest, felt the words. It felt so good to be held. Scott was quiet for some time. Jennifer slowly got comfortable with being held by him, began to relax.

"I'm sorry I didn't understand how badly you miss Jerry."

Jennifer stiffened.

Scott's hands moved up from her waist to gently

rub her back. "It's all there, Jennifer. The anger, the grief, the sense of drifting. The loneliness."

She didn't look up at him. "It's fiction."

"No it's not."

Jennifer finally decided not to hide from him. "No it's not," she softly admitted. She sighed. "If anything, I toned down the emotions."

His hands gently slid up to shoulders that were in tense knots. "Tell me about the day Jerry died."

"Peter, what are you doing back so early?" Jennifer glanced around briefly when she heard footsteps, then turned back to the oven. "Couldn't you get a court?" She set down the cookie tray she had pulled from the oven, reaching for the spatula. "Is Jerry putting the car away? I promised him the first batch of cookies."

"Jennifer." At the broken tone in her brother's voice, Jennifer looked up. She set down the spatula. "What's wrong, Peter?" she asked, fear gripping her heart.

"It's Jerry."

She leaned against the counter for support, burning her finger when it pressed against the cookie sheet.

"He had a heart attack, Jennifer."

The past tense didn't make any sense.

"He's dead, Jennifer." The blank whiteness on her brother's face told her of his own shock.

He couldn't be talking about her Jerry. They had tickets to a concert tonight. "Which hospital are they taking him to? I've got to get there." Jennifer pulled over her purse. "Memorial? Lake Forest? Condell? Where are my car keys? I need my car keys."

Her brother gripped her shoulders. "Jennifer, there were two doctors there when he collapsed. There was nothing that could be done. Jerry collapsed as we were walking down the hall to the locker rooms to get ready for our racquetball game. He suffered a massive heart attack. He died instantly."

His words began to sink in. A sob ripped through her. "Don't say that. Which hospital is he at?"

Peter shook her slightly, his own fear making his eyes almost black. "Heather is on her way. So is Pastor Kline. Don't go to pieces on me, Jennifer. Think about Colleen."

"God, you can't do this!" The cry came from the back of her throat.

Peter held her tightly. "Jerry loved you. Don't forget that, honey."

"Then how can he just leave?" Jennifer practically screamed. "If he loves me, he wouldn't leave. He didn't say goodbye, Peter." Her voice dropped to a whimper. "He didn't say goodbye."

The tears began to flow unchecked. "Peter, he won't get to see Colleen. What is my little girl going to do without a father?" The agony inside brought sobs to tear at her heart. "She won't get to grow up around her father. More than anything in the world, Jerry wanted to rock his baby girl to sleep in that rocking chair he bought."

Peter's tears silently matched hers. "I know, Jennifer. I know."

Jennifer told Scott some of the story. What she could put into words without breaking into tears.

Tell him about Colleen. The desire was there, but not the courage. She would not be able to control the tears, and she did not want to cry in front of this man, not tonight.

"I felt...*numb* I guess is the best word. There were lots of people here that night. My brother and his wife.

Friends from the church Jerry and I attended. Beth and her husband Les arrived late that night. I was tired by the time that evening came, it didn't really sink in that Jerry was not coming home."

Jennifer watched her finger trace along Scott's arm following the pattern in his shirt. "Peter took care of the arrangements for me. He had gone through the details only the year before when our parents were killed."

Scott carefully brushed away the hair from her face. "When did it begin to hit you, Jennifer, that Jerry was not coming back?"

"When I saw him in that casket." Her voice broke. "We went early to have a private visitation before people began to come. It was the first time I had seen him since the morning when he left." Jennifer wasn't brave enough to tell him the rest. *The last thing he said to me was "Take care of Colleen." And he kissed me. Then he left with Peter.*

She drew in a deep breath. "The funeral was rough. By that time I was exhausted, going through the motions. But not much of it really touched me. I don't remember what the funeral service itself was like. I do remember the carnations and mums. I hate the smell of those flowers now," she said intensely. *And I was sick. The stress making my morning sickness return so strong I couldn't keep anything down. The doctors wanted to admit me to the hospital, but I wouldn't let them.*

"The first night after everyone finally left, when the house was silent, I remember standing by the window. After an hour I realized what I was doing was waiting for Jerry to come home. I went to bed alone, and I lay watching the ceiling until it was time to get up again." She gave a grim smile. "I didn't think it was possible to cry for a month. I found out I was wrong."

Scott's arms tightened around her waist. Jennifer forced the story ahead a year, determined not to talk about the rest of it. "Once that first year was past, it got easier to come home to an empty house."

"You decided to stay here?"

"Yes. Peter and Heather wanted me to move in with them, but I declined. This house is lonely now, but it's still home. Little things Jerry and I did to make it fit us, the bird feeders in the backyard, the hammock we used all the time. I can't walk away from this place."

Scott rubbed his chin across the top of her head. "I'm very sorry you lost your husband, Jennifer. He sounds like he was a good man."

She nodded. "You would have liked him, I think."

Scott gently touched the dark circles under her eyes. "You still miss him a lot, don't you?"

"Yes." Jennifer pulled away from his arms to lean back against the couch. "I don't understand it, Scott. But I think about Jerry more now than I did a year ago. The memories are strong, almost painful, at times, they are so clear."

"Because of the book?"

"Maybe. When I eventually finished the book Jerry and I had been working on together when he died, I was pretty much caught in my 'I'm mad at you' stage. I had a very severe case of depression, Why had life dared to change on me? I was well past that when I began this book. When I started writing this book, it was more a matter of learning to live a new life without Jerry. If my life was going on, how did I want to live it if I was alone? I keep remembering the past, how good it was, the fun we had together. I can't see anything in the future that will compare with the past, and that is a very dangerous position to be in."

"You loved your husband," Scott replied, understanding.

Jennifer smiled. "With a passion." She sighed. "Really loving someone means being willing to let them die first. That was the most difficult lesson I have ever had to learn." Jennifer rubbed her eyes.

Jerry, I hope you like holding our daughter. I failed you. Failed Colleen. And God failed me. One simple prayer, Lord. Why couldn't you answer that one simple, specific prayer?

"Scott, it's late. Hadn't you better be going?"

Scott could see the pain still in her eyes. He knew she was closing the subject before she had told him all of it. But it would do no good to push. It would only cause more pain; he wanted to help ease her pain, not make it worse. There would be other nights. "Yes, I suppose I should." He reached out a hand to gently touch hers. "Thank you, Jennifer."

She smiled. "I still think you should go away and come back in a year."

He returned her smile, replying seriously, "I don't."

He touched the three-ring binder as he got to his feet. "Thanks for letting me read your book. I really did like it."

Jennifer got to her feet. "I'm glad." She carried the book over to the desk.

They walked together through the quiet house to the front door. "Are we still on for Thursday night, Jennifer?"

She nodded. "Yes."

He smiled. "Good. Get some sleep."

"I will. Drive carefully, Scott."

Jennifer shut the door after him, then leaned wearily against the door. The emotions of what she had not told him sent two solitary tears running down her cheeks.

"God, help me."

The prayer was broken, painful, so much emotion sitting beneath the surface. She was petrified of how Scott would react if he saw the pain. She couldn't show it to anyone, not Peter, not Rachel, only a little of it to Beth. They thought she had grieved for her husband and daughter and had begun to move on. The fact she had not only made her misery more deep. She should have grieved and moved on. But she hadn't. There was so much pain, the tears were so near the surface any time she even thought about her daughter. The wound in her heart seemed to only grow with time, not heal.

God, why didn't you answer that last prayer? Why?

She wanted to scream the words, but instead they were whispered with eyes full of tears.

Chapter Five

Jennifer was deep into writing the synopsis of the book her publisher would need for the sales and marketing departments when the phone rang. "Hello?"

"Hi, Jen."

"Scott." She put down her pen with a smile. "Hi."

"Are you going to be free after six? I would like to take you out to dinner and a movie," he asked, getting straight to the point.

"We have a date tomorrow night."

"Consider it a double feature. All I'm getting done here is creating more work. Please, give me a reason to leave."

She laughed. "I would love to," Jennifer replied, twisting the telephone cord around her fingers.

"Great. I'll pick you up about six-fifteen."

"Sounds fine. What movie?"

"I'm flexible," Scott replied. "There is a comedy, a murder mystery, three action adventures, and a Walt Disney film showing now."

"Who is in the comedy?"

"Tom Hanks."

"Let's see the comedy."

"Done. See you after six."

Scott was early. Jennifer was trying to fasten her left earring when the doorbell rang. She was wearing dress slacks and a light sweater, but the earrings were her absolute favorites, and she was determined to wear them. Her mother had given them to her on her twenty-first birthday.

Carrying the earring, she went to get the door. "Hi, Scott. Come on in. I won't be but a minute."

He smiled. "Take your time. I'm early."

She retreated to the bedroom. "Did the rest of the day turn out okay?"

He came to lounge against the door frame as she finished putting on the earrings. "Tolerable. I swear the paper just grows more paper."

She grinned. "The stories feel like that sometimes." She began looking for her shoes.

"They are under the bed, Jennifer," he commented, having spotted the black flats.

She pulled out the shoes. "Thanks."

"If you have a jacket, I would recommend you grab it."

Jennifer nodded. She went to the closet to retrieve her leather jacket. "I don't have anything lighter. I left my windbreaker at Peter's."

"This is perfect. You may need it before the night is over."

"Just what do you have planned?"

He held up his hands. "Just dinner and a movie. But it's good to be prepared."

She grinned. "Oh."

He smiled softly. "You're in a good mood tonight."

"Quite a change, isn't it?" She smiled, offered a slight shrug. "The book is about ready to go to Ann."

"Does that imply that when the writing is not going so well, you're not in a great mood?"

"How do you feel after a day dealing with one crisis after another?"

"Touché." He smiled. "You and Jerry had a warning system, didn't you? A way to tell the other when it had been a lousy day on the book."

She nodded. "If I told him to order in pizza, he got the message. Jerry," she grinned, "he would unwind by practicing on his trumpet."

"Was he good?"

Jennifer chuckled. "No." She picked up her purse. "Okay, Scott, I'm ready."

He locked the house for her. "Any preference tonight?"

"How about something Mexican?"

Scott held the passenger door for her. "I know the perfect place. About fifteen minutes from here." Rounding the car, he took the driver's seat. They left the subdivision. "I'm glad you decided to come tonight."

"So am I."

He looked over at her, shared a smile.

"Scott, you're driving. Your eyes are supposed to be on the road," Jennifer reminded him.

"You're a distraction."

"Of course I am. Watch the road," she replied with a grin.

The restaurant was a small place, tucked out of the general flow of traffic on a side street. "You'll like this place, Jennifer. It has great food." He offered her a hand from the car. As they walked to the door, his arm came firmly around her waist. He had not forgotten what she said about first times.

"Watch the number of hot peppers beside the name of the dish. They will tell you how hot and spicy it is," Scott warned her when they were seated.

Jennifer nodded. She read the menu with interest. "Everything looks delicious, Scott."

He smiled. "It is."

Jennifer finally settled on the burritos, extra spicy.

"You like hot and spicy?" Scott asked, surprised.

"I love it," Jennifer replied, raiding the bowl of taco chips the restaurant offered as a courtesy. They were homemade. And delicious.

Scott placed the order for both of them. He had chosen the same dish as Jennifer. "Try some of this." He pushed the bowl of hot salsa over to her.

"Not bad." Jennifer replied after a couple of samples.

Scott smiled. "Are you going to continually surprise me like this, Jennifer?"

"Doesn't everyone like spicy food?"

He chuckled. "No." He offered the chip he held. Hers had broken in the dish.

"Thanks. I've only known you a few weeks," she commented.

"That's significant?"

She nodded. "I've already seen you four times. This makes five. Tomorrow will make six."

"And?"

"Just how much are you planning for us to try and pack into this month?"

"Just as much as you'll let me."

"I was afraid of that. You look tired, Scott."

"A little."

"It's not good to rush this, you know."

"I know."

"So how come we're doing this?"

He grinned. "Because it really was the best idea I had all day." He lifted another chip and offered it to her. She took a bite.

Dinner arrived.

"Tell me about these Monday-night football games. How long have you and Peter been getting together?"

"Jerry started it. He and Peter were close friends almost from the day they met. Monday night became the guys' night out." She smiled at the memory. "Peter used to always come early, and they would disappear somewhere for dinner, play a little basketball in the church gymnasium. Jerry was the coach for the church team for a while, then they would come back to the house in time to catch the game. I invariably ended up on the couch with Jerry for the duration of the game." She chuckled. "He got an elbow in his ribs a couple times when he distracted me from the game. I love football, always have."

She hesitated. "After Jerry's death, Monday night was a way for Peter and me to both keep part of his memory alive. Peter uses it as an excuse to come over, see how I'm doing."

Scott was glad she was willing to share with him her life with Jerry. It mattered. It meant she was trusting him with the most important part of who she was. He wanted to understand her past. He needed to understand her past. "That takes courage Jennifer, to hold on to the good memories rather than to try to bury all the memories, good and bad."

"Maybe. As time goes on, the Monday nights have become easier. Those first few months, they were not so enjoyable." Jennifer sighed. "Peter blamed himself for Jerry's death. There was absolutely no reason to, but because he was the one with him, he felt like he should have been able to do something. I was afraid for a long time that I had lost my brother as well as my husband. Peter takes guilt very seriously. And there were some extenuating circumstances which didn't help." Like Colleen.

"What brought him around?"

"I yelled at him a few times. And he was worried about me. Had to be around to protect me. Time wore away the edge of the pain."

Jennifer needed the subject changed. "Tell me about your sister, Scott. What's she like?"

Scott followed her lead. "Heather? She is unique. Quiet. Shy. Has vivid blue eyes." He smiled. "Very strong willed. She knew who she was, what she wanted to do from the time she was five. Flowers. Anything she did was going to revolve around flowers."

"You said she's a florist now?"

"Yes. And has a thriving greenhouse business. She can make literally anything grow." He spun the ice in his glass, looked over at her. "I have to confess something. I stood Heather up in order to take you to the play *Chess*. That's why I'm on the hook to introduce you two."

Jennifer laughed. "Scott, you didn't!"

"I did," he admitted.

"How long a lecture did she give you?"

He smiled. "An earful. I told her you had pretty eyes. It quieted her down."

Jennifer had not laughed so much in months. "Scott, not while I'm this full," she protested. "Now how am I supposed to meet your sister tomorrow night without being nervous?"

"You two will get along just fine."

The waiter stopped to inquire if they would be interested in any dessert. Jennifer declined with a smile. Scott asked for the check. "The movie starts in about thirty minutes. It's time we headed over there."

He reached for her hand as they left the restaurant.

The movie theater was crowded. Scott bought their tickets, escorted Jennifer through the crowds both entering and leaving the theater. He gestured toward the refreshment stand. "Want some popcorn?"

Jennifer laughed at his hopeful expression. "And a large diet cola," she added.

He smiled. "Okay. Any candy?"

"Maybe an ice-cream cone after the movie," Jennifer said.

He nodded. Regretfully he let go of her hand. "No need for you to stand in this mob. I'll meet you by the doors to Theater Three?"

Jennifer nodded. "You won't need a hand?"

"I'll manage. See you soon." He went to find a place in line.

Jennifer made her way to Theater Three. She frowned. There were children everywhere. The Disney film was showing in Theater Four. She forced herself to take a deep breath. She started reading movie posters, anything to keep from looking at the children.

A little hand pulled at the fabric of Jennifer's slacks. "Hi." The child was holding a handful of bright red licorice sticks. "Would you like one?"

The girl could be at best three years old. Jennifer felt physically sick. Blond hair. Brown eyes. Dark eyelashes. A perfect grin. The girl could have been her own daughter had she lived. "Thank you, honey, but I already have a treat." Jennifer held up the piece of wrapped candy she had been carrying since they left the restaurant.

"Okay."

"Mandy, come over here beside Mommy."

The little girl turned. Jennifer looked up to see a lady carrying an infant coming toward them. The lady offered an apologetic smile on behalf of her daughter. Jennifer offered a soft envious smile in return. The little girl tottered off happily toward her mother.

The pain tore into her gut, and her heart stopped beating momentarily, held in the grip of a tight fist. Her composure already shaken, the encounter was enough to tip the balance. Lord, get me out of here. It was a desperate plea, and Jennifer was already turning to find the exit when Scott joined her. Never had she been more happy to see someone than at that moment. "Scott, would you please take me home?" She was desperate, and it came across in her voice and her eyes.

"Jennifer, what's wrong?" He set down the popcorn and drinks on the ledge of a display. She looked pale, shaky on her feet. He hadn't realized she wasn't feeling well.

"I need to leave," she replied softly, forcefully.

Kicking himself for not being more observant, Scott abandoned the food and maneuvered them toward the exit. Now was not the time for questions. Concern became alarm as they passed a family with an infant and a blond-haired little girl. Jennifer looked like she was going to pass out. His arm around her waist tightened. They reached the doors and she wobbled on her feet. "Let's get your jacket on, Jennifer," he said, quickly pulling it apart from his. She rested her head against the cold glass, letting him slip her jacket around her shoulders. He hurriedly found his keys.

Colleen. She tried to fight the tears. Didn't succeed.

His hand gripped hers. "Jennifer?"

She just shook her head.

Scott wrapped his arm firmly around her waist and pushed open the door. He was grateful they had parked nearby. Unlocking the passenger door, he helped her inside. Quickly, he moved around to the driver's seat. She was shivering. He started the car and turned the heater on full blast.

She took a painful breath and let it out slowly.

He watched her closely. There was very little color in her face, and her jaw was clenched as she tried to fight the tears. He'd never seen someone in shock before, and that was what he was seeing. "What happened?"

She turned her head against the seat to look at him, and it was obvious she didn't want to tell him, didn't know how to apologize for her request, didn't know what to say. "An old memory, Scott. I just wasn't ready for it," she finally said painfully.

Pain? This was agony. His hand reached over to comfortably grip hers. "Want to tell me about it?" Please, have the courage to tell me, he prayed silently.

How do I tell him about Colleen? Jennifer struggled to find the words and simply could not. The tears were already falling. To open up that pain would be devastating right now. "I'm sorry, Scott. I just can't."

If her refusal hurt, he didn't show it. He gently pulled her over from leaning against the door. His arms came around her and, very softly, he leaned down and brushed a kiss against her forehead. "It's okay, Jennifer," he said quietly, and the gentleness in his voice, his touch, told her the rest. He really was willing to give her the freedom to decide when and if she told him what was wrong. Scott kept her tucked close against his side and pulled the car out into traffic.

"Have you ever seen the city lights from Overlook Drive?" He asked a few minutes later when her tears had quieted.

She shook her head.

"They are worth seeing," Scott commented, looking down at her with a question in his eyes.

Jennifer was grateful he was not ending the evening early. She wouldn't have blamed him if he had. "I would like to see them, Scott." She rested her head against his shoulder. The arm around her moved, brushed the hair away from her face, before setting back around shoulders. "Close your eyes. Rest. We are several minutes from Overlook Drive. I'll let you know before we get there."

Jennifer could feel Scott's words as well as hear them. The last time she had been this close to a man was with Jerry. She had missed it. She closed her eyes, more than willing to just enjoy being beside him, to dream a bit about it being for real, permanent. Anything to stop her from thinking about Colleen. "These memories are never going to fade, Scott."

His arm tightened. "Yes, they will."

"How?"

"They get replaced. Eventually, they get replaced."

She sighed. "I sometimes wish I had never met Jerry."

"Jennifer."

"Okay, more accurately, I wish he had not died."

Scott knew she needed to talk. "How did you meet Jerry?"

He felt her smile. "English class. He was good-looking, outgoing. A journalism major. After class, eight of us were sitting at a table in the cafeteria, eating popcorn, studying. He joined us, taking the seat across from me. Introduced himself. Said he had seen me in class. Asked what my major was. Grinned, and asked what I wanted to be when I grew up. I finally got together the nerve to admit I wanted to be a writer. He didn't joke about it. His blue eyes got serious. 'Really?'" Jennifer smiled again. "I could tell he was impressed, Scott. He asked what I had written, which was not much at the time."

Scott chuckled. "Tell me the rest of it, Jennifer," he encouraged.

"He chose me as his study partner. He didn't need a study partner. He was smarter than I was. I liked his company. After a week and a half of his company every day, I stopped being shy around him. I liked him. He was the head of the campus Christian fellowship. He introduced me to half of the campus within the first week and a half.

"The lecture halls at college were like theaters, the wooden rows of seats angled up. I liked the tenth row in the middle. The professor couldn't see what you were doing, but it was not the back of the auditorium, either. Jerry would toss his backpack of books onto the chair beside me, offer a good morning, then mingle, saying hi to half the class before the professor arrived. A minute before class began, he would drop into the seat beside me with a smile.

"Our lit class was the first class of the day. Jerry

would bring the day's newspaper to class. I never took notes during class. I just listened to the lecture. Jerry took lots of notes. It was a two-hour class. The newspaper would come out quietly about twenty minutes into class.

"I had the habit of writing late into the night. I often slept until the last minute before racing to class. More than once I brought breakfast of a danish to class. By the third week, bringing both of us a danish was the rule."

Jennifer savored the memory of those carefree days. "Jerry soon figured out that my green notebook was my story notebook. He would see it come out, and he would offer a grin. He never read over my shoulder. That surprised me. It certainly made life easier. I didn't like most of what I wrote until the fourth or fifth draft. If I liked the story, I would slip the notebook over to him. He was like Beth. He liked everything I wrote. If I asked how I could make a story better, he would think about it awhile, then offer a different way the plot might develop, or a way to make a character more striking. Jerry loved a good mystery."

"Did you write your first book together?"

Jennifer nodded. "The sixth week of class I brought a special notebook to lit class. Asked him to read it. It was the first seventy pages of what turned out to be our first book. I had created private eye Thomas Bradford the year before, and the story had slowly evolved. Jerry was so thrilled by the book he came looking for me at the dorm. He had never come inside the dorm before. He wanted to know when I was going to finish the story. I was astounded that he liked it. I didn't think it was that good. When I told him I didn't know how it was going to end, he really got upset. He wanted to know how the case was solved, and I hadn't figured that out yet."

Scott laughed. "Is that when he got involved?"

Jennifer nodded. "He bugged me about the book for weeks. I finally told him if he wanted the book finished he was going to have to help me with it. He took me at my word. Tuesday, Wednesday and Friday afternoons he would drag me down to the bagel place, pick out a corner booth, buy us a late lunch, and we would sort out what had to happen in the book next. He started meeting me at my dorm and walking with me to lit class so he could read what I had written the night before."

Jennifer turned her wedding ring around. "I fell in love with Jerry that semester," she said softly.

"You have good memories, Jennifer. Be glad for that."

"I am. I just want those times back so badly, the memories hurt."

"They were all good times?"

Jennifer thought about it. "No," she admitted. "I was petrified I would not be able to sell my book," she said smiling, "petrified that I would. Worried about Jerry and what he thought of me."

With a great deal of reluctance Scott told her, "We are almost at Overlook Drive. When we reach the top of this rise, you will be able to see the city lights spread out below us."

Jennifer, with an equal amount of reluctance, sat up. And then she caught sight of the view. "Scott, this is incredible." The city was spread out before them, lights twinkling in a shimmering darkness.

"It helps to have a clear night." He pulled into the overlook. "Care to get out?"

She nodded. Scott turned off the car. Jennifer stepped out and slipped her jacket on properly. Scott went around the car to stop beside her. He leaned against the hood.

"I am surprised there are so many colors to the city lights," Jennifer remarked.

"Do you see the spotlight? There to the right?"

"What is it? A hospital?"

"Probably."

Jennifer smiled. "It looks like a lighthouse beacon." She leaned back beside him. "It's a nice night for seeing the stars."

"Know your constellations?"

"The Big Dipper. That is about it."

"Same here," Scott admitted. He leaned his hands back against the hood of the car to look up. "It's an awesome sight."

"Very," Jennifer agreed. She touched his arm. "You can see the Milky Way over there."

"Maybe someday we will understand the magnitude of what we are looking at."

"Maybe."

Scott looked over, hearing the shiver in her voice. "You're cold. Let's finish the drive."

She nodded. "I'm glad we stopped."

"So am I."

They drove along the mile drive slowly. The road began to descend. "Thanks, Scott. I enjoyed that."

He smiled. "So did I." He glanced at the clock on the dashboard. "It's just going on ten. We are near my place. Would you like some coffee?"

"Please."

It had been a pleasant drive, Jennifer thought.

"Jerry and I used to come to this beach years ago.

He loved the water," Jennifer commented as they drove along the lake toward Scott's home. She thought about those days and closed her eyes, fighting the sadness the memories brought.

Scott's hand reached over to hold hers.

"Make yourself comfortable, I'll be right back with the coffee," Scott said, escorting her into the living room of his home. It had a cathedral ceiling and was full of plants, beautiful pictures and comfortable furniture. She took a seat on one of the couches where she would have a good view out the windows. The moon was visible now. Almost full. Hanging low on the horizon.

"You look beautiful tonight." Jerry's arms came around his wife from behind, encircling the white, soft fuzzy robe she wore.

She smiled and leaned back against him. "Thanks," she said softly, but her attention didn't shift from the view. "You can see the sailboats in the harbor when the moonlight hits the masts just right."

"You're right," he said after a minute.

"I love this view."

"So do I."

Jennifer blushed. Her husband had turned his attention back to her.

"Did I pick a good spot for a honeymoon?"

"Perfect." She linked her hands with his. "Could we go sailing tomorrow?"

"Already planned."

"Jennifer."

She broke out of her reverie to accept the china cup. "Thank you."

He took a seat beside her, stretched his legs out.

"We had a view like this on our honeymoon. A big

full moon. The soft smell of the ocean in the air," Jennifer said softly.

Scott tilted his head to look over at her. "Where did you go?"

"Northern Washington state. A little town on the coast." Jennifer carefully tasted the hot coffee. A very faint taste of cinnamon. It was good. She leaned her head back against the high-backed couch. "You would like being married, Scott." She knew he was heading that way. It was written all over him. This man wanted to find a wife. The possibility was hard to consider. They were at different points in their lives, and sometime soon he was going to need to accept that and move on. She couldn't consider a second marriage. Not now. Not with so much grief so raw inside.

"What were those years like, Jennifer?"

Jennifer tried to give him a word picture of those years. "Morning devotions. Notes on the refrigerator. Constant deadlines. Tired eyes. Hard work. Libraries. Books. Lots of books. Late nights. Lazy afternoons. Chili dogs and baseball games. Naps in the hammock. Good books. Good movies. Good pizza. Raking leaves. Football games. Chocolate chip cookies. Hot cider. Hugs. Fires in the fireplace. Fuzzy warm blankets. Board games. Jerry cheating at cards. Christmas carols. Snowball fights. Laughter. Dinner parties. Quiet talks. No money. Lots of money. Sunny days in the park. Frisbee. Holding hands. Violets. Rainy days. Sleeping late. Breakfast in bed. Snuggling. Beautiful sunsets. Prayer. Arguments. Making up." She ran out of words.

Scott sat in silence for a long time. He had turned to watch her as she spoke, her gaze focused out on the distant lights, her attention in the past. "Describe life now, Jennifer," he asked quietly, already knowing what type of answer she was going to give. He wasn't prepared for its intensity.

"Lonely nights. Dark rooms. Tears. Anger. Lackluster meals. Being alone. Being scared. Pity in people's faces. Uncertainty. Silence. Drifting. Sadness. Broken things. Empty closets. Pity parties. Cloudy days. Shady salesmen. Bills. Isolation. Drowning. Doubting."

There was not a single thing he could say. He reached out his hand. After a moment's hesitation, she moved her own over to settle in his. His hand tightened around hers. "Thank you for answering me."

He got up and refilled her coffee. He didn't sit back down, instead moved over to lean against the window. "What plans do you have now?"

She sighed. "So many memories need to be settled. Maybe the next few months can deal with them, I don't know. I'll start on a new book."

"You're not looking forward to the change."

"I hate new things. I like comfortable, well-defined patterns. Not chaos and more uncertainty."

"Are you sure I'm not going to complicate things?"

She smiled. "Scott, you have disrupted my life from the day I met you. Of course you complicate things. But you are a nice disruption."

"Why are you so afraid of new things, Jennifer?"

She ran a hand through her hair. "I don't know. Mainly because I don't know what to do, what to say. I get flustered."

"If I throw you a first, will you at least consider it?"

She hesitantly nodded.

He walked to her side. Held out his hand. "Dance with me."

He lifted her to her feet, led her over to recessed shelves where she found a nice stereo. He slid the top CD into the player. The orchestra music filled the room. He held out his hands. Jennifer took the one step forward into his arms.

He was a good dancer. Jennifer rested her head against his chest, finding it easy to relax. "I could get used to this."

She felt him smile.

He was standing across the hall from the ladies' room, waiting for her.

He moved to her side when he saw her.

"Sorry about that," Jennifer said quietly, apologetically.

He studied her face for a moment.

"I brought you a drink. It looks like you could use it," he said finally, handing her one of the glasses he carried.

It looked like liquor. "Scott, I don't drink. Except under extreme duress," she qualified, remembering the anniversary of her husband's death.

"Neither, actually, do I. It's iced tea."

She blushed with embarrassment.

"Quit that, Jen. If you hadn't asked, I would have been upset."

Jennifer tilted her head to look at him. He was serious. She was never going to get used to this man.

Jennifer accidentally stepped on Scott's foot. It was the first time she had ever had a flashback about Scott instead of Jerry. It stunned her.

The arm at her waist tightened. "Okay?"

"Yes. Sorry," she replied, still thinking about that memory. She smiled. It was a nice memory.

The music eventually ended. Jennifer reluctantly

stepped back. Scott's hand reached up to gently brush her cheek. "Thank you, Jennifer," he said seriously.

She wisely said nothing.

"It's late. I should get you home."

The lake was quiet, still, steam rising with the dawn. Scott let the boat drift in toward the shore. With a smooth motion he cast out toward his right. He had been on the lake for an hour now, and the fish were striking at anything that flickered across the top of the water. He began smoothly reeling the lure back toward the boat waiting to feel the strike of a bass.

Jennifer was the one. Jennifer was the lady he wanted to marry.

It was a gut-level decision that he was making, but it felt right, it felt solid. He liked her. He liked her a lot. Okay, in truth, he was falling in love with her. He liked the idea of being married to a writer. He liked her personality and her preference for silence. He liked the sound of her voice. He could envision her being in his life twenty years from now.

She would make a great mom. Scott smiled as he thought about it, thought about what Jennifer was like when she talked about her niece, Tiffany, so much pride in her voice, so much love. He would love to have children with Jennifer. Two, maybe three children to fill his house. He would love to be called Dad. He could teach them to waterski, teach them to fish, teach them to love books and learning, teach them to love cooking. It was going to be great being a dad.

He couldn't wait for Heather to meet her. His mom and dad were going to love her.

Yes, Jennifer was the right one. She was perfect for him, an answer to his prayer.

Chapter Six

The last thing Jennifer felt like doing was spending an evening with Scott, going to dinner and meeting his sister. The argument she had had with God the night before had taken its toll. She wanted answers, and they were not being given. Her head was pounding. She had been in a rotten mood all day. She looked at the run in her hose. With a sigh she tossed the silk nylons into the wastebasket.

The mirror above the bathroom sink gave her a good picture of just how awful she looked.

She knew after a day of thinking about it that she had crossed the line from being honest to being disrespectful last night. God allowed her the right to be honest, to question him, to even be angry with Him, but being disrespectful was not acceptable and she knew it.

She looked up at the ceiling. "God, I am sorry."

Jennifer looked at herself in the mirror. Grimaced. She pulled her hair back into a ponytail, reached for a washcloth.

When Scott arrived an hour later, he found a very

subdued Jennifer sitting in the living room watching for him to arrive. Her dress was a beautiful sapphire blue, a simple, striking dress. Scott looked her over with pleasure. "I like it."

She smiled, his compliment helping assuage a very wounded spirit. She had discarded almost her entire wardrobe trying to find something which would not accentuate her pallor. Scott's second careful study of her face told her she had not totally hidden the effects of the day. The hand that took hers was gentle. "What's wrong?"

"I had a rough day," she admitted. "A lot on my mind."

"Would you like to take a pass on tonight? All you have to do is say the word."

"No. I'm okay. Just a little tired."

He nodded, understanding better than she realized that she really was emotionally exhausted. Her eyes told a message of their own. "We'll make it an early evening," he said.

He helped her on with her coat and locked the door for her.

Jennifer was surprised, at the same time relieved, by Scott's willingness to let the silence stretch between them. He had slipped a cassette into the player; the soft piano music was the only sound in the car.

Jennifer watched him as he drove. He really was a very handsome man. She now knew him well enough to be able to see the smile lines around his eyes, the little brush of silver-gray in his hair. She had found him in the past few weeks to be solid, dependable, trustworthy, gentle. A man who understood how to care, how to support. She had thought, after first meeting him, that he would be a man she would feel smothered being around. That the strength of his own personality would overwhelm her. Instead, she found him a very comfortable man to be around. He had never threatened her own carefully protected space. He listened. Let her choose how much to say. He was not threatened by silence.

He looked over and caught her inspection. Smiled with a question in his eyes. She shook her head slightly, her thoughts not something she could put into words. His smile deepened, but he chose not to break the silence.

The restaurant Scott chose surprised Jennifer. French. Quiet. Elegant. Their table, tucked in the corner, very private. Jennifer found herself on uncertain ground. She looked over at Scott.

His smile was gentle. "Relax, Jennifer. It's going to be a quiet evening, nothing more."

His soft reassurance made her blush with embarrassment.

"Stop that, Jennifer," he said, his voice suddenly stern, his hand reaching over to grasp hers. "Caution does not warrant an apology."

"It does if it's unfounded."

"No, it doesn't." He released her hand. "Please, Jennifer, trust me. You don't have to apologize for being cautious."

She lowered her eyes. "Thank you, Scott."

He frowned. "Jennifer, what happened today? Something is seriously wrong."

She looked up. The waiter joining them to take their orders, gave her a reason not to answer immediately. Their orders given, once again alone, Jennifer looked over at Scott and debated how to answer him. "I had a fight with God," she finally admitted.

His serious expression told her how strongly he took that news.

"It's not the first one we have had, nor will it likely be the last one. But the aftereffects are difficult to deal with."

"Why, Jennifer?"

"Scott, there is a great deal you don't know about me. I don't know that I can explain everything that is going on. I am still at odds with God over some basic issues involving Jerry." She sighed. "I pushed my case on one of those issues last night."

"Are you okay, Jennifer?"

"He's my Father, Scott. I don't like being at odds with Him. But I don't understand Him at times, and it is not an easy position to be in. It's just going to take some time to resolve."

"Jennifer, do you want to talk about the issues? I'll help if I can."

I would have to tell you about Colleen. I don't want you to see that side of me, Scott, that angry, hurting side of me. There is a limit to what a new relationship can support. I can't share that level of grief. Not yet. She reached over to touch his hand. "Thank you, Scott. I will take you up on that offer sometime. I can't tonight."

He squeezed her hand. "It's an open offer, Jennifer."

Dinner arrived. They both kept the conversation light during dinner, away from emotional subjects. Jennifer began to relax. By the end of the meal, Scott had succeeded in making her laugh several times. "Thank you, Scott," she said softly, gratefully, as they crossed the parking lot.

He hugged her. "That's what friends are for, Jennifer." He held the car door for her, closing it softly once she had slipped inside.

"Would you rather pass on meeting Heather tonight?"

It was a tempting offer. "No, Scott. Let's get it over with."

He smiled. "You don't have to be so nervous about this, Jennifer. Heather promised to be on her best behavior."

She's pregnant, Scott. That's the real problem. Jennifer forced a smile. "She's your sister, Scott."

"Don't hold it against her. As she so often says, she didn't have a choice in the matter."

Jennifer laughed. "Okay, Scott."

It was a thirty-minute drive to Heather and Frank's home. The house was two stories with white siding and a van parked in the driveway. As Jennifer expected, the yard was beautifully landscaped. The porch light was on. Scott pulled into the driveway behind the van.

Scott put a comforting arm around Jennifer's waist as they walked toward the front door. The door opened within moments of Scott ringing the doorbell. Heather's husband, Frank. "Scott. Jennifer. Welcome. Please, come in." Frank held the door for them with a smile.

"Jennifer, this is my sister's husband, Frank." Scott did the introductions once they were inside.

"Hello, Frank," Jennifer said with a nervous smile.

Frank took her hand. "It's nice to finally meet you, Jennifer. Let me take your coats. Come in and make yourselves comfortable. Heather's on her way down. The kids are already in bed."

The living room was beautiful. White carpet. Bold

red, green and blue fabrics for the two love seats, the easy chairs. Scott's hand on her waist, warm through the fabric of her dress, was a comforting guide.

"Scott! I am sorry. I was working in the nursery."

Jennifer didn't need to be told this was Heather. The lady was very petite, at most five feet two inches. She carried being pregnant beautifully. Scott met her with a hug. "Hi, Twig." He smiled at the paint splatters on her face. "Let me guess…you're working on the forest."

"Yes." She rubbed at the offending paint drops, her attention already turning to her guest. Scott reached back for Jennifer's hand.

"Jennifer, this is my sister, Heather. Heather, Jennifer St. James."

"Hi," Heather said softly, her natural shyness competing with an intense interest in Scott's new friend.

Jennifer bravely smiled in return. "Hello, Heather."

Both men were quick to step in to ease the tension. "Jennifer, Scott, would you like some coffee?" Frank asked.

"Please," Scott replied for both of them. "Heather, sit down, get off your feet. We won't stay long. How is the nursery coming?" Scott settled Jennifer on the love seat beside him, his fingers interlacing with hers, which were surprisingly cold.

"I'm almost halfway done with the forest," Heather replied. "I've been painting a mural around the nursery, something to make it different…not just white walls," she explained for Jennifer's benefit.

Jennifer found if she looked at Heather's face she could keep her nerves under control. "Did you create the design yourself, or are you using stencils?" she asked, working hard to keep her voice steady.

"Stencils. I found them in a children's book and then enlarged them."

Jennifer was intrigued. "Does the mural cover the entire wall?"

Heather grinned. "Yes. Frank gets to paint the part by the floor."

Frank came back in carrying a tray of coffee cups. He handed them around. A black Samoyed followed him into the room.

"Hi, Blackie," Scott greeted the dog.

"She's beautiful." The dog came over to say hello. Jennifer ran her hand along the warm fur of the dog's back.

"Would you like to see her puppies, Jennifer?" Heather offered.

"Yes, I would."

Heather waved both her husband and her brother back to their seats. "Stay put, we won't be long."

Scott felt the flutter in Jennifer's pulse. He gently squeezed her hand as she got up. The ladies left the room, walked through the house to the back patio where a small greenhouse had been built.

"Sorry, Jennifer, but it's rather difficult to talk about my brother when he's in the room. How do you like him so far?"

Jennifer chuckled. Heather was perfect. "I like him, Heather."

Heather smiled. "Good." She held open the door to the greenhouse. "The puppies have a home out here for the time being." She turned on the overhead lights. The room was warm, smelled moist, of earth, foliage and the fragrant smell of flowers.

Jennifer followed Heather slowly, captivated by the plants, the flowers, the violets. Jennifer stopped to carefully touch the leaves of a beautiful purple flow-ering violet.

"Do you like it? It's one of my personal favorites."

"I love it."

"I'll send you a couple of plants home. All they need is sunlight and water and they thrive."

Jennifer grimaced. "I just killed my last violets. The flowers around my porch are surviving by pure luck. I am not known for my ability to care for anything that is green."

Heather chuckled. "You can learn. Look at Scott. The man could turn anything brown within a week, but he's gotten better with time."

"Scott actually waters plants?"

Heather laughed. "You would be surprised."

The four puppies were curled up together on a quilt in a big basket, all sleeping.

"Heather, they are adorable." Jennifer gently stroked the soft fur of the two nearest puppies.

"I think so. The kids love them." Heather picked up the nearest puppy. "This is Pepper. He has the only markings in the litter. Two white feet."

Jennifer chuckled. "Cute. What are the others' names?"

"The nearest one is Choc, short for chocolate, then Gretta, and finally Quigley."

Jennifer reached across to stroke the last puppy. He woke enough to open his eyes, lick her hand. "Who thought up the name Quigley?"

Heather grinned. "Scott. He's planning to adopt him when he gets a few weeks older."

"He will have his hands full."

Heather set Pepper back down on the quilt. "Yes, he will." Heather groaned softly as she straightened.

"When's your baby due?"

"Eight more weeks. Would you like to see the nursery, Jennifer?"

Jennifer wanted to decline. Part of her also wanted to run the risk. She was curious to see what Heather had done with the nursery, see the mural. She took a chance. "Yes I would."

Heather led them back inside, up to the second floor.

Jennifer hesitated in the doorway to the room, then forced herself to cross the threshold. The room was lovely. The furniture had been shifted to one side of the room to leave the wall with the mural open. Jennifer looked around the room. "Heather, I love it." She could tell the colors had been carefully chosen to favor neither pink nor blue. "Do you know if you are going to have a boy or a girl?"

"No. We decided we would rather wait."

Jennifer smiled. "Do you have a preference?"

"Not a strong one. As long as my baby is healthy, I will be happy. I already know the delivery will have to be a cesarean-section. My rebuilt right hip will not allow a normal delivery. I'm not looking forward to that."

"If it's going to be necessary, at least you know from the beginning. To go through hours of labor and then have to have a C-section would be awful."

Heather groaned. "That is an understatement."

"I love the curtains, Heather. Did you make them yourself?"

"Mom made them for me."

"This will be their third grandchild?"

"Yes. Scott has disappointed Mom, she always hoped he would be the first to have a family."

Jennifer absorbed that remark, tucking it away as confirmation of something she already suspected. She walked over to study the mural design. If she looked closely, she could see the design yet to be painted penciled on the wall. "This looks very intricate."

"It is taking much longer than I originally planned. The leaves are so detailed."

"There's a leopard," Jennifer said is surprise, finding the penciled figure in the mural.

Heather joined her, carefully tracing the penciled figure. "He is going to be so key to the mural that I haven't yet had the nerve to begin painting him."

Jennifer nodded. "At least you have lots of leaves to practice on."

Heather smiled. "Exactly."

Eventually, after inspecting everything in the room, discussing future plans for furniture and colors, they left the nursery together. "How did you like the play?" Heather asked as they made their way back downstairs.

"I loved it. Scott told me he stood you up."

Heather laughed. "I forgave him. At least he was not using work as an excuse this time."

"Is it just a wrong impression, or does Scott work too hard?"

Heather considered the question carefully. "He's the first one in our family to reach such an important position, I don't really have a reference to say what is normal for a position such as his. I know he doesn't relax easily, that the job is always there weighing on his mind. He has to continually struggle to have a life away from his job."

Jennifer nodded thoughtfully. "Thanks, Heather."

"Sure. Scott tells me you recently finished another book?"

"Yes."

"I've read all of your books. You're a very good writer, Jennifer."

"Thank you," Jennifer said, caught off guard.

Heather grinned. "Don't be so modest. I envy you your talent. One of these days, we need to go to lunch together. I would love to hear what it's like to be a writer."

Jennifer laughed. "I would like that."

They joined the two men in the living room. Jennifer smiled for Scott's benefit as she joined him on the couch. The fact she had survived a trip to the nursery was her biggest accomplishment in weeks. She was very relieved to have the experience over, but also very glad she had agreed.

The evening ended shortly thereafter. It was late. Without anything being said, Scott knew his sister was tired. Frank was sent to the greenhouse to bring back two beautiful violets. Jennifer gracefully accepted the gift.

Goodbyes were said without being drawn out.

Jennifer leaned her head back against the seat as Scott pulled the car out of the drive. She let out her breath in a deep sigh of relief.

"Was it that hard?"

Jennifer didn't bother to soften her answer. "Yes."

Scott looked over at her, curious, wishing she would explain. Everything he had seen said Jennifer and Heather had hit it off, were already on the way to becoming friends. Jennifer's assessment did not match his observation. "Why was it hard?" Scott asked, feeling the need to push for an answer.

"She's pregnant," Jennifer finally replied.

"That's a problem?"

She nodded.

Scott looked over at Jennifer, needing answers. Her expression stopped his next question. She was seriously hurting. He reached over to grasp her hand. This is the issue Lord, isn't it? "Talk to me, Jennifer. What's going on?"

It was time to tell him. She abruptly changed the subject. "Could we go for a walk on the beach? Could you handle another late night?"

Her request surprised him. "Sure, if you would like to."

"Please."

Chapter Seven

Even with her coat on, Jennifer found the night air too cold to walk far, and her shoes weren't made for walking on sand. At Scott's suggestion, they went back to his place. He built a fire. With all the lights off, the living room took on a soft glow as the flames flickered around the logs, the only sound an occasional loud snap and sizzle as the sap in the wood burned.

He pulled her down on the sofa beside him and tucked her gently against him. Her head cradled against his shoulder, Jennifer watched the flames in silence for some time. She could feel Scott breathing, even hear his heartbeat. His arms around her waist were strong and solid. It felt so good to be near him. It felt safe.

"I lost a baby girl," Jennifer said softly into the silence.

She felt Scott's reaction. The sudden stillness as his breathing stopped. "When, Jennifer?"

He understood her pain. It was in his voice, in the way he was suddenly holding her. He understood her pain and was sharing it. Somewhere inside Jennifer a glimmer of hope began to form. She had taken such a risk in saying those words. Letting Scott see a memory that was still raw and unhealed. He could hurt her so badly with just a wrong word.

She was crying. She had been so afraid Scott would be angry that she had not told him earlier.

Scott looked down at the face of the most important woman who had ever been in his life and had to close his eyes at the pain he saw. His arms tightened around her. "Honey, it's okay. It's going to be okay." He was not able to think of anything else to say. He rocked her gently in his arms and let her cry. He felt a few tears slip down his own face as well. She had been holding the memory inside all this time. So much now made sense. Her anger at God. Her hesitancy to really talk with him. Scott groaned. Her reluctance to be around young children. How could he have missed seeing something so desperately wrong? She was a lady fighting a battle with grief so severe it had been crushing her heart and he had not understood. "Jennifer. Honey, it's going to be all right." He gently wiped away the tears streaming down her face. A baby. She would have made such a wonderful mother.

"Jennifer, tell me what happened." He needed to know. Please, Lord, help her to tell me.

There was a long silence as she tried to stop the tears. Scott waited, stroking her arms lightly, feeling the occasional tremor that ran down her back. She was in so much pain.

"I couldn't carry her to term. She was born badly premature." She let out a shaky breath. "She was so beautiful Scott. So awful tiny. She only weighed two pounds two ounces. Her feet were less than an inch long, her fingers couldn't even circle my little finger. She was less than eleven inches long. She was the most beautiful baby I had ever seen." She took a deep breath and let it out on a sob. "They said she wouldn't live. Her lungs were not developed, and the stress of having to breathe before she was physically ready to do so was such a crisis for her. But she was born, and alive, and she was going to live. You could see it in her blue eyes. She was such a fighter."

Scott gently brushed the hair back from Jennifer's face, watching her expression, the pain, seeing the incredible intensity of love she had felt for her daughter. He could feel the crushing pain inside his own heart at what was coming. God, why?

Jennifer smiled at a memory from the past. "But she did live, Scott. And she finally learned how to suck and she started to gain weight and she got stronger, and they even began to talk about miracles happening. I started to make her little clothes so she would have something to wear when she came home. I would spend my days at the hospital holding her and talking to her and telling her about her Dad and she would smile at me with those vivid blue eyes."

There was a very long silence and Scott did not disturb it. He couldn't.

"She was ten weeks old when she got the cold. In the last week when she no longer had the energy to move, she would lie in the incubator and watch me with her vivid blue eyes and blink at me as I talked to her. She struggled so hard for each breath. I got my hand inside the incubator around all the tubes and slid my finger under her hand and stroked the back of her arm, and I prayed a very simple prayer. Lord, she needs another breath. And when she breathed, I would say thank you and I would pray again. We were a team. I prayed and God answered and she breathed."

The words stopped. A heavy shudder shook her frame. "At 10:02 p.m. on Wednesday, December 10, I prayed, and God didn't answer, and my baby didn't breathe."

Oh, God. How could You crush someone's faith so callously? Of all the ways the baby could have died, why did you destroy Jennifer's faith in the process? Scott had never felt such anger before in his entire life. Never at a person. Never at his God. But it erupted full blown as he heard what Jennifer said.

"What was her name, Jennifer? What was your daughter's name?"

"Colleen." She said it on a whisper. "Colleen Marie St. James."

He didn't often call his sister in the middle of the night, but Scott picked up the phone at 2:00 a.m. when he got back from taking Jennifer home and dialed Heather's number. He had to talk to someone. She answered the phone on the third ring. "Twig."

"What's wrong, Scott? Mom?" There was alarm in her voice.

"No, all the family is fine. I need to talk about Jennifer."

There was silence for a minute as she woke up and regrouped. "What's wrong, Scott?"

"I just found out Jennifer lost a baby girl, Twig." He drew a deep, shaky breath. "I was okay when she told me, now I feel like I'm falling apart. I don't know what to do. She's been bleeding inside with grief because she lost a daughter."

"Oh, Scott. If I'd only known. I spent the evening talking about my pregnancy, showing her the nursery."

"You didn't know. Neither of us did. I should have put the pieces together earlier." He took another deep breath, fighting to stop the tears that wanted to come from deep in his gut. "Jennifer was pregnant when Jerry died. Did her best to keep herself together for the baby's sake. But the strain was too much, Colleen was born over two months premature. She beat the odds and made it through the first few days, apparently began to improve rapidly, after two months there was talk of letting her go home. Then she got sick and took a turn for the worse. She was three months old when she died.

"Jennifer has been blaming herself for the child's death, that it was her fault the child was premature. She could barely talk tonight, she was hurting so much." He ran a hand through his hair. "I don't know how to help her, Twig."

"Give her time, Scott. At least she's grieving. That's better than denying the pain of what happened."

"Without meaning to, I could really hurt her right now. Should I talk about it now that I know? Try not to talk about it?"

"Does she have any family in the area?"

"Her brother and his wife. Jennifer seems close to both Peter and Rachel."

"Then let her set the pace, Scott. From what you said, she's been fairly open about her late husband."

"Yes."

"She'll reach the point she can talk about Colleen the same way. It will just take time."

"Thank you, Twig. I'm sorry I had to wake you up."

"That's okay, Scott. I'll pray for you both. You can

handle this. Please, try not to worry tonight. Try to get some sleep."

"I'll try."

He put the phone down slowly after saying good-night. Time. His concept of how long he thought she needed had just been overtaken by a new reality. "Jennifer, I'll give you all the time you need. I promise you that," he whispered. "But I'm not going to let you retreat back into a shell now. Not after you have finally begun to face the pain. We'll get through this together. I'm not going to let you be alone in your grief anymore."

He lay awake for hours that night, fighting God over the senseless way Colleen had died, angry at the pain, angry at the brutal fact such a simple heartfelt prayer had not been answered. The anger did not change the circumstances, but he found in himself an intense willingness to go toe to toe with God to at least ensure Jennifer got an answer to the question of Why. She was going to be his wife. His God could not leave her like this. He had to at least heal the pain.

You've left her torn apart for three years, God. That makes no sense. I know You. You don't act this way. You don't rip apart and walk away. Why haven't You helped her? Why haven't You intervened? This isn't like You. You have to get back in this game and ease her pain. Is not one of Your names Comfort? I don't see love here, or comfort. Does it give You pleasure to leave her trapped in grief? How could You do this to the woman I love?

"Hi," Scott said quietly when she opened the door. He wished he had worn his sunglasses, taken more than the three aspirins, done something more to ease the pain radiating behind his eyes. He was at her door as early as he thought safe. He didn't want to have their first conversation be over a phone. He knew how the grief was going to hit her, and the last thing he wanted was distance between them when they talked. She looked awful but he didn't care. He felt as bad as she did.

"Hi," Jennifer replied softly, not meeting his eyes. She opened the door for him and Scott stepped inside. She felt very self-conscience this morning. She didn't know what to say after last night. She knew she looked a mess, and that didn't help any.

"I brought these for you." He took a ribbon-tied set of three roses from behind his back, one red, one peach, one white.

"Thank you, Scott," she said, fighting tears. Why did he have to be so nice? "They are beautiful."

Scott watched her as she carried the flowers into the living room and added them to the vase on the end table. He frowned. "Jennifer, did you sleep at all last night?"

She brushed away a tear as she wearily shook her head. "I thought I was over these crying jags months ago, Scott. Last night, every time I closed my eyes I was back in that hospital lounge, waiting for word about Colleen, or wearing that awful green gown I always had to wear when I was around her, trying to hold her despite all the machines around her," she grimaced, "remembering what it was like when she died."

Scott crossed over to join her, his hands lightly touching her shoulders, turning her toward him. "Look at me, honey."

She finally did.

He hated the look in her eyes. They were dying

again. "I am glad you told me. I know how hard it was. I'm angry with God for how Colleen died. She was your daughter, and you shouldn't have had to suffer the loss of both your husband and your daughter. But you have to deal with the grief and get beyond this, Jennifer. You've got no choice. You will have other children someday." It was the only thing promising that he had been able to find last night. She would have other children. God willing, they would be his. She was afraid of the idea right now, afraid of having more children, he knew it, he could feel it, but given time, her grief would eventually heal.

Jennifer didn't say anything. She blinked a couple of times, and he couldn't tell if she'd even heard him. She turned away to walk to the window, wearily rubbed the back of her neck, and he wondered how bad her headache was. "I'm sorry I didn't tell you sooner," she said. "Several times I have wanted to talk about her, but I could never find the right words."

The wall he had feared was up between them. He wasn't going to be getting close to her grief today. She had pushed it and the pain too far down to be touched. Scott closed his eyes and took a deep breath. Now was not the time to push. She desperately needed a break. The crisis the morning he had met her was nothing compared to the crisis that was coming, unless she got some help. She wasn't going to make it through this pain. She hadn't slept, and her emotions were becoming deadened. Mentally, physically, she didn't have the reserves to deal with what had happened. And if he wasn't careful she was going to see his presence as adding to her pain. He knew about the prayer, he knew the details of her crisis of faith. And her brother Peter didn't. He had realized that sometime during the night. She had never told Peter and Rachel about praying for Colleen to breathe. It had remained her private battle with God. The fact he knew made him dangerous to her now. If he wasn't careful, she was going to push him away, just as she was trying to push away the pain.

In an insight that seemed to come directly from the Lord, he asked, "Would you like to go out on the lake for a couple of hours? It's promising to be a relatively warm, sunny day. We could even do a little fishing if you like. It's peaceful out on the water and you don't have to think about anything, just watch your bobber. It might help you sleep. The wind and water always have that effect on me."

She turned to look at him—the quiet, calm, studying look she'd given on the pier the morning she had come back to the beach. It was radiating out from the strength inside, reserves he'd seen her tap that very first morning when she'd been so tired it had been hard for her to walk a straight line. "You're taking the day off work?"

"I figured you might like some company."

It earned him a soft real smile. It disappeared too quickly, but it gave him hope. She crossed back to his side, squeezed his hand. "Thank you, Scott. I really appreciate that. Yes, let's go out on the lake for a bit. I like to fish. Should I pack us a lunch?"

"I'll pack a cooler with drinks to take along. If we catch anything, we can fix them for lunch. If not, there is a restaurant built out on the lake down at the harbor. We can eat there," Scott replied, improvising everything.

She seemed willing to let him. "I'll just get changed and be back in a minute."

Jennifer changed clothes, her movements heavy and forced. Her reserves were gone, she was weary beyond words. She had already decided she was going to lean on Scott to the literal extent he would allow her. She was tired of fighting God. Tired of caring. Tired of coping. Today she was going to leave all the misery here at the house and ignore it all for as long as she could. It had been such a long, painful night. There were no more tears to shed. She had ended up standing in the doorway to the room that had once been prepared as her daughter's nursery, and she had sobbed there until she'd thought her heart would break. But her heart had stayed intact, and the hours had passed, and she'd eventually, wearily, headed to the kitchen to fix coffee and toast as the sun rose.

They left the house, Scott carrying her windbreaker for her, and he carefully made sure her seat belt was fastened once she was seated in the passenger seat. Jennifer leaned her head back against the headrest and closed her eyes and listened to the music Scott had turned on. She was almost dozing when they reached his house.

Jennifer looked over at Scott as they walked down to the pier together, her hand tucked firmly in his, and was incredibly grateful to no longer be alone. When she saw the boat she smiled. It had been designed for one specific thing, fishing, and the sight of it brought back ancient memories from her past, and she was glad she had come.

"Watch your step." Scott offered a hand to help her down into the boat.

The boat was designed to seat four. Jennifer moved forward to the middle seat.

Scott handed her a life jacket.

Once the cooler and the towels were stashed, Scott took his seat. He slipped the key into the ignition. The outboard motor started instantly. Leaving the motor idling, he got up to untie the mooring lines. "I'll run us over to the Harbor Stop to fill up the gas tank, get bait, then we'll head out to Westminster Bridge."

Jennifer nodded.

Once they cleared the No Wake zone, Scott opened the motor up, giving enough speed to lift the bow out of the water. Jennifer deliberately left last night at the pier and forced herself into beginning to relax. And unexpectedly she found her spirits beginning to lift as the bright sun and sky replaced her sense of darkness with the vividness of a beautiful day.

After close to five minutes of running, they passed Courtline Point and were out on the open water. The wind picked up.

Jennifer swiveled around to face Scott.

"Do you need me to slow down?"

Jennifer shook her head. "You're fine. The spray is cold even with the jacket."

"We'll be at The Harbor Stop in another four to five minutes."

Scott cut the speed down to comply with the No Wake rule as they entered the protected cove. Jennifer turned back to the front, impatiently brushing her hands through her hair to get it out of her eyes. She should have tied it back before she left. It was going to take twenty minutes with a brush to get her hair untangled.

The Harbor Stop turned out to be a supply store built out on the water, floating on pontoons at the lake level. A series of docks had slips to hold fifty boats. Scott piloted the boat to the east side of the store so he could moor within reach of the gas pumps. Intent on watching his distance, Scott didn't realize Jennifer had the forward mooring line in her hands, until, as the boat touched the dock with a gentle bump, she flipped the line over the tie point and brought the boat in snug to the dock. "Okay, Scott, you can cut the engine." She gave the line four figure-eights around the north-south prongs of the tie point, adding an extra turn to each loop. The line would not slip.

"Thanks."

"Sure." She looked around the boat. "Do you have a bait bucket for the minnows?"

"Behind you on the left. It's in the live well." Scott replied. He stepped out of the boat onto the dock. He had missed something. The bow moor line she had tied was a duplicate of the stern line he had tied. Jennifer was not a novice to boats.

Scott took the minnow bucket and offered her a hand out of the boat. She took his hand without hesitation. "Thanks."

Following Scott's example she dropped her life jacket back on her seat. "Gas first or bait?"

"Bait," Scott decided.

Leaving Scott to get the minnows, Jennifer wandered around to check out the store. There was a collection of paperbacks on the back wall. She paged through a mystery she recognized.

"Jennifer."

She turned, surprised to find Scott beside her.

"Try these on." He was holding a pair of sunglasses.

"Scott, I don't need—"

He cut her off with a smile. "Try them on."

Jennifer tried them on.

"What do you think? Do they fit all right?"

She smiled. "You made a good choice, Scott. They fit fine."

"Good."

He took the glasses. "Do me a favor and see if they have any chocolate cookies."

Jennifer laughed. "Okay." Her hands gently pushed his chest. "You're supposed to be buying the bait, Scott."

"Okay, okay."

Ten minutes later, Scott offered Jennifer a hand back into the boat.

"How far is Westminster Bridge?"

"About ten minutes west of here," he replied, stowing the minnow bucket where it would not shift. Jennifer clipped on her life jacket. She leaned forward to untie the bow moor line.

Scott started the engine. "Okay, Jennifer."

She released the line and pushed them away from the dock. Once they cleared the No Wake zone, he opened the motor up, sending the boat skimming across the open water. Jennifer slipped on her new sunglasses. It had been a long time since she had spent a day on the water. She was determined to enjoy this.

The lake was long, constantly branching, with a multitude of coves and inlets. Scott eventually turned into one of the side branches of the lake. The inlet was over three hundred feet wide at the opening, narrowing as it went back. Westminster Bridge was a railroad crossing, the concrete pillars farther down the inlet. "We'll start in on this side and make the half circle of the inlet," Scott explained, slowing the engine as he took the boat in toward the shoreline.

Jennifer nodded. There were fallen trees in the water beneath them, their massive root structures visible on the bank and the trees angling out into the water. The banks, however, appeared to drop off very quickly; there was no evidence to suggest they were actually floating over old trees the lake had swallowed up.

Scott dropped anchor once they were about fifteen feet from the shore. Jennifer slipped off her life jacket, draping it across the seat in front of her. Scott tossed his life jacket up front beside hers. Finding the right key, he unlocked the storage compartment where the tackle was stored. There were a dozen different rods, different makes, different reels. "Take your pick, Jennifer," he offered.

"The blue one with the open-face reel."

Scott lifted the rod out for her. He brought out the gray rod and open-face reel for himself, his birthday present from his dad.

Jennifer took a look at the rod. It had a swivel, hook and weight already. All she needed was a bobber. "Can you reach the tackle box?"

He passed it forward.

"Thanks." Humming softly, Jennifer found what she needed. Looping the line around the bobber, she slipped the metal spring back over the line to hold it in place.

She swiveled around to reach the minnow bucket. Jennifer closed her hand around one of larger ones. Smooth and slippery, it struggled to get free. She slipped the hook through the minnow's back behind its front fin. Studying the shoreline for a moment, she shifted around. Her cast sent the minnow and the bobber out parallel to the shore.

Watching her, Scott nodded his approval. She was not a novice at this by any means. She would get the best coverage of the territory by going parallel to the shore, rather than toward the shore. With a smile, Scott sent his line sailing out the other direction.

They followed the south bank, making their way toward the concrete pillars of Westminster Bridge. Scott was pleased to see the strain from last night beginning to fade from Jennifer's eyes. She was a born fisherman. She had a good eye for the water, a smooth cast, patience. She was clearly enjoying herself. She was also beating him hands down in terms of success. She had caught four bass, three of which were large enough to keep and dress.

Scott was enjoying watching her.

He needed to do something tangible to help her deal with her grief. It was the trauma of the loss that was so devastating. It was how Colleen had been born, how she had died that was the real problem he had to help Jennifer overcome. *Trauma.* The word kept coming back in his mind as he prayed. Jennifer was still caught by the event. When she had described those last few days when Colleen had fought for each breath, Scott had been able to see her there, sitting beside the incubator with her hand reaching inside and holding Colleen's, praying for each breath Colleen needed to take. He could see the shock that would have crossed her face when her last prayer for breath had not been answered. Colleen had died.

Trauma.

Scott couldn't comprehend the shock of what it must have been like to have such a simple prayer not answered. Jennifer had fallen so deeply in love with Colleen. It was in her voice, her face, her emotions. To watch her daughter die... Scott shook his head, flinching inside at the pain the image created.

How could he take Jennifer out of the place she was in now to a place where the trauma could lessen? Maybe it was happening already. The movie theater and the shock he had observed. The long night of tears last night. She was finally coming alive and feeling the pain and the grief and facing the trauma. And she had worked up the courage to tell him. They all had to be steps in the right direction.

He was furious at God for having put them in this situation. It was going to take more than one day for his own emotions to accept what had happened. He'd find a way. She needed him to be past the anger. But she had been working against the anger for almost three years, he'd been feeling it less than twenty-four hours. He needed time and answers, too.

They reached the bridge. Scott used the trolling motor to take them out away from shore and back into the main waterway. He cut the engine when they were some twenty feet from the base of the pillars; they would drift in closer. "I've had some luck around the base of the pillars," he offered. "It's deep here, around thirty feet."

Jennifer nodded. She cast her line out toward the first concrete pillar.

Scott watched her for a moment, before leaning forward to reach the minnow bucket and bait his own line. He cast his line out toward the second pillar. The bait dropped into the water a few inches from the concrete pillar. The bait had no more than hit the water then his bobber was gone.

Jennifer smiled. "You weren't kidding." She turned to watch him bring the fish in. The rod bowed down a foot as the line strained. The fish was trying to go deep. Scott turned him back.

"Nice fish." Jennifer commented as Scott brought him in over the side. It was a good-size crappie. Catching Scott's line, she slid her hand down to grasp the top of the hook and hold the fish still. Sliding her hand down the body of the fish, she lowered the back fins so she would not get spiked. He was almost too large for her hand. The hook came out easily, he'd been snagged through the side of his mouth.

Jennifer swiveled around so she could measure the fish. "Ten and three-quarter inches. Not bad."

Scott smiled. "He'll dress nicely," he agreed. He opened up the live well and Jennifer released the crappie in with the three bass she had caught earlier.

Jennifer leaned over the side of the boat to wash off her hands. Scott tossed her the towel. "Thanks." She wiped her hands and draped the towel across the seat.

The next fish went to Jennifer. It was a sunfish, which surprised her, given the size of the hook she was using. She leaned over the side of the boat and released it gently. She looked up to find Scott watching her. "What?" she asked, confused by his look.

"You've got a soft heart."

"Only for babies," she replied, but her smile was beautiful.

They fished along the pillars for a while, then moved to the north bank, slowly propelled by the trolling motor. Jennifer had not said anything, but Scott could tell she was getting to the end of her energy reserves. They had been out almost three hours. He was ready to suggest they head in when her bobber dropped below the surface with a jerk as the minnow four feet below the surface was hit.

She had a fighter. Scott pulled in his line to give her room to maneuver. Twice the fish turned in to the boat, then ran out again, forcing Jennifer to give up line or risk losing him.

The bass broke the surface on its third turn.

"Wow."

"He's a trophy, Jennifer." Scott hoped her line would hold.

Jennifer brought the fish to the side of the boat on the fifth turn. Scott got underneath him with the net and brought the bass over the side of the boat. The largemouth bass slapped angrily against the confinement. Scott took a firm grip on his lower lip. "Okay, Jennifer."

She slid the net free. "How's he hooked?"

"It's down in the side of his mouth."

Jennifer dug out the needle-nose pliers. "At least he didn't swallow it."

Scott held the fish firmly as Jennifer went after the hook. "Can you reach it?"

She got a firm grip on the eye of the hook, pushed it down. "Got it." She brought the hook out.

"Take him firmly by the bottom lip and put him against the tape, Jennifer. Let's find out how big he really is." Scott handed her back her prize fish.

He was heavy, cold. Jennifer laid him against the measuring tape on the side of the boat. "Twenty-one and a quarter inches," she finally decided. "He's the second largest bass I've ever caught." He was a beautiful fish.

"Would you like to have him mounted?"

Jennifer looked at the fish in her hands. "No. This one gets to go free." Leaning over the side, she lowered the fish down into the water. For a brief moment he remained motionless in her hands, able to swim free, but choosing not to move. Then he was gone with a slap against her hand.

Scott handed her a dry towel. "What's your record?"

"Twenty-six and a half inches. I caught him down on Lake Tahoe eight years ago," she replied.

"You've certainly got another story to tell with this one."

"You can say that again. He was beautiful."

"I think that one is going to be impossible to top. Shall we head in?"

Jennifer looked regretfully at the water, but had to concede she was exhausted. "Yes."

Scott nodded and moved back to his seat. Jennifer quietly began storing their gear in the lockers. She handed Scott his life jacket, than slipped on her own.

"Ready?"

She nodded.

"Where's the best place to clean the fish?" she asked as the boat pulled up to his pier.

"I have a cleaning table already set up in the boathouse. I can handle this part of it, Jennifer, if you would like to go ahead and take the cooler up to the house." He handed her the keys.

"Anything you need?"

"A pan of water to put the fish in. Try the cupboard to the left of the sink."

"No problem. I'll be right back."

Scott had already cleaned two crappie by the time Jennifer joined him. She set down the pan of water on the worktable beside him. "Thanks."

Jennifer watched him fillet the first bass. His movements were smooth. She could appreciate the skill. Jennifer quietly studied him as he worked.

Scott looked over, caught her look. He smiled. "For

lunch, how about if we wrap the fish in foil with a little garlic butter and almonds, put it over a hot grill? Maybe fix baked potatoes, as well? There is fruit salad in the refrigerator," Scott suggested as he worked.

"Sounds wonderful," Jennifer agreed. She smiled. "I just realized how hungry I am."

Scott chuckled. "Nothing is better than fresh fish when you are hungry." Their footsteps echoed across the redwood deck.

It had been a long time since she had done such a normal thing as setting the table, Jennifer realized as she set their places. It was odd, how being a widow changed things. It wasn't worth the effort to fix a meal for one, so she rarely had a need to sit at her dining room table. More often than not, she ate a sandwich at her desk while she worked. She had missed this normal routine.

She joined Scott on the patio when she had finished. "The coals should be ready in about fifteen minutes," he commented, adjusting the vents under the grill. He accepted the cold soda she had brought him. "To save time, I think we'll bake the potatoes in the microwave. I'm ready to eat."

Jennifer chuckled. "No debate here."

It proved to be a very simple recipe for fixing the fish. A piece of foil, several pats of butter, a little lemon juice, a dusting of garlic and lots of sliced almonds. The foil was twisted into a thin tube. "Nice," Jennifer commented.

Scott smiled. "Simple. I eat a lot of fresh fish."

Jennifer was pulling the hot potatoes from the microwave when Scott pushed shut the patio door, carrying a platter of fresh baked fish. "That smell's wonderful."

Scott set the platter down on the hot pad Jennifer had found for the table. "Wait till you taste it, Jennifer. It's unbelievably good." He held her chair out for her. "Be careful when you open the foil, there will be a lot of steam," he cautioned.

Jennifer savored her first bite. "This is delicious."

Scott smiled.

They talked casually over lunch, both avoiding talking about last night. Jennifer finished off two full packets of the fish, as well as the baked potato, before admitting she was full. The fruit salad made a delicious dessert. "That was a great meal." She stifled a yawn as she finished the sentence.

Scott debated offering her coffee, but the whole point of the day had been to help her sleep. If he took her home now she would probably fall asleep in the car, and that was not a very comfortable place to get some rest. "I have a lot of guest rooms here, Jen. Why don't you take a short nap and then I'll run you home. I have a couple of calls to return." The answering machine had been blinking when he checked it before lunch, but none of the calls had been urgent.

"Scott…"

"Please."

"A guest room would be very welcome."

He offered her a hand. "Come on, I'll show you upstairs." Jennifer let him escort her down the hall and to the stairway.

This was not a smart move. Jennifer was trying to form the words to back out and ask him to take her straight home, but they had reached the top of the stairs before she could get the words in order. Scott stopped by the first door. "Here you go." It was a beautiful bedroom. Delicate rose print wallpaper. Thick cream carpet. The dressers, the bookshelf, the bed, all early American antiques. A colorful homemade wedding ring quilt was folded neatly at the foot of the bed.

She looked lost. Scott forced himself to smile gently, leave her there. "I'll be in my office if you need me. Just turn right at the bottom of the stairs. You can't miss it."

"Thanks, Scott," she said faintly.

He closed the door softly behind him as he left.

Jennifer stood inside the door of the room for some time, getting used to the sounds of a foreign place, letting her nerves settle. She should not be here. She sighed. She was in no shape to leave. She moved hesitantly toward the bed. Scott was right, she needed to sleep.

She sat down on the edge of the bed. It was a nice mattress, not too soft, nor too hard. She slipped off her shoes. After a few minutes more thinking about it, she turned the covers down and stretched out. Immediately her body relaxed. Her sleep was that of exhaustion.

Chapter Eight

Scott quietly pushed the door of the guest room open. It was a little over an hour since he had shown Jennifer to the guest room. She was asleep, as he'd hoped. She had one hand tucked under the pillow, one hand curled under her chin. Her wedding ring was leaving a mark on her face. Scott carefully shifted her hand. He studied her for a few more moments before quietly slipping out of the room.

The grandfather clock in the downstairs hallway was chiming six-thirty as Scott again quietly pushed open the guest room door. She had not stirred in hours. Scott set a single rose down on the bedside table and tucked a note under the stem. Frowning slightly, he paused by her bedside. She was exhausted. But if she slept much longer she would not be able to sleep tonight.

"Jennifer." He gently shook her shoulder. "Jen, it's time to wake up."

"Go away, Jerry," she murmured, rolling over and taking the quilt with her.

He chuckled. "Jen, it's Scott. Come on, honey, wake up."

Her face appeared from beneath the quilt. She blinked at him a couple of times, then groaned. "How long have I been asleep?"

"About four hours," Scott replied.

She rubbed her eyes with the back of her hands. "I'm sorry, Scott. I could have slept at my own place."

He grinned. "No problem. I like having you here. I laid out fresh towels and a new toothbrush in the guest bathroom if you would like to freshen up. Dinner is in twenty minutes." He turned toward the door.

"Scott." He paused by the door and turned to look back. She ran her hand through her hair. "I need to go home. I can't impose on you any longer."

He just smiled. "Nonsense. Twenty minutes." He disappeared out the door.

Jennifer pushed back the quilt and sat on the edge of the bed. There was a single peach rosebud on the end table. "Oh, Scott. It's beautiful." She picked up the rose, gently fingering the soft petals. The note lying under the rose was clearly meant for her. She picked it up. "Jen, stay for dinner. Please. Scott."

The note folded in her hand. "Okay, Scott," Jennifer whispered quietly. She pushed herself to her feet. Her legs tottered beneath her. "Come on, Jennifer, wake up," she chided herself.

She found the towels and the toothbrush laid out on the bathroom counter just as Scott had described. Back in the guest bedroom five minutes later, her face washed and her unruly hair pulled back into place, Jennifer quickly straightened the covers on the bed.

Carrying her shoes, Jennifer went downstairs. She dropped the shoes on the rug by the front door. Scott was in the kitchen, humming a tune along with the radio as he tossed a large salad. "Something smells delicious," Jennifer remarked, pausing in the doorway as she took in the scene.

Scott looked up. He smiled. "Lasagna." Wiping his hands on a towel, he came over to join her. She looked so much better. Her eyes were clear, she had color back in her face.

"How are you feeling?"

"Not bad," Jennifer replied. "A little groggy."

They sat down to dinner a few minutes later.

He was in love with this lady. Scott didn't fight the growing conviction in his heart. Having her here made his house feel like a home. He'd give a lot to make this a permanent arrangement.

"Did your calls go well?"

"Yes. Most were just clarification."

She nodded. "What did you do while I slept all afternoon?"

I spent the afternoon thinking about asking you to marry me. He didn't say the words. She was not ready for that discussion. She wouldn't be until she dealt with what she had lost. Her husband. Her daughter. But the day was coming when she would be ready. He was an optimist man; someday she was going to be ready to get married and have a family again. He answered her question about his afternoon. "I worked on making a dog bed. Heather and Frank have offered me a choice from Blackie's latest litter."

Jennifer nodded. "Quigley is adorable."

"Thanks. I thought so."

They had finished dinner. "Interested in some coffee?"

Jennifer nodded. "Sounds good," she agreed.

They cleared the table together.

"Let's take the coffee into the library," Scott suggested. He led the way through the quiet house. Scott pushed open the French doors across from the living room. "This is the library, and beyond it, my office."

It was a small room, formal, with a love seat and two chairs, two antique mahogany tables. The four walls were recessed bookshelves. She could spend hours enjoyably browsing this room. She idly walked along the shelves, reading titles.

"Your books are on the third shelf to your left."

Jennifer looked over. She smiled. "They look impressive, all lined up together."

Scott smiled. "They certainly do."

Jennifer sat on the love seat. Scott chose the seat across from her, stretched out his legs.

"I love this room, Scott."

"I thought you might," Scott replied. "I'm glad you agreed to come today."

"I've enjoyed it," Jennifer agreed. She sipped carefully on the hot coffee. It was delicious.

"It's chocolate mocha," Scott said, noticing her surprise.

"I like it."

"Jennifer, would you come to church with me tomorrow?"

She didn't answer for some time. "I might," she replied. "Why are you asking?"

"You need to heal that relationship, Jen, or you are not going to be able to put this behind you."

"Scott, you can't fix things just because you want them to be different. My daughter died. God was the only one who could intervene. He didn't. That is not easy to move beyond. I feel like I was betrayed."

"Have you told Him that?"

"Yes."

"What has He said in reply?"

She didn't say anything for some time. "I haven't listened to find out."

"Are you at the point where you can listen?"

"Maybe." She had to admit she would like her relationship with God healed. "If I go to church with you, people will think we're a couple."

Exactly. "I'll do my best not to put you in any uncomfortable position."

She nodded. "I'll go with you."

"Thank you."

She smiled slightly. "I don't sing very well. Just to warn you."

"I won't hold it against you." She looked very peaceful sitting there, her feet tucked beneath her, her head resting back against the couch. He was beginning to recognize the expressions on her face. She was thinking about the past again.

"I wish I had a picture of Colleen with me so I could show it to you. She had such vivid blue eyes. She used to tilt her head just this certain way and look at you. Then smile.

"She was so tiny when she was born it was a struggle for her to be awake. It took all her energy. So she would lie there and blink at me with this surprised expression in her eyes. They had to feed her through patches on her back for the first two weeks. It was such a wonderful day when she began to suck."

"What do you miss the most, Jennifer?"

"The fact my life doesn't revolve around her anymore. She gave me a reason to get up every morning. Even if the routine consisted of going to the hospital for the day and sitting with her, she was there. It was devastating after she died not to have her there. I had grown so attached."

"Do you think about having other children?"

"No, never. Colleen was such a traumatic experience, it is going to take a long time for the intensity of those memories to fade. I couldn't risk going through that again."

"You loved Colleen. You would love another child with the same intensity."

"In my mind will always be the fact I lost my eldest daughter."

She opened her eyes to look over at him. "Scott, you don't watch someone you love die without carrying that image with you forever. There isn't room inside me to love another child, the grief for Colleen is too large. It shadows everything I have done in the past three years."

Scott wished he could ease the pain she felt. "Have you ever considered writing about Colleen?"

Jennifer just shook her head in reply and then sipped her coffee.

The room was silent for several minutes.

"Why haven't you ever married? You're not a bachelor at heart."

He smiled slightly. "I don't know. I've never met anyone I wanted to spend the rest of my life with."

"Are you close to your parents?"

"Yes. We have always been a close family. It's been that way for several generations."

"You have a large extended family?"

"I have five cousins, most with families, and my grandparents on my mother's side are still alive. What about you? Is it just you and Peter?"

"Yes."

He could not comprehend being that alone. It was a dreadful thought.

It was hard to let the evening end on such a heavy note. But he didn't try to lighten it. Jennifer needed the time to just have someone listen.

"I guess I'd better get going now." Jennifer set her mug down on the coffee table. Scott glanced at his watch and agreed that it was getting late.

They drove to Jennifer's house in a comfortable silence. She hugged him when they said good-night. "Thank you for today, Scott. I needed it."

"I'm glad I was able to help." He gently brushed her cheek with his hand. "I'll pick you up for church at nine. Try to sleep, okay?"

She nodded. "Good night, Scott."

Chapter Nine

There was a good crowd at the Sunday morning services. Jennifer smoothed down her floral dress nervously as she got out of the car.

"You look beautiful, Jennifer."

She barely heard the compliment she was so nervous. "You said Frank and Heather will be here?"

Scott nodded. "Frank is teaching Sunday school this morning, so only Heather will be in the services." He caught hold of her hand, carried their Bibles in his other hand. "If you would prefer not to sit with Heather, I can ensure they never even know we are here."

"No. I would like to sit with someone I know. Scott, I hate these first times. All your friends are going to wonder who I am."

He smiled. "Let them wonder. We'll slip in and out before they can come over to be introduced."

"No. If you do that they will really start to speculate about who you were with."

He laughed. "Relax, Jen. They are nice people.

They will like you. Would it be so bad for them to know we are friends?"

"I guess not." He opened the front glass door for them. "But I hate this," she whispered to him.

He hugged her waist. "Do you want to be introduced as Jennifer or Mrs. St. James?" he whispered back.

"Jennifer. Wait—no. Someone might take my wedding ring to be an engagement ring."

"If they do, we'll just say it's true," he teased.

"Scott."

"Spoilsport." It got him the smile he'd been trying to coax out of her.

They had reached the auditorium. Scott guided Jennifer toward the left section. "Good morning, Twig."

"Hi, Scott. Jennifer, I'm glad you could come." Heather's smile was genuine, and Jennifer realized she was also nervous. Scott had called his sister and told her they were coming, that was obvious. Jennifer slid into the pew to sit beside Heather.

"Jennifer, this is for you." Heather handed her a card. "I was so sorry to hear about Colleen."

"Heather, thank you," Jennifer replied, surprised. "You didn't have to do this."

"I felt so awful about Thursday night. I couldn't have been more insensitive."

"You didn't know."

"I should have been more observant, I'm so very sorry."

Jennifer opened the card and read it, had to fight not to cry. She had promised herself she would not cry today. "Heather, it's a perfect card. Thank you."

The services started. Jennifer felt herself pulled into the music. It felt good to be standing beside Scott sharing a hymn book with him. Not being in a position where others saw her and felt sad for her. It was one of the reasons she had stopped going to church with Peter and Rachel. It had been the church she and Jerry attended, and after he had died, she had simply not been able to deal with the pity.

Scott had a good voice.

It had been too long since she'd been in church. As the service progressed, Jennifer just tried to absorb it all. The choir was singing softly as the communion was passed.

As open as he was with her, the man seated beside her, deep in prayer, was a mystery to her. Scott had needed this morning she realized as she watched him searching out and finding God. This was where he got the strength to walk through his difficult weeks. Jennifer swallowed hard.

God, I'm sorry I have been fighting you so much. I know with absolute certainty that You did hear that prayer for breath. I don't understand why You answered it by saying no. Please help me accept what happened and go on, to accept the fact there will be no explanations for me to find. Only You. I still wonder if I prayed something wrong that time, if it was something I did that resulted in that specific prayer not being answered when the hundred prayers before that were answered. I'm still so angry, Lord. I'm trying to let that pain and anger go, but it's hard to the point of being impossible. When I see You face-to-face, I will understand why it had to be this way. Please, until that day, will You give me the grace to accept what happened and move on? I need you, Lord.

Heather was the one who silently slipped her tissues. Jennifer accepted them gratefully. All she seemed to do this past month was cry.

Scott gripped her hand. Jennifer wanted to lay her head against his shoulder and ask for a hug that would never end. Some things would have to remain a wish.

The sermon was good, but Jennifer remembered little of it.

When the service was over, neither Heather nor Scott questioned her earlier tears. They seemed to have a plan already worked out between them. Heather was the one doing all the introductions as they met friends. Jennifer was aware of the speculation going on. Scott had never dropped her hand. The people she met seemed very nice.

They walked out to the parking lot together. Scott was so proud of her. It had felt so right having her beside him. He longed for the day that would be permanent. He wished they could spend the day together again, but he didn't want to pressure her.

"That wasn't too bad, was it?" Scott asked as they drove to her home.

"No. I liked your church."

"I hoped you would."

He walked her to her door a few minutes later. He gently dropped his arms around her shoulders and pulled her into a hug. "Thank you," he said softly, brushing back the hair from her face. "It meant a lot to me that you came."

She hugged him back. "It helped."

"I'm glad." He hesitated before letting her go. "I'll call you," he said, stepping away, smiling.

She smiled back. "Okay."

Jennifer wandered around her house for almost an hour, cleaning things that were already clean, straightening things that looked fine. *"Have you ever thought about writing about Colleen?"* The words Scott had said Friday were haunting her. She picked up a pad of paper and went to stretch out on her bed. "If I were to write about Colleen, what would I want to say?" She wrote the question down on the top of the page. The tears began to come. "That I loved my daughter."

It was a soul-cleansing four hours. When she got up from the bed, her neck and shoulders were stiff, her eyes were sore, her hand tense from writing. But the raw pain was gone from her heart. It was on paper now. It was something that could be touched and shared and thought about. She set the pad of paper down on the nightstand and pulled down the comforter. Her feet were cold, there was a mountain of tissues tossed over the side of the bed, her eyes burned, and she desperately needed to sleep. But she felt better inside than she had in the past three years.

God, I can feel your peace inside for the first time in years. A safeness that feels like your arms wrapped tightly around me. Thank you for today. For all of it, the trepidation of going to services with Scott, the music, the sermon and the chance to begin healing by writing about Colleen. Please don't let this flicker of faith die. I know I've got such a long recovery still ahead of me.

She drifted to sleep with the light still on.

The phone was ringing, shrill and nearby and not stopping. It roused her groggily back to consciousness. "Hello?"

"Jennifer, I'm sorry. I didn't mean to wake you up."

She yawned and her jaw cracked. "It's okay, Scott." She rubbed her eyes and blinked hard trying to bring her clock into focus. "What time is it?"

"Seven-fifteen."

Did he mean evening or morning? She had no idea. "I was taking a nap. I didn't plan to sleep away the day."

"Andrew and I were just talking. I'm going to have to be out of town for most of this week. I need to visit two clients in Denver."

Jennifer forced herself not to feel the disappointment that churned inside. She wanted to discuss with him what she had been thinking about. "I'll miss you," she finally said, willing to admit the obvious.

"It's mutual," Scott replied, and she smiled at the frustration she heard in his voice. "I would give anything to get out of this trip. I don't want to be miles away from you. Would you like to go out to dinner Saturday night when I get back?"

"Sure."

"Thank you." She heard the relief in his voice. "I am sorry I woke you up. I know you need the rest. I'll give you a call from Denver."

"I would like that."

"Probably every night."

She grinned. Was this good or bad? She wasn't sure. But it felt good. "I'll be waiting for your calls," she replied with a smile.

They said goodbye, and Jennifer hung up the phone and looked at the ceiling and smiled as she groaned. "God, it was bad enough to be going on a date again. Why did You send a guy who wants to get serious? Are You sure I'm ready for this?"

"You went to church with him Sunday," Rachel said, sliding into the seat across from Jennifer at the kitchen table. Jennifer nodded as she took another bite of the bacon, lettuce and peanut butter sandwich. She had passed on the tomatoes. They had talked about church repeatedly since Jennifer had made the decision to stop attending with Peter and Rachel. Rachel understood her reasons—having attended the church with Jerry, having had a baby shower for Colleen there, having buried both Jerry and Colleen in that church—Jennifer simply found it too painful a place to be. She hated the pity in people's faces and constantly feeling like a widow. Rachel had offered to go with her to check out other churches in the area, but Jennifer had kept saying not yet, not willing to admit she was too angry at God to feel like going to church. Time had drifted by.

"I'm glad you went," Rachel said.

"So was I," Jennifer replied. "It helped, no one knowing about Jerry and Colleen. Has Karen forgiven me yet?"

Rachel smiled. "I think so. She makes a point of asking about you every week."

Karen had been a good friend at church, but her daughter had been born two weeks after Colleen, and Jennifer felt it necessary to keep her at a distance now. "I wish she understood it's nothing personal."

"She understands, Jen," Rachel said, passing her the bowl of fruit salad. "You'll go with him again next week?"

Jennifer nodded.

It was tough to plot a story when it came from real life. Jennifer tossed the pad of paper back on the round table and got to her feet. Ann had the final draft of the last Thomas Bradford book. Jennifer was trying her best to figure out what she would write next. Abandoning her office, Jennifer picked up a novel she was reading and walked out to the backyard.

She settled into the hammock and stared up at the blue sky and white puffy clouds. She and Jerry had both loved this hammock as a place to think.

Scott's suggestion that she write about Colleen was creating a real dilemma. Part of her wanted to accept the challenge. She wanted to share her love for Colleen with her readers. She just couldn't come up with a story line that would intrigue them. Her own story—a couple in love decides to start a family, gets pregnant, the husband dies; the baby, born early, also dies—wasn't an interesting story. It was emotional, but it missed a plot line.

She should abandon this idea and get to work on a mystery. She knew how to write mysteries.

Could she take her story and make it a mystery? The thought made her begin to toss the book she held up in the air and catch it, toss it up again.

The mysteries she liked to write had a detective. Maybe the husband was a detective? She rejected that idea. The man would die halfway through the book—hard to write a story around him. Maybe the husband didn't die of natural causes. Maybe the detective was trying to solve the case—the wife and the baby were an interesting complication to a straightforward mystery.

No. The detective thinks the wife is a suspect, he's pressing her for information, and she goes into early labor. When the baby dies, the detective is going to feel personally responsible. Jennifer missed catching the book, and it fell to the ground.

He couldn't be directly responsible. Maybe he's a cop and his partner wants to push for information, she's the prime suspect, and he's holding his partner back as long as he can from directly questioning her, but they reach the point they have to bring her in and she then goes into early labor. The detective falls in love with this premature little girl.

To even out the reader's sympathies, it's going to turn out the lady had actually, unwittingly, played a part in her husband's murder. When the baby dies, she confesses what had really happened. The final scene is the detective at the graveside of the baby.

Jennifer tumbled out of the hammock and headed for her office.

Jennifer wasn't going to answer. Scott held the phone and listened to it ring. It was after ten o'clock. Where was she? It was too early for her to have turned in for the night. He'd been calling her at ten o'clock every night and normally she was there on the first ring. He was about ready to hang up after six rings when the phone was suddenly answered. "Hello?"

"Jen, hi," he couldn't keep the relief from his voice.

"Scott." He could hear her smile. "How are you? How's Denver today?" She was certainly not getting ready for bed. He'd never heard her this alive before. She sounded like she had been very busy.

"Denver is fine. We've about concluded the negotiations for a new contract with one of our key customers. What about you?"

She laughed. "I've just about got the entire plot line for my next book sketched out."

"Really? That's great. What's it about?"

"It's another mystery. In fact, I think I've got another series. The key person is a cop. He's a detective in homicide. He's got a partner who is proving to be a great second character—sarcastic and cynical, great with one-liners. I'm going to have each book in the series focus on a specific case they are trying to solve." Jennifer settled back in the recliner. She was in her office, had been working on a pad of paper filling in the plot sequence for the book when Scott had called. She intentionally did not go into the details of the first case she was going to have the detectives solve. "Could you help me with a name? I haven't found one I like."

"What do you know about him?"

"He's thirty-nine. Five foot ten. Divorced. Plays basketball. A good character. Solid ethics. Honest. Tough, but can be compassionate. Slightly jaded by what he has seen people do to one another."

Scott thought for a few minutes. "Granite Parks."

Jennifer was shocked. It was perfect. "How did you do that? I've been wrestling with his name for days! It's perfect."

Scott laughed. "Beginner's luck. Anything else you need?"

She smiled. "Your company. I miss you," she replied, meaning it. "When is your flight back?"

Her reply had pleased him, she could hear it in his voice. "Mid-morning, Saturday. I'll pick you up at seven for dinner?"

"I'm looking forward to it."

It was storming Saturday when Scott arrived to pick up Jennifer. A crashing storm that came with heavy rain, wind and severe lightning. He pulled into her drive and hurried to the shelter of the porch.

"Hi, Jennifer." Lightning cracked as she opened the front door, and he saw her flinch. He stepped inside and quickly closed the door. She was dressed in a soft dove gray dress with a red sash and her hair pulled back by a matching red bow. She looked gorgeous. And slightly frightened. He slipped off his wet jacket and pulled her into a hug. "Okay?"

Her head buried in his shoulder, she nodded. Another bolt of lightning lit up the living room, and she flinched. "I don't like lightning." Her perfume smelled like lilacs.

"This storm is passing," he said gently. "Give it another twenty minutes and I doubt it will even be raining." He gently rubbed her back. "I really missed you," he said lightly.

She gave him a hug. "I missed you, too." She stepped back and picked up his jacket. "Could we wait till this passes before we leave?"

"Sure."

Jennifer put his jacket across one of the kitchen chairs and they went into the living room. Scott chose to sit in the easy chair instead of beside her on the couch. He would like nothing better than to kiss her, but he was not going to do so. At least not until this night was over. He smiled at the thought and forced himself away from the subject. "How is the book progressing?" he asked.

Her face lit up. "I love this period of writing a book. I don't have to worry about the details and the choice of words or the length of the scenes. I've just been sitting down and writing. I've made an enormous amount of progress. I love Granite. He is the perfect character. He is as clear in my mind as Thomas Bradford."

"I'm glad. I've been worried about how well you could make this transition. You've been writing about Thomas Bradford for years."

"I was comfortable, and I think that was becoming a problem. Great stories come from taking risks. This story feels more alive, more dramatic."

"Do you have any idea how long it will take to write?"

"At least six months. It will be significantly longer than my other books. How did Denver turn out?"

Scott told her about the people he had met, the places they had gone to eat, what the flight back had been like. The storm was beginning to drift west. The lightning had ended and there was simply a light rain falling when they eventually left for the restaurant. Scott had chosen a small Chinese restaurant that not many people in the city knew about. They were escorted to a private table in the back of the room where Scott held her chair for her. The menu was in Chinese.

"A friend owns this place. If you don't mind, I'll order for us. Is there anything in particular you don't like?" Scott asked.

"No."

The waiter spoke with an accent. Jennifer smiled. It was obvious Scott knew him well. The two men conferred for several minutes comparing dishes. The man left with a smile and a promise to bring hot tea.

Jennifer relaxed. She was going to enjoy tonight.

The courses came and kept coming. A ceremonial teapot and small bowls of soup came first. The waiter placed a second larger bowl between them. "The soup is a type of sweet-and-sour soup, it has shrimp in it," Scott said. "The other dish is a house specialty. They are wontons cooked in a very spicy chicken broth. I'll warn you, they are very hot."

Jennifer carefully lifted one of the wontons from

the dish. "These are delicious," she said after sampling the dish.

"I like them," Scott agreed.

The soup was followed by an assortment of fried rice dishes, a large platter of stir-fried vegetables, and then a shrimp and cashew dish that made Jennifer reach frequently for her water glass.

"I'm sorry. I should have ordered something less spicy."

"Are you kidding? This is wonderful. Jerry didn't like hot and spicy, and I love it."

Scott smiled and offered her one of the fresh-baked rolls to take away some of the effect.

She was going to make a wonderful wife, Scott thought, not for the first time. They had so much in common. Music, fishing, food. They both came from close families. Scott loved to listen to her laugh. She was relaxed tonight, and he was seeing Jennifer as she had been in the pictures before the death of Jerry and Colleen. Alive, happy. He could only hope she was drifting toward the same conclusion.

They left the restaurant almost two hours later. Scott held his jacket over her head as they ran to the car. It was barely raining, but it was an excuse to be near her. "I don't want to take you home," he admitted as he started the car.

Jennifer was grinning. "Let's go find somewhere to get a cup of coffee," she offered.

"Done."

He took them downtown to a five-star hotel that served gourmet coffee. At her suggestion they took the coffee into the atrium where a woman with a great voice played jazz standards at the piano. They settled into two comfortable chairs and shared a large chocolate chip cookie Scott had bought.

She was falling in love with him. Jennifer was laughing when the realization struck; Scott had retold a funny story he'd heard in Denver, and she had started to laugh. In that instant she knew she was falling in love in him. It was a sobering realization.

"Something wrong?"

She shook her head, absorbing the impact in her heart, and then she smiled, brilliantly. "Everything is fine."

It was almost midnight when they finally turned into her drive. Scott came around the car to open her door for her. He paused on the porch. "Jennifer."

She turned to look up at him, and he smiled. "Can I kiss you?"

It was a softly spoken query and it made her heart flutter. Jennifer wanted to blush, smile, put her arms around him. She simply nodded. Scott's hands very gently held her head and he lowered his head. The kiss held such tenderness that Jennifer nearly cried. She was smiling when he stepped back. Scott looked pleased. "You'd best get inside," he said huskily.

"Hi, Jerry." Jennifer sat down on the ground beside the headstone, her jeans and sweatshirt adequate protection for the cool, sunny afternoon. She had not been back to the grave site for over three months. She smiled sadly as she brushed the leaves from the smooth stone base. "I've got news I know you will be glad to hear."

She hugged her knees. She had woken up sad. "Scott's a good man. He makes me laugh. I miss him when he's not around. And it makes me incredibly sad, Jerry." She plucked at the dying grass. "We were suppose to have a lifetime together, you and I. I don't want to start over. How can love and sadness be so tightly intertwined?"

She glanced over at the second headstone, the reason she very rarely visited here. "Are you having a good time with your daddy, Colleen?" she asked, smiling, crying at the same time.

Chapter Ten

Jennifer watched the group of ten youths as they paired off and played pool, mentally putting names and faces together. Scott had encouraged her to join him for the pizza and pool, one of the events he was involved in organizing as a youth group sponsor. The kids ranged in age from twelve to seventeen, and as a whole were a close-knit, fun group. "The boy in the blue shirt at the far table playing by himself—what's his name?" Jennifer asked Scott's friend Trish as she surveyed the room from the vantage point of the long table and chairs, the remains of six large pizzas still around them.

"Kevin Philips. Fifteen."

"He's hurting," Jennifer commented, having formed the conclusion during the course of the evening. He had come across as angry and belligerent, and both Brad and Scott had spoken with him more than once. Jennifer looked below the surface, knowing there was a reason for the unreasonable behavior.

Trish nodded. "Adopted two years ago by Jim and Rita Philips. He'd been in foster care since he was seven, no place more than a year, had rough years before that in an abusive home."

"And now that he is in a safe and loving environment, he's letting himself feel the pain for the first time and he's angry as hell," Jennifer concluded. "Giving Jim and Rita an extremely rough time in the process, I imagine."

"Got it in one," Trish replied.

"It must be like trying to hug a porcupine," Jennifer said thoughtfully.

Trish smiled. "Sad, isn't it?"

"Yeah," Jennifer agreed, making a decision. *God, I've got the faith to try. Do you have a way I can reach him?* She picked up her glass. "Can you hold the fort here? I think I'll see if there's a way around the needles."

"Beat him at pool. He disdains amateurs, but he'll respect a professional."

Jennifer looked surprised at the comment.

"You're the one who came in carrying a case with your own stick," Trish replied. "Have you played Scott yet?"

"No," Jennifer replied with a smile. She had been watching Scott play, and he was good, but he wasn't aggressive enough to deliberately take shots away from his opponent. She did it as naturally as breathing. She hadn't played tonight, but she had a feeling Scott would probably wander over to see what she could do.

"Be gentle with him," Trish said with a smile.

"Who? Scott or Kevin?"

"Kevin. Scott can take care of himself," Trish replied with a laugh.

It turned out to be as aggressive a game as Jennifer had imagined. Kevin had consented unwillingly to actually play a game with her. When she'd drilled her first shot and placed the seven into a pocket off the bank and left the cue ball six inches away from a certain second shot, she'd got a look of surprise from him, but he'd said nothing, simply turned his full attention to the game. Jennifer didn't mind. She hadn't come over to talk. Respect was a good common ground to forge, and the pool table was as good a place as any to forge it. She beat him the first game and ignored the fact the others were rotating around to play each other.

"Twenty bucks on the next game?" she asked quietly, pitching the triangle toward him.

"Ten to four balls, ten for the game," Kevin replied. "You've been playing a few years longer than I have."

Jennifer smiled. "Agreed." He was conceding a win would be difficult, but if he got the cue ball early it would be possible to hit a run of four balls. She liked the way he thought.

The game had his full concentration, and Jennifer had to admire the way he could tap a side rail shot. He got the break he had hoped for—her break had left the table open, and he took advantage to run the table. She saw the smile as he sank his fourth shot, saw the sense of accomplishment take away some of the anger and knew most of its joy came from the fact he had an opponent that wasn't willing to make a win easy for him. He missed a tough fifth shot. Jennifer pealed off a ten from the money in her pocket and handed it to him as she circled the table to look at what kind of shot, if any, she still had left to take.

Scott, walking toward them with a frown, disturbed her concentration but only for a moment. She focused on her shots, saw the angles and the force and began placing balls in the pockets with deliberation. She wasn't worried about making Kevin look bad, the better she played, the more that ten dollars was going to mean to him.

"Jen, can I talk to you for a moment?" Scott asked.

Jennifer called the hole for the eight ball and sank it before she looked up. Ouch. Scott was not happy.

"Kevin, buy us a plate of nachos and a couple colas. I'll be back in a minute," she told the teenager, who actually gave her a smile. She walked with Scott toward the side door.

"He's already got a gambling problem, Jen. The last thing we need is for a church youth group function to be fostering the problem."

"He earned the cash by his effort. Don't knock that sense of accomplishment."

"It's not good. Please, don't do it again."

Jennifer sighed. "Scott, he's going toe-to-toe with everyone around him, looking for who and what to respect. That cash is a trophy, not a gamble for thrill. He's met someone better than him at the pool table and he knows it, and he earned that ten bucks with his effort. It mattered to him. He may not show it, but it mattered to him."

Scott conceded she was right. "I'm glad to see the fact you got beneath his edge, I'll grant you that. But please, go cautious, Jen."

"Relax. An angry fifteen-year-old can still be managed. As long as you don't suggest that's what you're doing."

Jennifer went to join Kevin and the plate of super supreme nachos he'd bought and had to smile at the interest coming from the other kids. She knew the game they'd played had been observed and commented on, and the food would certainly garner at least the guys attention. She slid into the booth across from Kevin and picked up the soda. "Who taught you to play pool?" she asked the boy.

Scott slid out a chair at the end of the table where Trish and Brad were sitting so he could see the entire group of kids and keep an eye on Jennifer and Kevin sitting together in one of the booths.

"She wiped the table with him. Did you see that five, seven split shot she took and made?" Brad asked him, his respect apparent.

Scott smiled. "When she mentioned she played, she forgot to tell me she played seriously." He could not believe some of the shots she had attempted and made. He wouldn't even think to attempt them. He would ask her for a game later, just for the pleasure of watching her play.

"I like her, Scott," Trish said, watching her talk with Kevin.

"So do I," Scott replied. He was proud of her, proud of the way she had mingled with his friends and the group of kids. He might not agree with her actions, but he had to respect the fact she was willing to tackle the toughest kid in the group. He hoped she succeeded. It was important that someone reach Kevin and help him heal.

"Jennifer's place. Can I help you?"
Interesting. Who was this? Scott found the young girl's voice made him smile. "Hi, it's Scott Williams. Who is this?"
"Tiffany."

Sixth grade. Twelve years old. Thought Steve Sanders was the cutest boy on the planet. Was trying to make the track team this year. "Hi, Tiffany. Is your aunt Jennifer around?"

"She's out back with Dad working on the yard. I can get her for you," the girl offered.

"That's okay. You might be able to answer my question. She said she was looking for one of the Precious Moments figurines. It's a set of train cars with zoo animals. My sister found a couple of the pieces, and I don't remember if she said she was missing the giraffe or the lion."

"Hold on and I'll go look. I'd have to go look, anyway. Aunt Jennifer doesn't go into that room anymore."

Out of the mouth of babes. Jen still had the nursery. Scott felt sick.

The girl was back in a few moments. "It's the giraffe."

Scott rubbed the tension is his forehead and tried to keep his voice light. "Thanks."

"Sure. Can I ask you something?"

He smiled. "Of course."

"Are you really getting a dog? 'Cause I'd love to visit, and Aunt Jen talks about you all the time, and I thought it might be okay to ask."

Scott grinned. "I get Quigley in a couple days. Tell your aunt Jen you've got to come. I would love to have you over. I'll need someone to baby-sit him when I have to be out of town, and Jen will need your help."

"Cool. I knew I was going to like you."

"Tell Jennifer I'll call her this evening," Scott said, pleased to have finally talked to the girl Jennifer bragged about with such love.

He hung up the phone, and Heather reached over to grip his arm. "What's wrong?" She was sorting the baby clothes she had found at garage sales that morning, the figurines she had also found sitting on the counter beside the clothes.

"Twig, she's still got the nursery. And according to her niece, Tiffany, she won't even walk into the room anymore. Tiffany said it in such a matter-of-fact tone of voice, like it's been this way for some time."

"You need to talk to her brother."

"Yeah. I do." Scott wearily rubbed his eyes. It had been a bad week at work, and it wasn't getting better on a personal level, either. The anger between him and God still sat there, tempered with time, but there and needing to be dealt with.

"Would you like to stay for dinner? I really appreciate you watching Greg and Amy for me."

Scott grinned. "You know I always have as much fun as your kids. Greg's turning into a good basketball player. I'll take a rain check on dinner, though, I've got mail to deal with and a youth group lesson to prepare. Frank gets back in town tomorrow?"

"His flight comes in around six, so it will be just me and the kids at church tomorrow morning."

"Plan for us to go out for lunch. I promised Amy pizza."

"Thanks."

Scott kissed his sister's cheek. "You're welcome. Now get off your feet, Twig, you're seriously pregnant."

She laughed and pushed him toward the door.

Quigley found his new home fascinating. Jennifer, sitting on the floor in the doorway of Scott's kitchen, watched the puppy circle the furniture in the dining room, suddenly turn and come full-speed back toward her when he got frightened by a dust ball. Jennifer caught him with a laugh. "What's the matter, little guy?" He was pure black, furry, his face too big for the rest of his body. He licked her face.

"I think he likes you." Scott had leaned over the counter to peer down at the two of them. He was grinning.

"I want to take him home," Jennifer replied, snuggling with the puppy.

"Sorry. You'll just have to visit often to see him," Scott replied. He came around and offered a helping hand to pull her to her feet. "Lunch is ready."

"I have to put him down?" Jennifer asked with regret.

"If you don't, he will eat your lunch," Scott replied. "I know, he's done it to me a few times." Scott took the puppy, and Quigley immediately made himself comfortable, resting his head on Scott's shoulder.

"No, I'd say you don't carry him around very much."

"He likes to go fishing," Scott replied.

Jennifer laughed and followed Scott to the patio for lunch. It was an Indian summer day, comfortably warm, not even a jacket necessary. Scott had fixed brats out on the grill. He set Quigley down and clipped on the hundred-foot leash so Quigley could go exploring without getting lost.

"Can you tolerate the onions?" Scott asked as he loaded his brat with condiments.

"What?"

"If we are going to be kissing, do you want onions on my breath or not?"

She slid her arm around his waist as she reached

around him for the mustard. "Taking a lot for granted, aren't you?"

He turned and kissed her. Both his hands were full, but he did an adequate job. "Nope."

"Go light on the onions," she requested, smiling.

The sadness was gone. She was in love with him, and she didn't mind if he suspected as much. For now, she just liked being with him. They needed some time together as friends.

Scott handed her a soda and a napkin, and Jennifer settled back in the patio chair to watch Quigley and laugh with Scott at his antics.

"I promised Tiffany she could come meet Quigley, so let me know what day might be good and you can invite Peter and Rachel and the kids over and we'll have a cookout."

"Scott."

She was going to protest that it wasn't good to bring family into the relationship this early but Scott didn't let her finish. Her family was likely going to be his most powerful ally. "If you won't ask them, I will." There was a twinkle in his eyes as he said it, but also the seriousness of his intentions.

"I'll talk to Rachel," Jennifer finally agreed.

They went walking on the beach later that afternoon. Scott let Quigley run without a leash. The puppy scampered around, flirting with the water's edge, pausing occasionally to dig furiously in the sand. "You're going to have to give him a bath when we get back to the house," Jennifer commented.

"He kind of likes the blow-dryer—hates the noise, but likes to put his face in the warm air," Scott replied.

Scott's hand was slipped into Jennifer's back pocket, her arm was around his waist. He liked afternoons like this. If he got his way there would be many more of them. He loved her. He no longer questioned that. It was only a matter of time now before he made that declaration. He figured the more afternoons they had together like this, the easier it would be for Jennifer to answer him.

"You want to come to Greg's birthday party Saturday? He's going to be nine. You could meet my folks. You've met everyone else in the family," he said.

He watched her bite her bottom lip. "Your parents?"

"They are going to love you," he said with a smile. "We'll bring Quigley along, too, for a puppy reunion. What do you say, Jen?"

Jennifer tilted her head to look up at him. She hesitated. "Sure. Why not?"

He leaned down and kissed her, slowly, taking his time. He could feel her smiling, and he was ready to haul her back to the patio chair where he could do it properly, when Quigley decided he needed to shower them with sand. "Quig, you've got to learn better timing," Scott protested. Jennifer just laughed.

She shouldn't have come.

Jennifer watched Scott in the backyard of Heather and Frank's home playing with six kids and four puppies and felt the joy of the last month disappear.

She shouldn't have come. There was no denying reality any longer. In a month of loving him, she had conveniently been ignoring one very obvious fact. Scott was going to want to have kids. Heather stopped beside her at the dining room table, smiled with her at the antics outside. "The kids are having a great time with the puppies." Greg had invited four of his school friends over for the party.

"Yes. They are all having a great time," Jennifer agreed. She was trying her best to not think about how pregnant Heather was. She liked Scott's sister a lot. Heather was a wealth of stories about Scott, and Jennifer wasn't above looking for information. Heather's due date was only two weeks away now, and as much as Jennifer liked her, she was doing her best not to think about the baby. Jennifer felt Heather look over at her and forced herself to shift back to a carefree appearance. "Can I help with the cake?"

"Mom is finding the candles. Then it's just a matter of calling the kids inside," Heather replied. They watched the antics in the backyard for a few more moments, then Heather slid open the patio door and stepped outside to call everyone in for cake.

Scott's mom joined Jennifer and smiled at the scene in the backyard. "I don't know who is enjoying themselves more, Scott or the kids. Amy and Greg are both having a great time."

Jennifer turned to smile at Margaret. Scott's mom had made her feel welcome from the moment she had walked in the door, and Jennifer was relieved. Margaret had looked at the way Scott had his arm around her, looked at the expression on Scott's face, and when she'd turned to look at Jennifer the deck had already been stacked in her favor. "Scott does seem to like kids," Jennifer said after a moment, dreading the second confirmation and knowing she had to hear it.

"That he does. He'll make a good father."

Jennifer nodded but didn't reply.

Scott came inside with the children, carrying his niece, Amy, in one arm and Quigley in the other, laughing over something Amy had told him. Jennifer smiled when Scott reached her, took the offered

Quigley. Amy looked so right in his arms. The little girl had her arms around Scott's neck and was clearly very pleased to be where she was. Amy had been at the door to meet them, been hoisted up by her uncle Scott for a smooch and had given Jennifer a wide grin and asked Scott if this was his girlfriend, like Jeff was her boyfriend. Scott had frowned and had wanted to know when he had been bumped as her boyfriend, and Amy had just giggled and explained that Scott didn't have a hamster and Jeff did.

Quigley chose that moment to stick his nose in her face, and Jennifer laughed and shifted him around so he could rest like a football in her arms. She loved this puppy. Scott hoisted Amy into one of the chairs and came back to join Jennifer. He stepped out of the way by standing behind her. He draped his arms around her waist, rested his chin against her shoulder. "How do you like my parents?" he whispered in her ear.

"I like them both," she whispered back. His dad had given her a hug and told her to make sure Scott behaved himself, that he was dangerous at birthday parties.

The dining room table was set with party decorations—streamers, balloons, party napkins and cups. After "Happy Birthday" was sung, the candles blown out, the cake was cut and passed around. Since Jennifer was still holding Quigley, Scott shared his piece with her. Jennifer giggled when he got icing on her chin. "Hold still," Scott warned as he lowered his head. She knew he had done it deliberately so he would have an excuse to kiss her.

"Don't you dare," she whispered fiercely. She didn't mind his family seeing them holding hands. Kissing was another matter. Scott grinned and rubbed the icing off with his finger instead.

"Scott, would you and Jennifer like some ice cream to go with that cake?" His mom's question had a touch of laughter in it. Jennifer blushed.

"Thanks, Mom, but I think we're okay with just the cake," Scott replied, not minding the question and not looking away from Jennifer. He hadn't seen this shade of pink before. It was quite endearing.

It was late. After midnight. Jennifer tossed another wadded tissue toward the bathroom trash can. She was sitting in the tub, crying her eyes out, and she was beginning to get mad.

Scott was going to want to have children.

What was she going to do?

She had tried to call Beth, but her friend wasn't home, and she didn't want to call Rachel. Not yet. Rachel would talk to Peter, and Peter would want to put his arms around her and fix it, and when he couldn't it would make him more sad, and Jennifer knew her brother had already carried more pain than any man should ever be expected to carry. The memory of his face as a pallbearer for Colleen was the last pain she ever wanted to cause him. The whole problem was the fact this couldn't be fixed.

It was a horrible dilemma. She was in love with him. But even the idea of having children petrified her. Jennifer couldn't think about children without thinking about the hospital, the doctors, the fear. The funeral. Colleen had struggled so hard to live. Jennifer didn't have the strength to risk losing another child.

How could she think about marrying Scott, when she knew she was going to deny him the fulfillment of his dream? She couldn't risk having another child. Not even for Scott. She was petrified of the idea. The tears came harder, and Jennifer gave up trying to stop them. She felt as if her heart was breaking. She loved him. And she was going to have to give him up.

Jennifer finally got hold of her friend Beth early the next morning. If anyone was going to be able to help her sort through what she had to do, it was Beth. Jennifer had reached the horrible conclusion that her only option was to say goodbye to Scott and not see him anymore. "Beth, could I fly out and see you and Les for a few days?" Jennifer asked when her friend answered the phone. Twenty minutes later, she stepped into a cab for a ride to the airport.

Scott paced the corridor of the airport terminal, waiting for Jennifer's flight to get in. To say he'd been surprised when she called from South Dakota was to understate his reaction. He had been trying to reach her for two days when she had called. Something was wrong. Jennifer hadn't said anything on the phone, only that she was visiting a friend, but Scott didn't need to be told that something had sent her running. Jennifer was not the type to simply up and leave without a reason.

Her flight finally landed, twenty minutes late. Scott was standing at the gate as the passengers entered the terminal. He saw her immediately. She looked exhausted, her eyes dark, her expression weary and sad.

"Hi, Jen." He took her carry-on bag and wondered if she would accept a hug. She removed the uncertainty by stepping forward to hug him. "Thanks for coming, Scott."

Okay. Whatever was wrong, it was at least going to be fixable. Scott held her tight, grateful to have her back. She'd scared him leaving like that and he took a deep breath and let it out slowly. "Have you eaten yet?"

"Yes. The food on the plane was not too bad."

"Let's get your luggage then, and I'll take you home." He kept an arm around her as they walked down the terminal to the baggage claims area. "How's Beth?"

"Beth is fine. I'm glad I went. The phone simply doesn't do a close friendship justice." Jennifer pointed out her one bag. Scott got her luggage and led her out to the car.

"Jen, why did you go?" Scott asked after several minutes of silence in the car. He had debated whether he wanted to ask the question or not, he was afraid of the answer, but he found the need to know was stronger than the fear.

"I needed to talk about Colleen," Jennifer finally replied. She turned and looked at him. "Beth knows the terrain. She lost a son in a drunk driving accident."

"How did it go?"

"Okay." Jennifer gave a half smile. "I cried a lot. Be glad you were not there."

Scott reached over and grasped her hand. "Don't. Don't hide the pain, Jen. It matters that you let me be part of this recovery."

She squeezed his hand. "I'm sorry. I know you want to help." Jennifer bit her lip. "I'm scared of having children again, Scott. Really, really scared."

His eyes closed briefly. No. Not this. Anything but this. He had been afraid she felt that way about children, but had hoped time had made her feelings less intense. Scott urged her over to sit beside him so he could put his arm around her. "It must be a very frightening idea to consider, after what happened with Colleen." His voice was husky, and he found it hard to speak. He could tell how much pain Jen was in, and he was sharing it. They had to be able to have children together. They had to.

"I keep remembering the hospital delivery room and the neonatal intensive care and the way she didn't breathe. The image is frozen in my mind."

Scott felt Jennifer take a deep breath. "I'm getting past the fear. I've got to. That's one of the reasons I went to see Beth."

Scott heard the determination in her voice and was so grateful she was working to heal. "What can I do to help?" he asked huskily, willing to do anything he could.

Jennifer eased her hand more firmly into Scott's. She loved him. She could do this. She could face having children again. Beth had helped make that choice clear. If she wanted a life with Scott, she was going to face her fears and deal with them. The bottom-line conclusion was simple. She loved Scott too much to let him go. A week with a friend who knew she could do it had helped make that decision possible. "Just be there, Scott. I'm going to beat this fear," she replied.

"Do you need a jacket?" he asked. Jennifer had on a sweatshirt, but the breeze off the lake was cool tonight.

"No, I'm fine," Jennifer replied. She had been home a week since she'd gone to see Beth, and her courage to at least consider children was still intact. She had begun to think about the possibility more, had actually got up the nerve to go into the room that had been set up as Colleen's nursery and sit for a while. Scott had invited her to his place for dinner and a walk on the beach tonight. She thought it was a good sign that he had let her drive over instead of coming to pick her up. The laughter of the last month had disappeared and been replaced with something more serious, more intense. The fun of a friendship was still there, but there were larger issues in front of them now, and they both knew it.

"Did you get much done on the book today?" Scott asked quietly as they began their walk along the beach, Quigley racing out ahead of them.

"I wrote about six pages. A moderately good day, I guess. I normally want to write about ten. How was work?"

Scott smiled. "Every problem in the entire company seemed to come across my desk today," he replied. "I was glad I had tonight to look forward to."

"Dinner was very good." He had made a thick beef stew.

He hugged her. "You're willing to taste my experiments. That must be one of the signs of a good friend."

"If you make something really bad, I probably will have to tell you," Jennifer replied with a smile. She bent down and found a smooth rock, sent it skipping over the water. "You must love having the water so close."

"I do. It is a very peaceful walk." Quigley chose that moment to coming running back to stop beside them, tail wagging, proceeding to shake all the sand off his coat. "Quigley, behave yourself," Scott said sternly, having to hide his grin. The puppy just nudged his leg. "If you find a stick, I'll throw it," Scott told the dog. Quigley took off down the beach again.

They had not talked directly about children since the car ride back from the airport. Jennifer did not want to broach the subject, and Scott fully intended to give her all the time she needed.

They walked back to the house forty minutes later, holding hands.

Jennifer found Quigley's brush and began to brush the sand out of his hair while Scott went to check for any messages.

"Jennifer." She looked up to see Scott in the patio doorway. "Heather has been admitted, in labor. Mom's message said they are planning to do the C-section at 7:00 p.m. That's just about now."

Jennifer felt part of her stomach drop. She wasn't ready for this kind of test yet. Not yet. She let Quigley climb from her lap and got up and dusted off her jeans. "Since my car is here, let's both drive to the hospital," she said, getting a firm grip on her courage.

Scott came to join her, tilting up her chin so he could see her eyes. "Are you sure?" he asked, worried.

Jennifer forced a smile. "I'm sure. Let me get my purse, and we can be on our way."

Scott hesitated, then nodded. "All right. I'll lock up the house."

Jennifer followed him to the hospital. If it had been the same hospital as where she had had Colleen, Jennifer would never have turned into the parking lot. As it was, she pulled in and parked beside Scott and found her hands were damp with sweat.

They walked across the parking lot to the main entrance of the hospital, followed the signs to the elevators that would take them to the fourth floor and maternity. Jennifer suddenly balked when the elevators opened and Scott moved to step inside. "I can't do this." She shook her head wildly, feeling the panic. She had spent too much time in her past on a maternity ward floor, in the intensive care. She couldn't go up there. The hospital smell was already making her stomach churn. She couldn't go up there and wait for a baby to be born. What if she were bad luck and the baby died?

Scott grabbed her in a bear hug, stopping a panicked flight. "Easy, Jen, it's okay. We're not going up there," he said firmly. She was shaking uncontrollably. "Come on." He walked her toward the hospital doors, waving aside a concerned front desk attendant and got her outside. He found them a private alcove where he could lean against a pillar and hold her.

She started to calm down. "Scott, I'm so sorry. I thought I could do this." She was crying, and he found a handkerchief and carefully wiped her eyes.

"It's okay, Jen. I saw when the panic hit. You did okay for several minutes. I bet that is better than you've done before," he said quietly.

"It is. But still. It's just a hospital."

"Don't beat yourself up. It's not going to help," Scott said softly. He was suddenly getting a firsthand taste of what he was battling, and the assumptions that he'd made were all proving woefully inadequate. "Come on, Jen. Let me take you home."

"No. You need to go be with your family. I live less than a mile from here. I can drive home."

"No way."

She smiled at his firm tone. "Yes. I'll be fine. Your family needs you upstairs."

He halfway conceded. "I'll follow you home and

make sure you get there safely, then come back," he replied.

She nodded her agreement, because there was going to be no way to dissuade him and walked with him to her car. He followed immediately behind her as she drove to her house. Scott got out and came up to the front door with her.

"Will you call me when you have news?" Jennifer asked him. She hated the fact she wasn't going to be there with him.

"I'll call you." Scott gently kissed her. "Please, don't think about kids tonight. Don't beat yourself up. Promise me?"

There were tears in her eyes as she nodded. "I promise," she whispered.

The phone rang at 9:00 p.m. Jennifer had gone to bed but was awake, snuggled under the covers, thinking. Her eyes were dry. She had checked the tears by force of will. She didn't know how to process what had happened, and the intense sadness was overwhelming. She'd had no idea that the fear had burned so deep inside, until she'd tried to walk past it.

"Heather had a baby girl. Mary Elizabeth. Seven pounds. Both of them are doing fine."

Jennifer squeezed her eyes shut and let out a deep sigh of relief. "Thank you, Scott. That's the best news you could have told me."

"How are you doing, Jen?" She could hear the controlled pain in his voice, the fact he wasn't coping with what had happened any better than she was.

"I'll be okay, Scott." She struggled to put some confidence in the words that she didn't feel.

"Can I come by?" She heard the plea and closed her

eyes. She had heard that plea before on the beach the first morning, and she had pushed him away then, and she was going to be forced to do it again and it was killing her. She couldn't talk right now, not until she dealt with the churn inside and could talk from some sort of level perspective.

"I've already turned in for the night. Could we get together tomorrow?"

His silence was so pain filled. Why did things have to be like this? Why did she have to hurt him like this? It was going to get worse, not better, and it was killing her. "I'll call you. We can go out for dinner and a movie," Scott offered.

"I'll look forward to it, Scott."

She hung up the phone after they said goodbye. Rubbed her eyes. It was there, staring them both in the face. The uncertainty of whether the relationship was going to survive. Prayer. She needed to pray.

Lord, I panicked. Deep inside, I panicked. And I couldn't control it. And I wanted out. And if I'd had to abandon Scott to get away I would have done it. What am I suppose to do now? It's there. It's not moving. I felt death tonight, felt the same icy chill of death I felt as I sat beside Colleen's incubator and realized she had not taken another breath. I can't fight death. I don't have that kind of courage. If it's going to stay there, sitting inside, cold and unyielding, I've got no choice but to tell Scott goodbye.

Scott walked the beach with Quigley late that night. If a few tears slipped that no one could see, they went unnoticed. Jennifer was hurting so badly. And he so badly wanted them to be able to have children.

Chapter Eleven

It was late when Scott arrived at Jennifer's to pick her up for dinner. He'd been forced to call her from work and move the time, when a late crisis in the day had necessitated another meeting. Andrew had been there at the meeting, and Scott knew his presence had saved his butt. He'd just about blown his temper at a line supervisor, and Andrew had stepped in and prevented it from happening. The guy had been wrong, but it had only been a mistake, not malicious, and blowing his temper would have been a lousy way to present himself.

He needed a break from this. He needed the pain to go away.

Lord, don't let the anger blow toward Jennifer. It's the situation that's triggering the anger, the fear inside, but she'll see it as her fault. I'm frustrated that there is so much left to do for Jennifer to heal. So much more time needed, so much fear inside me that we won't have children. What if it doesn't work out? What if Jennifer can't heal? What do we do then?

Scott parked the car and turned off the ignition and deliberately rested his hands across the steering wheel.

Lord, it's not going inside the house with me, this emotion. We both need a break. So take it, Lord, and help me give her what we both need, faith that You'll take care of this. Please.

Jen opened the front door when he knocked, and Scott was grateful to see the calmness in her brown eyes. She was in better shape than he had expected. He stepped inside and hugged her, and she hugged him back.

"I went ahead and fixed us dinner since I didn't know what time you might get free. I really would prefer to stay in tonight," she said as she took his coat.

"You can cook?" he teased, and she swatted his arm. "Well I didn't know. Not everyone can." He tugged her back into his arms as an apology. "What did you fix?"

"Pizza. And yes, I made it from the crust up. It's good."

"It smells delicious." He meant it. He could smell the yeast in the dough rising as the crust cooked, the cheese melting.

She leaned back in his arms. "Let's not talk about it tonight, okay? Not kids, not the panic, not Colleen. Not any of it."

His eyes closed when she made the request, and he rested his forehead against her hair. The sigh came from deep inside. Thank you, Lord. They needed time more than they needed words. "You have a deal." He smiled, not moving his head from where it rested against her hair. "But only if I get control of the TV remote." He'd known it would get a smile, but he hadn't counted on the gentle elbow in his ribs.

"Hey."

"At least Jerry would flip me for it."

He picked her up.

"A quarter, Scott, not literally." She was laughing, and it was the first time he'd heard the sound in a long time. It was a beautiful sound. Scott lowered her feet back to the floor and gently kissed her.

"Check the pizza and let's go surf the channels for something funny to watch."

They said nothing profound the whole evening, just sat on the floor in front of the couch and ate great pizza and laughed at old episodes of "Coach," and "Murphy Brown," and watched Doris Day and Cary Grant fall in love, and occasionally Scott would lean over and kiss Jennifer just for the pleasure of the contact.

Scott was traveling to San Francisco for a conference. The plane was somewhere over the Rockies and the view out the window was breathtaking, but he wasn't enjoying it. A folder was open in his lap and yet to be read; his mind wasn't on work, even though he was presenting a session.

The stress he had seen in her eyes was killing him. Jennifer was in so much pain. If only he could truthfully tell her he didn't want children. All this pain would go away. But he couldn't tell her that. He really wanted a family.

He needed to call her, just to hear her voice. Make sure she hadn't run. She was feeling so guilty, feeling like the fear was her fault. But it wasn't. Scott could see in her pain how badly the trauma of Colleen's death had affected her. The fear was a natural protective measure against the pain, and it was the pain that was the enemy.

He thought about three dates swiftly approaching, Thanksgiving, the anniversary of Colleen's death—he winced at that one—and Christmas. And he knew all of them were going to be hard on Jennifer. He couldn't keep hurting her. He had to let the pain go and give her the time she needed to heal. He had to keep the faith that she would be able to heal.

He was gone four days, and when he returned, it was to find Jennifer's message on his machine saying she was going to need to cancel their dinner date for the next night, that her editor needed her to turn around some revisions to the last Thomas Bradford book overnight. He listened to the message and rubbed his hand over his face and wished he could call her and be the lighthearted friend she so badly needed. Whenever he called her now he seemed to only add to the pain she felt; he was the reminder now of her fear and it haunted him.

Scott reluctantly didn't call her. They needed to be married. He needed to be able to hold her and not let her go, and if they couldn't talk, at least they could share the silence.

The house was empty and lonely. Knowing the pile of work at the office after four days of being gone was going to be steep, Scott decided he might as well spend two hours at the office getting started on the work he had to do. Work didn't take his mind off the problems, but it at least forced him to keep moving.

She couldn't put off talking to Scott about children any longer.

Jennifer sat beside him at the Thanksgiving table,

watched him with his family and knew she couldn't put off talking to him any longer. She loved him, and he wanted a family, and she knew the reality. He thought time was helping. It was going to kill her to admit the reality to him. She hid her troubled thoughts as best she could. Scott was relaxed, and she didn't want to rob him of that today.

The guys went out back to play some basketball after dinner, and Jennifer smiled as she watched them. Heather joined her, carrying a now-awake Mary Elizabeth. She was just finishing a bottle.

"How's she doing?" Jennifer asked, envious.

"Quite well. She is a very even-tempered baby. She only gets me up twice during the night," Heather replied with a smile, turning down the blanket so Jennifer could see her little hands.

"Could I hold her?" Jennifer asked, surprising herself.

"Sure," Heather replied. She slid the bottle to one side and handed Jennifer the second cloth diaper she was carrying. "She needs to burp."

Very carefully, Jennifer took the infant. The infant was waving her arms, trying to smile, with bright blue eyes and full cheeks, there was nothing frail or premature about her. She weighed double what Colleen had ever weighed. Jennifer eased the infant onto her shoulder and gently patted her back.

Jennifer grinned when the baby took a fistful of her hair and started to tug. "You find this very tempting, don't you, honey?" She gently loosened the baby's grip. It felt so wonderful to be holding a baby again. Jennifer blinked away tears that threatened to fall. She wasn't going to cry. She wasn't.

She tried to think about what it would be like to be pregnant again, have her own baby, and the joy she felt turned to almost panic. Mary Elizabeth suddenly looked like Colleen. Jennifer blinked hard and forced herself to take a deep breath. "Thank you, Heather." Jennifer handed Mary Elizabeth back carefully, grateful for the chance to hold her, her smile sad, knowing what she had just learned was going to change things for the worst.

"Jennifer, I'm sorry."

Heather did understand the tears that threatened to fall, and Jennifer gave her a tremulous smile. "You have a beautiful baby, Heather," she said, fighting for her composure.

The game outside began to break up. Jennifer forced the sadness away.

Scott came in with a smile, tugged Jennifer down beside him on the couch in the living room to watch the football game with him, kept her tucked firmly under his arm for the rest of the day. Jennifer loved him for it, for the comfort his presence brought.

They left his parents' house early in the evening. Scott took Jennifer home, and at her request came in for coffee. He leaned down to kiss her as they entered the house, and she tipped her head back and let the kiss deepen, feeling desperate. She loved him so much. She would give anything not to have to say what she had to say.

She was going to be breaking his heart and be breaking hers, and she dreaded what the next year was going to be like without him, and she wanted to cry and plead with God to change this, but the pleading was done, and the crying was done, and this was the reality she was going to have to live with. Holding Mary Elizabeth had forced her to face the irrevocable truth. She was afraid to have children again. *Too* afraid to ever change.

He knew something was wrong. His face was serious, his hands gentle on her waist. "Would you fix the coffee? I need to find something," she asked. He hesitated, then nodded.

Jennifer looked through the video tapes she had collected over the years, bit her lip as she found the tapes tied together with a blue ribbon. *God, I need some courage,* she said silently, opening the ribbon. She found the first tape she wanted and slid it into the machine, picked up the remote.

Scott came in with the coffee, and Jennifer nodded toward the couch. "Old movie night?" he asked quietly. Jennifer curled up beside him.

"I thought you might like to meet Jerry and Colleen," she replied. She felt Scott's sudden look of surprise, but she didn't look over at him. She turned on the tape.

Scott didn't say a word; he did put his arm around her.

Nervous was not a good enough term to describe how Jennifer was feeling. "The sound is not very good on this first part. It was taken at his bachelor party.

"There's Jerry on the couch." Jennifer indicated as the camera panned across the living room packed with people. "The man on his left is his best man. This was taken about a week before our wedding. Finals had just gotten over the day before. It's a Friday night, most of his college buddies stayed around to help him celebrate. They did a great job setting Jerry up. He thought we were going out to dinner and came over to the dorm to pick me up. Instead, he walked into four of his buddies who escorted him to the party."

Scott, watching the man on the screen, laughing with his friends, felt real envy. The man was a gifted speaker. Watching him, after catcalls of "speech," get up and off-the-cuff do a five-minute talk on why he was forsaking bachelorhood for marriage, made Scott realize just how much Jerry had loved Jennifer.

Jerry returned puns with his friends as he unwrapped the gifts. Items wrapped in the best bachelor fashion: brown paper bags. Tape was the first gift. "To ensure I keep my mouth shut at all appropriate times." Glue; a waste can. "If I can't fix it, I can always throw it away." Antacids. "No comment. Jennifer is bound to see this movie one day." A plunger. Jerry had dissolved into laughter when he saw that one. "Cute, guys. Real cute." A spade. "For shoveling out the dirt Jennifer likes to brush under the rug."

The last package was actually wrapped in real blue and gold wrapping paper. Jerry opened it, obviously puzzled. He turned deep red. A pair of blue boxer shorts.

"My gift," Jennifer admitted to Scott, her own face feeling hot.

Scott squeezed her arm, having heard the admission.

The next part of the video was from the wedding reception. Watching Jennifer and her new husband, Jerry, greeting friends, sharing cake, opening gifts, made Scott grow more and more silent. He was becoming more and more aware of just how much Jennifer had lost.

Jennifer changed the tape. "This is at the hospital with Colleen." Scott realized suddenly that in the past few months with Jennifer she had never shown him Colleen's picture. He leaned forward as the tape showed the hospital nursery. "Peter was taking the pictures?" he asked quietly. Jennifer nodded.

Colleen was a pretty baby, small, fragile, but all the more beautiful because of it. She had such tiny hands. Watching Jennifer hold her daughter made Scott feel like crying. He could see the bond between them. No wonder Jennifer had not shown him this tape before. He looked over, saw that Jennifer was silently crying. He wrapped his arm around her shoulder.

The tape eventually ended.

"That's Colleen."

He reached over and gently kissed her wet cheek. "Thanks for sharing her, Jen," he whispered softly.

She nodded. She took a deep breath. "We need to talk." She looked at him, looked away. "I don't want to have any more children. I can't do it."

She felt him freeze. She went on before her courage failed her. "I've tried my best. I even managed to hold Mary Elizabeth today. But I can't do it. I can't have children again. I can't risk going through the loss of a child again."

"Jen, the odds of that happening again..."

She shook her head. "To live with that kind of fear is something I can't do."

He hugged her toward him, rested his chin on the top of her head. "I know you've been thinking about this for some time. Is this definite? Will more time help?"

"It's definite, Scott." She was crying. "I am so sorry."

He brushed back the tears. He was silent for some time. "I really want to have children with you, Jen."

"I can't take that risk again, Scott. I just can't," she whispered brokenly.

The hard part was, he did understand.

Chapter Twelve

She wasn't going to answer the phone.

The machine picked up after four rings, and Scott left Jennifer another message for her to call him. She didn't want to talk to him. She was trying to put distance between them, and it was killing him to realize that was what she was doing.

What was he going to do?

Since that night three days ago, when she had said she couldn't risk having children again, his thoughts, his emotions, had swung in all directions. He wanted children. He wanted to have a family. She knew it, and in her own way she was trying to say goodbye.

Anger driving him to his feet, Scott left his office and paced through his house. Why did this have to happen? Why? It made no sense. God was supposed to be able to heal grief, give courage, but Jennifer had not healed. And his hope, his optimism which had been that time would heal the trauma and Jennifer would eventually accept the idea of having a child again, was up against a brick wall. Scott knew Jennifer's decision wasn't going to change. She couldn't risk losing a child again. It wasn't a matter of giving her another year, the trauma had irreversibly set her decision.

He honestly did understand. She couldn't risk losing a child again. But understanding did not lessen his own pain. He wanted children. He wanted a family. And he was now facing the loss of his own dream. No children. He was feeling the pain Jennifer must have felt when she lost Colleen. It felt like his heart was breaking.

Needing the space, Scott called for Quigley and headed for the beach.

Her decision had placed him at the point he was going to have to make a decision of his own.

He could begin to look for another lady to be his wife. If he wanted a family, that was his option. In his head he knew that, but the thought lingered only long enough for his heart to response. He loved Jennifer. There was no way he could walk away from her.

That left only the toughest road—to deal with his own grief of not having a family and reach the point where he could accept that cost. It made Scott painfully aware of what he would never have. An infant of his own to hold, rock to sleep, teach to walk. There would be no son or daughter racing to the door when he got home from work, eager to be picked up and hugged.

He could adjust to that reality. Eventually. He knew he could. If Jennifer gave him the chance. She might walk away from him for good rather than let him sacrifice his dream for a family. She had that kind of courage inside, and it scared Scott.

God, why did you do this? Why did Colleen die? Why did you let Jennifer get so badly hurt? Why am I being asked to lose my dream of a family?

The emotions tore into his words, and he stormed the beach for over an hour until his legs were spent and the anger was spent and one decision was burned into stone. He was not walking away from her.

Okay, God. What are we going to do?

The prayer came from his gut as he stopped at the top of a rise and looked out over the water. He had had his back to the wall before, and God had gotten him out, there had to be some plan for this time.

He didn't know enough.

He had seen the episode at the hospital, had seen the panic suddenly hit her. He knew she was afraid. But what specifically was she afraid of? What triggered the terror? Was it being pregnant? Was it the age of the child? Was it the hospital experience? Was she afraid of a second marriage, as well, losing another husband? He needed answers, because one thing was clear inside.

He was *not* walking away.

"Jennifer, can I get you anything else? A cup of hot tea maybe?" Rachel asked as she stopped beside the recliner where Jennifer was watching the kids play outside in the snow.

"Thanks, Rachel, but I'm okay for now," Jennifer replied, grateful for her friend's concern. In the past three days a cold had settled deep into her chest. The stress of the severed relationship with Scott was taking its toll on her mood as well as her physical health.

Tiffany, Alexander and Tom were all having fun out in the snow. It was not much, only a light dusting, but it was enough to enjoy. Jennifer smiled sadly as she watched them play.

Her decision had been the only one she could make,

but that didn't make the pain less. She had been ducking Scott's calls the past few days, afraid he might try to change her mind. Afraid to let him close. She had not told Peter and Rachel what had happened, but her friend seemed to know. Jennifer thought she had masked her grief about Colleen, but it was apparent Rachel at least suspected the truth.

"Christmas is three weeks away, and I've still got so much to do," Rachel said as she came back into the living room and took a seat beside Jennifer. "Christmas cookies and decorations and presents to buy." She smiled. "I love it. You are still planning to come for Christmas Eve, aren't you?"

"I wouldn't miss it," Jennifer said with a smile. "Can I bring anything?"

"Scott," Rachel replied, and Jennifer felt her smile stiffen. Three weeks from now Scott might not even be talking to her. "I'll ask him," she told Rachel.

It was so tough to love someone. She had to consider what was best for Scott, and she wasn't best for him anymore. She shivered. The thought of losing another child terrified her. She so desperately wanted him in her life, but not if it cost him his own dreams for a family. She would regret forever letting him give up his dreams.

"He's a good man, Jen," Rachel said, watching her.

"Yes, he is," Jennifer agreed, a catch in her voice. She paused to cough hard, feeling like her lungs were going to tear apart.

Jennifer smiled as her niece and nephews came bundling into the house, crowded around to ask if she had seen them make their snow angels. She loved these three kids. "Would a kiss make your cold better?" Tiffany asked as she pulled off her gloves.

"It might help," Jennifer offered, and Tiffany threw her cold hands around Jennifer's neck and gave her a big kiss on the cheek. "I want you to get better."

There were tears in Jennifer's eyes as she hugged the girl. "Thank you, munchkin."

"Jennifer."

She paused at the front door and turned, surprised. Scott. He was here. For five days she had avoided answering the phone, had played his messages and forced herself to not reply. She had hoped if she could make him angry, he would feel the pain less. And still he had come. She watched him walk up the front drive and her eyes looked at him, hungrily, having missed him so badly. He looked as rough as she felt. He had not had a good five days. "Scott. Why are you here?" she asked quietly as he joined her.

He took the keys from her hand and unlocked her front door. "To talk to you. Not answering my calls is not going to make the problem go away," he replied firmly, pushing open the door. He waited for her to precede him. She could see the determination in his face. He wanted to talk.

Jennifer tried to shore up her resolve and walked into the house before him. Ignoring him, she went into the kitchen, took off her coat and found a glass. She had been to see the doctor, and his diagnosis of walking pneumonia had somehow seemed fitting. She felt like hell. Scott was in the kitchen doorway watching her, as she opened the prescription bottle she had picked up from the pharmacy and swallowed the pills. She tipped her glass toward him. "Would you like something to drink?"

"A stiff drink seems fitting, but I'll fix some coffee

later," Scott replied. He was looking at her and she didn't like the fact he seemed to see everything going on inside her at a glance.

Scott's intense need to talk was fading. The fact he was simply with her again was changing his agenda. "Have you had lunch yet, Jennifer?"

She grimaced. "Half a bagel while I waited for the prescription to get filled."

He smiled and dropped his coat across one of the kitchen chairs. "Sit. I'll see if you have anything of interest for lunch."

"You don't have to cook for me."

He stopped in front of her and placed his hands gently on her shoulders. "I want to. It makes me feel useful. So just say yes."

"Yes." She leaned forward to place her head against his chest, and his hands closed around her. "I've missed you, Scott. I just don't have the energy to talk right now."

The hands holding her tightened. "Well I'm not letting you shut me out. Got that, Jen? If I have to push my way back in, I'll do so. I don't like you ignoring my calls."

"I'm sorry."

He kissed the top of her head. "You're forgiven. As long as you don't do it again. Now sit while I get to work."

Jennifer sat, her head in her hand, and watched him work. He moved around her kitchen, searching cupboards, looking through the refrigerator, and he soon had lunch underway. Jennifer smiled and watched him.

She had missed him so much. He was big and strong and solid and there, and she loved him so much.

She wished things were different, that they had met at a different time in their lives when they would have fit together and not now, when there was destined to be only hurt between them.

Another round of coughing stopped her thinking, and she struggled to regain her breath. Scott brought her a cup of hot tea and rested his hand on her forehead, clearly disturbed that she was sick. Jennifer wanted to lean into his hand. She was simply so weary. She wanted to curl up and go to sleep for hours. She pulled back, causing him to frown. She had been sick before in the last three years, it was just a bad cold, no big deal. It was weakness to lean on Scott after having told him the relationship could go no further.

Scott brought over lunch—soup, salad and fresh fruit.

"Thank you. This looks delicious," Jennifer said, doing her best to do the meal justice. "You took today off from work," she suddenly realized.

"Yes."

She closed her eyes, obviously in pain. "I didn't intend this, Scott. I should have called you."

"I still would have come," he replied. "I can tell you're feeling rotten. Do you want to go lie down for a while or could we talk?"

"There's nothing left to talk about, Scott."

"Yes there is. I love you, Jen, and you love me," he said with quiet confidence, and her eyes filled with tears.

"Well sometimes pain comes with love," she replied.

"I'm not letting you go, Jen."

"You need a wife who can give you a family," she replied, destroying her own hope for his sake.

"I need you."

"And if I can't accept that? What then?"

"I can out-wait you, Jen. Eventually your pain is going to fade to the point you can risk a second marriage."

"I won't let you give up your dream, Scott. You'll resent me for the rest of our lives, and I don't need the extra guilt to carry."

Scott sighed. "Don't sell us short, Jen. Would you rather I stay single for the rest of my life? That's what you're really asking me to do."

"You shouldn't be outside with your cold."

Jennifer turned on her heels to see Scott approaching.

"Peter told me where you would be," Scott said, not liking at all the puffy eyes and pale face he saw. Jennifer looked awful. He had been trying to reach her last night and this morning with no answer, just the voice of her machine saying to leave a message. She had asked both him and Peter to let her spend this day alone, but Scott couldn't honor that request. She needed someone with her on this day. He needed to be with her today.

There was nothing at the cemetery to block the wind, and it was bitterly cold for mid-December. Scott came to a stop beside Jennifer, looked with pain down at the two headstones on the grave site. He set the bouquet of peach roses he carried down on Colleen's grave. He wanted to take Jennifer's hand, offer some comfort, but she had both hands shoved in her pockets, her expression filled with pain as she looked not at the present but at the past.

When she still stood motionless some minutes later,

Scott grew concerned enough he reached out his hand and gently brushed her cheek. His heart was breaking at the pain she was experiencing. "Jen, can you tell me what you're thinking about?"

Jennifer was remembering a previous conversation with Scott.

"I wish I had a picture of Colleen with me so I could show it to you. She had such vivid blue eyes. She used to tilt her head just this certain way and look at you. Then smile.

"She was so tiny when she was born it was a strug-gle for her to be awake. It took all her energy. So she would lay there and blink at me with this surprised expression in her eyes. They had to feed her through patches on her back for the first two weeks. It was such a wonderful day when she began to suck."

"What do you miss the most, Jennifer?"

"The fact my life doesn't revolve around her any-more. She gave me a reason to get up every morning. Even if the routine consisted of going to the hospital for the day and sitting with her, she was there. It was devastating after she died not to have her there. I had grown so attached."

"Do you think about having other children, Jenni-fer?"

"No. Colleen was such a traumatic experience it is going to take a long time for the intensity of those memories to fade. I couldn't risk going through that again."

"You loved Colleen. You would love another child with the same intensity."

"In my mind will always be the fact I lost my eldest daughter."

"Scott, why did she have to die? She was so small,

so tiny, she had her whole life ahead of her. It wasn't fair that she died."

Scott wrapped his arms around her and simply hugged her. "I know it wasn't fair, Jen."

"I killed her." Scott felt something cut into his heart at those words. "If I'd only taken better care of myself, she wouldn't have been born early," Jennifer sobbed.

Scott tightened his grip. He couldn't take away the guilt Jennifer was feeling. "Jen, Peter told me a lot about those weeks. You held on long enough to give Colleen life. That was a miracle itself. Your doctors never expected you make it as long as you did, did Peter ever tell you that? When your blood pressure dropped the doctors were sure you were going to lose the baby. But you didn't. Colleen lived because you held on. Please don't feel this added guilt."

She was crying against his coat, and Scott was helpless to stop her pain. He let her cry and gently rocked her and read the two gravestones over and over.

"You need to get out of this wind," he whispered gently when her tears began to lessen. "Would you come with me? Peter and I will come back for your car."

She nodded, not lifting her head.

Scott walked her back to his car, carefully tucked her into the passenger seat. He turned the heat in the car on full blast and took a few extra minutes to rub her frozen hands. Because she was flushed he lifted his hand to brush her forehead and found she was hot, running at least a hundred-and-one temperature. "Have you eaten today?" he asked gently, tipping her chin up so he could see her eyes.

She shook her head. Scott wasn't surprised.

He called her brother from the car and told him

Jennifer was going to be at his place. Jennifer, beside him, barely indicated that she heard the conversation. She rested her head back against the seat and closed her eyes.

Scott looked over at her as he drove. He was convinced she had lost at least ten pounds since that awful day when she had said a definite no to having children. She was giving up hope. Finding her at Colleen's grave today didn't surprise him, but it did worry him. She had no equilibrium about her when she thought about Colleen. She had adjusted to, even accepted Jerry's death. She hadn't done the same with Colleen. She hadn't been able to let go of the trauma. But her comment at the cemetery was at least a clue why. She believed her actions had killed Colleen. Lord, what am I suppose to do? How do I best help her?

She was asleep when Scott pulled into the drive of his house. He didn't wake her. He unlocked the house, propped the door open and gently carried Jennifer inside and laid her carefully down on the couch. He found an afghan his mother had made to cover her with and then he went to the kitchen to fix something she might be able to eat. She needed to take something for the fever, but he would have to wake her to find out what she had taken, and Scott decided the sleep was more important.

He fixed potato soup and toasted bagels for their lunch, carried the food into the living room. "Jen." He shook her shoulder gently. She came awake, groggy, confused. "I brought you some aspirin for the fever. Have you taken anything recently?" Scott asked.

Jennifer struggled to think, lifted the cover back with a hand that felt too heavy to move. "No. Not since early this morning." Scott handed her the aspirins and she swallowed the pills. The lunch smelled so good, and her head, her eyes, hurt so badly.

Scott sat down beside her on the couch, gently brushed back her hair. "Do you want to try to eat?" he asked quietly.

Jennifer closed her eyes, relishing his touch, having missed him so much in the last several days. "In a minute," she replied softly. She opened her eyes a short time later, looked at him with such sadness in her eyes. "Thank you for coming today. I told you not to come, but I was wrong. It was hard to be there alone."

"I'll always be there for you, Jen, please remember that. I'm not going away." Scott could tell she wanted to argue the point, argue that he needed to go away, but the cold was too strong, and she didn't have the strength left to fight. "Try some of the soup," he said, helping her sit up. He sat beside her as she ate, finishing off his own bowl of soup in a fraction of the time it took Jennifer to eat a few bites. When she had eaten all she could, he turned her sidewise on the couch and pulled her to rest back against his chest, and he wrapped the afghan around her and simply held her. He wanted to talk, to ask questions and hear answers and work out a way to heal the pain, but it was not the right time, and there would be a right time; he had to believe that. He held her and let the warmth of his arms help fight the chills that still occasionally rippled through her. "I've missed you," he said gently.

"I've missed you, too." Scott was incredibly pleased to hear those soft words. Jennifer fell asleep in his arms.

Scott was content to simply sit and hold her. When Quigley came looking for them, Scott quietly directed the puppy to come curl up in Jennifer's lap. She woke enough to hug the puppy and drift back to sleep with him snuggled in her arms.

It was harder than last time to convince Jennifer to take a guest bedroom and get some real sleep. She had no intention of staying overnight, and Scott had no intention of letting her be home alone. He gave her the option of staying with Peter and Rachel, or staying with his sister, but he refused to consider letting her be home alone. With Peter backing him up, Scott was finally able to convince her to take a guest room for the night. He put her to bed with a drink on the nightstand beside her, aspirins she could take later that night and extra blankets to keep her from getting chilled.

Scott stood on the landing after finally saying good-night to his guest, and he had to smile. Jennifer was not a good patient.

She slept through breakfast the next morning. Scott was reading the paper around ten when Jennifer finally appeared in the kitchen. Scott wished he could say she looked better, but the fever had done a severe number on her appearance. He didn't care. At least she was up and walking. "Good morning," he said gently, getting up from the table to meet her.

"Is there coffee fixed?" she asked, her voice husky.

"Yes. I'll get it. Take a seat, Jen."

She sat down, weary beyond comprehension.

"How's the fever?"

"Coming down," she said, resting her chin in her hand. "I hate being sick."

"No one enjoys it," Scott replied, setting a cup of coffee and a slice from an apple danish in front of her. "Have you taken more aspirin?" She nodded, and he resumed his seat.

"You took another day off work for me."

He smiled. "I've earned it," he replied. "Jen, would you like to check out my library collection, find a book to read, or would you rather curl up and watch some television? I have several movies on tape," Scott offered.

Jennifer smiled. "Your care is appreciated, but I need to get home."

It was one of the few times he lost a debate with her. She wanted to go home, and he could not dissuade her.

It was hard for Scott to take her home and leave her there. They had to get married soon. He was tired of this.

"Jen, could I ask you a couple of questions?" Scott's breath fluttered some strands of her hair as his voice broke the silence of the room.

They were on the couch in her living room, his arms around her. She was resting back against his chest, her head against his shoulder, a quilt covering her legs. His arms were wrapped firmly around her waist and his hands were comfortably folded atop the quilt with her hands linked under his. The pneumonia had taken her strength, and although her fever was gone, he had no intention of allowing her to move very far.

It was time.

"If I can," she finally said. He heard the hesitation and offered a reassuring kiss across her forehead, and his arms tightened gently. "I've been praying a lot about what has happened, and I just need to understand some things. You might not even know the answers, and that's okay, because that would also help me understand."

She nodded and he felt her take a deep breath. "What're your questions?"

Lord, I could use some help here, Scott prayed.

"I want to know what you are afraid of, specifically. What is it that triggers the terror. Does the thought of being pregnant again make you feel afraid?" He kept his voice calm and steady, and he actually felt some of the stress in her body begin to lessen when he asked the question.

"No. The nausea is hard to handle, but being pregnant was okay."

"Does the memory of giving birth make you afraid?"

He felt the flinch. Okay. That was one answer he needed to know. "What about the memory makes you afraid? The pain? The hospital setting? The doctors?"

Her hands fluttered under his. "It wasn't supposed to be happening, it was too early, I knew I was losing my baby."

Scott turned her hands over to interlace his fingers with hers. She feared another premature birth.

"What if you had a healthy baby like Mary Elizabeth. Does that make you feel afraid?"

He almost thought she had not heard the question she was silent for so long, and then he felt her nod. "She might stop breathing," Jennifer whispered.

SIDS. Damn it. That one had been obvious. That one should not have been asked.

"If she's four, like Amy, does that make you feel afraid?" he asked, trying to pull that image of an infant from her mind.

Her hands eventually fluttered in his, signaling she didn't know how to answer.

"What about nine like Greg, or twelve, like Tiffany?"

She smiled slightly. "They feel like sturdy kids. Like maybe the worst would be a broken arm."

All right. He had his answers. Scott kissed her forehead and took a deep breath. "Just one last question. If the issue of children were not on the table, is a second marriage itself a problem? Does the idea of being married again make you afraid?"

"I won't rob you of your desire to have a family." It was a flat refusal and he was hurt, because it told him there was going to be quite a fight ahead.

"Does the idea of being married again make you feel afraid?" he asked again, determined to know that basic answer. He gave her time to think about it, and he felt the physical reaction in her body when she finally resolved the question in her mind. His eyes closed. He knew what was coming before she spoke, and it was the answer he had been afraid of the most. In all the pain about Colleen, she sometimes forgot the fact that unexpected death had also claimed Jerry. He had separated them intentionally, suspecting the truth. When she finally spoke, her words were barely a whisper, and they seemed to come as a shock to her. "Yes. The idea of being married again makes me feel terrified."

Chapter Thirteen

Jennifer tried to think through the stroke before she hit the cue ball, but her concentration was simply not there, and as the smooth wood slipped through her fingers and connected with the cue ball she shut her eyes and grimaced. She didn't even have to look to know that her finesse of the eleven ball had instead just left Bob Volishburg an open, easy shot for the game. Her friend called the corner for the eight ball and won the third game with ease.

"You want to tell me what's wrong?" he asked as he watched her pick up the triangle rack and place the balls inside.

I'm terrified of losing another husband so I'm going to walk away from a guy I love. Her face tightened at the awful place she was in. "Not really."

"Tell me, anyway," Bob replied.

Jennifer shook her head and broke the balls apart with a snap to start their fourth game. Bob had shown up about 10:00 p.m. and offered to play a couple of games. Before that she had simply been lining the balls up in a row and methodically nailing them into the pockets.

"Peter tells me you've been seeing a guy."

"My brother talks too much."

"Well, since I haven't seen you here in three weeks, I'm going to guess it's pretty serious."

"It was," Jennifer agreed.

"Ahh, was. Such an interesting word."

Jennifer smiled grimly. "Not interested."

"You expect me to tell you about Linda, you had better expect me to return the favor," Bob replied. "Jerry wouldn't mind you getting serious with a guy."

"I don't want to lose a husband again," Jennifer said, crushing the ten ball with an explosive shot that sent both it and the cue ball into the side pocket.

Bob placed the penalty ball and considered where he wanted to place the cue ball. "I imagine it's worse than losing a partner," he replied.

Bob had lost two during his career, and Jennifer knew what it had cost him. "It's bad," she agreed. Goodness knows Bob had played her a lot of pool late at night when she was avoiding going home.

"If you've got courage, you'll risk it again. You know what the worst is like."

She was grateful he didn't use the "it's unlikely to happen again" argument. It was an irrelevant argument, and they both knew it. "I don't have that kind of courage. I lost part of myself when I lost Jerry. If I let someone get inside again and I lose him, there won't be much of me left."

"The more rewarding parts of life are risky. You've never been one to play it safe. You don't play it safe when you play pool, you don't play it safe in your writing. You certainly didn't play it safe in how you loved

Colleen. But you wouldn't be who you are unless you did take those risks."

"Sometimes you have to pause and count the costs. You did when you left drug enforcement for homicide," Jennifer countered.

Bob shrugged. "I got tired of being shot at. Sure, it's healthy to reconsider the risks you are taking occasionally. But cutting yourself off from risk completely would leave you with a boring life." He smiled. "The last thing either of us can tolerate is boredom."

Jennifer smiled and nailed a ball into the corner pocket. "Maybe I'm getting old, Bob, but it's not as simple as it used to be. I don't want to get hurt again."

"And it's not going to hurt if you walk away?" Bob asked, going to the heart of the matter.

They could adopt. An older child, because Jennifer was going to panic with a child under ten, but adoption was still an option.

Scott tried to weigh what he thought about the idea as he walked the beach with Quigley. He had no rose-colored glasses about the idea. He had met Kevin's friends from foster care. Most of the kids were like Kevin. And while he honestly did like the boy, there was no hiding the fact the kid was troubled and a challenge. Any kid coming out of the system at that age was going to make Jennifer's scars look like paper cuts. Jennifer dealt with her pain remarkably well. A child, without the coping skills of an adult, would be a tangle of anger and pain and nearly impossible to get close to. They would hear "I love you" and likely remember a dozen people in their lives who had said it and then abused or abandoned them. They were kids who desperately needed love and someone to believe in them but who had been hurt so badly in the past they would reject the very thing they most needed to accept. They would likely be in trouble at school, with the law, make discipline and rules a constant battle while they processed the past pain.

She wouldn't marry him if she thought it meant him sacrificing his dreams of a family. The bottom line was that simple. Either she accepted the idea of adoption, or he was going to lose her, Scott understood that. She was serious about not marrying him at the cost of his dream. But to succeed in convincing her to accept adoption, he was going to have to be fully at the point where *he* could accept it. He wasn't going to be able to slide past the reality of what it would mean to adopt an older child and say lightly that it was okay. She would never buy that. He had to believe it was an acceptable solution before he could sell it to her. He couldn't have a doubt left inside.

Could he accept Kevin as his son? Mixed-up, angry, pushing-the-limits Kevin? They would probably have a child very similar to him to deal with. Scott felt the part of him that weighed risks look at and accept the risk. Putting a kid like that back together and through college and out into the world making his own way would be a profound accomplishment. One that was worth the cost.

His biggest fear was over the strain that would put on the marriage. Could they get to the point where they had a strong enough marriage to absorb the stress a child in that shape would cause? It wouldn't be easy dealing with anger and pain coming at them, not because they as parents deserved it but because something in the kid's past was finally getting expressed and they happened to be handy to take the fallout.

Scott called Quigley back to his side and bent down to pick up the puppy.

Lord, what do you want me to do? Are you really setting me up to be adopting older children? Is that what you have planned? I don't want to lose Jennifer. I don't. And if this is the only option, get me to the point I can accept it. Please.

Jennifer's fear of losing a husband was deep and going to be difficult to deal with, but Scott looked at that problem and knew it could be overcome. Adopting an older child; that was different. He had to get not only Jennifer to accept the idea, he had to first reach the point he could honestly accept the idea himself. At the moment, it still left his gut churning with doubt.

"Which ring are you looking at?" Heather asked as she gently rocked Mary Elizabeth back and forth in her arms. Her daughter was awake now and gurgling with delight as she wove her hands into Heather's hair. She and Scott had been walking the mall pushing the infant in her stroller as she slept, shopping for Christmas presents. This was the third time Scott had maneuvered them past this jewelry store.

Scott pointed to the back of the display case. "That one with the center diamond and the offset emerald. The engagement ring has another diamond and an offset ruby. Think she might like it?"

"She'll love it," she replied, getting to the heart of the matter. Jennifer would probably protest the expense, but she would love the ring. She watched her brother sigh and rub the back of his neck. "What's wrong?" Heather asked. Her brother rarely looked this troubled about life, and he'd had to work at showing an interest in Christmas shopping and that was not like him. He shrugged and didn't answer. As it now seemed likely that he was not going to be buying the rings today, Heather gently tugged his arm. "Come on, let's go eat lunch."

They went to a sandwich and soup shop on the lower level of the mall, slid into a booth. Their sandwiches and soup arrived and Scott smiled at how active Mary Elizabeth was. "Hand her to me, Twig, while you eat your soup," Scott offered, and his sister handed him the baby. "Hey, M, how you doing today? You like all these colors and lights, don't you? Are you going to like to shop like your mom does?" The infant smiled and gurgled and threw her arms up at him, her legs pushing against his thighs. Scott laughed and kissed her cheek. He settled her against his shoulder and looked over at his sister. His eyes were grave.

"We're not going to have children. She's so afraid, Twiggy." There were tears in his eyes that he didn't let fall.

Her hand covered his. "I'm so sorry, Scott."

He hesitated. *Twig, it hurts so bad.* "So am I," he finally said. It was his pain to cope with.

"You can borrow Mary Elizabeth anytime you like. The kids love having you as their uncle," she said, trying to help.

"Thanks, Twig. I'm going to do that."

"After lunch, go buy the rings, Scott," Heather told him, knowing that decision was the only one that was going to give him some peace.

"You really think she would like those rings?" he asked, fighting back the pain.

Heather couldn't remember her brother ever being

this uncertain. "Absolutely. Those rings are gorgeous," she reassured him, smiling.

"I found a gold band that I like, too."

"Come on in, Scott. Sorry I'm running late," Jennifer called from the kitchen.

Scott pushed open the door and stepped inside, shaking the light dusting of snow from the coat he'd taken off and carrying it into the kitchen with him. He dropped it over the back of a chair. The house was festive and colorful and Jennifer had Christmas music playing. "How did the cookies turn out?"

Jennifer smiled at him from the counter where she was boxing the iced cookies. "They turned out great. Tiffany, Tom and Alexander all approved."

Scott came over and rested his hands against her back, leaned over to kiss her. Her peach sweater felt soft and warm against his hand, and he rubbed her back softly. "There's no hurry. I told Mom we'd be by sometime this evening to drop the boxes off, but they aren't due to the nursing home until tomorrow afternoon. I think the youth group managed to make twenty dozen total, I picked up the last of them on the way over."

Jennifer paused in her work. "I'm glad your Mom does this. I don't bake cookies if it's just for me. And there are only so many I can pass on to Peter and Rachel and the kids."

"Which are the best? The Christmas trees, the reindeer or the candy canes?" Scott asked, studying the options.

"Try a candy cane. They break so easily when they're packed."

Scott picked up one and found the sugar cookie was

delicious. "You haven't eaten yet, have you?" he asked, hoping she had been willing to wait.

"I had a late lunch. Where do you have in mind? I'll need to change."

"The jeans are fine. I thought we would go split a sample plate at Shaw's," he offered.

"Sounds wonderful." She finished boxing the last cookies and added the box to the stack on the table. Her hands finally free, she came back to hug him. "How are you tonight?" she asked quietly.

He settled his hands around her waist and tucked her close. He liked the feel of her hands on his back. He kissed her leisurely. "I'm doing fine. I've missed you the past couple days," he said, studying her brown eyes, which reminded him so much of a young doe. She had beautiful eyes.

She sighed and leaned her head against his chest, and he took the opportunity to gently rub her shoulders and the back of her neck. He could feel the tension in her body. "I'm so glad you're around. I really don't like Christmas, and that's an awful feeling."

He rubbed her back, long soothing strokes across her shoulders and spine down to her waist. "I know." She had not been able to hide the sadness in her eyes, and he knew the memories were there and bothering her. "We'll keep you too busy to think about it. We're going to Rachel and Peter's for Christmas Eve?"

"If you're sure you want to. You ought to spend it with your own family."

Her protest caused him to smile. "You're going to be my family," he replied lightly.

"Scott…"

He tipped her chin up and kissed her before she could protest any further. "We'll go to my folks for lunch Christmas Day," he said. He nodded toward the boxes on the table. "It's cold outside. You'll need your long coat," he recommended.

She wanted the conversation to continue, he could see that, but after she looked at him she dropped her eyes and simply nodded. Scott squeezed her hands gently before he let her go. He was going to ask her tonight. He'd just made that decision.

Scott didn't have to persuade Jennifer very hard to get her to slide over on the seat and sit beside him on the drive to his parents'. He entwined his hand with hers as it rested on the seat. She was lost in thought, and Scott didn't try to break it. It felt right, having her with him, and it was so different from that night a couple months before as he had driven alone to his parents' for his birthday party. It was nice having her with him. His mom was home but not his dad, and Scott didn't linger at their place. He and Jennifer carried the boxes she had packed and those from the youth group into the dining room, where his Mom had several other donations packed. Scott kissed his Mom at the door and could see the question in her eyes, and he just smiled. He never had been able to keep a secret from her, and she knew something was different tonight. "We'll see you for lunch Christmas Day," he told her, giving her a hug.

Jennifer thought the restaurant would be packed with holiday gatherings, but the parking lot at the seafood restaurant was only partially full. Scott got out and came around to open her door, offer his arm across the slick parking lot. They were seated at a back booth of the restaurant and Scott ordered a large sample plate and two diet colas for them. "Is your Christmas shopping done?" Scott asked her as they both selected a freshly baked bread stick from the basket the waitress had brought.

She grinned. "Rachel's gift was the last one I needed, and I got that this morning. Did you find Heather's gift?"

Scott smiled. "I bought her an orchid. One plant that is flowering and several bulbs that she can plant."

"She'll love it."

Scott went silent for several minutes. "You're really missing Colleen, aren't you?" he asked quietly.

Jennifer wished he could not read the pain so easily. "Incredibly. She never got to see a Christmas," Jennifer sighed and wished there was some way to make the pain go away. "Most of the nursery was packed away shortly after Colleen died—the crib, the changing table. But I've still got the rocking chair, the clothes I made for her, the ankle ID band she wore. I keep telling myself I'm going to pack them away and turn the bedroom back into a guest room, but when I go in the room all I want to do is rock in the chair and cry." She felt so miserable admitting that.

"Jen, maybe that's what you need to do the most. Let yourself cry."

"I've cried enough, Scott."

His hand gently rubbed the back of hers. She had to force herself not to turn her hand into his and hold on. "You lost a lot, Jen. Allow yourself the freedom to grieve."

His concern and kindness was almost too much to take. "Could we talk about something else?" she asked, hoping he would not be offended.

He smiled.

"Tell me about your book," he offered. The sample plate of seafood arrived and they talked about her book over steamed scallops, garlic shrimp, mussels on the shell, and Louisiana blue crab claws. Jennifer felt the sadness inside lift as she sat talking with Scott. She loved him. It went as deep as it had with Jerry, and she wished so badly she could get past the terror of having children so they could have a future together. But she was resolute that she would do what was best for him, and right now, it was not her. But Bob was right. It was going to hurt so very, very badly to walk away.

They left the restaurant shortly after 8:00 p.m., and when Scott suggested they go for a drive, Jennifer gladly agreed. When she was with him, the pain was less.

Scott looked over at Jennifer as he drove, wishing he had some idea how she was going to respond to his proposal. There were times in his life when he put his heart into someone else's hands, and tonight was going to be one of them.

"Jen?"

She turned toward him and smiled, and it reached her eyes and made her so beautiful. "Yes?"

"Slide over here," he encouraged.

She slid over with a smile and his arm settled around her shoulders. "Where are we going?"

Scott smiled. "How does a fire, a cup of hot chocolate and a very enthusiastic puppy sound?"

"Delightful."

Quigley greeted her at the door with a cold nose and a squirming body. Jennifer scooped him up with a laugh after handing Scott her coat. "Hello, Quigley, my little beautiful boy." The puppy licked her chin and Jennifer laughed, and when she rubbed his ears he squirmed closer with a happy wiggle.

"Take him into the living room. I'll be right in with the hot chocolate. The fire is already laid and ready to start," Scott said as he rested his hand against her back and lightly ruffled the puppy's fur.

When Scott entered the living room some ten minutes later, the fire had been started and Jennifer had kicked off her shoes and curled up at one end of the couch with Quigley nearly asleep in her arms. Scott settled beside her and carefully handed her one of the mugs he carried. He smiled and ran his finger across the bridge of her foot. "I like the socks."

"Thank you, I thought the Christmas trees were appropriate."

Scott stretched his legs out and leaned his head back, watched the flickering flames surrounding the logs. They sat in silence for several minutes, both enjoying the stillness. Jennifer shifted around so she could rest against his shoulder, and Scott gladly welcomed her into his arms. "What are you thinking about so deeply?" she asked.

Scott took a deep breath. It was time. *Lord, help my words be the right ones.*

"What would you say to adopting an older child?" he asked quietly, then turned his head to look down at her.

"Adopting?"

"You know I want a family Jen, but I really do understand how terrified you are of the idea of having children again. We could adopt a kid like Kevin." Scott smiled. "He's anything but fragile, you know."

"Yes, he is, inside."

Scott gently stroked her hair. "I know you're right. People just forget it occasionally when they bump into that shell of his."

Jen gripped his hand. "You really would consider adopting an older child and all the problems that might bring?"

Scott wished he could read her voice well enough to know if that was hope or fear he heard, but all he could know for sure was that the calm, relaxed lady he had been holding a few moments before was now stiff and tense. His hands rubbed her arms, trying to dispel the tension.

"Jen, you need to be a mother. Having a family is as much your dream as it is mine. That dream didn't disappear when Colleen died, it just got badly battered." He kissed the top of her head. "You will make a good mom. I know that with certainty."

Her eyes were damp as he brushed her hair back from her face. He reached behind her for the gift he had set on the end table. "This is for you," he said quietly, placing both her hands around the small package. He smiled at her expression. "Go ahead, open it," he encouraged.

Her hands shook a little as she removed the ribbon and the deep green wrapping paper. She hesitated before opening the ring box.

"Will you marry me, Jen?"

The tears had begun to fall, and Scott wiped them away, wrapping her in his arms. He slid the engagement ring from the velvet slot and placed it in the palm of her hand. "I like this ring. It's special, just like the one you already wear. We could have something very special too, Jen, if you'll say yes."

Her hand closed around the ring and held it very tightly. "You're proposing and you want us to adopt." There was so much emotion in her voice...

Scott raised her hand and pressed his lips to the back of it. "Yes."

He felt her ragged breath, "I don't know what to say."

"Say you'll think about it," Scott said gently, his hands cupping her face, raising her face to let him fully see her. All the emotion was there in her eyes— the uncertainty, the fear, the love, the hope, the pain. He deliberately smiled, having just put his future and hers on the line. "I'm going to marry you, Jen. We're going to have a family, and we're going to make a difference in each other's lives and in the lives of whatever children God entrusts to us. I love you, Jen."

She buried her head against his chest and fought for her composure. "I'll think about it."

He kissed her forehead. "Think as long as you need to, Jen. I'm not going anywhere," he promised. He'd put it all on the line, and now it was a waiting game.

Chapter Fourteen

Could she adopt? Could she face the fear of being married again, adopt and raise a family? Or was she walking away?

The night was freezing cold, two weeks before Christmas. She couldn't stay out for long, even with the gloves and scarf, but Jennifer felt the need to see the stars, and so she sat on the hammock in the back-yard and leaned back and looked up. The stars in the Milky Way were bright and clear. Jennifer sat and looked at the sky and waited for the sense of being part of something enormous to settle into her soul. This decision was important, but it wasn't going to change the course of the universe. It would change her life and Scott's life and to a certain degree the lives of both of their families. She could make this decision. But what was the right decision?

The cold touch of death sat so close; incredible in its intensity. How could she risk getting married again? Even an older child. Could she really be a mom again?

Knowing what she had to do if she was to make a decision, Jennifer walked back inside, took off her coat and gloves, paused to hang them up and walked resolutely past her bedroom. She paused at the door of the nursery, took a deep breath and turned the handle. It was so quiet in the room, with a very faint scent of lavender from the dried flower display on the dresser. Walking slowly into the place she considered to be the heart of her home, she gently lifted from the dresser the clothes she had made for Colleen to wear, night-shirts and jumpers and very small socks. She smiled as she touched the soft fabric, remembering the love that had gone into making the garments, laughed as she remembered the sewing lessons Rachel had given her and how difficult it had been to make her fingers create what her mind envisioned. She took the gar-ments with her and sat down in the rocking chair, smoothing them out with care on the leg of her jeans. She refused to let the tears fall. There was pain here, deep pain. So many dreams had ended so abruptly.

Jennifer very carefully folded the clothes, leaned her head back and closed her eyes. For the first time in recent days she let herself go back in time to the funer-als, and actually think about what the experiences had been like. The first images that hit her were the cof-fins, polished oak, the wood grains deep and smooth. She had requested peach roses for Colleen's coffin, deep red roses for Jerry's coffin, and the flowers had rested on the center of the coffins, paying tribute to the memories she had of each. She felt and heard the music, felt the support of those standing with her, felt such a great distance from her God. In three years she had passed through the anger and despair—she now had a gentle peace with her God—but the taste of death still lingered. She couldn't lose Scott the same way. She couldn't. She would never survive.

It was time to accept reality.

The fear had won.

Scott dressed slowly, taking time to fasten his cuff links, choose the right tie, polish his shoes. He knew he was deliberately delaying the time he would leave his home to pick up Jennifer, even found himself amused at his actions, but did nothing to speed up his movements. He didn't know which way she was going to decide, but he was determined to hear her answer with as much dignity as he could. He'd either won or he'd lost for good. Either way, there would only be gratitude in his heart tonight for having known her. He loved her. He had placed her in the toughest position of her life, asking her to face her fear, without him being there to provide support. He picked up the single rose Heather had picked for him to give to Jennifer, a special rose—pale pink and white, perfectly formed.

Have courage, Jen. Please, have courage.

It was Christmas Eve and the music on the radio reflected the Christmas season. Scott drove slowly, carefully, eventually pulled into her subdivision, then her street, and finally into her drive. He parked the car, picked up the rose to shelter it from the wind and walked to her front door. She answered within moments of him ringing the bell and he smiled when he saw her. She was dressed for the Christmas Eve services, as well, her dress a wonderful deep blue velvet with satin trim. He kissed her cheek softly, and she hugged him, but there was nothing he could read in her eyes.

"Can we talk after we leave Peter and Rachel's?" she asked quietly, and he forced himself to take a deep breath. She wouldn't be so hesitant to share good news.

"Of course, Jen," he said quietly, wanting nothing more than to hold her tight and not let her go. But he owed her for adding a richness to his life he would have found nowhere else; he wasn't going to make the evening any harder on her than it was already destined to be. "I brought this for you," he said gently, pressing the rose into her hand.

She lifted the rose to smell its fragrance, touched the delicate pedals with the tips of her fingers. She lifted her eyes from the rose, an enormous sadness in those brown eyes, and she reached up and gently kissed him. "Thank you," she whispered.

He did hug her then, pulling her tight and simply holding her, and she clung to him in return, and minutes passed before she stepped away. "Let me put this in water."

He could see her reaching for strength deep inside, hear it in her voice. "I'll get your coat for you," he said, and she nodded and turned away. When she came back from the kitchen, the sadness in her eyes had been buried and replaced by calm acceptance. She slipped into her coat and pulled on her gloves. "I'm ready," she said quietly.

He locked the house for her, offered her his arm for the slick pavement, opened the passenger door. It was a silent drive to the area church Christmas Eve gathering. They both knew their respective families would be present at the area church gathering, but silently agreed not to seek out either friends or family. They sat together during the service, Scott firmly holding Jennifer's hand the entire time, and when the service was over, they slipped quietly back through the crowds. They waited for most of the parking lot to clear before Scott pulled from the church lot and asked Jennifer for directions.

Peter and Rachel's house was adorned with Christmas lights. Some were in the evergreens, others on the porch railing, some outlining windows. Jennifer drew a deep breath as they neared the front door, knowing that they would be expected and quickly pulled into the festivities, and knowing as well that she badly needed time to gather herself for the discussion later with Scott. Peter and Scott shook hands, and Rachel and Jennifer shared a hug. Jennifer didn't let her friend go for some time. "You okay?" Rachel whispered, and Jennifer nodded. Scott and Jennifer were escorted to the love seat in the living room, across from the Christmas tree and the presents the children had selected to be opened that night. There was cider and cheese and sausage, crackers, Christmas cookies. The boys gravitated to Scott, eager to have his attention. They made Scott smile, and Jennifer was grateful. She wished so badly the evening could end some other way. Scott reached over and put his arm around her shoulders, gently pulling her to his side. She looked up, surprised, and he tenderly brushed the hair back from her face and smiled. She could see the sadness in his eyes, but also a love so great that he would still offer comfort. She wished she could offer the same comfort in return.

As the evening progressed, Jennifer let herself relax and enjoy the time with her family. The children so enjoyed the celebration. The memories of past Christmas Eves spent with Jerry and her family returned, and they were good memories.

She couldn't give Scott up. She loved him. He had

just split a sugar cookie and offered her half of it with a smile. She loved him. She couldn't give him up. She'd come with a heavy heart tonight knowing she couldn't accept the risk of facing death again, had to say goodbye, but she couldn't carry out the sentence. She loved him. She was going to have to find a way to take the risk.

He knew something had changed. He held her gaze without wavering, his arm around her shoulder tightened, and he gently leaned over and kissed her.

They left Peter and Rachel's shortly after ten. Jennifer leaned her head back as they walked to the car; the sky was clear and bright with stars. Her hand was tucked firmly in Scott's, and it felt so right. "Where would you like to go?" he asked quietly.

Jennifer looked at the man she loved and quietly replied, "The beach, where we first met."

There was no wind, the water was calm, and the sand shifted as they walked. Scott had picked up both a quilt and a blanket at the house, and he spread the quilt out on the pier steps, helping her take a seat. He tucked the blanket around her legs. "Warm enough?" he asked, placing an arm around her shoulders and her coat. She smiled and slid another inch toward him. "I'm fine."

She didn't say anything for several minutes, her attention focused on the water and the starlit sky. "I was going to tell you *no*."

She felt his tension, and she could hear his deep, controlled breathing. "And now?" he asked softly.

She leaned her head against his shoulder. "I'm petrified of losing you, but I'll marry you." He laughed at the way she worded her acceptance, hugging her close. "I love you too much to say goodbye," she said.

He tilted her head up with both of his hands, his touch gentle, love in his eyes. "Jen, you won't regret this." Jennifer slipped her hands around his neck, gently moved them up into his silky hair. It was a deep kiss, full of love on both sides. "You are the very best thing that ever happened to me," he whispered, soothing away the lingering fear in her eyes with hands that gently stroked her face. "I'll help keep the fear away. You'll make it, honey, love can do it."

"The idea of adopting older kids…it doesn't feel too bad," she said, smiling slightly as she tugged his skewed tie straight again.

"Really?" His smile was delightful to see.

"Really," she confirmed.

He settled his arms around her waist under her coat, rested his forehead against hers. "How many children would you like?" he asked, interested.

She smiled. "Two or three would be nice."

His arms tightened. "Thank you, Jen."

She kissed him.

He got pragmatic. "Jen, I hate to disturb this moment, but it's cold out here. Let's go find your purse. I want to put that ring on your finger."

She laughed. He tugged her to her feet and picked up the blankets, escorted her inside. She found her purse and removed the ring box, handed it to him. He laughed softly at the way her hands were suddenly trembling, held them in his until they steadied.

"Important moment, isn't it?" he asked, breaking the tension.

She laughed, then, and relaxed. "It's big," she agreed. She moved the wedding ring she wore to her right hand and touched it, remembering. He gave her time, and she appreciated that. "Okay," she said quietly.

Scott gently slipped the engagement ring on her finger, smiled and kissed the back of her hand. "It looks good there." She hugged him, and he closed his arms around her to hold her tight. "Let's call Peter and Rachel. We'll tell my family tomorrow."

Neither Scott nor Jennifer minded the long drive to his parents' home. It was a chance to share the enjoyment of the moment. Jennifer sat close to Scott as he drove, her hand tucked in his.

"Marry me soon," Scott said over the Christmas music. He looked over at her, smiled. He'd read her fear correctly. She didn't need time to question her decision. It didn't matter what his friends and family thought. The wedding needed to be soon. When she didn't respond, he looked over again. Her brown eyes were calm and clear and slightly wet. "Bad idea or good?"

"Good one," she breathed. "Could we elope?"

He laughed. "No. Mom would kill me. How about thirty days? Third Saturday in January?"

Jennifer didn't have to think about it. "Yes."

Scott grinned. He could wait thirty days. Maybe.

His family was waiting for them to arrive, and when they pulled into the drive, Amy and Greg both came out to meet them, bundled up in coats and mittens. "Hi, Uncle Scott." Scott picked Amy up with a laugh and tickled her. He ruffled the boy's hair.

"Hi, Greg. Is lunch ready?"

"We were waiting for you," Greg replied.

"Then let's get inside," he agreed. He caught Jennifer's hand as they walked up the porch steps, shared a private smile with her.

It was his mother who first noticed the ring. Jennifer was taking off her coat and handing it to Scott's father when Margaret caught her breath and immediately looked over Jennifer's shoulder to Scott. He smiled and linked his arms around Jennifer's shoulders.

"Mom, Dad, we've got some news." He didn't have to say more, his smile said it all. Jennifer was swept into a hug by his mother who was now laughing and wiping away tears, his father was hugging him, and both Heather and Frank were crowding into the entryway to celebrate the news. The kids were thrilled, their eyes sparkling with excitement.

The family was sitting down to lunch when Scott paused behind Jennifer's chair, put his hands on her shoulders and looked around at his family. "We are getting married the third Saturday in January." Surprise, shock, bewilderment, he saw them all on their faces. He smiled. "This decision is right for us. But we could use your help, there are details to sort out."

Within an hour of the Christmas lunch announcement, Rachel and Peter and the kids had been invited over to make it a family celebration. Scott sat on the couch with Jennifer, watching his sister and mom tossing wedding details back and forth with Rachel. This felt right. This felt perfect. Their two families meshed so well. Jennifer had chosen colors for the dresses, and the wedding party had been decided on; they were working on the reception plans now.

From where he was sitting Scott could see Quigley trying to wrestle a tennis shoe underneath the great blue spruce in the foyer. Too tall and massive to fit in any conventional room, the Christmas tree towered in the curve of the stairway, reaching toward the skylight. He and Jennifer had helped decorate it, a process that involved leaning over the stair railing to reach the high branches. The gifts were gone now allowing Quigley a place he considered to be his new home, hiding down in the fluffy red-and-white tree skirt under the low branches. Scott saw Tiffany chase him down again, try to convince the puppy not to drink out of the Christmas tree base.

It was tradition in the neighborhood to go Christmas caroling on Christmas Eve, and as twilight came the adults began sorting out coats and gloves. All the kids wanted to go. Neighbors would have hot cider and cookies for the carolers. "Can I ride on your shoulders, Uncle Scott?" Amy asked, tugging at his hand.

"I'm staying here with Jennifer," he replied, and Jennifer saw the disappointment on the little girl's face.

"Go with them, Scott. There's no need for you to stay simply because I'm getting over a bad cold."

"I think the doctor called it pneumonia," he reminded her.

"Mom, aren't you coming?" Greg also looked disappointed.

"Mary Elizabeth is asleep upstairs. I need to stay here," Heather told her son.

They were the only two holdouts, everyone else, including Peter and Rachel were going. "Listen, both of you, go with the kids. I can listen for Mary Elizabeth. She's only been asleep half an hour. She'll never know you were gone," Jennifer insisted. She could see that this was a long-standing tradition, and she knew how much fun it was to go caroling.

"Jen, are you sure?" Heather asked.

"Positive."

She looked at Scott. He reluctantly removed his

arm and got up, leaned back down to kiss her. "I was hoping for thirty minutes on our own," he whispered, and she laughed.

She saw everyone off, watched as they joined up with neighbors who were also out to go caroling. She closed the door with a laugh as Quigley tried to sneak through. "No, you don't, friend. You get to keep me company. Tiffany will be back in an hour."

The house was silent with everyone gone. The massive Christmas tree blinked its colored lights, the smell of greenery wonderful. It had been such a beautiful day.

Jennifer went over to the baby monitor and made sure it was turned all the way up. She sat on the couch and played tug of war with Quigley using an old rag someone had found for him. He grew tired of the game after about ten minutes, and Jennifer let him run again. He was going to eventually be one very tired puppy. Smiling, she picked up the glasses and dishes around on the tables and carried them into the kitchen, loading the dishwasher.

Twenty minutes and she had heard nothing from Mary Elizabeth. Jen knew what was driving her desire to check on the infant but went, anyway. She walked up the stairs with Quigley underfoot, quietly pushed open the door of the guest room where Margaret had a crib set up. The baby was sleeping peacefully. Jen watched her breathe, reached out very gently to touch the softness of her little hand. She was so beautiful. So big. So healthy. Jennifer watched her and smiled, quietly left the room.

The kids would be cold when they got back. Finding that Margaret had set out all the ingredients for hot chocolate, Jennifer read her recipe and set to work.

She tasted the drink as it heated and knew she was going to have to get a copy. The recipe had a pinch of Dutch chocolate in it. It was delicious.

Quigley yelped. Jennifer tilted her head, trying to figure out where it had come from, but it was not repeated. Not liking the fact he hadn't come bolting back into the kitchen after encountering another dust ball surprise, Jennifer carefully turned down the flame under the large pan heating the hot chocolate and set aside the long spoon. "Quigley? Where are you, boy?"

Jennifer walked through the living room, expecting to find him stuck under one of the couches. The flicker of orange caught the corner of her eye, and she turned. She froze. Flames were licking up the back of the Christmas tree. Smoke was beginning to billow up and fill the stairwell. The fire alarm went off just as she understood what was happening. The tree was big and dry, and the flames were engulfing it so quickly.

The baby. Quigley, who must be beneath the tree, she had to leave to fend for himself. There wasn't time to call for help. There was only one way upstairs and it would soon be impassable. Covering her nose and mouth with her hands, Jen plowed through the smoke accumulating on the landing and made it to the upper hallway. The smoke was only beginning to collect here. It was still filling into the skylight.

Mary Elizabeth was crying at the piercing noise of the alarm. Jen gathered the infant and all her blankets together, tried to not let her own terror make her hold the baby too tightly. She lightly covered the baby's face with the edge of a blanket to protect her from the smoke. She was not losing another baby. She would claw death in the face before she would let that happen.

The hallway was filling with smoke as she exited the guest room. She kept her head low. She could hear Quigley now, barking in a panic from somewhere downstairs, and she felt the relief. She loved that puppy.

"Hold on, Mary Elizabeth, it's time to see what our exit looks like," Jen told the child, trying to keep low to keep the screaming infant from breathing in smoke. Jen could feel it already burning her eyes and making her stressed lungs choke. She turned the corner and felt the intense heat hit her. The blue spruce was totally engulfed. The edges of the stairway carpet were on fire, and she couldn't see to the bottom of the stairs, the smoke was so thick.

Jen swore and ducked back away from the corner and the heat, choking on the smoke.

There was no other way off this floor but a window. It was the smoke that would kill them. Mary Elizabeth wouldn't be able to survive even a couple of breaths of this acidic smoke. She couldn't drop her from a second floor window. Knowing her options were limited, Jennifer rushed toward the nearest bedroom. There was not a single person on the street. Swearing, she grabbed the blanket off the foot of the bed and ran to the bathroom. The shower drenched it in seconds and Jennifer didn't waste time shutting the water off. She heard glass shatter. The fire had burst thru the skylight.

The flames now had a vent, and while the air fed the flames, it actually gave Jennifer one great big break. The smoke rushed up, the skylight becoming a large chimney. For the first time she got a look at the entire stairwell. None of the stairs had collapsed, the outer wall was still free of fire, the carpet showing itself surprisingly resistant to the dropping embers. It was melting, Jennifer realized, not burning.

"Mary Elizabeth, I love you," Jen sobbed, kissing the still screaming infant, "please hold your breath." She had to make the front door.

She wanted to run and could only hurry, forced to take the steps at a pace where she would not trip. She held the baby wrapped in the soaked blanket and turned toward the outer wall. The searing heat on her right came right through the wet blanket and drove her almost to her knees as she tried to slide past the burning tree. She was at the landing, and she could see the front door, near, and yet so many steps away. Her lungs stopped drawing air. The smoke combined with the lingering effects of pneumonia was too much to handle. Quigley was having a fit down below, desperate to reach her.

Mary Elizabeth was going to die in her care. Oh, God, no. Not again. Tears flooded her eyes, and she was choking.

She cleared the final step, whimpering at the pain and the desperate need to breathe, Mary Elizabeth tucked and protected in her arms.

God, please help me.

She didn't make it to the front door.

"Look, Uncle Scott. Smoke!" Amy tugged his hair to get his attention. She was perched on his shoulders, looking all around. She had actually tugged his head in the direction of the smoke, and Scott couldn't help but see it.

The girl came tumbling off his shoulders. "Dad, that's Grandma's place!"

There were fifteen adults in the caroling party, all

neighbors. They were a block to the west of the house. They were seeing the vent of smoke billowing through the skylight.

"Mary Elizabeth!" Heather screamed.

Frank, Scott and Peter made the block at a dead run, cutting through flower beds and bushes. Flames were coming through the skylight now. There was no sign of Jennifer and the baby. The fire was in the worst part of the house, blocking the stairs, the hallway, all the exits. Scott got to the front door first, scalded his hand on the hot metal only to realize someone must have turned the latch, locking the door when it closed. Frank headed toward the back of the house.

Peter broke out the living room window.

If Jen was upstairs with the baby... Scott forced himself not to think about it. They would never get to them in time. The bedroom window above him blew out, showering them with glass.

Scott followed Peter through the window. The smoke billowing around the room choked him. "There!" Peter screamed to be heard over the deafening roar of the fire. She'd made it past the burning tree and to within touching distance of the front door. The wallpaper and hallway was totally engulfed in flames, the stairwell was gone. The burning tree was threatening to fall in her direction.

Peter scrambled to yank the burning floor rugs away from her face. "Get them out of there!"

Scott dropped to his knees and dove for her, feeling the heat try to burn him alive.

"Mary Elizabeth!"

"Here," Scott yelled to Frank. Jen was curled around the infant.

Scott grabbed the two of them and yanked them

clear of the leaning tree. Kneeling, he passed the crying infant to her father. Her cries were a wonderful sound.

The sodden blanket had protected Jen's hair from burning, but she wasn't moving, and she wasn't breathing. "Grab her!" Scott yelled, lifting her toward the window. Peter got through and took her weight, and Scott yanked himself through the window after them.

Peter had her on the driveway, the blanket off and the cinders on her clothes stamped out, but he wasn't getting any air into her lungs. Her blood, no oxygen in it, had turned her skin blue. There was enough medical training present to deal with a trauma victim, but no one could bring the dead back to life.

Scott sat on the cold concrete next to her, held her burned hand and watched his sister do CPR, and Peter trying to get her to breathe, and he started to silently cry.

Chapter Fifteen

"Hi, precious." She would know those blue eyes anywhere. Jennifer held out her arms and Jerry handed her the baby, gurgling and smiling and waving her arms, happy. Colleen hadn't grown, but her eyes were bright, her small body strong. She grinned and flirted with her Mom, bubbling kisses at her, delighted at the long hair she could tug. Jennifer grinned and offered her necklace instead.

There was fire in the dream now, fire between her and her husband, her child, then they were gone.

Mary Elizabeth. No!

God, I can't do this. I can't. Not another child.

"Jennifer!" It was a strong voice that compelled her attention. "You keep fighting, you hear me? Mary Elizabeth is fine. She's home. Do you hear me? Don't you dare give up!"

She was not fighting to live. That was the hardest part for Scott to grasp. She'd been on the respirator five days now, slowly growing worse. But he thought he understood. She had collapsed in a burning house holding a baby, her last conscious thoughts the realization Mary Elizabeth was going to die because she had not made it to the door. Jennifer wouldn't want to live, knowing that. He told her Mary Elizabeth was fine, over and over again, and she heard him, her hand flinched when he spoke to her, but she only got worse. *Please Jen, don't do this. Don't leave.* It was like she didn't believe him. It began to make him mad.

"Jen, I had Rachel reserve the church this morning, and Mom is sending out the wedding invitations. You've got twenty-five days left before your wedding so I suggest you try fighting this respirator. This give up attitude is not appreciated."

If one set of tactics did not work, it was time to try a second. Scott watched her hand flinch, knew she could hear him. She had been hearing him for the last five days, but hadn't been willing to fight back to consciousness. Her burns had to hurt, her right hand and arm had blistered, but they were all first degree, they would heal with only minor scars. He had told her that, but nothing was getting her to fight.

Her hand twitched and this time slightly turned.

"You have to open your eyes, Jen. You can't sleep anymore. Open your eyes," he ordered.

She did. She looked annoyed and she closed them again, but she'd opened her eyes.

Scott laughed around his tears. "Oh, no you don't. Get back here. Open your eyes."

They opened again and she blinked at him. It was hard to see a smile around a respirator, but her eyes softened. He gently kissed her forehead. "Mary Elizabeth is fine. You did good, Jen. You did good."

Chapter Sixteen

Jennifer woke early on Saturday morning, her wedding day, the house quiet and still, though it would change in the next hour as Rachel and Beth arrived. Jennifer listened to the peaceful quiet, her last morning in this house, and smiled. She was going to miss this place. She considered burying her head under the pillows again and letting the next hour drift by, but knew she didn't really have that luxury. She flexed her stiff right hand, feeling the tightness in the skin around her fingers that still lingered even after the blisters had healed. The stiffness in her skin, the inhalator she used twice a day, were the only remaining marks of the fire. The doctors told her another month would remove even them. After ten days in the hospital she had been ready to get home. She rose, stretched, slipped on her robe and walked through the house to the kitchen to start coffee. The stress in her system was totally gone, and it made her feel like a new person. Fear had been her companion for three years, and it was gone now. She felt wonderful. Peaceful.

His parents' home had been a total loss, but they

seemed to be handling it without too much despair. Jennifer hadn't been back. She didn't want to see the burnt-out shell, and the wrecking crews had come in ten days later. Margaret in particular had taken the loss calmly. They were people who grasped material things lightly, and when they were taken away, those people were not crushed. The picture albums had actually been at Heather's that day, and some of their more precious keepsakes from the master bedroom had been recovered. That was all Margaret considered irreplaceable. They were staying with friends in the neighborhood, planning to rebuild in the spring. Scott had offered them his home, and Jennifer had urged them to accept, goodness knew it was spacious enough, but they had declined. Olivia and Jack had been friends for thirty years and their children were grown, Margaret and Larry were more comfortable staying with them, where they could walk to the site and oversee the construction.

Jennifer drank her coffee standing up, looking out over the front lawn, white now from snow that had come down overnight. They had chosen wedding colors to match the winter season. Beth's and Rachel's gowns were deep green, Scott's and Brad's tuxes were black with deep red accessories; poinsettias would dominate the decorations in the church. Heather, of course, planned to see that the flowers were spectacular. There would be guests, over a hundred had already confirmed, and Heather's friend Tracy was providing the music. Jennifer knew her dress would look spectacular against such a setting. She had done away with the long train and instead gone for simplicity, choosing a white silk classical gown.

Scott had made the honeymoon plans and given

her not a single hint of where they were going, only that they would be gone a week. Even the clothes he had suggested she pack gave her no clue. She walked through the house carrying a fresh cup of coffee. There were gifts to wrap. Jennifer smiled at the thought. She went to her office and picked up the packages. She had gifts for the wedding party, but those were already wrapped. The gifts still to be wrapped were for Scott.

It was a little thing, letting him choose what she wore at night, but it was an important gift. A few of the boxes she wrapped were to make that gift possible. The other gifts, they were simply things that would serve as memories for both of them—a copy of a book Ann had helped her get autographed, a sweater she had found for him, an engraved watch. The gifts were small, but they would make a memory, and that was the reason for them.

The gifts were wrapped and Jennifer was putting the final touches to what was packed in her suitcase when Rachel and Beth arrived. Her friends carried breakfast with them, and their excitement made Jennifer smile. Jennifer sat at the kitchen table with them, sharing a raspberry danish and listening as her two friends went through the details for the day. Jennifer put herself in their capable hands—her hair was brushed silky smooth, her makeup was done with an expert hand. When they arrived at the church her dress and veil had been laid out in the dressing room, a room filled with a profusion of flowers from Scott.

She dressed quietly, smiling at the excitement around her. Margaret was going to be a wonderful mother-in-law. She had brought the bouquet of flowers Jennifer would carry. The children were in and out of the room. Both Tiffany and Amy were going to carry flowers down the aisle, and all of the boys, Greg, Tom and Alexander were recruited to help Scott. Jennifer knew at the reception she would be meeting much of Scott's extended family, and she took a deep breath as she left the dressing room, escorted by Rachel and Beth. "They are seating the family," Peter told her as she joined him at the top of the stairs. He smiled at his wife. "Two minutes," he told them. "Are you nervous?" he asked, offering Jennifer his arm. He was going to give her away.

"I'll be fine once I'm down the aisle," she replied. "The church is full?"

Peter smiled. "Yes. Scott looks calm on the outside, but it's covering one very nervous guy. He was pacing earlier, when he thought he was alone."

The doors to the auditorium were opened, and the music began. It was time. The girls went first, followed by the bridesmaids, then Peter squeezed her hand and Jennifer was walking into the church on the arm of her brother. The flowers in the church were overflowing with color and fragrance, Heather had outdone herself. She could see Scott standing at the front of the church with Brad at his side. He looked so dignified: tall, strong and confident. As she caught his gaze he smiled, and she saw him start to relax. She smiled back.

When she reached the front of the aisle, Scott took her hand in his, and Jennifer relaxed, finally, where she felt safe and protected. His grip was firm and strong and confident.

She listened to the service, and when the time came to exchange vows, she placed both of her hands in

Scott's and faced him, enough love for a lifetime shining in her eyes.

"Jennifer St. James, do you take Scott Williams to be your lawfully wedded husband, to love, honor and cherish, for richer or poorer, in sickness and in health, till death do you part?"

"I do," she answered, smiling at the man who was to be her husband.

"And do you, Scott Williams, take Jennifer St. James to be your lawfully wedded wife, to love, honor and cherish, for richer or poorer, in sickness and in health, till death do you part?"

"I do," Scott replied with conviction, smiling at Jennifer.

She gently squeezed his hands.

Brad handed Scott Jennifer's wedding ring, and he smiled and kissed the back of her hand before sliding it on her finger. Jennifer accepted his from Rachel. Her hands trembled as she slipped it on his finger, annoying her, but making him smile and softly whisper, "I love you," as they turned to face the front of the church again. She looked up at him and grinned. "Did Peter tell you I almost fainted at my first wedding?" she whispered.

"Now you tell me," Scott replied in a whisper, amused. "No wonder he said Brad had smelling salts in his pocket. I thought they were for me." He still held her hand, determined not to release it again, now that the service was almost over. They lit the large candle on the table, shared communion, then Rachel was handing Jennifer back her bouquet, and the minister was turning to the congregation. "Ladies and gentleman, may I present Mr. and Mrs. Williams," the minister said with a smile. "Scott, you may kiss your bride."

Scott took his time, amusing Jennifer, who stood patiently as he smoothed back her short veil, linked his left hand with hers, gently tipped her chin up with his right hand and lowered his head to share their first kiss as husband and wife. He was smiling, a deeply satisfied smile, and it made her smile in return.

They walked down the aisle holding hands, Jennifer very content to leave the details now to Scott.

"Doing okay?" Scott leaned over to ask, taking advantage of a slight break in the guests coming through the reception line.

"Yes," Jennifer told her husband, loving the word *husband.* "My hand's taking a beating with all the handshakes, but I'll make it."

"Pain?"

He would get her out of the line if she so much as hinted at pain. Jennifer could tolerate it. "No, just annoyingly stiff."

"Does that mean your pool game might be a little off?" he asked with a grin.

"Don't count on it," she replied.

Jennifer enjoyed the reception, mingling with Scott's family, her husband never far from her side. He was a dashing figure in his tux, and she loved watching him. It seemed to be mutual, because he had her blushing more than she could remember doing in recent months. Everyone wanted to ask about the fire, and she found herself trying to keep the details to a minimum. Heather, who now considered Jen second only to an angel, gave her a happy Mary Elizabeth to flirt with for the pictures everyone requested.

Scott maneuvered her to the back of the reception hall. "Let's slip away and get changed. If it fits, wear the outfit I had Rachel put in the dressing room for you. I'll meet you in the lobby."

"We'll miss the rice."

"Not with Tiffany and Greg around, but I figure it's worth a shot," he replied with a chuckle, kissing her at the top of the stairs where they needed to part company. "Hurry."

Rachel helped Jennifer slip carefully out of her wedding dress, and they both laughed when they saw the gift from Scott. He had sent jeans, socks with wedding bells on them, new tennis shoes. It was the sweatshirt that brought the laughter. It was white with a beautiful red heart with Scott Loves Jennifer written on the front and Jennifer Loves Scott written on the back, all the kids' initials at the bottom as the designers.

Jennifer met Scott at the top of the stairs. He had changed into jeans and a company sweatshirt. He grinned and gave her a hug. "Thanks for wearing it."

"Are you kidding? I love it."

"Brad has brought the car around, it's been appropriately decorated, though I was able to talk the kids out of tin cans attached to the bumper. We've got friends standing two-deep in line to toss rice."

"You're loving this."

He grinned. "Of course. Now that all the ceremony is over, it's time to have fun."

She laughed and let him tug her to the door. "Ready to run?" he asked.

As they came through the doorway, the rice began to fly amidst laughter from their family and friends. They hurried to the car through the shower of rice.

Scott came around to open Jennifer's door, get her safely seated. She had to bat a few balloons from inside the car before she could get in. Scott circled the car, grinning at the Just Married wording on the windows. Brad handed him the car keys. "The car is filled up, sodas are in the cooler, and I made sure all your luggage is still there."

"Thanks, friend," Scott said with a grin.

Scott found his sunglasses and slipped them on, looked over at his new wife and grinned. "Ready to go?"

She laughed as she tried to get the rice out of her hair. "Please."

She watched where they were going until she saw Scott turn onto the interstate. She settled back in her seat and made herself comfortable. The stress was over, and she was now conserving her energy for the evening. It had been a very long day already. She closed her eyes with a sigh.

"You were beautiful today."

She turned her head on the seat and smiled. "You looked dashing in your tux."

"You think so?"

"Most definitely. Can you tell me where we are going?"

"I thought we could use a little uninterrupted time. We are borrowing the home of friends for the next week. It's a country place, secluded. There's a pool table in the den, so we can play a few friendly games. There are horses to ride and cross-country trails to ski if we get some snow. I also thought you might enjoy the peace and quiet to work on your book. Rachel transferred everything to my laptop, and your notes are in the briefcase."

She reached over and hugged him. "Thank you."

"You're welcome." He gestured to the map on the seat beside him. "It's a four-hour drive, so it's going to be late when we arrive. Why don't you try to get comfortable and catch a nap? There should be a couple of pillows in the back seat, complements of Trish."

Jennifer found them. "Thank you, Trish." She piled them up against the door and made herself comfortable.

Scott looked over, a short time later, to find Jennifer had fallen asleep. Her hands were slack in her lap, her breathing low and level, and her head was leaning against the locked side door, the seat belt holding her still. He smiled. His wife.

Thank you, Lord. I owe you one.

Her eyes had been so crystal clear since the day she had come awake. No fear, no tension, no stress. It was the Jennifer he had seen in pictures from years ago. She hadn't told him why the fear was gone, and he didn't intend to press. She'd tell him when she was ready.

It was a glorious sunset an hour later, wonderful in color. Scott considered waking up Jennifer to enjoy the view but decided against it. She was sleeping so peacefully. She woke about twenty minutes before they arrived, stretched her arms and settled back, relaxed.

It was a beautiful home. Scott led Jennifer to the front door and, with a smile, carried her over the threshold.

Scott found Jennifer in the kitchen when he came downstairs from carrying in the luggage. "They left a nice note," Jennifer said, gesturing to the counter. "They also left dinner. There's Italian beef and a wonderful cheese dip, all the fixings for salad. Interested?"

"Very. I don't remember lunch."

Jennifer smiled. "See if you can find the plates, and I'll get started on the salad."

They played four games of pool after dinner, effectively dispelling any notion of her stiff hand having affected her game. After soundly beating her husband for the fourth time, Jennifer couldn't prevent a giggle as he swept down on her after she sank the eight ball and picked her up off the floor. "You are lethal at this game. I think it's time we did something else."

She wrapped her arms around his neck. "What did you have in mind?"

He nibbled along her jaw before finding her mouth. "Let's go to bed." His husky request got a blush, an intimate smile and a nod. "I like that idea." She thought about the gifts and whether to mention them but decided against it when her hand found its way inside his shirt as he carried her toward the steps. The agenda for the night was not going to need help. She let her hand play across his chest as he reached the first landing and watched his eyes turn dark with passion. She smiled and slid her hand lower. "Jen, I need thirty seconds of good behavior here, or you're going to get dropped on your tush," he warned. She chuckled and kissed his jaw. She had missed being married.

"Which side of the bed do you prefer?" he asked as he carried her into the guest bedroom.

"Yours," she replied with a smile.

He claimed a kiss as he very gently lowered her to the bed. "I love you," he whispered.

She wrapped her arms around his neck. "I love you more," she said with a smile.

He was laughing as she tugged him down.

It was sometime before dawn when Jennifer awoke,

tucked beside Scott, held safe and secure by his arms, her head resting against his shoulder. She moved to restore circulation in her left hand and felt his arms tighten.

"Hey, you're awake," he whispered drowsily, awakened by her movements.

She kissed his jaw. "Told you I liked your side of the bed," she murmured.

Even half-asleep, he smiled at her comment. "You can have it every night. I like sleeping with you," he replied, enjoying immensely waking up with a wife instead of alone. She chuckled at where his hands moved and leaned over to kiss him. "It's mutual."

Epilogue

"Do you think something might have happened? He's late."

"Twenty minutes," Scott replied, folding his arms around Jennifer's shoulders as she stood watching out the front window.

"His first night on his own with the car. Are you sure he was ready for this?"

Scott smiled. "He'll be fine. And there will be a good reason he's late. He's been a model of good behavior since we put the possibility of a car before him. He's not going to lose the privilege he's worked months to achieve by doing something stupid the first time he gets the keys. Let's wait and see what he says."

"Well, I worry about him."

"Of course you do, you're his mom," Scott replied, leaning over to kiss her.

She leaned back, letting him take her weight. "How are our other two? Asleep?"

"Hopefully," Scott replied, having been the one to get soaked giving the twins their bath. Not that he minded. The three-year-olds both looked like their mom and they loved to flirt. "Kay wanted Quigley to sleep in their room and April practically pleaded with me to say yes, so I let the shaggy beast have the rug."

Jennifer grinned. "What did April do, flutter her eyelashes at you?"

Scott smiled. "She likes to think it makes a difference, and who am I to dissuade her? April is easier to resist than Kay. Kay has that Daddy smile." He slid his hands around to link with hers. "Come on, it's not the in thing for parents to stand at the window and watch for their kids. You have to do it with some class. Like sit on the couch." Jennifer reluctantly let herself be pulled away from the window. Their adopted son, Paul, had just got his license, and it was tough to let go, accept the fact he was growing up, would turn seventeen in a few weeks. After five years, the first two of which had been marked by incredible battles of will, their son was now pushing straight A's in school, lettering in track and able to wipe the table with both of them at pool. She loved him with a passion. Add Kay and April who formed Paul's personal adoring fan club, and Scott who thought his son should be a fighter jock or president, and Paul had the deck firmly stacked in his favor.

"It's a chaperoned date, you don't have to worry about him. Kevin won't let him get into any trouble," Scott reminded her.

Jennifer smiled as she leaned her head back against Scott's arm. "I know. Kevin has turned into a great youth minister."

He stole a kiss. "Are we ready for Morgan?" Their lawyer was coming out in the morning to discuss a fourteen-year-old runaway that desperately needed a home.

"I think so. Are you sure we're ready to do this again?"

"I think it's the mission God dropped in our laps," Scott replied seriously. "I love being a dad. You're not having any reservations, are you?"

Jennifer shook her head. "No."

The lights of a car came through the living room window. "Thirty minutes. Not too bad," Scott commented, glancing at his watch.

Paul swooped in the front door, dropping his jacket across the banister. "You know, one of these days I'm going to catch you two more that just smooching on that couch," he remarked, dropping into the leather chair across from them with a grin. "I'm in love," he said dramatically.

"Really?" Jennifer asked, sitting up. He and Tiffany had been spending a lot of time together, and tonight wasn't their first date.

He rolled his eyes. "No...the car. Even Kevin says it's cool." Praise from his idol. "Tiff's not too bad, either," he told his mom, amused at her look. "I was late because Kevin had to pop the hood of the car and take a look. Oh, and he wants me to be the junior high social director this summer. I told him I would ask you."

Scott grinned. "Do you want to?"

"Me? Have lots of munchkins around looking up to me and hanging on every word I say? Now who would like that?" he replied, grinning.

"You," Scott replied. He glanced at Jennifer. "Sure, it's fine with us. You might want to ask Tiffany if she'd like to help out."

"I kind of planned on doing that," Paul replied with a grin.

Jennifer settled herself into the crook of Scott's arm with a smile. She loved being a mom.

* * * * *

Dear Reader,

Thank you for reading *The Marriage Wish*. It holds a special place in my heart as my first book published. As a preemie myself, I've often thought about what would have happened had I not lived. This story was born while looking through the baby photo albums my mother kept through my long hospital stay.

I would love to hear from you. You can find me online at www.deehenderson.com, email me at dee@deehenderson.com or write me c/o Love Inspired Books, 233 Broadway, Ste. 1001, New York, NY 10279.

Sincerely,

Dee Henderson

GOD'S GIFT

Take delight in the Lord,
And He will give you the desires of your heart.
Commit your way to the Lord;
Trust in Him, and He will act.
—*Psalms* 37:4–5

Chapter One

"Go back to the States, rest, see the doctors, shake this bug and be back here at the end of August to take the Zaire project." His boss's words still rang in his ears. *Medical furlough.* The words dreaded by every missionary. Six years in the field in remote locations. He should feel lucky to have made it this long. He didn't.

James Graham moved down the aisle of the plane, following the other passengers, a heavy jacket bought in New York folded over one arm. It had been eighty-two degrees when he left the capital of Zaire yesterday afternoon. The pilot had announced Chicago was forty-five degrees and raining, a cold April evening.

The pain was bad tonight. It made his movements stiff and his face taut. He moved like an old man and he was only thirty-five. He wanted to be elated at being home, to have the chance to see his friends, his family. It had been six years since he had been back in the States. Pain was robbing him of the joy.

He would give a lot to know what bug had bit him

and done all this damage. He would give a lot to have God answer his question, *Why?*

He stepped through the door to the airport terminal, not sure what to expect. His former business partner Kevin Bennett had his flight information. James had asked him to keep it quiet, hoping to give himself some time to recover from the flight before he saw his family. His mom did not need to see him at his worst. For fifteen years, since his dad died, he had been doing his best to not give her reason to worry about him.

James could still feel the grief from the day his mom had called him at college to gently let him know his father had died of a heart attack. He'd been ready to abandon college and move back home, step into the family business, but she had been adamant that he not. She had compromised and let him return for a semester to help, then told him to get on with his life. She had sold the family bakery and begun a profitable business breeding Samoyeds, a passion she had shared with his dad for years.

When he'd felt called six years ago to leave the construction business he and Kevin had built, to use his skills on the mission field, his mom had been the first one to encourage him to go. She was a strong lady, a positive one, but she was going to take one look at him in pain and while she wouldn't say so, she was going to worry.

"James."

He turned at the sound of his name and felt a smile pierce his fatigue. Six years was a long time to miss seeing a best friend. "Kevin." He moved out of the stream of people toward the bay of windows that looked out over the runways.

They had been close friends for so long, the six years blinked away in a moment. His friend looked good. Relaxed. A little older. They had gone to high school together, played baseball as teammates, basketball as rivals, he on the blue squad, Kevin on the red. They had double-dated together and fought intensely over who would be number one and who would be number two in all the classes they shared in college.

"I won't ask how you're doing. You look like you did that time you fell off that roof we were replacing," Kevin remarked. "I'm glad you're back."

James smiled. "I had to come back just to meet your wife."

Kevin laughed. "I have no idea how I ended up married before you did. You'll like Mandy."

"I'm sure I will. She got you to settle down before you were fifty."

"Without you around as my business partner, there was too much work to do without help. I hired Mandy's brother—he's good by the way—and before I knew it, I was thinking more about Mandy than I was about work. I know a good thing when I find it."

"I'm glad, Kevin."

"It's your turn now."

James smiled. "Later, Kevin. We need a few dozen more clinics built before I want to think about coming back to settle down." He had come to the conclusion early, having watched his parents and other close friends, that marriage took time, energy and focus if you wanted it to grow and survive, and unless you were ready to make that kind of investment, it was simply better to wait. He had at least fifty more clinics to build. On the days he wondered if he had made the right choice, he had only to flip open his wallet and look at the pictures of the children the clinics had saved to know that for now, he had made the right decision. He was a patient man who planned to live a long life. There would be time for a good marriage, someday, not now—not while there was work that needed his attention. "You were able to keep my arrival quiet?"

"They think you were delayed by visa problems in Zaire. They aren't expecting you until late tomorrow."

"Thanks." James rolled his shoulders, hating the pain that coursed through his body and up his spine, making every bone ache. "An hour ride should give me time to let another round of painkillers take effect."

"Do the doctors know what made you ill?"

"No. It was probably an insect bite. They don't know what it is, but they're of the opinion that it will eventually run its course. I think Bob kicked me back to the States just to get me out of his office. He knows I hate a desk job."

He had told Bob to replace him. In the remote areas where the crews worked, it was critical that every man be able to pull his own weight—lives depended on it. They couldn't have a man who winced every time he swung a hammer managing a crew, no matter how intensely he wanted to keep the job.

James could tell that Kevin understood how deeply he had felt the loss; it was there in his eyes. He was grateful it wasn't pity.

"Fifteen weeks of your mom's good cooking, a baseball game or two and you will be back in Africa swinging a hammer, pouring cement, and wondering why you were crazy enough to go back."

* * *

The house had been painted, the color of the shutters changed from dark green to dark blue, the flower beds extended along the length of the house as his mom had planned. He had grown up in this house, built in a subdivision of similar homes, the asphalt driveway going back to the garage the place of many impromptu basketball games. His dad had liked to play and James had liked the chance to razz him about getting old. James felt a deep sense of peace settle inside. He had really missed this place.

Kevin pulled into the drive behind a blue Lexus. James glanced at the car, impressed. His transportation for the last six years had been four-wheel-drive trucks. He had always appreciated a nice car.

"I'll bring in the bags," Kevin offered.

"Thanks," James replied absently, stepping out of the car and looking closer at the house. In the evening twilight he could see the porch still needed the third step fixed; it slanted slightly downward on the left end, and it looked as if the gutters were reaching the age when they should be replaced. He made a mental note to look at the window casings and check the roof, see what kind of age the shingles were showing. The grass was going to need to be mowed in another few weeks; he would have to make sure the mower blade was sharpened. The thought of being useful again felt good.

"Looks like your sister is here, that's her van."

"The Lexus?"

Kevin shook his head. "Don't recognize it. You were the one who remembers cars."

James led the way up the walk. "Do you still have my old Ford?"

"Runs like a dream. You would never know it's got a hundred eighty thousand miles on it. It's yours if you want it for the summer."

"Thanks, I might take you up on that. You must have found a good mechanic."

Kevin laughed. "With you gone, I had to."

James quietly opened the front door.

His mom had redone the entryway with new wallpaper, a modern design with primary colors and bold stripes. The hardwood floors were slightly more aged but polished until they gleamed. The living room to the right had white plush carpet and new furniture, a gorgeous couch and wing-back chairs. The place was filled with light even though it was now dark outside, the room warmed by a crackling fire in the fireplace. A CD was playing country music.

The house smelled of fresh-baked bread.

There were puppies sleeping in front of the fire on a colorful braided rug. Two of them, white fluffy bears that were maybe three months old. They reminded James of the little polar bears he had seen in the Coca-Cola commercial on the flight home.

"James!"

His sister Patricia was coming down the stairs, had reached the landing when she saw him.

He met her at the base of the stairs with a wide smile, a motion to lower her voice, a deep, long hug. His ribs ached where she hugged him back, but he ignored the pain as best he could. He had missed her, his companion in mischief. "You've gotten even more beautiful," he said, holding her at arm's length to look at her. Her hair was longer and her face serene for being the mother of two children. Paul must be fulfilling his promise to keep her happy.

She laughed, her eyes wet. "What are you doing here today? We weren't expecting you till tomorrow."

"I like surprises," he replied, grinning. "Where's Mom?"

His sister returned the grin. "In the kitchen. She's been so excited at the idea of seeing you."

"James, I'll leave you to the family. Call me tomorrow?" Kevin asked, touching his arm.

James smiled and reached out a hand. "I will. Thanks, Kevin." He meant it more than he knew how to put into words.

James caught his sister's hand and pulled her with him down the hall to the kitchen at the back of the house. He had snuck down these halls as a kid to raid the refrigerator during the night, and had spent a good portion of his teenage years sitting at the kitchen table dunking cookies in his coffee, telling Mom about the day's events. Unlike most of his friends, he had loved to bring girlfriends home to meet his mom.

He leaned against the doorpost and watched his mom as she cleaned carrots at the chopping board. He felt tears sting his eyes. "Is there enough for one more?"

Mary spun around in surprise at his words and he saw the joy he felt mirrored in her face. The knife clattered down on the cutting board.

He steadied them both as her hug threatened to overbalance them, then leaned back to get a good look at her. "Hi, Mom."

"You rat. You should have told me your flight was today."

She had aged gracefully. He grinned. "And ruin the surprise?"

He stepped farther into the kitchen, his arm around her shoulders. "What's for dinner?"

"Vegetable soup, beef Wellington, fresh asparagus."

"And maybe apple pie," added a voice touched with soft laughter from his left.

James turned. The lady was sitting on the far side of the kitchen table, a bag of apples beside her. She was wearing jeans and a Northwestern sweatshirt, her hair pulled back by a gold clasp, her smile filled with humor. The black Labrador he had entrusted to his mom when he moved to the mission field was sitting beside her.

The lady was gorgeous. She gestured with her knife toward the peels she had been trying to take from the apples as an unbroken strand. "Your mom swears this is possible, but you're not supposed to arrive till tomorrow, so I have time to find out."

James grinned at the gentle rebuke. "It's all in the wrist," he remarked as he moved toward her.

"Rachel Ashcroft. Most people call me Rae. Your mom is giving me a baking lesson," she said lightly, holding out her hand.

James took her hand and returned her smile with one of his own. Rachel the Angel. His building crew had named her better than they knew. "Mom's a good teacher."

"And I'm a challenging student," she replied with a grin. "It's nice to finally meet you, James."

He liked the sound of her voice, the fact his mother liked her. Baking lessons were more than an act of kindness, they were a hallmark of the days of the bakery and James knew his mom didn't just offer lessons to anyone.

He tugged a chair out at the table and turned it so

he could stretch his legs out and greet his dog. The Labrador was straining to push his way into his lap, his tail beating against the table leg. "Easy, Jed, yes, it's me," James told the animal, stroking his gleaming coat, glad to see at fifteen years that Jedikiah appeared to still be in good health.

Rae leaned over to look past him. "Patricia, he's not nearly as tall as you claimed," she said in a mock whisper.

Patricia laughed as she pulled out the chair between them. "Now that he's here, he's not nearly as perfect as we remember."

"Rae, I think the problem is he's been gone long enough I've forgotten all the mischief he use to get into," his mom said with a twinkle in her eye as she brought over a glass of ice tea for him. She lightly squeezed his shoulder. "It's good to have you home, James."

"It's mutual, Mom," he said softly, smiling at her, relaxing back in the chair. His journey was over for now.

It felt good to be home.

"Rae, you mean to tell me you actually volunteered for the junior high lock-in?" James teased.

They were stretched out in the living room enjoying the fire and relaxing after a wonderful dinner. His mom was beside him on the couch and his sister was sitting in the wing-back chair to his left. His dog was curled up at his feet. Rae was wrestling with the two puppies over ownership of a stretched-out sock.

"Staying up all night was no big deal. Patricia just forgot to tell me I would also be fixing breakfast for twenty junior high kids. Your niece, Emily, saved me. She's great at making pancakes."

"Let me guess…you taught her, Mom?"

"She's a natural," his mom replied, smiling.

A pager going off broke into the conversation. Rae glanced at the device clipped on her jeans. "Excuse me." She reached across the puppies to retrieve her purse and a cellular phone.

"Hi, Scott."

She listened for a few moments, the animation in her face changing to a more distant, focused expression. "How many yen? Okay. Yeah, I'm on my way in. See you in about twenty minutes."

She closed the phone, got to her feet. "Sorry, I've got to go. Thanks for the baking lesson and dinner, Mary."

"Anytime, Rae. I enjoyed having you here."

"Call me about this weekend, Rae, maybe we can do lunch after church," Patricia asked.

Rae nodded. "Let me see what is on my schedule."

James saw the uncertainty in her eyes as she pulled on her jacket, glanced at him. "I'm sure we'll be seeing each other again," he commented with a smile. If he had anything to say about it, they would be….

She gave a slight smile. "Probably. Good night, James."

"Good night, Rachel."

The drizzling rain made the road black and the streetlights shimmer as she drove to the office. Rae's hands were tense around the wheel for the night reminded her too much of the one on which her partner Leo had died.

She had been in New York when their mutual friend

Dave called, pulled her out of a pleasant dream and abruptly flung her into the harsh reality of Leo's death. Dave had chartered a plane to get her back without delay, and her girlfriend Lace had been waiting at O'Hare to meet her.

There hadn't even been time to grieve during the following ten days. Days after Leo's death, the markets began a ten percent fall. Rae, trying to learn to trade with Leo's skills overnight, felt crushed under the stress. Yet, it had been good, that crushing weight of work; it had insured she had a reason to get up each morning, a reason to block out the pain and focus on something else.

Her friends were good and loyal and there for her. She had survived. Part of her anyway. Part of her had died along with Leo that cold, wet, October night.

The mourning had started a few weeks later, the blackness blinking out her laughter for over a year.

She had promised Dave and Lace she would start getting out more. She knew they were worried about her; it had been eighteen months since Leo's death, but it still felt like yesterday. She wondered at times if the pain was ever going to leave.

In some respects, she knew the pain was a blessing. She had been to the bottom, the pain could not get worse. No matter what the future held for her, there was a certain comfort in knowing she had touched the bottom and she had survived. Life could offer her nothing worse than what she had already tasted.

She was picking up her life again, resuming activities she had enjoyed before Leo's death. She had begun to bowl in a league again, was back as a sponsor with the youth programs at her church, had decided to try once again to learn how to cook. She pursued the activities though the enjoyment was still hollow.

Tonight had been nice, relaxing, if a little intimidating to meet the man everyone spoke of so highly.

James Graham had been in pain tonight. He had downplayed his answers to his mother's questions, but Rae had observed and drawn her own conclusions. He had moved with caution, as if expecting the pain.

She had seen Leo through too many broken bones and pulled muscles; she knew how unconscious movement was, how easily you moved first without thinking and then were caught by surprise. James had been living with pain so long, he had relearned how to move.

He was worried. She had seen it in his face when he thought no one was watching. It had made her wish she could do something, anything to help. She hated to see someone suffer.

He had the guest room on the east side of the house. The shadows of the oak tree outside his window danced across the ceiling as cars passed by on the street below. The bed was comfortable, more comfortable than any he had slept in for the past six years.

He couldn't sleep.

His body was too exhausted, his muscles too sore.

James watched the play of shadows across the ceiling, absently flexing his right wrist where the pain was unusually intense. He had learned many weeks ago that it did no good to try to fight the fatigue. Eventually, sleep would come. Still, he knew he would feel exhausted when he woke, no matter how many hours his body slept.

It had been a good evening. He couldn't remember

when he had enjoyed an evening or someone's company more.

Rachel the Angel. His crew in Africa had given her the name because of the packages she sent twice a month via Patricia. It had taken James almost four months to get an answer from Patricia on who was taping the Chicago Bulls basketball games for them. They had rigged up a battery powered TV/VCR to travel with them so they could enjoy the games.

Those tapes had been like water to his thirsty men. His crew had been mostly short-term help—college graduates and missionary interns there only for a specific building project. They had all been homesick for something familiar. Rachel had no idea how important those gifts had been to him and his men.

He owed her a sincere thank-you.

He had watched her over dinner and as she had played with the puppies later. He had watched her when her face was relaxed and when she smiled.

She wasn't all she appeared to be on the surface.

Rae had been friendly, polite, and slightly flustered at the idea of interrupting a family reunion by staying for dinner. But the lightness and the laughter and the smile she had shown this evening had seemed forced. When she laughed, it didn't reach her eyes.

James had seen grief tempered by time before. He knew he was seeing it again.

The picture on the nightstand was the last thing Rae saw before she turned off the bedside light. Leo, his arm thrown around her, grinning. They had just won the skiing competition at Indian Hills. Their combined times for the run had put them in first place. Rae had to smile at the memory. He had forgotten to tell her how to slow down.

Hanging by a slender ribbon looped over the corner of the frame was the engagement ring Leo had bought her.

It was after 2:00 a.m. The Japanese stock market had gone into a decline and the rest of the overseas markets had followed it down. She had spent hours at her office deciding strategy for the opening of the New York markets. She could feel the tension and the stress through her body as she tried to cope with what she knew the coming day was going to be like.

She had never missed Leo more.

Leo had loved the trading, thrived on it; she just felt the fear. There was an overwhelming number of decisions to make rapidly, simultaneously, and it wasn't a game you could prepare for ahead of time, you just had to react to the markets and sense when to move in and out and when to hold and sweat it out. She would be back at her desk in three hours; she already wanted to throw up. She had never felt so angry at someone for dying as she did at Leo now.

Rae blinked back the tears and rolled onto her side to look at the moon visible over the trees.

God, why did Leo have to die? Why did he have to be driving too fast? If he hadn't chosen that road, at that time, he would be here tonight, as my husband, sound asleep beside me. He would be looking forward to facing the markets tomorrow, instead of me dreading it.

God, I miss him so much. Is this ever going to end?

Please, I can't afford to play "I wish" tonight. I need some sleep. I need the ability to act decisively

*and with speed tomorrow. There are thirty clients de-
pending on my actions, and six employees who are
going to be taking their cues from me. I'm going to
need Your help tomorrow. Remember me, Lord. I'm
depending on You.*

Chapter Two

"Lace, I've got too much work to do. I can't afford the time to go with you guys on vacation."

It was Saturday and Lace had come over early to drag Rae out of the house for a walk down to the park and back. Rae had groused about being woken up on the one morning she could sleep in, but now followed Lace down the path with the loyalty of a friend reluctantly conceding defeat. By the time she had convinced Lace she really should be allowed to sleep in, she had already been fully awake.

As she brushed her hair before the mirror, pulling it back into a ponytail, she noticed dark circles under her eyes. She heard Lace in the kitchen.

Rae didn't know what Lace had hoped to find. There was nothing left in the house. She had taken the last of the saltines to work with her to try to settle her stomach, ordered in food there when she got hungry. It had been an eighty-hour work week and it was only Saturday. She needed sleep, not exercise.

She had survived. It was the only good thing she could say about the week. The managed funds had crept up 1.24 percent against an index that had dropped two percent. She had traded her way out of the correction quite admirably.

Lace had insisted they stop for breakfast before they walked to the park. She had also frowned at the sweats Rae wore, but hadn't pushed it. Lace was saving her energy for another round of negotiations about their vacation.

They had been going on vacation together ever since their college days—Leo, Rae, Lace and Dave, plus whoever else they could tempt to come along. Rae loved the week in the country, fishing, hiking, relaxing. She just didn't see how it was possible to go this year; it had not been possible last year, and fundamentally, nothing had changed.

"Jack wouldn't mind coming out of retirement for a week to keep tabs on the accounts."

"Lace, it's not that simple."

The path widened and Lace dropped back beside her.

"Make it that simple. Rae, if you don't slow down, you're going to burn out. Do you honestly think Leo would have wanted this?"

Rae stopped walking, blinking away the unexpected tears.

"I'm sorry. I didn't mean to touch a raw memory," Lace said, her arm slipping around Rae's shoulders.

Rae nodded, knowing it was true. There was deep sympathy in her friend's eyes; Lace would hand over part of her own heart if she thought it would cure the pain. "I'm doing exactly what I have to, Lace. Keeping the business together while I look for a new partner to replace him. And you are right. Leo thrived on the day-to-day trading. For me, it's nerve-racking. But I'm not working any harder than he did."

"He took breaks, Rae. You don't. If you don't stop soon, you're going to crash. Please, you need to come with us on vacation this year."

"The bridge games are just not the same without you," Lace added when Rae hesitated, dragging a smile from her. "Tell me you will at least think about it?"

Rae hugged her friend back and started walking down the trail again. "If I say no, is Dave going to be showing up at my door?"

"Now, would I do that?"

They had been best friends since Rae was nine years old, the year Rae's parents had died and she had come to live with her grandmother. Lace had lived down the street. They had a lot of history between them. Rae didn't buy the look of innocence. "Yes, you would."

They walked together down to the park benches where mothers could watch their children play on the swings and slides and rocking horses. Rae sat down, annoyed to admit to herself she was tired; Lace joined her on the bench. Her friend was fit and active and had the stamina to go for hours. Rae just felt old. She kicked a bottle cap on the rocks in front of the bench and watched it flip over, tilting her head to read the words inside.

"Dave says he's going to make senior partner next month."

Rae looked up in surprise. "How? The senior ranks are age sixty plus, he's thirty-six."

"He snagged some major client, and the firm is

worried about the message it conveys to have a simple 'partner' working such a major account."

Rae laughed and the sound was rusty but felt good. "He got the Hamilton estate."

"Hamilton Electronics?"

"That's the one."

Even Lace looked impressed, and she didn't impress easily.

"When is he getting back from Dallas?" Rae asked.

"Tonight. I told him I would meet his flight."

Dave McAllister stepped off the plane from Dallas, and with a thank-you and generous tip accepted the sheaf of faxes and the ticket a courier was waiting to hand him. Then turned his wrist to glance at his watch. He had thirty-eight minutes before his flight to Los Angeles, barely time to find his luggage, get it on the right plane and check his messages, certainly not time for dinner.

There were days he hated being this good a lawyer.

"You eat, I'll read."

"Lace." He felt the relief at seeing a friend's face. She fell in step beside him, took the briefcase and papers, and handed him a chili dog. He didn't even protest the onions and eating a chili dog in a suit. She was a lifesaver. You didn't protest a lifesaver. Not at ten o'clock on a Saturday night.

"Jan told me about your abrupt arrive and depart schedule."

There was amusement in her voice. Any time now she would be telling him to get a real life. He liked her too much to care. It was business. Sometimes it demanded a little sacrifice.

"Read me the important stuff," he asked her, fin-

ishing the chili dog and wishing she had bought
him two.

She was flipping pages as they walked. "Oh, here's
a good one." She skimmed the legal document with
the ease of someone who wrote a lot of them. "Your
client Mr. York is going to loose his shirt." She sum-
marized the brief for him as they took the tunnel from
terminal C to baggage claim.

"It's smoke. They are going to ask to settle out of
court."

Lace grinned. "No, they won't."

"If they do settle, you owe me for that parking ticket
you managed to pick up on my car."

He found his luggage and wished he had thought
to pack for a longer trip. He hadn't been planning this
trip to Los Angeles.

"Is Rae going to come?" It was the reason Lace had
met him, the reason they had been playing phone tag
across the country for the last several weeks.

"I got nowhere. You would think after twenty years,
I would know how to convince her to budge, but the
only thing I managed to do was make her cry."

Dave frowned. "Lace, you were suppose to be helping, not making matters worse." He saw the look on
Lace's face and lightened up, fast. He was going to
have Lace crying, and one lady in his life in tears was
enough. "She's having a down week, Lace, the markets turned, I bet it was nothing you said. She cried
on me one time because I wore a tie like the one she
had given Leo."

Lace blinked and put her lawyer face back on.
"Good save, not great, but good. You're her silent partner, you've got to do something."

"Give me a clue what to do, and I'll do it. Anything," Dave replied, frustrated at the situation, frustrated at not being able to help one of the two most important friends he had left. "But I'm just as much at a loss as you are."

Lace nodded. "She's got to come on this vacation. That I do know."

Dave sighed. "Okay, I'll see what I can do when I get back to town Tuesday." He checked the monitors to find the gate for his next flight. "What are your plans for the rest of the week?"

"Sports stadium zoning and salary cap contract language."

"Sounds like a whale of a good time."

She elbowed him in the ribs. "Beats playing divorce attorney. I thought you were going to get on the happy side of marriage for a change."

"I'm working on it, Lace," Dave replied, tweaking a lock of her hair. "Want to have dinner Thursday before Rae's game?" They were Rae's acting cheerleader section on nights she bowled with the league. It gave them an excuse to try to make her laugh again.

"Not Thai again, or Indian. I don't mind spicy, but I draw the line at curry."

"Need some help?"

The church nursery was busy with activity as one service finished and another prepared to begin. There were name tags to match with diaper bags and parents for children being picked up; new infants and diaper bags and instructions to write down for children being dropped off. Short-handed because two of the helpers were out with the flu, Rae was finally sitting down again. She looked up at the question and smiled.

James.

He looked good.

The unexpected thought made her blush, which really confused her and changed her smile to a momentary frown.

She looked down at the active infants she held. She had to grin. They were twins and she had her hands full. "Which one do you want?"

She watched him step into the nursery, careful to avoid letting any of the toddlers get past him and out the door. His movements were stiff and she wished their prayers on his behalf would be answered. She hated to see someone in pain. His week back in the States had faded his tan slightly. He sat down in the rocker beside her. "Give me—" he paused to read the name tags on their sleepers "—Kyle."

Rae carefully handed him the infant, watched him accept the six-month-old with the ease of someone comfortable around kids. The infant was fascinated with a man to look at.

"Patricia said I would find you here."

"I hide out here most Sundays," Rae replied, tempting Kyle's sister Kim with a set of infant car keys. She had been keeping up with infants and toddlers for the last hour and a half with her teenage helpers. She couldn't believe he'd shown up here of all places. She pushed her hair back as Kim reached for it again.

"Like kids?"

"Babies," Rae replied matter-of-factly.

"They grow up fast. Emily was barely walking when I saw her last. Now she's reading," James commented.

"Six years is a long time."

Rae snagged an infant that was in danger of falling backward and scooted him over to lean against her knee. James nudged a ball over to him with his foot.

"Thanks."

"Is it always this lively?"

Rae smiled. "No one is crying so this is calm. But I normally do have two more adults to help keep order. They're both out with the flu. Thanks for the offer to help."

"My pleasure. I wanted to thank you for the Chicago Bulls tapes."

She was surprised and pleased that he had sought her out for something so simple. "Kevin said you were a fan."

"Your packages would make my week and that of my entire crew."

She looked down at the infant she held, embarrassed. "I'm glad you liked them."

"I'm afraid I've been thinking about you for two years by your nickname," James added.

His remark made her look up. "Really?"

He smiled. "We named you Rachel the Angel."

Now she really blushed. "They were just game tapes."

"They meant a lot to us. I promised the guys I would convey their thanks." James set the rocker in motion.

Rae had no idea what to say. "Should I apologize for not liking hockey?"

Her question brought a burst of laughter.

Rae left work Monday night after nine, stopped at the grocery store for a deli pizza and a six-pack of soda, and on impulse picked up a carrot cake. She needed to grocery shop to actually stock her cabinets but didn't have the energy.

She had decided she really, desperately, wanted a break. She was going to read a good book tonight, set her alarm to let her sleep an extra half hour and try to rebuild her energy. It was bad when she started the week exhausted.

She put the pizza in the oven, forgot and then came back to set the timer, walked down to the den as she poured the soda over ice. She wrinkled her nose and chuckled softly as she tried to drink around the fizz. She was parched.

Work would not be so bad if it were simply not so long. She had given up trying to record her hours in February; tracking her time had been one of her New Year's resolutions. Knowing she was averaging 64.9 hours per week did not make coping with them any easier.

The library shelves were packed with books she considered worth keeping—thrillers and suspense and mysteries intermixed in the fiction, medical texts, financial texts and law references taking the rest of the space. She had a hard time choosing, there were so many books she would like to reread. She finally pulled down a hardcover by Mary Clark.

She settled into the recliner, kicking the footstand up. This was the way she liked to spend an evening.

She opened the book.

A small piece of red colored paper fluttered down between the arm and the cushion of the seat.

Rae shifted in the seat, balancing her drink and the book in one hand to reach the item.

A Valentine's Day card.

Leo's bold signature signed beneath his "I Love You."

The sob caught her off guard, emotion rushing to the surface before she could stop it.

No. No, she was done crying!

She wiped at the tears with the back of her sleeve, caught a couple deep breaths and forced them back. No. No more. She *was* done crying.

She got up.

It was hard, and her hand wavered, but she resolutely tucked the beautiful card in the box on the bookshelf where she kept the pictures she had yet to file in her scrapbook.

She wasn't going to let a card do this to her. It was beautiful, and there was no one to send her I Love You cards anymore, but she wasn't going to let the card affect her this way. No. She couldn't.

The desire to read was gone.

She left the book resting on the armrest of the recliner and returned to the kitchen. The pizza had barely begun to cook.

Was it possible to simply decide to stop grieving?

She leaned against the counter and watched the pizza cook.

Was it possible to simply decide not to grieve anymore?

Rae rubbed her burning eyes and reached to the medicine cabinet for the aspirin bottle. Her head hurt.

God, I've decided I'm not going to cry anymore. My head hurts, my eyes hurt, and crying over the fact I flipped open a book and had a Valentine's Day card he sent me fall out has got to stop. My life is full of reminders of him. He was in my life for ten years. He's there, in scrapbooks, in snapshots, in little knick-

*knacks around the house. He fixed my car, and helped
build my bookshelves, he even tried to teach me how
to make pizza. Work is filled with reminders of him, he
is there in every decision and in every stock position
we hold. God, I'm not going to grieve anymore. You've
got to take away the pain. But I'm through crying. He's
gone.*

She felt like she had been sideswiped by the same
semi that had killed Leo.

When the pizza came out, she ate one piece and put
the rest into the refrigerator, not hungry, not caring
that she really needed to eat more than she had been
in the last few months.

She took a hot shower and let the water fill the
room with steam, cried her very last tears until she
felt hollow inside, and quietly said goodbye.

She was going on with life. She only hoped it held
something worth going on for.

"What do you think?" Kevin asked, leaning against
the side of the construction trailer.

James looked out over the eighty acres of land
Kevin was turning into a new subdivision of afford-
able homes and felt slightly stunned. "Kevin, you have
done wonders with the business in six years."

His friend laughed. "Believe me, it has more to
do with you than you realize. The early days of the
business established such a high-quality standard that
almost overnight the business opportunities began to
come to us faster than we could meet them.

"It was that house we built for Ben Paulson that
turned the corner. He considered the construction so
top-notch, that when he began to put together this
community, he approached us with the business."

"How's the business mix—new construction versus additions, reconstruction?"

"It's tipped sixty-forty toward new construction now. You want to take a look?" Kevin asked, motioning to the current homes being built.

"Please."

They walked across the site to one of the framed-in homes. "We have five basic models going up in this subdivision. Most are selling before we even pour the foundation. This is the most popular model. Three bedrooms, two baths, with an open great room."

"You've got a good architect."

Kevin stepped into the studded kitchen. "Not as good as you," he replied with a grin, "but Paul has an eye for both space and cost. He's been a good addition to the team."

Kevin stepped through what would someday be a patio door. "Of course partner, when you get tired of Africa, we've got a lot of work to do here."

James laughed. "I think you've got things well under control." He looked around the staked-out lots and thought about what this place would look like in five years, full of homes and families and kids, a place for dreams to be born. It felt good knowing the business here had thrived while the work in Africa had thrived, as well. There were times when he could see God's hand at work and this was one of them. Instead of building only here, they were building both here and overseas.

The doorbell rang.

Rae was sprawled on the couch with the book that had come in the mail that day. It was Tuesday and it had been a long day. She had decided on the drive home that it was time to pick up the final part of life she had left idle since Leo's death, the book she had been working on. When she had found the package with the medical text waiting for her on her doorstep, it had solidified her decision.

She glanced at her watch. She wasn't expecting anyone.

With some reluctance, she put down the book and went to get the door.

"Dave." She was both surprised and pleased to see him.

"Dinner?" He was carrying a pizza box from the place down the street and his smile made her grin in reply.

"You angel. Sure. It's what? Only ten o'clock?" she teased.

"I just got off work, and it's time for congratulations."

"Oh? You won your case?"

He rolled his eyes. "You, my little friend. When were you going to call me?"

Her...? Oh, the stock that went public... Her smile widened. It had been such a long day she had actually forgotten. "It was only a little killing," she demurred.

"Sixty-four percent in one day. And you had an even hundred thousand on the line. I would have brought ice cream as well, but they were out of pralines and cream. You look good," he said, seriously.

She wasn't in the mood for serious tonight. "Thanks a lot, friend. Go get silverware, the game's on."

He moved around her town house with the ease of an old friend, finding plates and napkins, the pizza cutter he had put in her stocking last Christmas.

The living room coffee table had served as a table

for many such late-night dinners. Dave discarded his suit jacket and tie, rolled up his sleeves, kicked off his shoes. He settled on the floor, using the couch as a backrest. "Who's winning?" The Chicago Bulls game was muted on the TV.

Rae handed him one of the sodas she had snagged from the bottom shelf of the refrigerator, helped herself to a slice of the thick-crust supreme pizza. "The Bulls are up by eight in the third quarter, the Sonics are having a bad night."

He nudged the book on the edge of the table around so he could see the title. *"Cell Microbiology?"*

"Research for my book," Rae commented easily, sinking back against the pillows she had pulled from off the couch. "This pizza is great. Thanks."

"No problem."

"What were you doing at the office till ten o'clock?"

"Some pro bono work. Yet another father not fulfilling his child support obligations."

"Will he come through?"

Dave shrugged. "I can force it here as long as he doesn't go underground with a cash job or change states."

"You'll let me know what the family is short?"

Dave nodded. "The fund got enough cash?"

"Eight thousand. It will last about another ten weeks."

"Let me know when it runs dry. I'll match you again."

"Thanks."

Dave nodded.

Rae smiled quietly at her friend as he snagged the remote and turned the sound back on. They frequently supported families they knew were in financial need.

He was as generous as she was, he just didn't like people to know it.

They watched the game and ate pizza, the silence between them that of old friends. "So, have you thought about coming with us?" Dave asked finally.

Rae laughed. "Lace sent you, didn't she?"

"Rae, you did not come last year. We understood. But you need a vacation. I'm not accepting any excuses this year. If I can get a week off, you can too."

"Dave, I've got new clients to deal with, a load of new stock issues to evaluate, and a market that's so high it makes me cringe. I can't afford to be gone a week."

"That is exactly why you have to come. There is never going to be a good time to take a break. When the markets are good, you're worried about them dropping, and when the markets correct, you're worried about losing other people's money. You're coming."

She tipped her soda can toward him. "When did you get so pushy?"

He chuckled. "Rae, I've always been pushy, you just like me too much to care."

Rae sighed. She had thought about the problem at length. She did want to go.... "I'll call Jack tomorrow and see if he's free." Jack had been Leo's and her first backer in the business, and as an experienced stockbroker, she trusted him to keep the accounts stable while she was away from the office.

"He is. I already called him."

Rae chuckled. "I should have never given you that power of attorney." It had made sense at Leo's death to have another partner officially on the books in case something happened to her. Dave had been the natural choice.

"I'm your biggest backer, not to mention one of your more wealthy clients. You have to listen to me," Dave replied with a grin.

She thumped him with a pillow. "I think it's time I get some new friends," she remarked and had to duck when a pillow came back at her.

"The doctor said fresh air and rest?"

"That's taking a little liberty with his prescription, but yes, that's essentially it. That, and some medication that is making the pharmacist rich." James was sitting at the dining room table at his sister's house, his chair turned and his legs stretched out before him, watching her finish clipping pictures for the Sunday school class she taught. He had managed to sleep until ten and for once had awoke with some energy and only moderate pain. Either the medicine or the downtime was helping. He had eaten lunch with Mom then come over to see Patricia and the kids.

"Then camping fits the bill. Come with us."

"Patricia, it hardly seems right to invite myself along on your vacation."

"Nonsense. The cabin can easily sleep ten, and we had planned the food assuming Paul was going to be able to come. Since he can't, you might as well take his place." His sister nodded toward the window. "The kids would relish having you around for an entire week."

James motioned his coffee cup toward the kids. "Last night you were worried about them wearing me out," he replied with a twinkle in his eyes.

Patricia grinned. "That was before I knew Paul was flying to Dallas. You're new, male and a relative. They will listen to you. I'm just Mom."

He laughed. "Ahh. Kid patrol. I get it."

"Seriously, you wouldn't have to do anything but sleep in, eat wonderful food and watch a bobber. It would do you good."

"What are the odds there are bugs that bite?" he asked, smiling. He had already made the decision to go, he just liked making his sister work for it.

"I will personally tell even the mosquitoes to leave you alone," she promised.

He set down his coffee cup and absently rubbed his aching wrist. "What do I need to pack?"

"Yes!" Her eyes danced with delight and he laughed.

"The days are comfortable but the nights can be a little chilly since we are beside the lake. I would bring whatever you want to read, the selection there is eclectic and quite old."

Now he had reason to laugh. "You just described a weekend on a building site, Patricia."

His sister grinned. "Then it will feel like home."

Chapter Three

"I can't believe you talked me into this."

Dave tossed her suitcase in the trunk.

"A vacation will do you good," he replied, reaching over to drop a college cap he had snagged from his bag onto her head. "Lighten up. You're officially on seven days of R and R. Besides, it's Memorial Day Weekend."

She wrinkled her nose at him and adjusted the cap. "Dave, my idea of a camping trip is slightly different than yours. I suppose you brought that jazz CD for the trip again, didn't you?"

"It's tradition."

"You don't like jazz. You just don't have the heart to tell Lace that."

He blushed slightly. "It was a birthday gift. One that I appreciate," he stressed.

Rae grinned. "Why don't you just ask her out and end her misery?"

"And ruin a great friendship?" He rolled his eyes. "Please, you've got to be kidding."

She pushed him aside to rearrange the bags he had

crammed in the trunk. "You're just gun-shy about making a commitment. It's past time you got married, you know."

"Don't start acting like my mother, Rae. I've got a life I enjoy. The marriage bit can wait."

"You wait too much longer, friend, and she's going to find someone else," Rae replied. She gestured to the walk. "Bring me that black bag next."

He picked it up and the smaller one beside it, giving her a dirty look. "A few books you said? You're taking your entire library."

"I told you my idea of a vacation was different than yours. I plan to sleep, read and do some writing."

"No fishing?"

She took the smaller bag from him. "I might drown a worm if you promise nothing will bite it."

She reached for the other bag, but he held it back.

"This feels like a computer...."

She put her hands on her hips and grinned at him. "Don't push it, David, you'll lose the argument."

He handed it over. "Am I going to get nagged into finding you a copy of the *Wall Street Journal* every morning?"

"I'll read it on-line," she replied, slipping the laptop into a cushioned spot between her jacket and his. "Okay, let's pick up Lace."

"Mind if I relegate you to the back seat for the trip?"

Rae grinned. "I thought you said you weren't interested?"

"You're just going to stick your nose into a book. Lace likes my jokes."

Rae laughed. "There are some she likes just about as much as you like jazz."

"She laughs."

"She's got a sweet heart. And if you break it, I'm going to make your life miserable," Rae replied.

"Rae?"

The question nudged her away from her research. "Hmm?"

"We're going to stop at the welcome station and get new state maps. You want us to bring you a box of their free popcorn?"

Rae shifted the pen she had clutched between her teeth. "Sure. While you're there, check and see if they have new maps of the lake. They were planning to update them to show the new trails."

"Okay."

It was almost four in the afternoon. Lace and Dave had been chatting for most of the drive. Rae had lost track of the conversation a couple of hours ago.

She stretched her back and considered putting her research notes and books back in order. The cabin was about thirty minutes away now. A glance at the spine of the book showed she had more than a hundred pages still to read in this latest medical textbook.

She should have become a doctor.

Yawning, she slipped her page marker into the book and closed it, reached over and slipped it back into her briefcase.

The actual manuscript she was working on was in her suitcase, the three hundred pages too hefty for her briefcase. Writing was her one persistent hobby. Crafts, sewing, watercolors had come and gone over the years; she always came back to her writing. She was getting better. Lace and Dave both liked this story. Leo had liked it so much he'd tried to convince her to cut back her hours at the office so she could finish it.

She wanted to finish the novel and write a dedication page to Leo. She thought it might be a way to help her say goodbye.

She smiled. She wouldn't mind seeing her name on the spine of a published book, either. For all this effort, there should be some payback.

She felt lighter in spirit than she had in the last year. They were right. The vacation was going to do her some good. She was looking forward to days not driven by the markets, a chance to read for pleasure, the freedom to sleep in, the right to be lazy.

The edge to the grief was beginning to temper. The sadness was still there, heavy, and so large it threatened to swamp her, but the pain was less. She had prepared for the vacation. She knew it was going to be hard, not having Leo with them, not having him there for the game, or messing up the kitchen with his creations, or dragging her hiking.

It was going to be okay.

She should have picked up working on the book months ago. It was good, and when she worked on it, she felt better than she had in a long time.

She was determined to smile, laugh, and do her best to have a good time.

"Emily is asleep."

James glanced in the rearview mirror to see his niece collapsed against the bright yellow Big Bird pillow she had brought with her. He smiled at his nephew Tom, sitting in the front passenger seat. "It was only a matter of time. Your mom was asleep hours ago."

"She was up late with Dad," Tom replied. "They've been talking about having another baby."

James choked. "Do you want a brother or sister?" he asked, trying to keep his voice neutral.

"Sister. That way Emily will stay out of my stuff and have another girl to play with."

It was a big deal when you were nine.

"I hear your dad has been coaching you for the football team."

"He's trying. I still can't throw a spiral. Jason can, and he makes a big deal out of it."

"You'll get it with more practice."

"Want to play catch with me?"

James flexed his aching ankle and was grateful the van had cruise control. "I'd be glad to, Tom."

"Thanks. Mom doesn't catch very well."

James grinned. "She never could. I spent years trying to teach her how to catch a baseball."

"She says she was pretty good."

"It's relative, Tom. She was pretty good for a girl who shut her eyes when the ball got close."

Tom grinned. "She does that with a football, too." He grimaced. "I hit her in the face one time by accident. She wasn't very happy."

James glanced back at Patricia, curled up awkwardly in the back seat with her head tucked against her jacket and a pillow. "She's your mom. I bet she's forgotten all about it."

"I hope so. My birthday is next month."

James laughed.

"Check your mom's directions again, Tom. I see exit fifty-eight coming up."

Papers rustled as Tom found the map and the handwritten directions. "That's the one. Then take Bluff

Road north for five miles. She'll have to direct from there. I know it's lots of trees and water."

"Got it."

Fifteen minutes later, the van pulled up in front of the vacation getaway.

It was a beautiful cabin, built at the top of a hill looking out over a calm lake that the map showed went for miles. They were half a mile from the nearest neighbor, and ten miles from town.

James stepped out of the van and stretched, fighting the pain in his spine that came from sitting too long, the muscles in his ribs aching with every breath he took. He smiled at the sound of birds. "Who did you say owned this place?" he asked Patricia.

"A friend of Dave's. There are a couple canoes and a fishing boat in the boathouse and a neighbor has horses he lets us ride."

Patricia pointed to the shoreline to the north. "Just around that bend is a large meadow and what is practically a sandy beach. It makes a great place to picnic. The fishing is good everywhere along this inlet. The kids were catching crappies off the end of the pier last year."

"It looks like we're the first to arrive. Do you have a key?"

"It's off the silver star on my key ring."

The porch was solid oak and extended around the cabin, the front door snug and smooth to open. James stepped inside and paused to enjoy the sight. The place had obviously been designed by an architect who knew his stuff. A large fireplace with open seating around it, a spacious kitchen, a large dining room, an encompassing view of the lake. The deck on the back of the house led down to a pavilion built beside the water.

He turned as Patricia came in with a bag of groceries. "This is going to be a good place to relax."

She smiled. "I'm glad you came."

She turned at the sound of another car. "That must be Dave and the others now."

"Lace, do you want the Wedding Ring quilt or the David's Star quilt?"

"The blue one," Lace replied from somewhere inside the massive walk-in closet.

Rae laughed. "They are both blue."

"Then you choose." Lace stepped back into the room, having hung up her clothes. "I do love the smell of cedar in a closet. You want me to unpack your suitcase?"

"Sure, though I doubt the jeans and T-shirts will care much where they are tossed."

"Didn't you bring anything nice?"

Rae grinned. "Why should I? I can borrow from you."

Lace groaned as she saw the contents of Rae's suitcase. "I'm going to get you fashion conscious if it takes my entire life to do it."

"Lace, face it. I've got a very limited sense of aesthetics. If it's comfortable, I wear it." Rae pulled out the small bear Leo had given her and tossed it on her bed near her pillow. "You ready to eat? The guys are probably raiding the food even as we speak."

"Sure. We can walk it off tomorrow. Dave wants to try that trail that wanders up to the eagle viewing platform."

"A five-mile hike, mostly uphill, is not my idea of a good time," Rae replied.

She laughed at Lace's expression. Her friend had discovered the romance novel tucked in the side pocket of the suitcase.

"Want to borrow it after I'm done?"

Lace grinned and tossed it on the nightstand. "With two good-looking, single guys on the premises? Why bother to read?"

Rae tugged Lace to the door. "Come on, friend, there is mischief to make. I still owe Dave for that ice down my back two years ago."

Lace laughed. "The long arm of revenge is about to strike one unprepared man. What are you planning?"

"I have no idea. But that has never deterred me before."

James couldn't decide who he liked more, Lace or Rae. They were sprawled out on the floor battling it out over a checker board, both having soundly beat Dave an hour earlier.

Lace was the more outgoing of the two, Rae more contained and likely to be the one who smiled quietly. They were obviously old, lifelong friends.

No, it wasn't really a contest. Lace was nice, but Rae... Rae had him almost regretting he was going back to Africa in a couple months.

Dave dropped a new log on the fire and both ladies jumped. He ruffled Rae's hair. "Sorry. Want a toasted marshmallow if I get the stuff?"

"Sure."

Patricia came back and James slid over, gestured for her to put her feet up on the couch. She had finally convinced two worn-out kids that ten o'clock was late enough for bed. "Thanks, my feet are killing me."

"Maybe you should have passed on the game of tag."

She laughed. "And lose out on the opportunity to hug my son? It's worth a few aches."

James pushed off her tennis shoes and gently massaged her feet. Both her ankles were swollen. He smiled. He was almost positive she was pregnant.

He would be back in Africa when the child was born. His face tightened at the thought.

"Ribs still bothering you?" Patricia asked quietly.

"Not bad," James replied. The pain was tolerable. He'd live. "What's that you're eating?" he asked, noting the sandwich she had brought back with her.

She looked guilty. "Roast beef and hot mustard."

She was pregnant.

James grinned. "Next time you go scavenging for something to eat, I'll teach you how to make Manallies. You'll love them."

Lace won the checker game and Rae rolled over onto her back with a groan. "Lace, you are a devious, underhanded, world champion of world champions. What is that now, the last fifteen games we have played?"

"Leo could beat me," Lace replied, sliding the pieces back into the box.

"Leo could beat anyone at anything," Rae replied, pushing herself up and redoing the ponytail that was holding back her long hair.

Dave offered a golden toasted marshmallow. "Careful, it's hot."

Rae slipped it off the stick. "Thanks." She stood

up. "Anyone need a drink? I'm going to go raid the ice chest."

"See if we've got another Sprite," Lace replied. Rae glanced at Dave who shook his head and at Patricia who indicated a soda at her feet, stopping at James with a raised eyebrow.

"Root beer."

She nodded. "Coming up."

She was gone a long time for someone simply getting sodas from the ice chest. She came back with three soda cans. She handed the Sprite to Lace. "Dave, you want to help me carry in more wood for the box? The radio said we might get some rain tonight."

"Sure. Be right there."

James caught a private byplay between Lace and Rae, saw a smile pass between them, and wondered if the guys should stick together. They *were* outnumbered two to one. Rae looked at him as she handed him the soda he had asked for; James decided Dave was on his own.

They disappeared out the front door and James saw Lace struggling to contain her laughter.

"Sorry, I've got to see this. It's two years overdue." Lace slipped over to the window to look out at the porch.

"What did he do?"

"Put ice down her back when she and Leo were dancing."

James glanced at his sister. "Who's Leo? He's been mentioned several times," he asked softly.

"Rae's business partner. He was killed in a car accident a year and a half ago," Patricia replied.

"They were close?"

"Yeah."

His heart tightened. No wonder he saw sadness behind Rae's smile.

There was a crash from the front of the house and the roar of a surprised man.

Lace was laughing. "Good job, Rae." She came back and dropped into one of the plush chairs. "We're going to need to get more ice," she remarked, reaching down to pick up her soda. "Dave is sitting in it."

Dave came in brushing water off the back of his jeans and shaking ice out of the back of his sweatshirt. "Rae, that was excessive," he mildly remarked, scowling at her as she slipped under his arm.

"That was two years of interest," she replied with a twinkle in her eyes. "You want a towel?"

He tweaked her ponytail. "Bring me two."

She came back with two bath towels, draped one around his shoulders. He took the other and rubbed under his sweatshirt.

"You know I owe you one now."

She laughed. "Got to catch me first."

She dropped into the chair opposite Lace. "Lace, he's got six days to retaliate. I think I should have waited a few days."

Dave came in carrying a soda and Rae ducked when he stopped behind her chair, half-afraid she was going to get a bath with it.

James chuckled.

It was going to be quite a week around these three friends.

Chapter Four

"Tranquil morning."

It was the crack of dawn. Rae, seated on the porch steps, turned, surprised. She knew neither Dave nor Lace were likely to be moving at this time of the morning.

James.

"Couldn't sleep?" she asked, concerned. He was in pain, she could see it in his movements and his face.

"Overdid it yesterday. I pay for mistakes like that," he replied, sinking down onto the porch steps beside her. "Thanks for making the coffee."

She smiled. "Not a problem. I don't wake up without it."

"These days, neither do I," he replied. "Why aren't you sleeping in?"

How was she suppose to answer that? The truth or something that made sense? Rae shrugged a shoulder, then changed her mind and decided to tell him the truth. "Ever have one of these experiences in life that just stops you in your tracks until you figure it out?"

She liked his smile and the frank way he turned

and met her gaze. "Like God just grabbed your jacket collar, tugged and said, 'No, think about this'?" he asked softly.

Rae nodded. She drew her knees up and folded her arms around them. "I woke up about 2:00 a.m. with Psalm 37 running through my mind. I don't know why. Feels important."

He leaned back on his hands, his expression thoughtful. "It's an interesting Psalm. Trusting God with your dreams, the security He provides, the promise of refuge in times of trouble. What were you thinking about when you went to bed—if you don't mind me asking?"

Rae smiled at the room he was trying to give her. She didn't know if it was the conversation topic or the fact it was her that had him slightly uncomfortable. "Nothing earth-shattering. The book I've been writing."

He looked surprised. "I didn't know you were a writer."

"Have been for years. I'm not published, just enjoy doing it." She tipped her coffee cup to see if there was any left.

"Sounds like fun."

She smiled. "It's a different kind of work."

A blue jay dropped down past the porch steps to land on the flagstones and check out what looked like a dropped dime. He took back to flight with a raucous cry.

"Most of the time when a scripture comes to mind like you described, it's because it is an answer to a question you were asking."

The only thing I've been asking lately is where do I go now that Leo is dead....

"Could be," she replied, knowing he was right. She nodded toward his coffee mug. "Want some more? I need a refill." She didn't want to think about Leo and the past. Not on this vacation.

He knew. It was there in his eyes. He knew she was avoiding something God wanted her to deal with. He handed her the mug. "Sure," he said.

He'd probably never been afraid to face anything in his life. Rae wished she had that kind of courage. She didn't. Not when it came to saying goodbye to what she might have had. "Black?"

"Please."

When she came back out with the coffee, he had moved, stretched his legs out fully, was slowly working his right knee. He was doing his best not to grimace with the movement.

Rae felt an intense sense of empathy for him. He was like Kevin, a man accustomed to days of physical work. The pain had to be hard to cope with. She sat back down beside him, leaving a foot of space between them, turning slightly so she could lean against a porch post. "Patricia said the bug was damaging your joints," she remarked, handing him the refilled mug.

"It's doing damage like lupus, fibromyalgia, or the aggressive forms of arthritis. The joints lose the ability to move freely."

"Is it getting better?"

He grimaced. "At a snail's pace. They don't know what bug I picked up, and they don't know how long the symptoms are going to last."

"Is it the pain that messes up your sleep?" she asked, curious.

"Yes and no. The sleep study showed there is a lot

of alpha wave activity during what should be delta sleep. My body isn't sleeping properly anymore. They don't know why."

"You weren't praying for patience by any chance, were you?"

He smiled. "I was praying for someone to show up in Africa who knew how to train medical staff. We were building clinics faster than we could staff them."

"What's the problem with getting staff?"

"Money. Doctors who have been in practice for a few years have grown to like the income and don't want to go, doctors straight out of medical school are so deep in school debts, they can't afford to go."

"I don't know why that surprises me. We've got the same problem staffing the Crisis Centers here."

The door behind them opened. "Would you two like a hot or cold breakfast? We've got everything from fruit and cereal to bacon and eggs," Patricia asked.

"I want you to give me another pancake making lesson," Rae requested, scooping up her mug. "The squirrels can eat the ones I burn."

James laughed. "Rae, she's not the best at it either."

"She's better than I am. That's all I care about," Rae replied with a grin as they both went inside.

"Dave, Rae is *cooking*." It was a whispered warning overheard from the hall. James had to smile at Lace's reaction. No one could be that bad a cook.

He changed his mind thirty minutes later. Rae had tried, but the pancakes were not like the ones his mom made.

Rae chuckled at the expressions on her friends' faces around the table, pulled back the plate of re-maining pancakes she had set on the table and reappeared with a plate of pancakes Patricia had fixed. "I'm getting better, you didn't try to stifle a gag."

"Rae, why don't you just give up?" Dave asked. "It's not your fault your grandmother refused to cook. Cooking is something you either learn as a child or it's a lost art."

"Nope. I'm going to learn how if it kills me," she replied, helping herself to two of the pancakes Patricia had fixed.

"It might kill one of *us* one of these days," Dave replied, then yelped when someone kicked him under the table.

"David Hank McAllister, be nice."

"She knows I'm teasing, Lace."

"Hank?" Rae burst out laughing.

Dave turned to Lace. "Now see what you've done? You promised you wouldn't tell."

Rae's laughter intensified. "Hank. Oh this is rich."

"I'll give you rich, *Amy.*"

Rae wrinkled her nose at him and did her best to stop her laughter. "I can't believe I've known you ten years without knowing your middle name."

"What's so funny?" Emily had joined them, wiping sleep from her eyes. James lifted her up into his lap, his own laughter hard to contain. "Just adult stuff," he told her, smiling.

The threesome quieted down. "Sorry, Dave," Lace whispered, then giggled.

He snagged his coffee mug to get a refill, his head shaking as he walked to the kitchen. "Women."

Rae leaned across Dave's empty chair toward Lace, a smile dancing across her face. "I think I know what we should get him for his birthday."

Lace had to stifle her laughter at the whispered

suggestion. "Think we could still find the CD?" Lace asked. "He hates country music almost as much as he does jazz. It's perfect."

"You knew?"

Lace grinned. "He hides a cringe every time I choose track four. He is so easy to get."

"Lace, you are good," Rae said, sitting back in her chair and looking at her friend with new respect.

Lace leaned back in her chair. "I'm better than good," she replied with a smile. "He's never going to know what hit him."

Laughter was good medicine, James thought. He hadn't felt this good in weeks. Watching Rae and Lace, he couldn't contain his smile.

Rae caught him watching her and grinned. "You'll get used to us, James."

"I'm enjoying it," he replied, watching her blush slightly.

Lace saw the blush and turned to look at him. He winked. James saw Lace hesitate a moment and glance back at Rae. Then a wide smile crossed her face. "Dave," Lace called, "we want to go canoeing this morning. But I'm riding with you. Rae sent me into the drink last time."

Dave appeared in the doorway, munching on a piece of bacon. "Only if I'm steering."

"You can steer," Lace agreed, getting up to clear her place.

"Lace, I wanted to lounge on the patio with a book," Rae remarked, stacking the plates.

"No, you don't. You want to go canoeing."

Rae looked at her friend, puzzled. "Okay." She glanced over at Patricia and James. "Either one of you want to go canoeing?"

"The kids and I have a date with a pair of horses," Patricia replied, smiling.

"Can I steer?" James asked quietly.

Rae looked at him, finally caught the byplay between him and Lace, flushed, then laughed. "Sure." She snagged her friend's sweater. "Come on, Lace. You need to put those plates in the sink."

Lace let herself get tugged out of the room. "I need to put these plates in the sink," she agreed, winking back at James.

Dave watched them go with a rueful smile. He tugged out his chair with his foot. "It is going to be a *long* week."

James laughed. He had a feeling both he and Dave were going to enjoy it.

"Do you want to beach the canoe and rest your wrists for a while?"

James smiled. "Relax, Rae. I'm fine. That's the fourth time you've asked."

"You're here to recover, not make matters worse."

She rested her paddle across the bow and leaned over to watch a school of sunfish slide by near the surface.

She had a nice back. He'd been admiring the view for the last hour.

His wrists were sore, but not intolerable. His shirt was almost dry. There had been a laughter-filled water fight between the two canoes about forty minutes back. He hadn't felt this relaxed in months. Nothing to do but drift with the current and spend time with a beautiful lady.

The canoe way ahead of them rocked wildly and

Rae ducked her head so as not to look. "Tell me she isn't trying to stand up."

James chuckled. "Okay, I won't."

Lace somehow managed to turn around without tipping the canoe over. "Want to catch up with them?" James asked.

Rae shook her head. "They are probably debating the ethics of civil litigation again. I'll pass."

"What does Lace do for a living, anyway?"

Rae resumed paddling, her movements sure and smooth. It added a slight sway to her back. "It's more a question of what she hasn't done. She's the daughter of a federal judge and a district attorney. She's got a law degree, but more because it's what the family does, then anything else. She's forgotten more law than most lawyers ever learn. She doesn't like to settle down. She's worked in international banking, edited textbooks, worked for Senator White. She's currently doing some consulting work for a sports management firm downtown."

"Was that where you three met? College?"

"I've known Lace since I was nine. We met Dave and Leo at Northwestern. We made an awesome foursome. Dave the fighter for justice, Leo the energy, Lace the constant new interests, and me the practical planner."

James smiled. "You're also the hub they revolve around."

"That's because I'm always there doing the same thing," Rae replied with a smile. "I'm a creature of habit."

"You grew up with your grandmother?"

"My parents died in a car wreck when I was nine. We were living in Texas at the time. The next day this wonderful lady in her fifties appeared and said, 'Don't worry. You've still got me.' I had heard about her all my life, got Christmas presents and birthday gifts, but not seen her since I was about five. The day we arrived at her house in Chicago, five inches of snow fell. I thought I had moved to another planet."

James smiled. She had loved her grandmother a lot, he could hear it in her voice. He caught a glimpse of golden brown and dipped his paddle deep, turned the canoe twenty degrees to the left. "Look behind that fallen tree." A deer had come down to the water's edge to drink.

"She's beautiful," Rae whispered.

The animal raised its head, paused, then went back to drinking.

They watched for several minutes. The animal picked its way over driftwood, then slipped back into the woods.

"Want to try out those sandwiches Patricia sent?" There was a clearing up ahead of them.

Rae picked up her paddle. "Sure."

"So, did you have a good time?"

Rae rolled onto her side in the spacious bed, half smiled at the question from the other side of the dark room. "I can't believe you set me up."

"He's a nice guy."

Rae smiled in the darkness. "Yes, he is. He's also leaving the country in less than three months," she pointed out, being practical.

"That's tomorrow's problem," Lace replied. "It was good to see you enjoying yourself."

"Lace, I always enjoy a vacation."

"Not since Leo died."

Rae bit her bottom lip. "I really miss him, Lace."

"I know you do," came the soft reply. "You okay?"

It had been a nice day, but it had been hard. The cabin was yet another place filled with memories of Leo. She had missed Leo's tap on the door, waking her up at 5:00 a.m. to go fishing, missed having him fix breakfast for them. She had enjoyed the afternoon with James. He didn't seem to mind the silence or the space she preferred. It was almost better, knowing he was going back to Africa—easier at least. The last thing she wanted to even consider was risking getting hurt again. "Yeah, I'm okay." She would be. When God helped her fix the hole in her heart. "Remember those canoe races Leo and Dave use to have?"

"Holding that rope across the water for a finish line was not one of our more well thought out actions," Lace replied.

Rae laughed softly. They had both been pulled into the water when the guys reached up and grabbed the rope. "They had to have been planning that one for weeks ahead of time."

"You got Dave good last night, by the way."

"Thanks. Watch my back for me, okay? I have no idea how he's going to retaliate."

"I'll do my best," Lace promised. "'Night, Rae."

"'Night, Lace."

Rae wished she had brought her jacket. It was late afternoon. The breeze coming up from the lake made it cool in the shade. She had hiked to the highest point near the cabin, a hill that let her look out over the water. They had been at the cabin for three days, and the slow, easy pace had taken away a sense of strain that she had not been aware she was carrying.

*God, You know what Psalm 37 says. Take delight
in the Lord, and He will give you the desires of your
heart. I feel like that promise got broken.*

The prayer was a soft one. Rae settled back against
the trunk of a tree and watched the water.

...the desires of your heart... That's what she felt
had been taken from her with Leo's death. She'd had
a relationship with him, a deep one, a relationship that
had been heading somewhere. Leo knew her, inside,
where she rarely let many people in.

*God, why did You rip away what was the desire of
my heart?*

She tilted her head back and watched puffy clouds
drift across the blue sky. For the first time in over a
year, she felt a sense of peace settle inside.

"What's wrong? You're frowning."

A cold soda appeared at her elbow. Rae looked up
from her laptop. James had begun to join her most afternoons on the patio, and while she would not admit
it to Lace, she had begun to look forward to his company.

"I think I need to rewrite chapter eighteen."

"Rae, the story is fine." He'd been up until
2:00 a.m. reading the manuscript. It was more than
fine, it was wonderful. She just needed the courage
to finish it.

"I think it's slow."

He pulled over a chair. "Give me the printout. Let
me see."

She shifted the book holding down the manuscript
pages and gave him the last four chapters. She gratefully drank the soda as she watched him read.

It was odd, how far their relationship had come in

five days. She'd never expected to be so comfortable around him. She'd relaxed, and he'd turned into a very good friend.

"Read it again without page 314, I bet that's what you're sensing is wrong."

She paged back and forth in the on-line text. "That's it. It's too technical."

He picked up his own drink. "I want an autographed copy when it's published."

"James, it may never get finished, let alone find a publisher."

He smiled. "You'll finish it. You've got, what, another five hundred pages to go?"

She laughed. "Trust me to choose a big story to tell."

"I *like* the fact you think big."

She blinked. Smiled. "The kids catching any fish?"

"Emily's got six and Dave's only caught two. Emily's decided it is time to start giving him pointers, he's letting the team down."

Rae laughed. "How are Lace and Tom doing?"

"Scheming. They disappeared about an hour ago for what Tom called a 'super-duper' spot."

"That sounds like Tom. Got the time? Patricia asked to be woke up at four."

He glanced at his watch. "She's got another half hour."

"She's pregnant, isn't she?"

James grinned. "I sure think so. She was eating pickles for breakfast this morning."

He leaned back in his chair to pick up the book on the lounge chair that Rae had been reading that morning. Richard Foster's book on prayer. He liked her reading selection. "Is this one good?"

"Very."

"Bookstores and hot fudge sundaes were the two things I missed most about the States."

"I don't imagine the vanilla ice cream in Africa is the same as a Dairy Queen here."

"Didn't even come close. Want to ride to town with me to find some good ice cream?"

His offer caught her off guard.

Interesting…she looked like a doe caught in a car's headlights. "I promised Tom a banana split for having thrown a perfect spiral," he said gently. He'd just walked into something that caused her pain and he had no idea what it was.

"I think I'll pass."

There was the clatter of feet and the sound of laughter from the front porch. James squeezed her shoulder gently before walking inside to meet the fishing champs.

Several hours later, James carefully set the sack he held down on the kitchen counter. He flexed his wrist, which had threatened to drop the package. The rest was helping, but he had such a long way to go before his body recovered. The only thing predictable was the pain. He would be so grateful to be able to do normal tasks like carry in the groceries without having to think about them first. Tom had disappeared down to the pavilion.

"Thank you, James," his sister said, walking in behind him. "I didn't mean to leave you with the groceries to carry in."

"It was three bags, Patricia," he said ruefully; the pain made it feel like thirty. "How's Emily's hand?"

"It's barely a scratch. A Band-Aid fixed it." She

started putting away the groceries. "Since we've got cornmeal, should I deep-fry the fish as well as make hush puppies?"

"Most of the fish are bluegills—they are going to dress as popcorn pieces, so I would plan to deep-fry them. Do we have some newspaper we can use?"

"Under the sink, there's a stash just for cleaning fish."

James found them. "Thanks."

He glanced around as he left the cabin, then walked down to join Dave and Lace and the kids where they were preparing to clean the fish they had caught that afternoon. Rae was nowhere in sight.

It bothered him that he'd upset her with his earlier invitation to get ice cream. He had unintentionally touched a raw memory, and he needed to know that she was okay.

She'd been disappearing occasionally, taking some long walks. Hopefully, that was where she had headed this time.

She was getting her endurance back; she had made it to the top of the trail without being so out of breath she felt ready to collapse. Rae settled on the big rock that made a comfortable perch from which she could see most of the sandy stretch of beach. She had forty minutes before dinner, and had decided to take advantage of the time. She thought best when she hiked.

James's invitation had touched a raw nerve. There was no way he could have known Leo had taken her to that Dairy Queen the last summer they'd spent here. It bothered her that a simple question could throw her so badly.

She knew one reason the pain was lingering.

They would have had a child by now.

She wanted children. Deep inside, being a mother was part of who she wanted to be. She and Leo had talked at some length about having children, how they would restructure the business to let her work from home. She had been looking forward to having children almost as much as she had been looking forward to being married. She liked being single, but for a season in her life, not forever. She had been looking forward to his proposal. Learning he had been carrying the ring with him the night he had died had nearly broken her heart. It had simply been another indication of how unfairly life had treated her. She had been so close to the life she wanted, longed to have. It wasn't fair that it had been wrenched away from her.

The dream of having children was growing more distant.

She had lost so much of her life when Leo died.

It was so hard to keep letting go of pieces of her life. She propped her chin on her hand, rubbed her eyes. She liked to think, to plan, to look at the future. At times like this, she wanted to curse that part of her nature.

She had her work left, her book. Dave and Lace. An indefinite time of still being single.

The passion to earn money for her clients had disappeared during the last year. Two years ago the business had been something she had been willing to pour her life into, she had valued its success. Since Leo's death, the work had lost its compelling fascination. She was still good at it. She was even learning how to do Leo's job with reasonable skill. But it worried her that her heart wasn't in it, that her drive was gone. She had thought the vacation would help her be prepared to go back to work strong and focused and full of energy. Instead, the vacation was only contrasting how strongly she really didn't want to go back.

She was going to have to make some changes. She knew that. There were no margins left in her life, no time left in her schedule. It had been good and necessary in the past year to be so overwhelmingly busy, but she knew she could not continue in that mode another year.

There had to be a partner she would be comfortable working with, someone who could take Leo's place. She had been looking for a year to find someone who was a good trader, who had a track record to match Leo's. She wasn't having much luck. It was time to find someone who could replace her function, be the primary analyst, so she could consider moving permanently to Leo's trading position. It made her slightly sick to think about it, but the reality was, she couldn't carry both jobs indefinitely.

She tugged the notebook out of her pocket, looked again at the list she had been writing. So many components of the job had fallen behind due to lack of time. They weren't visible yet, but in another six months they would be. She had to hire a trader soon to free up her time to do the analysis. Every time she looked at the list of work to be done, Rae knew the decision had to be made.

The decision would have been made in the past over a cup of coffee and a stolen few minutes in Leo's office. It would have been decided and acted upon in a day. She hated running the business alone. The risks had been shared in the past, the decisions balanced by two opinions and two points of view.

She needed to accept and go on, build a life she would enjoy living.

It was a difficult proposition.

She didn't want the life she had.

She wanted the life she had lost.

"What's wrong?" Lace dropped down beside James on the steps. He gestured toward the campfire they had built down by the pavilion.

"Rae. She's restless tonight."

She had also been avoiding him all evening. He watched her get up from where she had been sitting, studying the fire, and pace down to the lake again. He hadn't meant to stir up her pain, and it was obvious that he had. She had looked strained when she came back from her walk, tired, and the sadness had been back in her eyes. He hated seeing it.

"How close were they, Lace?"

"Rae and Leo?"

James nodded.

"That last year, you would swear they were able to read each other's thoughts."

Lace pushed her hands into the pockets of her jacket. "Leo lived life with intensity. That's what drew people to him. He had the energy and boldness and courage to switch directions on a dime, take big risks. Rae was the perfect fit for him. She has the focus and depth and thirst for details necessary to break apart the problems, quantify them and see a way to make his vision happen."

James, watching Lace, saw deep concern etched in her face. "She hasn't been the same since Leo died. The sparkle that used to be inside when she talked about work is gone. They fed off each other, and she's lost without him. I think she's found the business was Leo's dream, one she had borrowed, and now that Leo's gone, she's trying to learn to do what he did naturally—take risks—and she's scared to death. She's not designed to take risks, it's not in her personality. To compensate, she's working hours that will put her into an early grave. About the only time I see glimpses of the old Rae is when she's working on her book."

For the first time, James was starting to understand some of the complexity in the lady he had met. "She's using work to cope with the grief. That's not unusual, Lace."

"She's at the office at 5:00 a.m., doesn't leave until 7:00, sometimes 8:00 p.m. She makes Dave and I look like loafers. We haven't been able to shake her out of that routine."

"How much money is she managing?"

"About twenty-five million for thirty clients," Lace replied. "It could be seventy million if she said yes to even half the offers she gets."

Rae was driven by her own internal standards of excellence. Watching her with her book had shown James that. Add that kind of money to the equation, it was no wonder she was responding in the way she was. "She's good at what she does."

"Rae and Leo were the only money managers in the midwest to have beaten the S&P500 every year for the last seven years. Rae did it again on her own last year. She's on track to do it again this year. She's good. But her heart's not in it, James, not like it used to be."

"It would be a big risk to sell the business, walk away, Lace. You said yourself she's not going to easily take that kind of risk."

 Their serious conversation was broken up by a shout of laughter from the pier.

 "Dave just threw Rae into the Lake," Emily told them, racing past. "She really needs my towel."

 Lace got to her feet. "Excuse me, James. On behalf of my out-of-commission, best friend, Rae, I'm going to go help Dave join her."

 "He's crazy to take both of you on."

 "That's why we love him," Lace replied with a grin. "Keep what I said to yourself, okay? Rae's opinion about her work is different than mine."

 "I will. The background helps, Lace."

 She nodded, looked down at the group by the pier. "Mind if I borrow your flashlight?"

 He handed it to her. "Just don't hit him with it."

 She grinned. "I'm more refined than that. I think I'll suggest a late-night boat ride and let him swim back to shore."

 The cabin was quiet, except for the sounds of the night drifting in—the soft sounds of rustling leaves, the distant call of an owl.

 James had long since given up on trying to sleep. He lay in bed listening to the night, thinking, working out construction plans for the clinics he was going to build in Zaire.

 He had loved the past weeks in the States with his family, his friends, but his heart was in Africa with the work that needed to be done. It was comforting to be able to focus on that and lay his plans. He would be able to hit the ground running when he got back in late August. They should have the first of the four clinics built and equipped by early November, the next one by the end of the year.

He needed to see about getting the equipment for the clinic expedited while he was in the States. A face-to-face meeting would ensure the urgency was understood.

He moved to shift the quilt and felt a familiar hot pain coarse through this elbow. He frowned, annoyed.

He had stopped asking God to heal him. He understood scripture, he understood the power of persistent prayer. He also understood the reality that nothing was going to stop God's plans from moving forward, not lack of money, not lack of building materials, not lack of government signatures, not lack of physical health for him. God knew what he needed and by when. James had stopped worrying about it. He had seen too many miracles in the last six years as God brought all the right pieces together for him to even worry about this need.

It would be nice, however, when he didn't have to fight this pain every time he moved.

He was on a vacation. He hadn't had one in six years. He was going to enjoy it and let tomorrow take care of itself. As long as the vacation was temporary.

This was nice, but it wasn't his dream.

He wanted to be back in Africa.

The sound of running water made him tilt his head to the side on the pillow, listen more closely to the sounds from inside the cabin. Someone was up.

He listened for the light steps of Emily or Tom to come back down the hall but heard nothing. Someone else was up at 3:00 a.m.? He had been the one to lock the cabin, set the dampers on the fireplace, turn off the lights at midnight. Everyone else had already turned in.

Not concerned, but curious, and wide awake anyway, James dressed in his sweatshirt and jeans.

Rae was curled up on the couch in black sweats, a book in her lap, a drink beside her on the table.

"Care for some company?"

She looked up, surprised. "Come on in, I didn't realize you were still up."

"I could say the same thing about you."

"Catnap. It's really annoying to wake up at 3:00 a.m., wide awake. Normally I would find a financial report to read, but the cabin doesn't run to anything that dry. No use waking up Lace with my restless turning."

James settled into the chair opposite her. "What did you find?"

She glanced at the spine of the book. *"Biomechanics of the Human Hand."*

"I'd say that qualifies as light reading," James replied, tongue-in-cheek.

"Actually, it's quite good. Some of their math is wrong, however. I spent twenty minutes looking at their torque calculations because I didn't understand their answer, only to realize they made a mistake in their math. It makes sense now."

"Let me guess, you took engineering classes as electives."

She grinned. "Doesn't everyone?"

"No," he replied, chuckling.

It was a nice time to talk, the dead of the night, no hurry to give a fast answer, no reason to break the silence until a new question occurred. Rae asked about the work in Africa, and James relaxed, enjoying the chance to talk about it.

He asked her about work, and while she hesitated

to answer at first, she was open and frank in what she said. He had heard Dave and Lace talking, had his conversation with Lace to go on. He knew how hard the past year had been on her. He avoided asking about Leo and she never volunteered his name.

Even so, he learned a lot, both about business and about Rae.

"What are the critical few pieces of information that drive your decisions? The day-to-day trading trends? The company earnings reports? The industry segment? The overall economy?"

"Most of the planning I do is around the company's ability to increase market share. That's the critical factor for knowing which companies I want to recommend. The right price to buy is driven by an analysis of the books and the style of management—are they aggressive in growing the business or conservative? How well do they use the assets they have? A company with small reserves but a willingness to use them is invariably a better buy than a company with large reserves that passes up opportunities. When to sell is a crap shoot—I know the fundamentals, but it's hard to judge how far the market will take a stock that is rising beyond what its fundamentals can support. Invariably, I sell too soon."

He listened to her, observed her and he realized something. Rae on her own turf, in her domain of expertise, was decisive, clear and confident. She loved the analysis, being able to make the call with confidence, having the facts to make the right decision. Her job perfectly matched her talents and gifts. She was known as one of the best at what she did because she was one of the best—others could only imitate what came to her intuitively, naturally, by instinct.

* * *

"No, a red card does not mean it is a diamond," Rae informed Dave, picking up the cards, overriding his appeal that he had won the hand with a trump card. "A bluff only works if the other person buys it."

"Face it, Dave, I can read you like an open book. I knew you didn't have it," Lace told him, smirking.

"Lace, you can't be successful all night," Dave replied, tossing a piece of popcorn at her.

James had figured the bridge game would be a serious event. He should have known better.

The ladies were killing them.

Rae had managed to bluff and win two hands and Lace had just nailed the ladies' second hand.

Tom, acting as Lace's partner, finished scoring the hand. "Lace, you really are good."

"Thank you, Tom," Lace said, pleased.

Rae shuffled the cards with the ease of someone who had handled a deck of cards for years. "Want to cut?" she offered Dave.

He offered the cards to Emily, sitting beside him.

The little girl grinned.

Rae dealt the cards, a flip of her wrist landing the cards directly in front of each person at the table. "Your bid," she told James.

"Two clubs."

Dave and Lace ended up going head to head again, both holding the last of the trump cards.

Dave laid down the three of hearts. "Sorry, honey. You've been got."

Lace laid down her last card with a smile. "You need to count better, friend." The five of hearts.

Rae burst out laughing at Dave's expression.

"Next year we're going to play Monopoly," Dave told Lace, as Rae collected the cards.

"I would love to be your landlord," Lace replied, grinning.

"Rae, mind some company?" James asked quietly, stopping at the bottom steps to the pavilion. The bridge game had concluded a little over an hour ago. He had left Dave and Lace haggling in the kitchen over the best way to reheat spaghetti left over from dinner, and come out to walk along the lake before turning in for the night. He had thought Rae had already gone to bed, instead he found her sitting alone in the pavilion, looking at the water.

Tomorrow they would be packing up and heading home.

"Come on up," she replied, her voice quiet.

He touched her shoulder as he reached the bench. She was cold.

He slipped off his jacket and draped it over her shoulders.

"Thanks." She buried her hands into the warmth, one last shiver shaking her frame.

"You should have come back to the cabin for a jacket."

"I didn't realize I was this cold."

James settled on the bench beside her, pushed his hands into the pockets of his jeans. The water was tranquil tonight, the moonlight reflecting off its surface, dancing around. A multitude of stars were out. Nights in Africa had been like this—panoramic in their display.

"What's wrong?" he asked quietly. She didn't disappear in the middle of the night without something driving her actions.

She eventually sighed. "I don't want the vacation to end."

He turned to look at her. There was so much sadness in her voice. "Why, Rae?" he asked gently.

"I've enjoyed the last several days working on the book. I don't want to give it up." She leaned back, looked up at the stars, a pensive look on her face. "It's simple to say I'll make time to write when I get home, but the reality is, there won't be time. There is so much work to do, it's overwhelming."

"You're tired." Tired of the pace of life, tired of the weight, tired of carrying the responsibility, tired of being alone.... How well he understood tired.

She sighed. "In three days, this will all be only a distant memory. I'll be living on adrenaline again, going from one crisis to another."

"Rae, you can change it. The schedule is reflecting your choices."

"I have a responsibility to my clients to see that the job is done well. I've been looking for someone to step in and help manage the business, looking hard, but it just hasn't happened yet."

He knew what it felt like to be the one carrying the responsibility to make sure a situation worked out. You did whatever had to be done, it was that simple. The early days in business with Kevin, most of the last six years in Africa...a commitment was kept, even if it meant long hours and a lot of lost sleep. But the doctors had been pretty frank—they didn't think his symptoms would be as severe had he not been pushing himself so hard for so long.

"I've watched you this week. You're one of the best planners I have ever met. You can manage the business until you find someone. Just don't let yourself get overwhelmed. Set some limits, do what you can and walk away from it," he advised, wishing he had learned to heed his own advice at some point in his past.

"I've never learned how to walk away and really leave my work at the office. It's been haunting my sleep the last few months," she admitted quietly. "I don't want to go back to that, James. It's not worth it."

How he wished he could take away the burden or make it easier to carry. Words were such a limited help.

He thought about how dramatically the past five months had changed him. He had that to offer, the reality of what it was to know the tasks exceeded the resources to meet them. "Rae, I've had to learn the hard way that you have to accept and live with the limits you are dealt. You're going to have to set limits around how much energy you can pour into work, how much stress you can carry. When you reach your limits, walk away. The world won't stop functioning if you take twelve hours for yourself."

"No, I might only lose my client's shirt."

He smiled. "Somehow, from what I hear, I doubt that is very likely. You've got to learn, Rae, that taking a break is just as legitimate a use of your time as continuing to work."

She sighed. "I feel guilty when I leave a job unfinished."

How well James understood that guilt. "Believe me, I feel the same way. Limits are never easy, but Rae, in the long run, they prove their worth. Maybe I'm fortunate with this illness to have at least learned that. My body no longer allows me to exceed my limits. It forces me to stop and rest. I wish it would do it in a somewhat less drastic fashion—the pain and fatigue are intense. But it's made me learn to set priorities for what I will use my energy to do."

"It's come down to prioritizing good versus good. I can either ensure the day-to-day decisions are right and on time and risk sacrificing the big picture, or I can focus on the future analysis and risk the day-to-day trading. It's a no-win situation," Rae said.

James stopped his train of thought, realizing something. "Rae, do you like your job?"

She was surprised by the question. Surprised enough to stop and think about it before she tried to answer it. When she did, her answer seemed to surprise her. "I want time to work on the book. I want time to spend with friends. I want the job, but not at the expense of those two needs." She smiled. "Ambivalence. I never thought I would feel that about work. In the past, it's been the passion and driving goal of my life. I don't know when it disappeared."

"Leo's death," James said softly.

She thought about it. "No. It changed before that. The day I said yes to going out with Leo. What I wanted in my life changed. I'm good at the job, I just don't want it to be the only thing in my life anymore. I shifted gears inside to planning for a marriage and a family."

She sighed. "I don't know what I want anymore." She considered that statement for a moment. "Yes I do. I want Leo back."

He liked her honesty, her ability to be frank. "It's tough to adjust when you know what you want isn't going to happen," he commented, knowing some of what it felt like from his own frustration with this medical furlough. "Figure out a way to put time into your schedule to write, to spend time with Lace. Re-evaluate what you think about work when you've fixed those problems," he suggested.

She really did love her job. He was convinced of that. She just needed it to be her job again, instead of her life. Rae was tired, but the love of the job was still there, buried under the weight of the responsibility she was carrying.

"I've been trying to think about ways to make my time during the day less fragmented—the trading is a reactive job, something I didn't have to deal with before. That's what's killing my ability to do the analysis work. There has to be a way to improve the situation."

James was grateful to hear some of the tension had left her voice. "You'll find it, Rae. Think of it as a puzzle to solve."

She laughed. "A puzzle called Rae's Day on the Job. That's what it is, too, a problem to be analyzed and solved. It can't continue as it currently is."

"I hate to be the one to suggest this, but it is getting late. We had probably better turn in for the night."

She had yawned twice and her face was showing her weariness. She needed to be in bed.

Rae nodded, pushing herself away from the bench. "Thanks for being willing to talk work, James. I know it's not the most interesting subject."

He smiled. "Oh, I don't know. It's a good chunk of your life right now. I'm interested."

"Why?"

"Just because," James replied, dropping his arm around her shoulders as they walked back to the cabin.

He stepped back as they entered the back door, let her precede him. Patricia had put the kids to bed a while ago. Dave and Lace had turned in; the cabin was quiet. "I'll see you in the morning, Rae. Sleep well."

He was surprised by her attempt to contain a smile. "You, too, James. Good night," she said softly.

It was as he was climbing under his covers that James realized he'd been truly enfolded into this close-knit family of friends.

They had short-sheeted his bed.

Chapter Five

Fifty laps. James touched the wall, breathing hard, and let the water lap around him as he let his body relax. His endurance was back. His body ached, not with pain, but with the exertion of a good workout.

Smiling, pleased, he swam at a leisurely pace to the ladder.

He was over the worst of the symptoms.

Eight weeks of a lot of sleep, a lot of medicine, and careful exercise had paid off. His joints no longer ached.

He had already talked his next step over with Kevin. He thought his body was ready to tackle a building project again. It was time to know. Three weeks working on a house with Kevin would tell him if he was right.

The smell of chlorine was strong in the air as James crossed the tile deck to the chair where he had left his towel and locker key. The health club was surprisingly empty for a Thursday afternoon. A glance at the wall clock showed he had just enough time for ten minutes in the whirlpool followed by a quick shower before he needed to leave to pick up Dave.

Rae was bowling in the finals tonight.

She was still too busy to suit any of them, but James had watched her eyes begin to smile again, knew Rae was adjusting, finding a balance between her life and her work.

He'd become one of the group.

His initiation had been one short-sheeted bed. He still had no idea which one of them had done it, but they had all obviously known about it.

In the six weeks since, he had come to profoundly appreciate their offer of friendship.

He was part of the group.

He'd never experienced anything like it, a camaraderie coupled with loyalty that went so deep as to be nearly unbreakable. He had begun to realize the significance of it the day Dave flew back on a chartered flight from San Diego during a trial to be at an awards banquet where Lace was speaking, and from the awards banquet went back to the airport for a return trip in the middle of the night. It was Rae networking her contacts to donate the medical equipment he would need for the clinics then pulling more strings to get even the shipping costs donated. It was Lace putting in an all-nighter with Dave to prepare a court defense, then getting on a plane herself to make a major presentation the next day. It was Friday night dinners at Dave's place, movies at Lace's, basketball games at Rae's. It was a network of names and contacts and favors that they used freely to solve problems for each other, from getting plane tickets on a moment's notice to getting phone calls to the top executive of a corporation put through. It was inconceivable amounts of cash flowing from one individual or another to needs the group spotted. It was a common "what I have is yours" use of their time, resources and talents. Cementing it all together was a lot of laughter.

They were friends.

They had chosen him to be one of them.

As the weeks went by, he had grown to appreciate how big a blessing God had dropped in his life.

He had become their expert advisor on cars, construction, real estate, large organization management, and, somehow, their elected chief arbitrator of decisions. There would be options on the table for what to do, where to go, whom to call, priorities to set. And when he finally stated what he thought, they would go that way. He had finally understood a few weeks back that they were doing it intentionally. They wanted him to be part of the team, not a newcomer.

He was going to miss them when Africa put him half a world away.

Six weeks, and he would be standing on scrubland, putting a clinic together where there was only a dream and a need.

He had a feeling that the three of them had simply decided they were going to extend their network around the globe to follow him. Dave had been adding contacts in the State Department to his Rolodex; Lace had already put her international banking contacts at his disposal; Rae, through the foundation money she managed, was already picking his brain for details about the type of doctors he needed to staff the clinics.

They were being friends.

They hadn't been able to solve his medical problems, but they had literally put in his hand access to one of the best health clubs in the area, the private cards of the best doctors in the city, even season tickets to the White Sox games.

There were times he marveled at the blessings God chose to give. This group of friends could have only been conceived and put together by the hand of God.

"Anything else, Janet?" Rae asked, pausing on her way back from a telephone conference with Gary in Seattle and Mike in Houston.

Her secretary glanced down her running list. "Mark said he would fax the corporate resolutions over tonight, Linda had a question on the tax distribution from March—I had the information she needed so I faxed it to her—I need a decision on when you would like to meet with Quinn Scott, and Bob Hamilton wants to have lunch next week to follow up on your proposal."

Rae felt like doing a dance, but settled for a significant smile. "Accept any day next week that Bob Hamilton has available—I'll call and apologize to whomever you have to bump from my schedule. Remind me to send Dave a thank-you. Pencil Quinn in for either late Tuesday or Wednesday afternoon next week."

Janet added the information to her list. "I'll leave you a confirmation message on your voice mail and update the board with what I can arrange. That looks like it."

"Wonderful. Thanks, Janet."

Rae was going to be able to leave the office by 6:00 p.m. The changes made in the past six weeks had finally begun to pay off.

She entered the trading room for one last review of

the day's events. She had the place to herself, a rare occurrence.

Mr. Potato Head was smiling.

Rae grinned and tipped his pipe down. Leo's toys still dotted the room. She'd never had the heart to remove them. This was still his domain, even today. Besides, she liked his toys, they each had a story to tell that made her smile.

It was a spacious room made crowded by the volume of equipment. She glanced at the news feeds, three televisions monitoring CNN, the financial channel and the news channel, all three taped for playback in case of breaking news, then at the bank of stock price monitors. Leo had written the software driving the price monitors. One monitor showed prices and movements for all the stocks they owned, another monitor showed prices and movements for stocks on their watch list, and the last monitor showed prices and volumes in the market as a whole.

Scott was breaking down the stocks that had dropped or jumped up during the day, would give his recommendations by voice mail tonight; she would do her own analysis of the data in the morning in light of his recommendations and make some decisions.

Rae settled down in the captain's chair and tipped back, sipping the cup of coffee she had brought with her as she watched the terminals on the trends desk flip through the daily, monthly and yearly graphs for each stock they owned. She paused the progression of the graphs occasionally, adding a few of them to her work list for the morning. On the whole was satisfied with what she saw.

A touch of a key flipped the display to client portfolios. Rae took her time reviewing the thirty-two screens, looking at the effects the day's markets had had on her clients' portfolios.

It had been a good day overall.

All the information she was looking at was available in her own office, but she had decided after coming back from vacation that it would be a strategic move to separate the analysis and planning work she did from the trading work she also directed.

After six weeks, her office felt like a haven again. She had to worry about instant decisions and responding to events when she was here in the war room; outside of this room, she could back off to her more natural planning mode. It had been a good compromise.

Hiring two more excellent secretaries and thinking through carefully what data she needed to see each morning had let her focus that critical first forty minutes of her day. At Lace's insistence, she now had breakfast being delivered for everyone in the office at 7:00 a.m. Her appetite was still nonexistent, but Janet was keeping a watch on her, showing up with a plate of food if she forgot to stop working to eat. Rae was pretty sure the dozen roses on the corner of Janet's desk were from Dave. Trust her friends to have a spy in her office.

A glance at the middle clock on the wall, the one set for Central Standard Time, showed ten minutes before six. It was time to get moving. She needed to swing by Lace's condo and pick up Dave's leather jacket on the way to the bowling alley. How Dave's most cherished possession had ended up at Lace's place in July was a mystery Rae intended to solve before the night was out.

Lace had been in Canada for a conference, it could

have conceivably been cool enough she would need a jacket, but Dave's leather jacket? It wasn't fashionable. And Dave didn't exactly just hand that jacket out. Letting a lady wear that jacket was Dave's equivalent of giving a class ring.

"Nail it, Rae."

She stopped the swing, the loud call coming just as she began to step forward, the momentum spinning her around. "Would my cheering section please quit interrupting my concentration?" she demanded, amused.

"Why? You bowl better when we interrupt you," Dave said.

"Your only strikes came with our help," Lace confirmed, her patent leather shoes resting on the back of the chair in front of the bench. She was shelling peanuts. She looked about sixteen with the outfit she had on—the poodle skirt was vintage sixties if it was a day, the bubble gum had to be interfering with the peanuts, and her hair was in two ponytails. Two. It was carrying cheerleading beyond the call of duty. It did explain the leather jacket.

"How many strikes is that?"

"Two," James added cheerfully from his seat as acting scoring secretary.

She scowled at him. She was having a rotten game.

"Try to behave, you're embarrassing my team."

"They're okay, Rae," the rest of her bench chimed in. Dave tipped his can of soda in thank-you for the support. He had bought the first round of soft drinks for the entire league. He was everyone's pal tonight.

Rae reset her position, considered what Leo would have done in this situation, and laid a blistering twist

on the release, crossing her ball over the fifth board.
She watched it flair out to the second board, cross
the second set of diamonds and promptly hook into a
pocket with a vicious pop.

"All right, Rae!"

She walked back to the bench, smiling.

She slapped hands with her teammates and picked
up the towel she had tossed on her seat.

"You're a pretty good player, aren't you?" James
leaned forward across the back of the seat to whisper.

"Sort of," Rae whispered back. "We promised the
league we would make the games competitive this
year."

"So, where are we going from here?"

It was late, and the foursome paused in the parking
lot to consider Dave's question.

Dave had his arm draped around Lace's shoulders.
James could understand why he didn't want the evening to end. He didn't particularly want to see the evening end, either.

Rae paused beside him as they considered what
they would do, shifting her bag holding two bowling balls to her other hand. He had offered to carry it
for her, but she had declined with a smile and a soft
thanks. He hadn't made an issue of it. The symptoms
were gone, but she was still being cautious. Either that,
or she didn't want his help. He preferred to think she
was still being careful of his wrists. The first time at
the bowling alley, weeks ago, he had picked up a bowling ball and the pain in his wrist had made him nearly
gasp in pain. Tonight, he bet he could bowl a game and
not feel even a twinge.

"James, will a late night be a problem?" Rae asked

him in an undertone, confirming his suspicions of what she was thinking.

He appreciated the question, but he really was okay now. "No."

"We could go to Avanti's for a pizza," she suggested to the group.

"Great idea. They have the best garlic bread sticks," Lace commented.

"Garlic? Lace..." Dave began to protest.

Lace slipped out from under his arm. "Don't go making assumptions, Dave. I'll ride with Rae and we'll meet you two there."

Dave sighed. "Sure."

James hid his smile, aware, as was Rae, how Lace and Dave were skirting around actually dating. "Come on, Dave, ride with me and give me directions. I'll bring you back here to pick up your car."

They walked across the parking lot to the car Kevin had loaned him, listening to the laughter of the ladies as they walked in the other direction to Rae's Lexus.

James unlocked the car, catching sight of Dave's expression as he turned to watch them. "She does like you, you know."

"I thought getting a kiss when I was sixteen was a big deal," Dave commented. "It's nothing like trying to get one from Lace. I've never met a lady with more contrary signals in my life."

"She doesn't want to mess up a friendship."

"No, it's not that. Rae was like that. I think Lace just likes to be contrary. I made the mistake of asking her out only after I found out she was dating some tax attorney. She's miffed at me."

James smiled. "She looked really miffed tonight."

Dave gave him directions to the restaurant. He

smiled. "She does make nice company. But James, I swear, she's going to have me going in circles for months before she says yes."

"So, ask her to something you know she can't refuse. She's into art in a big way isn't she?"

"Impressionists."

"Find a showing she would love to see, make it hard for her to turn you down," James suggested.

"That's a good idea."

James turned east on Hallwood Street, easily keeping Rae's Lexus in view up ahead.

"What's Rae like to do?" he asked casually—too casually—a few minutes later. He had a few weeks before he left the country; he wouldn't mind spending some of that time with Rae. He enjoyed her company.

Dave laughed. "Not aiming low, are you?" He thought for a moment. "Rae? I guess I would put bookstores at the top of her list, pet stores, charity auctions, medical conferences. Any conference related to work—financial planning, taxes, stock selection. She's always been pretty hard to pin down."

"Does she dance?"

Dave looked troubled. "I would recommend that you stay away from it. Leo was trying to teach her."

Dave pointed out the restaurant. "They were two days away from being engaged, James. She's still dealing with a lot of big issues. I'm not saying don't pursue it, but I would move cautiously if I were you."

Engaged.

Lace hadn't told him that.

James slid out of the booth as the ladies came to join them, allowed Rae to slip back into her seat. She was sitting beside him in the booth.

It had been a laughter-filled last thirty minutes. Rae was still riding high with energy, her team having won the competition, and Dave was in usual form tonight, keeping them laughing at his stories. James was finding it hard to join in. He kept considering the implications of what Dave had said.

Engaged.

There was a lot of pain to process when you lost someone you loved. It may have been almost two years, but when he looked at Rae, he knew she had a long way to go before she had processed all the grief. The implications of how her life had changed—the work pressure, the added weight of responsibility, were still fundamentally affecting her life.

How well he could remember the first time he met her, how deep the grief had been in her eyes. Now, after weeks around her, he was catching glimpses of Rae without that pain; moments when the glimmer of laughter would reach her eyes, moments when her smile would cause her eyes to twinkle. As a friend, he wanted to see that healing continue. He wanted to help in any way he could. As a man, he wanted her to be able to move on from the past.

He liked her.

It was a pretty profound emotion, because he wanted it to be more than a casual friendship.

He knew the reality. He was returning to Africa in six weeks. He had an obligation and commitment there to finish what he had begun, and the need was there, but the part of him that looked at the cost of that commitment was chalking up Rae as one of the steeper costs he was going to be paying.

Before he went back to Africa, he would like to see the smile in her eyes there all the time.

He wouldn't mind spending more time with her before he went back overseas, simply because he enjoyed listening to her and being with her. But he no longer could treat her past as a casual fact. It was big and powerful, and to be a friend he had to at least appreciate what that past meant to her. Until tonight, he really hadn't understood.

It made the idea of asking her out take on a whole new implication.

She hadn't been on a date since Leo passed away. He ought to have at least realized that before he popped off a casual question. No wonder his suggestion of going into town to get ice cream had startled her.

She hadn't been prepared to hear such a casual offer.

He would know better in the future.

He smiled as he listened to Rae debate Dave over the merits of the latest tax cap proposal for the county, Lace interrupting occasionally to add her concerns. The three of them had a passion for politics and legislation that made him wonder why none of them had ever gone into politics. The debate came down to point of interpretation and all three of them looked at him.

He grinned as he picked up his soda. "Sorry, I can't even give an opinion."

"We've got to stop doing local politics," Lace apologized, pushing her plate to the side.

"Who wants the last two pieces of pizza?" Between the four of them, a large Canadian bacon pizza had nearly disappeared.

"Rae," he and Dave said at the same time.

Rae rolled her eyes. "I don't need to gain that much."

"A bird has been eating more than you have. Take it for lunch tomorrow," Dave insisted.

Rae conceded because she was outvoted.

James leaned back in the bench and watched Rae, a smile on his face because she was beside him and because occasionally she would turn to ask him a question in a low voice so the other two wouldn't hear and her eyes would be sparkling. She had chosen him, since Dave and Lace were skirting around actually dating each other, to be the one she would turn to when she needed a partner. She sent him to get her soda, asked him to find the hot pepper shaker for her. Little things that made him smile. She'd returned the favor by announcing Dave was buying the pizza. Dave had groaned and protested and she'd just looked at him, prompting laughter around the table when Dave didn't say another word.

Rae was happy tonight and he didn't want the night to end.

She needed more breaks like this. He'd been thinking about it as they sat and talked tonight. He had one option up his sleeve, something he thought might get a yes from her even though everything he had seen so far said she was comfortable in the group of friends, but not beyond that group. Puppies were a hard date to turn down.

"Have a nice night?"

His mom was still up, seated in the recliner in the family room, knitting, the late show just finishing, credits scrolling by on the screen. It was like walking back in time. So many times during his high school and college days he had come home and found her in just that chair, reading a book, watching a late show, occasionally sleeping. It was his dad's chair.

James leaned against the doorpost, tucked his hands in his pockets, smiled. "Real good, Mom."

For all the pain and trouble the bug he had picked up had caused, the fact that it gave him a few weeks back with family almost made it worthwhile. He was storing up memories of his mom and his sister and her family. He was going to miss them all.

"I'm glad." She set down the sweater she was making, then touched the remote to shut off the television. "I do love Cary Grant. He made such good movies."

His dog levered himself to his feet, came over to greet him. "Hi, boy." James stroked the dog's coat and he lazily leaned against James's jeans, loving the attention.

His mom picked up the bowl of orange peels beside the chair and the empty glass off the table. "Your dad and I watched that movie on our honeymoon." She touched the light switch. "There were a couple phone calls for you tonight. Jim Marshall called from Germany and Kevin called, said to tell you Monday was good on his schedule. I left the notes on the kitchen table."

"I bet Jim's got a new baby to announce. Heather was due about now," James remarked walking back to the kitchen to get the message.

"It would be his second?"

"Third. He's got a boy and girl." He confirmed the number was the one he remembered. "I've got a couple guys coming over tomorrow to help me rehang the garage door so it won't stick anymore. I'll be over at the kennels after that. Did your dog Margo have her puppies yet?"

"Not yet, but the vet says she's due anytime. Bobby said he would be sure to check on her tonight when he makes his rounds."

"I've got someone I think I'll invite over to see them," James said casually.

His mom smiled, that smile she use to get when he said he was bringing a girl home with him to study.

"I'm leaving in six weeks, Mom."

His mom nodded, but her smile only got wider. "Six weeks is a long time. Rae will like the puppies. Lock up before you turn in?"

James knew he had said nothing about Rae recently, he'd seen her only as part of the group. He spent his time with Dave or Kevin or over at Patricia's. Trust his mom to figure out his interest before he did....

"I'll lock up."

"It's good to have you back, James," Kevin said, handing him the second cup of coffee he was carrying.

It was the crack of dawn, dew was still on the cars and trucks, and they were looking at what was essentially a hardened pad of concrete. Not a piece of lumber had been laid for this house that was slated to be ready for the electrician and plumber in three weeks.

"Remember how to be a carpenter?"

James laughed. "I've forgotten more than you ever learned," he replied, drinking the coffee and looking over the blueprints spread out before them across two sawhorses. He was eager, impatient to get to work; he had always loved these initial few days, framing in a house and making it appear from nothing.

His devotions that morning had landed on Psalm 127. *Unless the Lord builds the house, those who build it labor in vain.* It was just like God to note the arrival of this day with the same expectation James felt.

It was nice to know this morning he was going to be helping God build a home.

"The rest of the crew should be arriving anytime. Find the chalk and let's get this house underway," Kevin said. "I've missed this, James. I've been stuck behind a desk too much the last couple of years."

"Have you sold this one yet?"

"A real nice couple from Georgia, moving with his job. They've got one little girl, about six years old."

The lumber for the frame had been delivered and rested on pallets on what would someday be a sodded backyard. James started hauling lumber. The first nail drove into the wood in two decisive blows of the hammer, making him smile and reach for the next nail.

He was back.

This was who he was.

A carpenter who made homes and clinics rise where there was only a dream.

It felt good. Really, really good.

God, thanks. The prayer came from his heart. It was followed with another nail, pounded in with a smile. There was a day coming in heaven when he was going to get the Master Craftsman in a workshop to show him the things He had made when He was a carpenter. There was something uniquely satisfying with sharing the profession Jesus had chosen for thirty years.

Jesus could have been a farmer or a fisherman, or a shopkeeper. He had chosen to be a carpenter. James could understand why.

Chapter Six

"James, can you join us? We're at Rae's tonight,"
Dave asked.

Ten hours on the job studding in the kitchen had
left him dripping in sweat and physically tired, a good
tired that came after accomplishing a good job, but
still ready for some downtime. He had been headed for
a shower and a ball game when the phone had rung.
His mom was out tonight with Patricia and the kids.

"What time, Dave? I'll be there."

It was Rae. Any other offer he would have declined.
Going to Rae's put the request in a different league.

"Seven-thirty. Lace is coming out from the city."

"I'll be there."

"Great. Come hungry. I'm doing ribs on the grill."

James hung up the phone. Rae. He hadn't seen her
for eight days. He had checked the nursery Sunday
morning to find he had just missed her. Eight days
was too long.

Margo had four gorgeous puppies, but James had
decided a phone call was not the way to extend the
invitation. He needed to do it in person, when he

knew it was a favorable time and he would see her expression.

Tonight.

Ask Rae over for dinner and a trip to the kennel to see the puppies.

Add his mom to the picture. Dinner at his mom's kitchen table. That should be low-key enough to get a yes. Nothing threatening. It would get him a few hours of her company, that was the objective.

He went to take a shower, his fatigue easing with the plans for the night.

After four days of construction work with Kevin, his body was complaining about the physical exertion, but so far it was the aches and pains he would expect from having been sidelined for so many weeks. It wasn't the pain he had learned to dread, pain burning in his joints; it was the normal ache of muscles getting used to doing some heavy work.

He was relieved.

He had been more worried than he was willing to admit about how this first week of construction would go. He wasn't out of danger of a physical surprise yet, but every day that went by put him all the more closer to being able to return to Africa. He prayed for that every morning when he got up, every evening when he went to bed.

Africa.

It was work he did well. It was work that saved lives.

He was enjoying the comforts of a hot shower, a good meal and a soft bed while he had them. They would soon be memories. He had learned to enjoy good things while they were there. It was a cost of the mission field. He had accepted the cost once before, and he would accept it again.

There was a world in need, and he had the skills to meet it. To not go would be to deny the call God had placed on his heart.

Someday, there would be a payoff worth the sacrifice.

It was time to quit wishing for something else and enjoy what God had given now. Good friends. A wonderful lady. Ribs.

Dave was awesome with charcoal and a grill.

"Dave, did you need matches?" Rae shifted the casserole dish of scalloped potatoes to the top of the stove, careful to keep a firm grip on the hotpad. She had already burned her thumb once tonight.

"Got them, Rae. Were you able to find the long tongs?"

"Yes, but I need to wash them," Rae called out to the deck. "I'll have them for you in a minute."

She blew a strand of hair back from her eyes. Company was coming and she was a wreck. Still in her skirt and blouse from work, rumpled, hot, running late.

"Would you quit fussing over the food and go take a shower? It's just James and Lace," Dave said, joining her in the kitchen.

Exactly, Rae thought. She preferred James to see her with a semblance of her act together.

Dave laughed and took the pot holders. "Go. I can manage the kitchen."

She hugged him then deserted him, leaving him to try to put together the menu.

The shower was hot, the steam taking away the

marks of the stressful day. It had been a day where she had been silently pleading by noon for God to send her some relief. The markets had been volatile, one of the computer feeds of data had gone down, and Janet had been called for jury duty.

Rae rapidly washed her hair.

God, we've talked about it so many times in the past six weeks. I'm glad You're using James to help pull me out of the grief, but God, just between You and me, this is getting embarrassing. He's a friend, he's going back to Africa in six weeks, and I'm acting like I've got a crush on him! I'm not cut out to be acting like I'm twenty again. I'm not ready to emotionally deal with a guy and a relationship again. So would You please ease this emotion and use tonight to help me back off?

Oh, and God, if I get a chance to talk to Lace alone tonight, help me find the right words to say. She's been quietly hoping for Dave's interest for three years. Now that he's asked, she needs the courage to say yes. I understand her fears, Dave has not exactly shown a desire to settle down in the past, but I've seen something different in him the past few weeks, and I want Lace to at least give him a chance. I think they were made for each other, Lord. They complement each other, and they've already got the commitment to each other as friends.

The silent prayer helped steady Rae's nerves. Ten minutes later, standing in front of her closet biting her bottom lip, she had to make a decision. She wanted comfortable and Lace would argue she should go for knockout. Rae hated waffling about clothes. She had no idea what she should wear. She finally chose a black knit top and a pair of pressed jeans. She added her mother's pearls. It was a compromise.

It took forever to get her hair to dry. When she finally clicked off the hair dryer, she could hear voices from downstairs. She glanced at the clock. Lace had made better time than she expected.

Rae hesitated, then reached over for the perfume bottle.

It was a night of friends over for a meal and a televised baseball game. She had to get over these nerves. She finally had to order herself to get downstairs and be the hostess.

James parked behind Lace's car in the drive. As he walked up the drive to the town house, he could hear laughter coming from the deck at the back.

Rae had a beautiful home. He let himself in, having concluded they were all outside. It was a comfortable place, nice furniture, beautiful paintings, restful because it was lived in. Rae had her mom's books—eight novels—prominently displayed in the living room. Her mail had been dropped in a basket on the kitchen bar, magazines tossed in a basket beside the couch.

There were books everywhere, on bookshelves in the living room, a stack on the hallway table to be returned to the library, a half-dozen more piled up on the floor at the end of the couch, most with a bookmark indicating where she had left off reading.

The first time he had seen her home, he had been impressed with how well it reflected her personality. It wasn't coordinated as a decorator would do it, but it was visually restful and functionally useful.

Rae was a lady who liked pictures, most of the shelves and a few of the tables had framed snapshots. Her family. Dave and Lace. Leo.

Rae had a picture of Leo on the shelf beside her

mom's novels. It was a candid snapshot, obviously taken by either Lace or Dave, at the cabin where they had vacationed. Leo had been in the kitchen making waffles, Rae leaning against his back and reaching around to swipe a strawberry. The snapshot told James a lot. Leo had turned to say something to Rae, and the expression on his face as he looked at her had been unguarded. Leo had been in love with Rae. It was there in his face and his eyes.

He had been a good man.

Everything Dave and Lace said, everything Rae herself reflected, told him that.

The fact Rae had kept the snapshot, displayed it as she did, was a tribute to the fact the love had been returned.

The pictures of Rae with Leo, other pictures around, had given him a glimpse of a Rae he had not met, one who was relaxed, happy, not yet touched by grief.

Her smile was returning, but it was a slow process.

God, are You sure an invitation is the right thing to do? I'm back to waffling again.

James followed the sound of laughter to the deck just in time to see Dave duck the spray of the water hose Lace was holding. She had obviously been trying to help with the flaring flames licking the charcoal and threatening to burn the ribs, but she hadn't been ready for the fact Rae had turned the valve on.

James bit back a laugh at the scene.

Lace meekly turned the hose over to a Dave who was now standing in wet shoes. "Sorry, David."

Dave wiped the water off his forearm, gave a long-suffering sigh. "You know, the first time I could write it off as an accident, but the third time? I swear you just like to get me soaked, Lace."

"Would some ice tea make it better?"

He tweaked a lock of her hair at the amusement in her voice. "Make it a soda with caffeine. I have a feeling I'm going to need it tonight."

The wind shifted and James got a smell of the cooking ribs. A day working on a house made a man hungry. He stepped out onto the deck.

"Hi, James." Rae walked onto the deck, pausing beside him.

She was beautiful tonight, her hair pulled back in a gold barrette, the length brushing her shoulders. The pearls were a sharp contract to the black sweater. He didn't see her wear jewelry very often. "Hi, Rae. Looks like I got here just in time."

"Be glad you weren't here a few minutes earlier, you would have probably gotten doused, as well."

She seemed a little uncertain around him, not meeting his glance. James wondered ruefully what was wrong. He wished she would relax around him like she did with Dave.

"James, can I get you a drink?" Lace asked.

Lace, as always, was dressed casually, yet looking like a fashion model. "A soft drink would be fine," he replied, returning her smile.

"I made my special sauce I was telling you about. You are going to like these ribs." James accepted the inevitable and went to join Dave.

James settled in with Dave, talking food, and looking around the yard, noting a few things that needed done. Rae didn't have enough time in her life to keep a yard landscaped, he knew that, but there was evidence that in the past she had tried.

The trellis with the grapevines needed to have a few slates added to bear the weight of the full vines. And her rosebushes were in full bloom, though a couple needed to be trimmed back.

He missed not having a house and yard to work on. Years before, when the business with Kevin had finally begun to turn a modest profit, he had bought an older two-story home near where Patricia currently lived and used his free time to fix it up. He had enjoyed the work, both inside and out in the yard. When he had sold the home the summer he went to Africa, it had been like parting with an old friend. He had made good money on the investment, but it had been a sacrifice, selling the place.

He was a man who liked having a home that showed the benefits of his labor. For six years on the mission field, he had accepted living in temporary housing, often staying with members of the local church, their hospitality appreciated and generous, but it was not the same as having a permanent home.

Dave had a restless, nomadic streak. James was different. He looked forward to the day the clinics were built and the job was done, coming back to the States to settle in one place, buy a house and use his labor to make it a nice home.

Lace returned with the soda he had requested.

Dave flipped the ribs over, added more barbecue sauce.

Ten minutes later, they settled around the table for dinner. Rae and Lace sat across from Dave and James.

Rae was quiet, but her smile was genuine, her laughter making her eyes twinkle. Although she was still avoiding catching his glance, he had a long evening to work on getting her attention.

Rae passed him the bread and he finally caught her eye. He smiled and it was tentative, but he got a smile back from her.

James relaxed.

Lace was back to flirting with Dave.

It was a wonderful meal. The food was delicious, and the company enjoyable. By dessert, the conversation had turned to Rae's book.

Rae didn't like being the center of attention; she was the one who preferred to listen. James found her slight blush tugging his protective nature.

He was pleased to hear that she had been able to get an average six hours of writing time in each week since the vacation, and was now working on chapter twenty-four. When she talked about the book, she came alive in a way that made her face light up. He loved to see that expression.

They eventually moved to the living room and the baseball game, Lace accepting a small gesture from Dave to join him on the couch. Rae settled into a chair, and James sat across from her, watching her as much as he did the game.

Often, he would see her eyes drift from the game to the pictures on the mantel. She looked less hurt, but still sad.

It was not the time to ask her. He could have arranged a chance to ask her, but he didn't try. Tonight was not the right time.

There was a day coming soon that would be the right time. She needed to know a future did exist beyond what she presently had; she needed to know the sadness could be left behind and she could look at options beyond just her career. He had heard the weariness in her voice as she talked about how work was going, her progress in looking for a business partner.

She wasn't going to leave the sadness behind without someone taking the step to ask her on a date. He cared too much about her to leave for Africa without having helped her open that door.

He would be opening the door that someone else would eventually walk through.

He wanted her to still be single in five years, when he figured he would be coming back to the States for good. It wasn't fair to her. She wanted children. He had only to look at her at church around the children to see the obvious. It wasn't fair to rob her of a dream just because he would prefer to have her wait for him.

The sixth day working on the house was a physically challenging day. It was a hot, eighty degrees by 10:00 a.m., the sun and heat and humidity making them sweat and go through gallons of ice water. James paused on the bandsaw, having cut the last lumber they would need to finish framing in the master bedroom and master bath. Wearily, he wiped the sweat from his face with the towel he had slipped in his back pocket.

The pain was back.

He had woke to it that morning, a burning sensation in his chest muscles that had made him groan as he moved to get out of bed. It was mild compared to what it had been like in the past, but after two weeks without feeling it, it had been a surprise.

A hot shower had eased the pain, so that by the time he reached the site that morning he could almost believe he had imagined it. Almost.

He was going back. He was determined to be back

in Africa on schedule. The pain this morning had only strengthened his resolve.

He didn't have to be a hundred percent to do the job. A little stiffness of a morning was something that could be managed.

It was coming up on four o'clock. He had worked through the day, able to do his job, and do it well. His work hadn't suffered, and the activity had not made the ache worse. This morning was a slight glitch, but not something that was going to stop him. Still, he was grateful when Kevin suggested they call it a day. He would spend the evening resting, and tomorrow would be better.

"James, Rae is going to be coming over for dinner tonight. She and I need to talk about the upcoming children's musical. Are you going to be in tonight? Should I set you a place?"

James paused as he reached for a soda can on the bottom shelf of the refrigerator. Trust his mom to act before he did. He retrieved a drink and popped open the tab. "I'll be in," he replied, smiling; he reached around her to swipe a finger across the edge of the icing bowl.

"You're as bad as the children," she scolded, smiling.

"I like fudge icing." She had baked a chocolate cake that afternoon.

"You've got your father's sweet tooth. Go see what kind of mail we got today," she asked, banishing him from her domain.

James kissed her cheek. "Sure, matchmaker."

He met Rae at the door two hours later. She was tired, he saw that immediately, and while she had changed into jeans and a short-sleeve top, it was clear she had come immediately from work. "Come on in, Rae, Mom's in the kitchen. What can I get you to drink?"

She gave a grateful smile. "Ice tea, please."

She followed him to the kitchen, greeted his mom and pulled out a chair at the table, sat down. James watched her try to push the fatigue back, focus on his mom and the conversation.

He got her the drink she had requested, then pulled out the chair across from her, and settled back to watch and listen.

It didn't take long for her and his mom to come up with a plan for the children's musical, agree on who each one of them would call and recruit to help.

When dinner was served, Rae did her best to convey her appreciation to his mom, but James noticed that she barely ate. The phone rang soon after dessert was served. His mom waved him back to his seat and went to answer it.

"What happened today, Rae? You look...shell-shocked for want of a better word."

"I lost two hundred fifty thousand dollars," she replied. He heard the shock in her voice. "The last hour, the markets simply fell apart."

"Rae, I am sorry." He had no way to convey how deep his empathy went for the type of day she had obviously had.

She spun the ice in her water glass, her thoughts obviously a long way away. "We haven't had this bad a day in three years."

"Are you going to be okay?"

She gave a rough laugh. "I'm petrified of tomorrow. Hardly what my clients would want to hear me say tonight."

James pushed back his chair. "Come on, let's go for a walk."

It was a sign of how hard the day had been that she didn't even ask why. James interrupted his mom to softly to tell her where they were going, and ask if she wouldn't mind fixing a piece of the cake for Rae to take home with her. He was worried about how little Rae was eating, but it didn't make sense to push it tonight.

The sun was getting ready to set. James watched Rae tuck her hands into the pockets of her jeans. Walking beside him, a weariness made her shoulders droop. "It's a beautiful sunset," he remarked quietly.

It got her to look up and notice. "Yes, it is."

James wanted to reach over and tuck her hand in his, tell her it would be okay. He couldn't. He had to settle for what he could do. The first thing to do was get her back in a positive frame of mind. "Okay, what's your game plan for tomorrow?"

She smiled, resigned. "I don't have one yet."

He slipped his hands into his own pockets and hid a wince at the way his left wrist complained in pain. "What are your options?"

"Sell and take profits before the stocks slide further. Do nothing. Sell strategically and use the cash to buy stocks that seem to be below their worth."

"How are you going to decide which one to do?"

She shrugged, then stopped walking for a moment, bit her bottom lip. "It hinges around one conclusion. I've got to decide if this is a short-term adjustment, or the warning shot of a long-term correction."

She started walking again, and he shortened his stride to hers. "Which do you think it is?"

"I don't know, James. I'm not current with my overall analysis, I don't have the facts I need to support a call either way. I'm kicking myself for being so careful to do the trading correctly, that I had not left adequate time to prepare for this. James, I cut my analysis time back so I could work on my book. Finding those six hours a week to write just burned my clients."

She was wrong. Those six hours of time writing had kept her able to do the trading and the analysis. They had kept her from burning out.

"What would Leo do in this situation?"

"He would be selling and taking profits, using the cash to go back into the market, buy stocks that slipped too far in the correction."

"Are you comfortable doing that?"

"Not at the speed he would do it. I don't know when a stock that is sliding down should be bought. I end up buying too early and having to watch it slide further before it bottoms out."

A slight breeze rustled through the branches and leaves of the trees they were walking under. It was an older neighborhood, the sidewalks lined with fifty-year-old oaks.

"You need to decide on a course for tomorrow, and go with it. When you have more information then you can adjust your plan," James said.

"Thanks." Rae nodded and lightly touched his arm.

They walked in silence for most of the way around the block and soon they were back to his mom's house.

"Would you like to go see some puppies?" James asked, wanting to distract her when he saw her frown at something she thought of.

His suggestion accomplished his goal; it broke her focus on her job. "I love puppies," she replied, slightly wistful.

"I know where there is a litter of four puppies, recently born. It's a five-minute drive. Would you like to go?"

She nodded.

Pleased, James gestured to his car. "Come on."

The kennel was quiet.

James saw Rae look around with interest as they walked through the quiet hall toward the back of the building. "Never been here before?"

"No."

"I'll show you around later," James offered.

He opened the gate and was not able to stop a wince of pain at the action.

"James, what's wrong?" Rae had seen the pain cross his face.

When he didn't answer, her face grew more intent as she made her own conclusions. "Your wrist hurts, doesn't it? Your wrist hurt when you opened the gate." There was alarm in her voice.

"Rae, it's nothing. My body is stiff after a long day working on the house. That's all."

"That's not all it is. You winced, James."

"It's nothing, Rae," he insisted, stepping through the gate to the kennel runs and waiting for her join him.

"James..."

He smiled. "Rae, I promise, it's nothing. I'm fine. Come see the puppies."

Margo had the first kennel run, a spacious indoor and outdoor kennel she could move between at will. The dog was awake, having heard them enter the building. She was stretched out on a soft quilt, four furry bundles sprawled around and over each other asleep beside her.

"They're beautiful."

James opened the gate and felt the pain burn in his left wrist but refused to let any indication show on his face. "Hi, girl. How are you tonight?"

Margo raised her head and her tail began to beat against the blanket. James stroked her fur, greeted her as the old friend she was.

Rae knelt down beside him, cautiously offered her hand to Margo to inspect, had it licked in approval.

Two of the puppies stirred and tried to get up, only to roll as they tangled each other up. James laughed and caught them.

"This is Benjamin, and this is Justin."

Rae sat down on the kennel floor and Benjamin came over to climb in her lap. The puppy yawned and Rae laughed. "They are adorable, James."

James sat against the concrete wall and stretched his legs out, Justin in his lap. "I thought you might like them," he replied, rubbing Margo's coat and playing tug-of-war with the puppy over ownership of a towel.

The stress he had seen on Rae's face over dinner had eased. She was absorbed in the puppy she held. James smiled. He was glad she had agreed to come. Now if he could only convince her to take a puppy home... Nothing made a stressful day fade faster than an animal that wanted all your attention. He laughed as the puppy tried to figure out how to get his front paw inside her jeans pocket.

"How are you doing this morning?" Kevin asked. Kevin's question pulled James away from his

thoughts. "Ready to get to work," he replied. He was
going to need the time today working on the house to
sort out his confusing thoughts from last night. He had
loved the couple of hours he'd spent with Rae, walking with her, playing with the puppies, watching her.
It had been a night he really enjoyed, and when she
had left for home about nine, he had been able to tell
the break had helped her, too. She'd left in a positive
frame of mind, relaxed. For a while he had regretted
Africa, until perspective cut back in, late that night.

He doubted a carpenter would be her first choice
of a guy to date. With her background, her interests,
a doctor or lawyer would be a better fit. He had never
been one to hold a dream that did not have at least a
corner of it rooted in reality. He had enjoyed the night
and he hoped to enjoy another like it before he left for
Africa, but that was the sum total of what he would
hope for.

Kevin smiled. "Then let's do it."

James looked at the framed-in house. He was going
to build this house and then he was going to go back
to Africa. It mattered to him. He was going to make
it happen. No matter what it took.

His wrist twinged as he grasped the ladder rung.

"Rae, how are you doing?"

Dave's call had been transferred to the war room,
and his voice distracted her momentarily from the
numbers she was studying.

"Dave, it's chaos. I'm busy and it's going to be a
long day. Say a prayer for your finances, I'm currently
losing your money." She winced as another group of
numbers caved in and went red. "Anything you need?"

"For you to relax. You'll do fine. We'll bring dinner by the office around six."

Rae smiled. "Thanks, friend."

She leaned back in her chair to drop the phone in its cradle.

It was like trying to patch together a leaking dam with bandages, the cracks in the market were spreading so rapidly. She was grateful she had made the assumption she was looking at the beginning of a major market correction, at least that decision was proving to be accurate.

"Scott, let's start moving about forty percent of the airline stocks to cash," she said quietly, mentally reviewing the holding lists for where her profits were the most vulnerable to the correction.

Some positions she was selling today had been held for five years, bought during the last major correction. Sooner or later, everything changed. Today had become that day.

She was playing it very conservative, choosing to ride it out and do nothing in most of the stocks she held, making moves only where it seemed strategically beneficial. It was going to be a long day.

"Rae's got a nice location," James commented, following Dave across the atrium of a major office complex. The building interior was marble, gold, modern, with plants and a multilevel waterfall.

"The builder of the complex was a friend of Leo's," Dave replied. "She's on the fifth floor."

A small sign by the suite door, stenciled in gold, told him they had arrived at Rae's office.

The reception area was a formal living room, with comfortable couches, chairs, and a glass-topped table set discreetly to the side. "Lace decorated for them," Dave commented, smiling. He indicated the hall to the right. It opened into a large spacious room that was obviously the hub of the research area. The lady filing reports smiled when she saw them. "Hi, Dave."

"Hi, Janet. Have you met James, yet?"

"Not officially, no. Hello, James."

"It's nice to meet you, Janet."

"Where would you like the dinner we brought?" Dave asked, looking around.

She nodded to the conference room behind him. "Over there would be wonderful. We appreciate it. We're all behind today, there was so much happening so quickly."

"Where is she?"

"The war room."

"Any screams during the day?"

"She's been so calm you would think the market was flat," Janet replied.

"How did she do?"

Janet grinned. "Unbelievably well."

"She made money?"

"It's a tad insulting that you sound so surprised," Rae commented, causing Dave to look around.

"I brought pot stickers. Forgiven?"

She smiled and joined them. "Depends on how many you brought. Hi, James."

"Hi, Rae." She looked exhausted. It had obviously been a long stressful day, but her smile told him a lot about how she felt. She had done well today.

"Would you like a fast tour while I find everyone?"

"Sure."

"Dave, what should I bring you to drink?"

"Something cold."

Rae laughed. "I think I've got that. Janet?"

"A cream soda."

Rae pointed out doors as they walked back toward the reception area. "This is primarily the analysis wing of the suite, my office, another conference room, Janet's office." She took a turn just before she reached the reception area. "This is the trading wing, Leo's office. Scott—one of my key traders—Ann and Jeanna." She paused by one of the doors. "This is the trading room. I'll warn you in advance, it's normally a little neater."

She pushed open the door. James stepped inside. The amount of information and how it was correlated and displayed was incredible. It was like nothing he had ever seen before. He felt slightly overwhelmed. This was her domain?

"Rae, do you want to clear the rest of the position in five-year treasuries tomorrow? There is a working spread we could take advantage of," a man in his early twenties asked from the far side of the room.

"Punch it up to the monitors," she requested. He pressed a couple keys and the data he was looking at appeared on the main screen in front of her. Rae studied the data, nodded. "Good idea. Put them on the list to move early in the day. Scott, have you met James?"

"Spoken on the phone, but no. It's nice to meet you, James."

James shook hands, liking the man on sight. Dave spoke highly of him. "Same here. This looks like an interesting place to work."

Scott laughed. "Challenging," he replied.

"Dinner is here," Rae commented, picking up the stacks of notes she had scrawled during the day. "What can I get you to drink, Scott?"

He gestured to the table behind him. "Got it covered, Rae. The main conference room?"

Rae nodded.

"Give me another couple minutes to finish the file transfers, and I'll be there."

"This has been a long day for you," James commented as they stepped into a small kitchen. It was six-thirty and Dave had mentioned Rae had called him from the office at 5:00 a.m. that morning.

Rae opened the refrigerator to get the requested drinks. "It will take a couple hours longer to wrap up today than usual, but seven o'clock isn't that uncommon. Did the building go okay today? I was worried about you."

James smiled as he took the drinks, careful in how he gripped the cans because his hands wanted to drop them. There was no way he was going to even hint how harsh the day had been. He had a weekend to relax and recuperate. The pain that had been in his ribs the day before had settled into all his joints with the viciousness of a disease that had never left.

But he had worked through the pain again, and it had not crippled him. It was different now; he knew what to expect, he knew how to adapt.

"We put the roof joists in place today. The work is going well. I've missed it, Rae, building a place."

"I'm glad you're able to do it again. The pain is okay?"

"I'm fine," he replied.

She hesitated, then nodded. "Let's go eat."

It was a fair day—sunny, moderate temperature, slight breeze. A builder's ideal day. James was on the roof with Kevin laying the roof sheeting in place. They had set the joists that morning and by evening should be ready to lay the shingles. James slipped yet another nail from the bag and held it in place. He had been using the nail gun across the seams, but there were some corners that required a hand-driven nail.

Pain radiated through his entire body with every blow of the hammer.

The weekend had only let his joints grow more stiff, the pain more severe. It was a losing battle, and James knew it, but wouldn't let himself admit it.

He was losing a dream and he refused to simply give up.

Six months ago he would have thought nothing of laying the entire roof sheeting by hand. There was rarely electricity to power tools where his crews worked. James pulled another nail from the bag. The sweat was pooling around his eyes, sweat from the pain and not the physical labor.

He was not going to let this disease win. The nail dropped from fingers that could not hold it in place and he sighed heavily, hating the pain, hating the way his body was letting him down. He reached for another nail and tightened his grip on it, hating the burning pain that flared in his muscles in response to the action.

Kevin took the hammer out of his hand. "It is not going to help to let the pain cripple you."

James wanted to swear at his helplessness but it was intangible; Kevin was there. "Give me the hammer back, Kevin."

"It's not the end of the world if you can't be a builder anymore."

"I am a carpenter, Kevin. That is who I am." His anger was hot, directed at the illness, at his friend for putting into words what he knew but had not been willing to admit.

"There was a day Jesus walked away from his carpentry shop and did not go back. You've got to let it go, James. It looks like God has got other plans for you."

James had seen the grim look on his friend's face that morning. Kevin had been observing him for days. He knew the reality. James could deny the pain to his family, but Kevin knew better. It was minor consolation that his friend looked as pained by the reality as James felt.

James walked to the edge of the roof and took the ladder back down to the ground. Tired, exhausted, hurting and deeply discouraged, he pulled off his work gloves and unbuckled the tool belt he wore.

Kevin joined him. "James, this is not the end of the world. You just need more time."

"It's been six months, Kevin. Just how much longer do you suppose it will be before I can hold a hammer again for any length of time, be useful on a site?" James replied, feeling his body fighting against the pain in his joints. It was so crippling he would be lucky to be able to move tomorrow.

"It takes more than sweat equity to build a house."

"I'm not the type to be behind a desk, Kevin," James replied, angry at the situation, the brutal unfairness of it. He was good at what he did. The clinics he helped build saved lives. He loved the work. And the most black reality he had ever looked at was staring him in the face.

He wouldn't be going back.

Chapter Seven

"James?" The soft voice called from the front of the kennels.

James rested his arms across his knees, and three puppies immediately attacked the towel that no longer moved. The fourth puppy was over by the gate, growling at a grasshopper that had dared to enter their playground. Margo was stretched out beside him, keeping watch on all her children.

"Back here, Rae." This was the very last thing he wanted. He did not want to see her, he did not want to see any of his friends.

It had been three days. He supposed he should be grateful they had waited this long. He glanced at his watch. It was after seven o'clock. His mood had been so black, the pain so great, his anger so hot, that for the past few days he had tried to make himself scarce. His friends didn't need to be around this.

He had left the doctor's office this afternoon and come to the kennel. Puppies didn't know how hard life could be; they only knew how to play and sleep and eat. They were good company—they didn't ask how he was doing, and he didn't have to tell them.

The disappointment was overwhelming, to know his dream was over. He wanted to go back. It wasn't easy to set aside that disappointment and act polite, friendly, calm. The last thing he wanted to hear was that this was God's plan. James couldn't believe this disease was part of God's plan. He might have permitted it, and He would eventually make some good come out of the situation, but it didn't make sense as part of His original plan.

He understood now Rae's comment that she wanted the past back. Leo had died young and Rae's dreams had been ripped away. This disease would hit and take away his dreams. The reality of such losses was heartbreaking.

"Hi," Rae said softly, stepping outside to join him in the fenced-in run.

He was tired—tired of the situation, tired of the pain, tired of wondering what he was going to do now. But when he saw her, he smiled. He was glad to see her. He had missed her.

She had changed into jeans and an oversize Chicago Bulls T-shirt. She sat down on the grass near him, and the puppies tumbled over to join her.

She didn't say anything, just sat playing with the puppies. He sat and watched her and was grateful.

He carefully rubbed his aching wrist. Even playing tug-of-war with a puppy was too much strain. He wondered who had called her. He had told his mom and Patricia about his doctor's appointment before calling and having a long talk with Bob. Dave had probably heard from Kevin, and from there Lace and Rae would have heard.

James had no idea what had happened with the markets these past two days, didn't know what Rae had been trying to deal with. He knew she had spent the weekend at work. He should have at least caught the evening news the last few days. He wasn't being much of a friend.

She looked weary. The kind of weariness that came from carrying a heavy load for a long time without a break.

One of the puppies tried to eat her shoelaces. James reached over and pulled the puppy over to him, offering the towel as compromise.

"Thanks."

James smiled. "Sure."

She looked at him, wanting to say something. James took pity on her, opened the door she needed. "I called Bob, canceled my plane tickets."

"I heard," she said quietly. "I'm sorry, James."

He knew she was. Of all his friends, she was the one most able to understand and empathize with the loss. "How have the markets been this week?"

"Ugly."

She didn't say anything else, and James knew her struggle to keep her job to sane limits was being lost. "How many hours has it been this week, Rae?"

"At the office from 5:00 a.m. to about 7:00 p.m., followed by late evenings at home trying to get the analysis work done. I am so tired of work."

No time to work on her book, that went without saying. "I'm sorry, Rae."

She smiled. "We've both got pretty big burdens to carry this month. I know you need some space for a few days, but I desperately needed a break, that's why I decided to come by."

"Rae, I'm glad you did. I'm not exactly good company right now, but I am glad to see you."

She helped a puppy settle in her lap. "Dave is dragging me to a baseball game Sunday afternoon. Would you like to come?"

He considered it for a few moments. "Yes."

She smiled. "Good."

"Have you had dinner yet, Rae?"

She blinked, surprised to realize she had not. "I meant to, but no. I think I left a plate of pasta in the microwave."

James chuckled. "Come on, I'll buy you a hamburger at the diner down the block. I want some ice cream and they make an awesome sundae."

He expected her to decline, pleading lack of time or that she was not hungry or something. Her silence did last a few beats too long, but she nodded yes.

"Should we put the puppies inside?"

"Margo will corral them inside when she's ready for them to settle down," James replied. His body argued in pain as he moved to stand up, making him clench his jaw. Rae saw, but didn't say anything. She did maneuver to be the one who opened the gate. James was almost grateful—almost. He intensely disliked needing the help.

The diner was a locally owned, popular place. It was late enough in the evening they were seated almost immediately. Rae glanced at the menu and ordered a bowl of soup and a salad. James frowned, but didn't say anything. She was losing weight; she needed to eat more.

"I don't want to talk about work, and you don't want to talk about the pain. So what do we talk about?"

"Dave and Lace?" James offered with a smile.

Rae grinned. "A favorite subject. I hear they actually went out on a date last night."

"Really?"

"Lace called me shortly before midnight. She woke me up—had to tell me all about it."

"Let me guess, a museum showing?"

"Actually, dinner with a private collector Dave had met a year ago at a conference."

"I'm glad. They make a good couple."

"Do you really think Dave is ready to settle down? Lace has had a crush on him for so long, she doesn't need to get hurt by being one of a list."

James thought about it. "He's ready to settle down. It's in all the little things he does, the way he looks at her, the way he talks about kids."

"Dave being a dad. That I never expected to see."

"What about Lace? Does she want kids?"

"Very much. I think that's why she started dating the tax attorney—she knows her time is running out."

James wanted to know what Rae thought about the subject of children. She was the same age as Lace, so it had to be a concern for her, as well. Had she written off that dream when Leo died? It would be a shame if she had. Rae would make a good mom.

Her meal and his ice cream arrived and neither one said much as they ate.

Did this constitute a date? James wondered as Rae pushed aside her soup and salad, both only half-eaten.

"Not hungry?"

"Food doesn't settle well anymore," she admitted. She gave a rueful smile. "Lace will kill me if I've developed an ulcer."

"Rae…"

"Don't push, James. I'll deal with it."

"Do it soon," he insisted.

"Yeah. I hate doctors."

He smiled. "Now that I can understand."

She realized what she had said, smiled back. "I bet you do."

She glanced at her watch and sighed. "I've got to go. Work is waiting."

James knew ignoring the work was simply an option Rae didn't have. "Rae, remember to pace yourself, okay?"

"I'm trying. Honestly."

He walked back with her to the kennel and to her car. He said goodbye with surprising reluctance.

It was a quiet spot, a bench in a local park that could look down on a ball field or over to a small playground, a place to pause and rest during a walk. James sat down, physically needing the break. He was trying—trying too hard—to exercise enough to keep his body improving, but not too much to cause more damage.

The recuperation was slow at best.

He sat down and carefully stretched his legs out.

God, I don't understand.

I loved Africa. I loved serving people, building clinics, saving children's lives. Now, Father, here, I don't have a purpose. I don't even know where to begin.

I don't understand why You ended such a long ministry in such an abrupt way. Why not some warning? Why not a sense that maybe I should start thinking about coming back to the States? Why so abrupt? One day I'm fine, the next week I'm in so much pain I can barely move. I feel like You abandoned who I was and what I was doing. You didn't give me closure, Lord, You just took the ministry away.

What am I suppose to do in the States?

If You've taken away my ability to hold a hammer and saw, You've pretty much taken away who I am.

You have thousands of good architects here, Lord, thousands of good builders. Why take away a ministry that was doing some good for people?

I don't understand.

All my life, even through the rough times, I have known You had a plan. For the first time, here, now, it feels like You've forgotten me.

The sun woke him Saturday morning, the light streaming into the bedroom and making him blink as he tried to read the time.

He moved cautiously to pull over a pillow, take the strain off his neck. His joints were stiff, his spine taut, but the burning pain was not as severe. James had begun to dread the first hour after he woke up, he was grateful that today was not as bad as the other mornings had been this last week. Time and rest were beginning to ease the symptoms.

If he was staying in the States, what did he want?

It had taken days to shake off the anger, the frustration of the situation and face the reality.

If he was staying in the States, what did he want to do?

It was time to accept reality and go on.

If he was building a new life in the States, then it was time to do it and quit wishing for what was not going to happen. Returning to Africa was not in his future.

He lay in bed looking at the ceiling, thinking.

Buy a house with a yard, that was definite.

Kevin wanted him to take over some of the architecture work and the idea was worth considering. He could work from home, do it at a pace he could tolerate.

Rae. He wanted to get to know her. More than just the surface he knew now. He liked her. He liked the twinkle in her eyes, her smile, her laugh, her willingness to do what was required despite the personal costs.

He didn't want to be alone anymore.

It was a big aching hole in his gut. He didn't want to be alone anymore. If he was back, then he wanted what he had been delaying and saying "not yet" to for years—marriage and a family.

Patricia was due in mid-January. James knew seeing the baby was going to bring back lots of memories. It had been his favorite part of Africa, seeing the children at the clinics.

Rae liked kids. At church most Sundays he found her in the nursery, and the wistfulness in her eyes had not escaped him. She would like to be a mom.

Leo was a big problem. The sadness hadn't left Rae's eyes yet. She was still locked in the past, still grieving. The grief was easing, but it was still there. James wasn't sure how to help her, how to ease that pain she carried.

He had to wait for his own health to stabilize again, but give him a few weeks and he would be fit again. He had to be. He could not imagine life where this pain didn't eventually ease off. Three weeks to get Rae to say yes to a date. He had faced tougher assignments, not many, but a few.

* * *

She was an avid White Sox fan.

James looked over at her, surprised, when she stood up and yelled to get the attention of the third base player. The man turned, found them, smiled, waved back.

Dave looked around her. "Before he moved downtown, he used to hang out with us," he explained.

James nodded, somehow not surprised.

Rae sat down again, and James reached over to snag the drink she was waving around. "You're surprising me," he commented with a smile.

"Really? That's good," she replied, a twinkle in her eyes.

She leaned back and put her feet on the empty seat in front of her, picked up her binoculars again. They were five rows behind the White Sox bench; the binoculars were not really necessary.

It was a good day, with good company. Lace was somewhere, having disappeared to find nachos. Lace had hugged him when she saw him. The hug had hurt, but James had no intention of ever mentioning that, pleased to have her acknowledge without words what had happened. He had grinned when Lace had maneuvered them so Rae was sitting next to him.

James relaxed in the seat, stretching his legs out as best he could. The pain was moderate today, manageable.

They went out to eat after the game, an early dinner. Lace took them to a new Mexican place she had found. Rae, sitting in the seat beside him at the table, competed with him for the dish of hot sauce for the tortilla chips. "Rae, this is going to make your stomach a mess," James cautioned quietly.

She hesitated over a chip. "You're right. But I could be wrong about the problem. I'll risk it."

By the end of the meal, James could tell she was regretting the risk. Her face was pale and she had pulled back from the conversation.

"Dave, Lace, I hate to be the one to break up a party, but Rae and I have plans. We need to be going."

Rae looked at him, surprised, but didn't hesitate to take the silent offer, getting up and pushing back her chair.

"Stay and enjoy dessert," he told Lace and Dave, smiling at the surprised look on both their faces.

"Of course," Dave replied, smiling. "I'll pick up the tab for dinner, go enjoy the night."

"Thanks," James replied, wishing it really was what he was trying to imply.

"Date?" James saw Lace ask Rae silently.

Rae just smiled and picked up her handbag. James quietly moved back to let her precede him as they walked through the restaurant tables. She hesitated as they stepped outside, looked around the parking lot. James reached for her hand and was shocked to find how cold and clammy it was. He looked at her, alarmed.

He put his arm around her waist and walked her across the parking lot to his car.

"That was so stupid…"

He carefully tucked her into the passenger seat, clipped on her seat belt. He could hear the self-directed anger. "Relax, Rae. It was a mistake, not a crisis."

As he drove, she leaned her head back against the headrest, closed her eyes, fought to keep her stomach from cramping. James settled his hand across her clenched ones. "Don't forget to breathe, Rae."

She gave a tight laugh. "It hurts."

James's hand tightened. "I know."

He thought about stopping somewhere, a pharmacy, a drugstore, to find something that might help, but he didn't know where one would be in this area and the car ride was not helping her. Getting her home seemed more important. There were stores near her town house; he would get her settled in her own home, then swing back to the store to pick up something that might help her.

She had been quiet for too long, and her hands were damp with sweat. "Doing okay?"

"I feel awful," she replied softly, not opening her eyes.

James squeezed her hands, hurting for her.

He pulled into the drive at her town house behind her Lexus, came around to open the door for her. He watched her take a deep breath before she moved, and saw her wince as she stood.

"Where are your keys?"

She found them in her bag.

He unlocked the door, stepped inside and made a sweeping inspection to make sure the place looked undisturbed. "Do you have something or should I go down to the pharmacy?"

"Buy me some of that pink stuff if nothing else," she asked, grateful. She eased off her shoes. "I'm going to go lie down."

He carefully brushed her damp forehead with his hand. "I'll be back as quick as I can, Rae."

"Go on, I'm okay."

He gave a soft smile. "Sure you are."

He locked the door behind him, taking Rae's keys with him. Ten minutes later he was back at Rae's, unlocking the front door.

"Hey, lady," he called softly. She was not downstairs stretched out on the couch, so he walked quietly up the stairs.

The master bedroom was at the end of the landing, a large room, decorated in several shades of deep green and gold. A beautiful and neat room. Rae was lying on the comforter, curled up slightly, her knees pulled up.

"I brought you some stuff," James said, sitting down carefully beside her.

She opened her eyes cautiously. "Thank you." The words were barely a whisper.

James gently stroked her hair back. She looked so different from the lady in control he had come to know. He opened the sack and read directions, found the bottle that promised to act the quickest. "Let me get you something to drink to take this with."

"There's a glass in the bathroom."

James ran the tap until the water was cold, filled the glass.

"See if this helps."

She gratefully took the medication he offered, then lay back down. She was shivering. James reached over and caught hold of the end of the comforter, then folded it up around her to keep her warm.

"James, at the restaurant…how did you know?"

"You were turning the color of unsalted butter," he replied, smiling, glad to have her somewhere she could rest and recover.

"Thanks for what you did."

"Don't mention it," he replied gently. "Need some soda, something else to help?"

She shook her head. "I don't think I'll risk it."

She grew quiet and James sat beside her on the bed, idly smoothing her hair with his hand, watching her, thinking.

"I can't miss work tomorrow."

James hesitated. "You just took the medicine, Rae. In a couple of hours you will feel much better."

"Have to be," she replied, her voice slurring slightly as she grew drowsy.

"If something really bad happened and you couldn't go in to work, what would you do?"

"Dave has power of attorney, and Jack would step in, manage the accounts temporarily until I was back or Dave could arrange a more permanent situation."

She stirred restlessly. "Hot."

James pushed the comforter back. Within moments she was cold again.

"My stomach wants to be sick," she warned him, groaning suddenly as she coiled up again.

He rubbed her back.

"You'll survive," he replied, glad he had stayed, glad she had not made a big deal of his staying.

She was on her feet a few minutes later, staggering to the bathroom, waving him away. He ignored her wishes, staying with her to keep her hair back as she was violently sick. He handed her mouthwash and used a hand towel to gently wash her face.

He tucked a blanket around her shivering frame and sat with her on the bathroom floor, leaning against the wall. "You're off Mexican food for a while," he told her firmly, rubbing her icy hands briskly between his.

She was buried in the blanket, her head tucked against his chest. "Not a problem," she agreed with a weak laugh.

James hated seeing anyone sick, but it certainly was one way to get her to forget her normal reserve around him. When he let go of her hands, she curled them against his chest, gave a soft sigh.

James rested his arms around her waist and waited for her to feel better, to risk moving back to the bed to lie down. He liked having her in his arms.

"Going to sleep?" he asked, amused, when she was still leaning against him motionlessly several minutes later. She was almost limp.

He felt her relax at the amusement in his voice. "Hardly. Not on the bathroom floor. Although I have been known to drift off if I'm somewhere warm and comfortable. I don't care how good the movie is, chances are I'm going to fall asleep."

James tightened his arms and really considered kissing the top of her head. "I'll remember that."

"I like mushy movies." He could hear the amusement in her voice, and a yawn that cracked her jaw.

"Does this mean if I ask you on a date, you might say yes?"

"Depends on what, where and when," she finally replied.

"Tomorrow night, Shaw's, eight o'clock?"

"Day after. Eight o'clock is fine."

He smiled. "You've got a date."

She nodded. "Good."

They sat together in silence, Rae trying to drift off to sleep and James content to hold her and think. A few more minutes and he would urge her back to bed where she could rest in better comfort. For now, here was just fine.

She suddenly stiffened. "Let me up."

She jerked forward.

She was sick again.

He felt her spine ripple with the spasms. "Easy, Rae, easy. Don't fight it."

He was helpless other than supporting her weight. He hated this. There were tears running down her face now. He gently wiped them away, eased her back onto the floor when the worst was past.

Whatever medicine she had taken earlier had been lost, but he couldn't risk giving her more. She protested weakly when he eased her out of his arms, forgave him when a cold cloth pressed against her cheeks.

"Don't tell Dave about this. I'll never hear the end of it."

"I won't," he promised softly.

He eased her into bed twenty minutes later when it looked as if she were past the worst. She sank back into the covers, her eyes closed. A nightgown and the lights off would be a lot more conducive to rest, but he didn't intend to leave until she had more medicine and was clearly feeling better.

His own body was aching with the unforgiving costs of sitting on the floor. He pulled over the chair she had in the room, silently scanned the stack of books she had beside her bed. Most were medical texts, but he found a Spencer mystery and pulled it from the stack. It was a good book, but he read only a few pages at a time, as he quietly watched Rae, worried about her.

The picture beside her bed…*the ring*…held his attention for a long time. It was a beautiful ring, hanging from a ribbon looped over the picture frame.

What had it been like to be handed that ring after Leo had died, to have such a tangible indication of how much had been ripped away? Was it a comfort to have his picture, the ring in sight each night, or was it making it harder to let go and move on? He looked at the ring and back at Rae and felt slightly sick himself. She might say yes to a date, but she was a long way from stepping beyond the past.

God, what's the key to get past her pain? You know. Will You help me understand how to help her let go of the past? At least not make it worse?

Finally toward midnight, he got more medicine into her. She seemed to be feeling better.

He eased the covers around her, leaned down and gently kissed her forehead. "Call me in the morning, Rae."

Her eyes were serious when they locked with his. "Thank you, James."

He looked back, just as serious. "Good night, Rae," he finally said. He reached over and clicked off the light. "Sleep well."

He pulled her door partly shut, took the book with him downstairs. He didn't want to leave until the medication had a chance to work.

She had said yes. He wanted to smile, to feel the anticipation, but the impulse was tempered by the fact that he knew how careful he needed to be. He couldn't afford a mistake with Rae. She had a lot to deal with without him making a careless comment and making things worse. She was a beautiful lady, a wonderful friend, someone he wanted to get to know at a much deeper level. He couldn't afford a mistake.

He left for home about one-thirty, Rae sleeping peacefully, her face looking relaxed in the moonlight.

Did she really want to date James?

Rae eased back against the counter, sipping her coffee, considering the question. She was in her robe and slippers; the dawn was still just a twilight. It was a quarter past five. She had allowed herself to sleep in an extra half hour, hoping her stomach would remain settled. So far, she felt a little tentative, but she was still on her feet.

She didn't want to date him.

It was her gut reaction—a strong one—not wanting to risk being vulnerable, not wanting to risk letting someone really get to know her. She had been down this road before, let Leo get close. Love was a powerful thing that made life so full of joy. When you lost it... Rae didn't want to get hurt like that ever again.

Did she want to date James?

She didn't want to wake up alone for the rest of her life. She wanted someday to have a son, a daughter, someone to call her Mom. She wanted that.

To date James meant she had to risk getting hurt again.

Very rarely did she let herself think back to what the first year without Leo had been like. It was too painful, too raw, too black. She never wanted to experience that again. She didn't want to get near a situation like that ever again.

She rubbed her foot on the flooring, tracing a pattern in the tiles.

She didn't have a choice.

Of every man in her life, James was the only one she could see as potentially being her husband. She already had a crush on him, not that she would admit that to Lace. She liked him. She liked what he had done with his life, how he related to his family, who he was as a friend. She had been around him and she had been watching him. His faith and his actions were consistent with one another. His words and his actions were consistent. He would make a wonderful husband.

She was going to have to risk her heart—and hope and pray for the best.

"His car was still here at 1:00 a.m. It must have been quite a date."

Rae tried to reach the book she had just knocked behind the headboard. "Lace, it wasn't like you think." Her friend had shown up shortly after eight-thirty with a gallon of ice cream and a video they had not seen before, interrupting Rae in the middle of cleaning house.

Lace pulled yet another dress from the back of Rae's closet, considered it, and put it back with a slight shake of her head. "Oh, really? When are you seeing him again?"

Rae couldn't stop the blush.

"I thought so," Lace said, smiling. "When?"

"Tomorrow night," Rae finally admitted. "He's picking me up at eight."

"Casual or dressy?"

"Casual."

Lace went back to inspecting the contents of Rae's closet. "This might do," she finally decided, pulling out a green silk dress.

"That is not casual," Rae said.

"Casual means low heels, less jewelry. It is a simple dress that will go anywhere."

Rae bit her lip, considering. "Maybe, but only if I can wear my hair down."

"It looks beautiful down. Wear that gold necklace Dave gave you for your birthday, and maybe the bracelet from Leo."

Rae considered, then moved past Lace to look for shoes. "These?"

"Perfect. Where are you going?"

"Shaw's."

"Nice place."

Rae wished she had said no when he asked her. An actual date. Maybe she could plead still feeling ill.

No. She was not a coward, even if she felt like one. She had another day to get over her nerves.

"What did you and Dave do last night after we left?"

Rae was astounded to see Lace blush. "Lace?"

"We went to see a movie."

"That hardly explains that blush," Rae said, sitting down on the side of the bed. "Give."

Lace sighed and sank down on the bed beside her, picked up the bear Leo had given Rae. "He kissed me."

"Dave."

Lace nodded. Her expression was so morose, Rae didn't know what to think.

"And?"

"And we're going to mess up a great friendship. He doesn't have a settle-down bone in his entire body."

"That's all?"

Lace nodded.

"Thank goodness. I was afraid for a moment. I thought it was a bad kiss."

"It was a great kiss," Lace said, more depressed.

"Dave really does want to settle down, Lace. He's

just been kind of slow to realize that. He's been thinking about it lately, even thinking about having kids, if James is to be believed."

Lace visibly perked up. "Our Dave?"

Rae smiled. "One and the same."

"He could have mentioned that to me, the turkey."

Rae laughed. "We're suppose to be having a girls night, and here we are talking about guys. Come on, let's go watch that movie. I hear you need a box of tissues by the time it's over." She tugged Lace to her feet.

"Can I ask one more guy question?"

Rae hesitated. "Sure."

"James is a serious kind of guy, Rae. He isn't the type to date casually. Are you sure you know what you're doing? I don't want you to get hurt," Lace said softly.

"Lace, I'm scared to death that this is a mistake, but I said yes. I guess I'm going to find out."

"This house has the space you were looking for, James. And the yard. It needs work, but the structure is sound and the price is certainly right. I think you ought to buy it," Kevin concluded, standing on the drive and looking over the property again.

They had already been down in the crawl space, up in the attic, on the roof, done a detailed inspection. It was a good property.

"I'll think about it overnight, but I agree. This is the place." James looked over the house. His transition to the States was going to feel so finished the moment he bought a house. He would be settled here for the long-term. "You said the schools in the area are good?"

Kevin raised a single eyebrow at the question, but replied, "Excellent."

James nodded. He would be raising a family here, knowing about the schools was an important factor. The house had the room he would need to set up an office, let him resume work as an architect in a consulting capacity with Kevin. It had room for his wife to have a large office, and still leave bedrooms for children. There were some structural changes to be made—two walls would go when he remodeled—but it was a house with possibilities.

The yard needed work, but there was almost an acre of land. Plenty of room for kids to play.

What do You think, God? Is this the place to settle down and make a new start? It's certainly a wonderful place with great potential.

"You thinking about settling down in more ways than just buying a house?" Kevin asked.

James weighed how to answer. "Possibly," he hedged. He needed to get this bug back under control, work the pain out of his system again. He had done it once, he could do it again. He had been thinking a lot about a lady with twinkling blue eyes.

Kevin smiled. "Wonderful idea. I would act on it."

"I'm thinking about it," James replied, smiling.

She should have chosen a different dress. Rae turned one way and the next, trying to decide if this was really an acceptable choice. It was a beautiful dress. But she had bought it to wear to a concert with Leo. They had never gone, but still, it was a dress that had some history.

God, what do You think?

She had never been so nervous about a night in her life. At work it had been difficult, if not impossible to concentrate. The whole office had seemed to know that something was up.

God, I hope Your sense of humor holds. I'm probably going to need You to pull my foot out of my mouth a few times tonight.

She was blowing this out of proportion. It was a date, yes, but that was all it was. She needed to relax, quickly.

The doorbell rang, the chimes sounding throughout the house, and her muscles tensed. She forced them to relax.

She descended the steps, moved to the front door.

He stood in the doorway, relaxed and comfortable in dress slacks and a tailored shirt. "Hi."

It was the soft greeting, the relaxed way he smiled, that made her relax and smile back. "Hi, James."

"You look very nice tonight."

She blushed slightly, looked at the dress. "Thank you."

"Dave said roses and Lace said orchids, but I decided on something more unique." He picked up a bouquet of wildflowers from the rail. The flowers were delicate, fragile, the bouquet a riot of color.

She accepted them, touched by the thought and the attention he had paid to the detail. Every color of a rainbow was present. "They are lovely, James."

"They are flowers whose beauty will eventually fade, your beauty won't."

Flowers she had expected…the compliment she had not. "James…"

He grinned. "It took two days to come up with the line, but I haven't had much practice in the last six years. My delivery still needs a little practice."

She leaned against the doorjamb, grinned. "Oh, I don't know. You did pretty well."

He reached out and touched her hand. "Go find a vase for the flowers and let's get this night under way."

She joined him a few moments later, carrying a lace wrap should the night turn cool.

He locked the front door for her.

Rae walked with him down the drive, liking the attention as his hand touched the small of her back, the fact he matched his pace to hers. "Can I ask one question, if I then promise to drop the subject for the night?"

He opened the car door for her, smiled. "Somehow I think I would prefer to have you ask it now, than have this question in your mind for the evening," he replied. He walked around the car, slipped behind the wheel, turned the key in the ignition. When the car was running, he rested his hands across the steering wheel and turned toward her. "What's your question, Rae?"

"How bad is the pain today?"

He nodded, conceding it was a good question. "On a scale of one to ten, one being so bad I don't want to move, ten being I no longer notice any symptoms, today is about a six."

He pulled out of the drive and headed toward the restaurant. "Can I ask one question, if I promise to stay off the subject for the rest of the evening?"

Rae hesitated before nodding. "I suppose fair says you get at least one."

He chuckled. "Tell me about work."

"That's a complex question. Anything specific you would like to know?" she asked, looking at him. She saw him nod.

"Do you still like your job?"

Rae leaned her head back against the headrest. "I love the challenge. I love the fact I am good at turning data into a concrete conclusion. There are times I even think I may learn to like the trading. But I hate the hours. There has been no time for the book lately, and I really hate that."

"Tonight is taking time away that you could be using to write."

Rae was grateful that he understood the cost she had paid when she said yes. "Yes. But I don't regret my choice."

"I'll make the night worth it."

Rae smiled. "It already is."

They arrived at the restaurant.

Rae took her time looking over the menu. "Do you think baked trout would be safe?"

He grinned. "I would say that is a good choice."

Rae liked the evening with him, sharing a meal. He told her stories about Africa, stories from the days working with Kevin building their business. He made her laugh and it made the stress of the workday fade.

They lingered at the restaurant for almost two hours, enjoying the chance to talk together. When James finally suggested they should consider leaving, she agreed, knowing she needed to call it a night before it got much later, but regretting the ending of a wonderful evening.

"Would you like to see someplace special?" James asked her as she fastened her seat belt.

She looked over at him, surprised. "Sure."

He nodded. "It's not far."

He took them to an established neighborhood a couple miles from her own home, where the trees were ancient and the houses set back on large plots of land. He drew to a stop in front of a two-story house, put the car in park.

Rae looked around with interest.

"My new place," James said quietly.

She turned to look at him. "Really?" He had bought a house? She looked back at the place. He had bought a place. A deep spot of uncertainty inside her dissolved. She had been afraid he might end up settling in a different city, with a different job. He had bought a house. This was good.

He smiled at her surprise. "Come on, I'll show it to you," he offered, turning off the engine.

Rae slipped out of the car.

It was a beautiful home. James had arranged to have the key and he opened the front door for her, gave her a guided tour, pointing out the structural changes he planned to make. Rae wandered around behind him, enjoying listening to James in his element, the house having replaced his discouragement with something positive.

They walked back to the car, James quiet and Rae enjoying the beautiful night.

It was eleven o'clock when James escorted her up the walk to her own front door. "I'm sorry I made it such a late night for you."

Rae leaned against the doorpost, not entirely ready to say good-night yet. "I'm not. I had a good time, James."

He rocked back on his heels, smiling. "So did I. Would you like to do it again?"

Rae considered the offer. "Would you like to come over for a movie Thursday night?"

He smiled at her. "You go to sleep with a movie."

"Only with guys I like."

He grinned. "What do you say I pick out the movie?"

"I like this plan."

"Say eight o'clock again? I'll bring dinner?"

"Deal." She smiled and reached forward, touched his hand. "Thank you, James."

His hand turned over and gently grasped hers. "Have a good night, Rae."

Chapter Eight

The ground was soft; it had rained during the night. Rae's heels sank into the grass as she crossed the landscaped grounds.

"Hi, Leo." She carefully settled on the bench near his headstone. "I've missed you."

It was a weekday morning, at an hour she should have been at the office. Instead she was at a cemetery, her beeper on, her cellular phone in her purse, trying to shake off the effects of a rough night of no sleep.

"I'm scared, Leo, and I don't know why."

The dreams had been nice, at first. She had been with James, she had been happy, she had been in the house she had visited, but the dreams had always ended with her being abandoned.

She sighed, and looked over the grounds, looked up at the beautiful sky. There were no answers to find here. She had thought the dreams reflected what she was still feeling from Leo's death, but she had been wrong. It was peaceful here today; there was sadness, but the grief was gone.

The grief had moved on without her realizing it.

The trip here had been worth that much at least. It was an hour's drive. She rarely came, instinctively knowing it was better to let the memories fade.

The troubled sleep did not originate from here.

The car ride back to the office was made with her thoughts deep in options. To think ahead for months at a time, to consider options, was part of both her personality and her training. She had some serious issues to resolve.

She was dating James. It had been one date so far, but he was buying a house nearby. Lace had read him right, he was not a man to date casually. The next several months were going to see a relationship being developed. Did she want that?

Yes. She had made that decision the night she had agreed to the first date.

A relationship meant time.

She still had a book to write. That book mattered to her, more than any of her friends understood.

No matter which way she laid out her schedule, she simply did not have enough time to do her job, write a book, and get to know James. Something simply had to give.

The job.

She had to find a partner. She had to. It was that, or sell the business.

James was early.

Rae descended the steps quickly, paused at the bottom of the stairs, took a few deep breaths, trying to make her anticipation less obvious. She flipped the locks on the door.

"Hi." She was past the point of being nervous. She had missed him.

"Hi, lady."

His smile made her feel so good inside.

She held the door for him as he had his hands full. Something smelled wonderful.

"Mom was making Italian, so I brought us home-made ravioli."

Rae settled her hand on his arm and liked the strength she felt. She looked into the sack. "Cheese-cake?"

"Homemade, too."

"You can bring dinner over whenever you would like."

He laughed. "Come on, let's eat while it's still hot."

Rae had struggled with how to set the table. She had wanted it to look nice, but not overly romantic. It was dinner and a movie. She had compromised with elegant placemats and her bouquet of flowers as the centerpiece.

James unpacked the sack. Salad, strawberries, ravioli, homemade rolls, cheesecake.

James told her about progress on the house purchase as they ate, and Rae told him about her day, glossing over the stress. It was a comfortable conversation, but it was impersonal, leaving Rae feeling slightly discontent.

They moved to the living room after dinner, James taking the remaining strawberries with them.

Rae hesitated for a moment, then chose the couch, pushing the coffee table out with her foot so she could sink down in the cushions and use the table as a footrest. "What movie did you end up choosing?"

He slipped it into the VCR, and used the remote to

click on the television, set the volume. "An old one. A mushy one."

She blinked, surprised. "You got a mushy movie?"

He chuckled at her expression, nudged her over to free a pillow, sat down beside her. "It's a date, Rae. Mushy is good planning on my part."

"If it had not been a date?"

He stretched his legs out and grinned. "A Western, definitely."

Rae leaned against his shoulder. "I like Westerns, too," she whispered.

"Do you?"

"Anything but horror," she confirmed.

His hand gently brushed through her hair. She loved being this close to him, able to see the expression in his eyes, feel his chest rise and fall under her hand. The movie came on, interrupting the moment. She didn't move away; instead, settled against him. His arm slipped around her. His hand captured hers.

It was a love story.

Partway through the movie, Rae shifted to rest her head against his chest, snuggle her hands against his shirt, relax further as she watched, captivated by the story.

James's hand gently stroked her hair.

It was a movie that required a box of tissues.

She was crying toward the end but had no desire to disturb the pleasure of the moment with James. She was supremely comfortable, tucked in his arms.

James grabbed the tissue box and gently wiped her wet cheeks.

When it was over, she dropped her head down against his chest, hiding her face. "Next time, don't get a mushy movie. I look awful when I cry," she said, laughing, as she tried to wipe away the damage.

James settled her against him. He studied her face seriously, smiled gently. "I think you look okay to me."

"You're being kind."

His hands brushed her cheeks dry. "No, I'm not," he said simply.

Rae eased her hands to his shoulders. "James."

"Hmm?" He drew her closer.

"Isn't this going pretty fast for a second date?"

"I've wanted to kiss you for about twelve weeks now, it feels kind of slow to me," he replied with a slow smile.

She blushed softly. "Really?"

He grinned. "Quit fishing for a compliment."

If she leaned forward even a little, they would be kissing. She wanted to kiss him too much to let herself do it.

She dropped her gaze. She wasn't used to this emotion.

"We need to take a walk," James said abruptly.

It took Rae a few moments to remember how to breathe again. He got up and held out his hand and she had to shake her head a couple of times to clear it before she could focus on his hand and accept it.

She steadied herself with a hand braced against his forearm. "A walk is a real good idea. Where are my shoes?"

Having him tie her tennis shoe laces helped break some of the tension inside her, the cool air outside helped finish the task.

James put his arm around her shoulders as they began walking down the block. Rae took advantage of the opportunity to tuck herself as close to him as she could get.

"It would have been quite a kiss," she offered, teasing softly.

He laughed. "Oh yeah, it would have been quite a kiss."

She wanted this relationship to progress. The realization made her shiver. Her mind was thinking marriage and children. It was too much transition. Fifteen weeks ago she had been grieving over Leo, thinking her life was over, and now she was at this point with another man.

She eased slightly away from him. "It's been almost two years since I kissed a guy."

"Try six years since I really kissed a lady," James replied. He let her ease away, but kept hold of her hand. "I think we would be wise to avoid the situation for a while."

They walked together in silence. Rae felt herself begin to relax again. Nothing had changed, not really. They were dating. They were both going to have to decide how serious they wanted the relationship to be, where it was heading, how fast it was going to move. It was good to know the potential for a lot more than just friendship was there.

"Rae?"

"Hmm?"

"Can I ask you a tough question?"

She turned and looked up at him, saw how serious he was. "Sure."

"Were you and Leo planning to have kids?"

Rae felt the wistfulness well back inside. "Yes," she whispered, looking out at the night. "At least three. He liked the idea of a big family."

James squeezed her hand. "I didn't mean to touch a raw memory."

"That's okay. We were planning it all, the house, the kids, the dog."

He tucked his arm around her again, pulling her close. "Tell me to butt out if you don't want to talk about this."

She nodded. "What do you want to know?"

"Has the anger faded?"

"At Leo?"

"And God."

Rae considered it as they walked. "Mostly. It's just a profound sense of disappointment that lingers now, that the dreams and plans ended so abruptly. How are you doing with losing Africa?"

"Resigned. There's nothing short of a miracle cure that can bring it back."

The silence stretched between them. Rae wished they were further along in the relationship so that she didn't feel so...awkward. She wanted to know what he thought about getting married, having kids...not necessarily with her, but in general, she told herself as she bit her bottom lip.

"What?" He sounded amused.

She looked up at him, this man she had dreamed about, had decided to let past her reserves to say yes to a date, to say yes to possibly a lot more. He was smiling at her.

"What question is circling around in that mind of yours, wanting to be asked?"

She blushed.

His expression grew serious and gentle. He brushed her cheek with a finger. "It's okay. Ask."

"Did you buy that house planning to have children?"

"Four," he replied, smiling. "At least two adopted. I've got a wallet full of snapshots of children, I want a few of my own to add to the collection."

"Four."

James tugged her hair lightly. "My wife will have a little say, of course."

"That's kind of necessary," Rae reminded him, grinning. So what if it was only a second date? Nothing had been conventional in her life or in their relationship to this point. She might as well ask the questions she would like to have answers to. "What's your ideal honeymoon?"

Her question amused him. "That's a tough one." He thought for a moment. "Three weeks. Somewhere with a private beach, a lot of sun. Maybe Maui."

"Wedding?"

"Big."

"Ten-year anniversary gift?"

"Rae..."

"I'm curious."

"My wife would learn to play golf."

It was such a specific answer that Rae couldn't help but laugh. "You play?"

"Not yet. If I get married, I figure I'll learn."

"No more questions?" James asked after a moment. "No."

He tugged her to a stop. They were in the shadows of a tall oak, moonlight flickering between the leaves. "Then I have a question for you."

Rae looked up at him.

"Can I kiss you?" he asked, seriously.

There was nothing she would like more. "I'm not

so sure it would be a good idea," she found herself replying.

He linked his arms around her, bringing her close. "Just one kiss?"

She reluctantly nodded. She wanted to kiss him, to find out if it would be as special as she imagined it might be. She eased herself forward, her arms resting on his shoulders.

The kiss was gentle, soft, careful. It made her more vulnerable than she had been in two years. She was letting him inside her heart. It made her tremble under his hands.

He broke the kiss off before it could progress. "Kissing is going to be a problem."

"We could not do it again," she felt honor bound to offer. She was still trying to sort out the emotions, how much she had enjoyed that kiss.

He hugged her.

"Rationing. One kiss per date. We might survive."

She leaned against him and returned the hug. "Come over tomorrow."

They both laughed.

"Come on, lady. It's late. You've got to go to work in a few hours. It's time I took you home."

Rae reluctantly let him start them walking again. After they reached her town house, it took only a couple of minutes for the movie to be rewound, the dishes from dinner to be repacked.

Rae stood in the doorway after James stepped out onto the porch, the sack balanced in his hand.

"I'm not going to do more than simply say goodnight," he cautioned, even as he stepped closer.

"That's wise," Rae agreed.

"Do you feel like the rug just got pulled out from under your feet?"

It was nice to know she wasn't the only one.... "Yanked out," she clarified.

"What do you want to do about it?"

He was so close she could touch his face if she only raised her hand. "Take it one day at a time," she replied softly, wisely.

He leaned down and gently kissed her cheek. "Good answer, Rae. You like sandwiches?"

She blinked at the change of subject. "Sure."

"I'll bring lunch tomorrow if you can get twenty minutes away. Your complex has a pond, ducks, and a park bench."

Her smile lit up her face. "Thanks."

He smiled back. His free hand gently stroked her cheek. "Tell me to go home, I'm in trouble here."

Her hands gently touched his shirt. She took a deep breath and pushed him a step away. "Go home."

He stepped back, made it two steps down the walk before he turned. "Rae?"

She hadn't moved, didn't have the strength or the will. "Yeah?"

"Sweet dreams."

Her face tensed.

"What?" He came partway back.

She forced her smile. "Nothing. I'll dream sweet dreams," she promised. "I'll see you tomorrow, James."

He hesitated. "Good night, then."

"Good night."

"The duck on the end looks annoyed."

Rae bit into the center of her sandwich, trying to

keep the inch-high stack of condiments from falling off. She was near the end and it was becoming an adventure to eat. "You would be, too, if your wife was flirting with another guy," she remarked when she could speak again. "That's Bradley. His wife is the one in front flirting with the mallard."

"You've got them all named."

She finished the sandwich. "The same ducks have been coming back here for years."

James shifted his arm across the back of the bench. Rae took advantage of the situation to lean her head back. "Thanks for lunch."

He smiled. "My pleasure."

"You look tired."

"You don't," he replied with a grin. "In fact, I would suggest you might have overdone the caffeine this morning. You're...perky."

She pushed him in the ribs with her free hand. "I'll give you 'perky.' And quit ducking my question."

He laughed at her pun.

"Ohh." She gave up and joined him, his laughter contagious.

"I didn't sleep because I was busy thinking," he told her when his laughter died down.

"Serious thinking?"

"Hmm. Got a question for you."

She rested a hand on his chest. "Oh, boy. Another question. Am I going to like it?"

He grinned. "Well, it took me several hours to phrase it, so you should."

She ducked her head against his chest. "Ask."

He rubbed her shoulders.

"You're not asking..." she said with a chuckle.

"Forgot the question. You're distracting, lady."

She sat back up, laughing. She hadn't felt this light-hearted in ages.

"I think we can safely say we are past the preliminaries in this dating adventure, wouldn't you agree?"

She thought about it carefully. "Yes," she said with a decisive nod.

He tickled her for that exaggeration. "Here's my question."

She was still laughing. She struggled to get serious. "Okay."

"This is a really important question," he reminded her, waiting until she nodded. "Will you…" He paused. "This is a really important question, Rae," he reminded her.

She tried to stifle the giggle. "Okay, okay. Ask."

"Rae, will you…help me pick out the wallpaper for the kitchen?"

She blinked at him. "Wallpaper."

He nodded, his expression serious. "Wallpaper."

She giggled. "I could probably do that."

"Will you help me hang it?"

"Only if you buy the brush-with-water kind. I'm dangerous with paste."

"Important point," he agreed. "Wallpaper with self-stick adhesive."

"I'm not very good at vertical stripes."

"I am," he replied smugly.

She was laughing so hard she was having a hard time catching her breath. "James, you spent last night thinking about your house?"

"I wouldn't want you to think I spent it just thinking about you."

"That wouldn't do," she agreed, solemnly.

She reluctantly checked her watch. "I've got to go back to work."

He gently brushed her hair back from her face. "Thanks for lunch."

She grinned. "I loved lunch."

"Come here," he whispered, tugging her toward him.

Her hands came to rest against his chest.

He kissed her, softly, gently. "Go back to work. Think about me occasionally."

She reluctantly got to her feet. "If I think about you, I won't get any work done."

He quirked one eyebrow with his smile. "Your concentration is that distractible?"

"I think I will plead the fifth," she replied with a smile, reluctantly slipping her hand from his. "See you later."

"I'm sure you will."

"Dave, the paint is supposed to be on the porch, not on me," Rae protested, tugging the sleeve of her shirt around to check out the latest white splotch.

"Sorry."

She gave a resigned sigh. "Sure you are."

There were footsteps behind them. "Aren't you two done yet?"

"Lace, you stuck me with someone who bites the tip of her tongue when she paints and who insists we leave no brush strokes visible anywhere. We are still going to be painting this porch next week."

Lace laughed and tweaked Dave's collar. "Did you know you've got a white handprint on your back?"

"Rae!"

She shrugged, even as she grinned. "Sorry."

"Would you two children like to come and eat? The pizza is here," James announced from the doorway. He and Kevin had been plastering the new wall they had built after tearing down two others.

Rae looked up from where she sat on the porch. "Sounds good to me."

"Feed her, James, please. She's driving me nuts."

James laughed and offered his hand to Rae, pulled her to her feet. "Hold it." He rescued her ponytail from shifting through the wet paint on her T-shirt. He tugged his baseball cap off and tucked her hair up in it. Grinned. "Okay, you're safe now."

"Dave should not be allowed to have a paintbrush."

James turned her around to inspect what had once been a pair of blue jeans and a hockey T-shirt. "Rae, you sat in wet paint?"

She glared at her friend. "He lied."

"I only said the step was going to need painting again. It did. You sat in it," Dave explained.

"I was naive this morning," Rae told James.

James tried to hide a smile. "Apparently."

"You're supposed to be on my side," she protested, seeing the smile.

He leaned down and kissed her paint-freckled nose. "I am." He tugged her hand. "Come on, let's eat."

Rae sat beside James on the backyard deck sharing pizza off his plate, sitting as close to him as she could get on the stoop. It had been nice, spending the last three weeks dating him. If she had to put it in one word, the last three weeks had been...*fun. Wonderful* was a good word. Or maybe the word she should choose would be *cautious.* No. Neither one of them were being cautious, per se, they both knew where they were heading, though they were taking their time.

One of these days she was going to admit to herself she was falling in love again. One of these days...

"I'm glad you came."

Rae smiled. "So am I." She lifted his soda can.

"Rae—" Lace pushed open the patio door "—come settle this debate. Dave insists I've got this striped wallpaper upside down. It doesn't have an up or down."

James smiled. "Go." He watched Rae head inside to settle the debate between her friends. He loved being around them, their laughter and their jokes, their teasing. A day with all of them meant a lot of inevitable laughter.

He was in love with Rae. In the last three weeks, any doubt about that had been removed. He loved her. He loved the way she looked, the way she smiled, the way she moved, the way she liked to snuggle, her confidence, her willingness to look at something that needed to be done and not shirk back, her willingness to give of herself to her employees, her clients, her friends—even at a personal cost. James could understand now why Leo had been so firm about making sure Rae had time to work on her book. Rae would give herself away and leave no time for herself.

James finished the soda.

They had some major issues to sort out. She needed time to think through what she wanted to do about her work. He wished he could solve the dilemma, find her a partner, but after several long talks with Dave, he better understood the obstacles she was dealing with. He couldn't add the pressure of an engagement to what she was already struggling with.

A few more weeks of time. It was the best gift he could give her right now.

She was going to say yes. He could read that in her eyes when he kissed her.

She was going to make a wonderful wife.

He carefully rubbed his left wrist. He was back to about an eight on his ten-point scale. A few more days, and even the stiffness should be gone.

He owed Rae some dance lessons.

"Rae, are you sure I can't get you something? A sandwich? A bagel?"

Rae shifted from where she was stretched out on Lace's couch, turned to look over at her friend. "Thanks, Lace, but really, I'm fine."

It was a quarter past eight on a Thursday night. At the office, Rae had looked at the clock, decided enough was enough, and tossed the work into her briefcase. The briefcase was sitting in the front seat of her car now, would eventually get opened. The conference call was for 7:00 a.m. She still had eleven hours to get the work done, get some sleep. She would manage. "I like your dog." The little dog was curled up on Rae's chest, loving the attention.

"It looks like Tiger likes you, as well." Lace sat down in the chair. "You need to get a dog."

"Someday," Rae agreed. "What time is your flight to New York?"

"Six a.m. I'm on the return flight at two."

"That means you will get to see the airport, the inside of a cab, and the law offices of Glitchard, Pratt and Walford."

"Basically."

Rae struggled to hold a yawn back. Lying down was reinforcing how tired she was. Work was under control for a change, but it was costing her a lot of sleep.

"Rae, are you really thinking about getting married?"

The question caught Rae off guard. "Why do you say that?"

"Little things. The way you smile when you're with James."

Rae bit her bottom lip. "I've been thinking about it," she finally admitted. "It's scary, Lace. I let Leo get so close, and then I lost him. What if something happens to James?"

"Are you really worried about that? Losing James?"

"I don't know. It's not like I think he will die in an accident like Leo did. It's more my cautious side putting up a reason to not let the relationship go any further."

They both grew quiet.

"I don't know if I could handle getting married. It changes your life so much," Lace finally said.

"I don't mind being single, but I've been single for a long time. I'm ready to change that. I still want kids, Lace."

Lace smiled. "A Sunday morning in the nursery makes that pretty clear. You're right. It's one thing to be single for ten years. It's another to think about being single for your lifetime." Lace slid over a footstool. "James will make a good husband, Rae."

Rae moved the dog so he would not tumble off. "Probably. I don't know if I'm as cut out to be a wife though."

"What bothers you about being a wife?"

"His expectations. Leo knew me before he fell in love with me. He knew the reality of who I was and who I was never going to be. James—I'm worried that he sees what he wants to see. You know me, Lace. You know how focused I get at work. You know what I think about decorating, and keeping house and cooking. I'm worried about the little things that James doesn't consider a problem now being a big deal after we have been married five years."

"You have to learn how to be married. You both will. I'm sure there are things about James that will bug you the same way in five years."

"Really? What? That's my problem. The guy is too perfect. He likes his mom. He's reliable, honest, kind. He knows where he is going. He is good at his job. He thinks for himself. It's kind of scary."

Lace laughed. "Oh, Rae. You have got it bad."

"Change the subject. I'm getting nervous just thinking about it. Can you imagine what the first week of the marriage would be like? What every meal would be like?"

"Let him teach you to cook. In five years, you should have the basics down."

Rae grimaced. "Thanks a lot, friend."

"Have you decided what you are going to wear tomorrow night for our night out with the guys?"

Dave and James were taking them out for dinner, then dancing. "No. What are you going to wear?"

"Probably the blue silk. Why don't you wear the black dress? I'll loan you my short black velvet jacket."

"It is a beautiful dress." It was one of her favorite outfits.

"Dave made dinner reservations for seven-thirty?"

"Yes. Will you have time to get ready, given your flight schedule?"

"As long as the flight is not delayed, I'll be fine."

* * *

James was early.

Rae hurried to gather her clutch purse and shoes, carried them with her as she went downstairs.

"We should have done this a long time ago," James finally said after a slow appraisal of her, his expression one of frank appreciation.

Rae couldn't control the blush. She stepped back as he came inside. "I'm glad you like it," she replied, smiling, trying to keep her voice light. She had never been very good at the emotional interplay and she was on uncomfortable ground, immensely glad he appreciated her appearance, at the same time flustered by the frank attention.

James reached out and caught her hand, drew her toward him. "I think…"

When he didn't finish his sentence, she looked up. His eyes were studying her face, waiting for that movement. He smiled, his hand reaching up to caress her cheek. "…that we should start this evening with a kiss."

She suddenly grinned.

She liked being close to him. She could see the laughter and the love in his eyes. It was okay to be a little nervous. It didn't last. She stepped forward a little so she could lean against him. "Do you really?" she asked, tilting her head back to watch him.

His hands locked behind her waist. "I do."

She paused to consider the offer. "I like the idea…."

He smiled. "But?"

"It's going to be really hard to keep my mind on dinner and dancing if every time I look at you tonight, I'm remembering this kiss," she replied, answering his smile.

"I can fix that."

"Really?"

He nodded. "Close your eyes."

She giggled; she couldn't help it. "James."

"I'm not letting you go until I get this kiss," he remarked.

Rae thought about it and quietly closed her eyes. She could feel him lean down. Ready for the kiss, she held perfectly still...and the kiss didn't come.

She opened her eyelashes a fraction.

He was waiting for her to do just that. He smiled and swiftly kissed her. She loved this man so much.

His forehead rested against hers. "We need to go eat." His voice was reluctant.

"Hmm." Rae sighed and slowly stepped back, knowing he was right.

James tweaked a lock of her hair. "Do you have a wrap? It's chilly tonight."

Rae stepped into the living room where she had a coat that went with the dress.

James held it for her as she slipped it on.

His attention to the details, locking the door for her, walking beside her to the car, holding her door for her, were noticed and appreciated. He did it naturally, and the attention meant a great deal to Rae.

"Where did you and Dave decide on for dinner?"

"Tobias House. It is quiet, elegant, but still has a really good steak."

Rae chuckled. "Okay. I can tell where your priorities are."

"I was working on the upstairs guest room today, I'm ready for a good meal."

"You got the window replaced?"

"Just about. Since we had to open up the wall already to put in the larger window, we decided to go ahead and move some of the electrical wiring, put in more insulation. Another day, and the guest room will be finished."

"The house is almost done."

James smiled. "Just needs a woman's decorative touch," he agreed.

Rae decided not to touch that comment. They were heading somewhere; she just wasn't sure how ready she was for the next step. It was hard enough admitting to herself how deeply she had fallen in love with him. That knowledge should be filling her with joy. It was, but it also felt a little scary.

James reached over and gently touched the bottom lip she was biting. "Don't. We've got all the time in the world, Rae. I'm not suggesting anything."

She stopped the unconscious gesture. "I know, James. It just feels really big sometimes, this relationship."

He clicked on the right turn signal. "I know what you mean. It's scary from my side, too."

She turned to look at him, surprised. "Really?"

"Really. I got a surprise with you, Rae. I wasn't expecting to come back to the States to stay, let alone find you. I like to plan my life, and I wasn't planning this."

Rae leaned her head against the seat headrest and smiled. "We're even, then. I wasn't expecting to meet you, either."

James laughed, reached over to pull her hand into his. "Don't get me wrong, Rae. Now that I've found you, I have no intention of letting you go."

"I think that's one of the sweetest things you've ever said to me."

He raised their linked hands and kissed the back of her wrist. "Just don't tell Dave that, he already thinks I'm way too mushy. Lace wants him to follow suit."

Rae laughed. "I'm sure he told you to be on your best behavior tonight, didn't he?"

"Why do you think I wanted to get the kiss in before we joined them?"

Dave and Lace had not yet arrived at the restaurant, so James and Rae requested their table and went on in to be seated.

The restaurant had subdued lighting, white linen tablecloths, romantic music. "I can't believe I've never been here before," Rae remarked, accepting the cloth-covered menu.

"It is a really nice place," James agreed, glancing around.

They agreed on an appetizer plate, went ahead and ordered soft drinks.

"How is Patricia doing?"

"Fine. Eager to have a baby in the house again. She started decorating the nursery this last week."

"She's feeling okay?"

James nodded. "Seems to be. She's still very active."

"Are you looking forward to having another niece or nephew?"

"Definitely. I used to babysit Emily."

"You did?"

"I like that stage where they are just learning to walk. Every day you would get surprised with the latest hurdle they had mastered. One day she couldn't walk, and the next day, there she is, on her feet and wobbling across the room. It was great."

"I like that age with the kids in the nursery, too. They change from being infants to toddlers almost overnight."

Dave and Lace arrived with apologies for being late, and the conversation shifted to greetings. They looked adorable as a couple, Rae decided, watching as Dave held the chair for Lace, leaned down to whisper something to her. Lace looked flushed, the apologies had been a little overblown. They had probably been stealing a couple moments together before coming into the restaurant. James had apparently reached the same conclusion, because his greetings to Dave were accompanied by a slightly raised eyebrow.

Dave sat down beside Lace. "We got detained," he said simply, choosing not to go further. "Have you already ordered?"

A trip to the ladies' room would have to be engineered, Rae decided. Lace was in love. It had her confused, and off balance, but Lace was most certainly in love.

Rae took pity on her and ensured the next ten minutes of conversation were focused on Dave and how the case he was defending was coming along. It put the evening back on the normal casual friendship tone for all of them. They ate dinner talking, laughing together, as four old friends, not as two couples.

It had been a wise move to make. When dinner reached the dessert stage, Rae felt as if she had finally relaxed. She caught James watching her a few times during the meal, shared a private smile with him, but otherwise the tone stayed in neutral territory.

It was Lace who suggested where they should go dancing, a club that was known for its good blues. The place was typically busy, but not packed on a Friday night. Her suggestion was readily adopted.

Rae indicated she was going to stop at the ladies' room before they left and Lace joined her.

They were fixing their makeup when Rae finally decided to broach the subject. "What happened before dinner?"

"He wants me to go with him to a dinner party being hosted by one of the firm's senior partners."

"That's big."

"That's huge. They don't like the idea of having a senior partner who is single. That's the only reason they are throwing the party, to see who Dave will shake out of the woodwork to bring."

Rae understood. Lace didn't like being considered a solution to Dave's problem. Rae was blotting her lipstick when she had a brilliant idea. "Why don't you accept that job offer from Olsen, Richmond, and Quinn? There is no way Dave would take the member of a rival firm to a party thrown by a senior partner unless he cared more about you than he did about what the other senior partners thought."

Lace paused, touching up her blush. "That would be devious and underhanded." She was smiling even as she said it. "I couldn't do that."

Rae picked up her clutch bag. "I know you couldn't. You're in love. But the thought does makes the situation seem more palatable."

Lace chuckled. "I think I'll be more direct. It will cost him that watercolor painting I found at the gallery last week."

"Bribery works well," Rae agreed, smiling. Her friend looked good, being in love. It made her eyes glow. Rae wondered if she had the same expression, hoped hers was a little more contained. "Are you glad you came tonight?"

Lace smiled. "Yes. I like having Dave know he has to act like a gentleman. He even brought me flowers."

James made a point of taking hold of Rae's hand when they reached the club. They walked across the parking lot to join Dave and Lace. He liked holding her hand. She was his date, and he didn't intend to leave that to anyone's interpretation. She willingly interlaced her fingers with his.

Dave had his arm around Lace's waist.

As they opened the door to the club, the music drifted out into the night. Stepping inside was like entering a contained world, the music, the lights, the large group of people, most on the dance floor, some sitting at tables grouped along the walls.

They checked the ladies' coats, and Dave scanned the room for a table. "Over here."

James kept his hand on the small of Rae's back as they followed Dave and Lace through the crowd. It was a beautiful room, decorated in cherry wood, polished gold fixtures, and an abundance of greenery. The tables were packed close together and they stepped to the side several times as waitresses and other guests moved through the same small aisle.

Dave had found a table on the raised-floor platform, near the band. James held Rae's chair as she took her seat, let his hands gently squeeze her shoulders before pulling out the chair beside her.

"Would anyone like something to drink?" Dave asked, catching the eye of a waitress.

"A ginger ale," Lace requested, scanning the room to see if she knew anyone present.

"Diet soda," Rae replied.

"Make it two," James agreed. "Rae, shall we check out the dance floor?" They could sit and talk or they could dance. James would prefer to dance. She had gone tense as they walked to the table; the fastest way to ease her apprehension was to show her she would do fine.

She wanted to decline, but he held out his hand, smiling, and she conceded, putting her hand in his. "Sure."

He had yet to figure out what perfume she was wearing, but he liked it. He liked it a lot. She had brushed her long hair back and secured it with a gold clasp, the pattern in the clasp shining under the lights as they walked down to the dance floor.

James paused at the edge of the floor, gently caught both her hands to turn her toward him. She had such a beautiful face. He thought about kissing her but instead simply smiled. "Why don't you show me what you know?"

His request made her smile, her eyes reflecting her laughter. Her hands rested softly on his shoulders. "I suppose that would be a good place to start," she agreed demurely.

James settled his hands on her waist with a smile. "Concentrate on where you place those high heels, Rae."

She chuckled. "Okay, teach me how to dance, I'll leave you alone."

James laughed and willingly moved them onto the dance floor.

She fit in his arms, followed his lead, obviously loved to dance, her problem was more a lack of confidence than skill. He solved that problem by keeping her totally distracted. They managed two songs before he couldn't resist leaning down to kiss her. "You are doing great."

He loved her smile.

They spent two hours at the club. It was an evening that James was reluctant to see come to an end, but eventually out of courtesy to Rae—he knew how long her week had been—he suggested they call it an evening.

Rae slipped off her shoes as she watched James's car pull out of her driveway. It had been hard to say good-night. She loved being with him, loved being near him. He had stopped at the front door, kissed her good-night, and quietly said thank-you for a wonderful evening. Rae had echoed his sentiments.

Church Sunday and the chance to sit with him was too far away.

She took off the velvet jacket and the dress with care. It had been the perfect choice for an outfit. She smiled as she took off her makeup. James had liked it.

She was tired, a deep tiredness that had settled on her as James drove her home. She longed for bed and the chance to sleep until her body decided to wake up.

Leo's picture on her nightstand made her pause. She picked it up, carefully slid off the ribbon and the ring. Her smile in the picture was of a woman in love. She had seen that smile again tonight, a few minutes ago, as she washed off her makeup. She was in love with James. The same kind of love she had felt for Leo.

Her finger gently traced over the glass.

She was ready to move on. The past was behind her. She thought about it for a moment, then carried the picture with her to the drawer where she kept her mother's diaries, gently set Leo's picture there.

The ring. She closed her hand around it, feeling the cool metal, the beautiful diamond; she put the ring with her mother's wedding ring.

The past was closed.

Chapter Nine

"What's wrong?"

James instantly masked the pain. He hadn't heard Rae come back into the room. He had moved to get up from the plush couch and the pain in his hips and knees had brought tears to his eyes. "Nothing. I've been sitting too long," he said, dismissing whatever she had seen.

She handed him the drink she had brought for him. It was a sign of how hard her day had been that in the dim room she didn't realize he was lying. She dropped down on the couch beside him. He had only a few seconds' warning to clench his jaw against the motion. What has seemed mild three hours ago had become agonizing pain now. It was so bad, even holding the glass of soda she had brought him hurt.

They were at Dave's, the movie paused yet again, this time while Dave answered a call. Rae had arrived late and had been interrupted by six pages during the past two hours. She rested beside him now, her head back, her eyes closed, and he could feel the weariness enveloping her. The weariness was one reason he was doing his best to shield her from what was happening again, the return of the pain.

"Go home and get some sleep, Rae. You don't need to be here." She looked as if she had barely slept in the last three days.

"Dave's got trust papers being delivered here tonight that I need for tomorrow," she replied, too weary to open her eyes. "I'm sorry, James. I'm lousy company tonight."

He gently brushed her hair back from her face. "Rae, quit apologizing for the markets tumbling. I know how hard you've been working lately."

"I've never lost so much money so fast in my life. Why Taiwan and China had to go at it this month, of all months..." She struggled to open her eyes. "If I sit here, I'm going to fall asleep, and then I'll be groggy for the drive home, and end up being a danger to everyone around me. Maybe Dave can bring the papers by my place in the morning."

"Of course I can," Dave agreed, coming back into the room. "Go home, Rae. And turn off the pager for six hours. You need some uninterrupted sleep."

She raised herself tiredly to her feet, her hand on James's arm, leaned over to quietly kiss him goodnight. "Sorry," she whispered. "I need to get some sleep."

"Go. Drive carefully."

"It's two miles. I'll call when I get home."

He kissed her back, hating to see the exhaustion in her eyes. "I'll be waiting for the call."

Dave walked with her to the door, making arrangements for the morning.

James winced when Dave came back, turned the room lights back up. "Okay, what's going on? Rae put her hand on your arm for leverage and you went white as a sheet."

"Quit being a lawyer, Dave, and get me some aspirin."

He crossed the room. "Can you even get to your feet?"

James laughed, ironically. "Dave, I can't reach forward to set the glass down right now, my joints are so painful."

Dave pushed the coffee table back with his foot, took the glass. "What happened?"

James eased himself forward to the edge of the couch, sweat coursing down his forehead. "Something set it off, I don't know what. A virus, something. Three hours ago it was discomfort, now it's excruciating."

"Let's get you to the hospital."

James shook his head. "Get me the phone, and that cane you loaned me once before. I know this routine by heart. Whatever the doctor is going to prescribe, I've already got at home."

It was agonizing waking up. Agonizing to breathe. Every breath forced his chest muscles to expand, every breath meant pain.

The doorbell had woken him up. He was on the couch. Apart from the fact that the painkillers the doctor prescribed had stopped him in his tracks last night, the stairs were something he had no plans to climb anytime soon.

It took him a very, very long time to walk from the living room to the front door.

Rae.

There was sweat from his journey marking his forehead, and nothing could disguise the white, taut jaw; he was enduring the pain and it showed.

He saw tears fill her eyes.

"You should have told me."

He had to smile. He had known her response would be this, but still, knowing it was not the same as experiencing it. It mattered a great deal that she was here, at his place, to check on him in person. She wasn't at the end of the phone, or at work where she rightfully needed to be right now. "Rae, I'm fine. Go on to work."

"You always answer the door walking with a cane?"

He leaned against the doorjamb, easing the pain in his spine by finding a solid support to take some of his weight, wanting to invite her inside, but not wanting to endure the walk down the hall.

"I'm sorry. I should have told you. Or at least called you this morning."

She reached out her hand to touch him, uncertainty making her hesitate before she very gently rested her hand against his forearm. "I am so sorry you're in pain again."

She was. It made him ache, knowing he had added to the load she was carrying. He hated the malicious randomness of this disease. "Come here," James said quietly, reaching for her hand. He drew her a couple steps closer to him. It was difficult, looking at the strain she carried from several nights without sleep, knowing he had added to the weight she carried, seeing the tears. He loved her. He didn't want to cause this.

He wiped away her tears, then very carefully leaned down to kiss her. "Go on, Rae. I can maneuver around just fine, if a little slower than normal. Go to work.

It's nothing new, nothing I haven't dealt with before. It's the same symptoms, the same disease. I will be okay. Come tonight and crash on my couch and see for yourself I'm really going to be okay."

"You'll need someone to carry things for you, fix you lunch…"

He grinned.

"Okay, maybe not fix you lunch…but answer the phone, answer the door. I should be here."

His fingers gently silenced her. "You need to be at work. I need those things to keep me fighting the pain, working to defeat it. Go do what you have to do today, call me occasionally, and when you are honestly finished, not before, come back and keep me company." He smiled. "I'm not going anywhere today."

She bit her lip.

"Rae, I promise. I won't keep any more surprises from you."

"Is this what a day you would score a one looks like?"

James hesitated. "This is a two, Rae. You'll know one when you see it."

"I hope I never do."

"I hope that, too." It would scare the daylights out of you if you did.…

"Will you page me if you need anything? Anything at all?"

"I will," he promised softly. "Go to work, beautiful."

She had elected to sit in a chair rather than beside him on the couch. He was exhausted to the point of wanting to collapse, but he didn't have the heart to tell her to go home. It was seven o'clock and she had arrived only a short time before.

Trust the illness to rob him of even a hug from her. He hated this unnamed disease, he hated it tremendously.

She knew. "I should go, you're tired."

"No," James protested, so that she hesitated as she rose from her seat. "You haven't told me how your day went yet," he encouraged.

He could do so little for her, the one thing he could offer was a willingness to listen.

"You don't need more bad news and I don't want to think about it."

"Tell me. If you don't, you'll be replaying the day in your dreams."

Rae sighed. "The total market was down another two percent today. That makes eight percent this week, twelve percent in the last seven trading days. Even companies I thought of as stable are in trouble. And clients are calling, feeling the need to make changes, forcing me to sell positions I would normally have allowed to ride out the correction. A broker got shot today in New York by a client holding big option positions he was going to be forced to cover. It's becoming that kind of a panic."

"Are you holding up, Rae?"

"It's a walk in the park compared to what you're dealing with."

"Oh, I don't know. At least I can clear my schedule to deal with this. Have you been able to clear your weekend to give yourself time to sleep?"

"James, I want to be here. I'll sleep in, then come over."

"Not before noon. You need the sleep, Rae."

She reluctantly nodded. "Noon. I'll stop somewhere and bring us lunch."

Saturday came. Four days and the pain was still excruciating. James shaved, having to pause frequently because his hand could not grip the razor. He hurt. Every joint, every muscle. He looked in the mirror and hated the fatigue, the pain. He had not been able to sleep, the pain was too intense, and his face showed it. Rae did not need to see him like this.

He could hear his mom downstairs, moving around in the kitchen.

He turned on the faucet, suppressing the pain from his wrists. It was wearing him down. Wearing down his ability to be optimistic about anything. How many times was he going to have to endure flare-ups like this? Each time it happened, his body took longer to recover. Longer to heal.

Was this the time he simply wasn't going to recover?

He forced himself to move, to ignore the question.

He was not going to let fatigue rob him of his optimism; he was going to recover, he had done it before, and he would do it again. Small step, by small step. He had made it upstairs today. It was progress. He smiled wryly. Just as long as he didn't fall down the stairs going down.

He was tired of this. Tired of being tired. Tired of being in pain.

It was the last thing he wanted Rae to see.

God, why this? Why now? I don't understand.

He was sitting at the kitchen table, glancing at the paper, eating an iced cinnamon roll his mom had recently taken from the oven, when the doorbell rang. James looked at the cane. His body protested at the thought.

"I'll get it," his mom called from the living room. She had been cleaning his house again even though he had a cleaning service that came in each week. James had realized his mom was going to do what she decided to do and nothing would stop her. He had kissed her cheek and let her go to it. He was grateful for the love behind it.

He knew it was Rae. He had told her to come over no earlier than noon and it was now five minutes past the hour. He got to his feet as she entered into the room, ignoring her "Don't get up." She had slept in, but not enough for what her body desperately needed. She looked…wiped out.

"How are you?" she asked, stopping close to him, her eyes searching his face.

He leaned forward to gently kiss her. "Better now that you're here." He meant it, even if his body ached at the movement.

"Rae, would you like some coffee?" his mom asked. "I've got homemade cinnamon rolls, too. Fresh from the oven."

Rae pulled out a chair beside James at the table. "Both sound wonderful. Thank you."

James sat down carefully.

"You didn't get much sleep," Rae said softly.

James smiled. "Not much. But I don't think you did, either."

She grimaced. "No."

He motioned to the paper. "It sounds like the markets finally had a quiet day yesterday."

Rae nodded. "Probably the prelude to a bad

Monday. There is concern the economic numbers being released Monday morning will prompt a rise in interest rates."

He studied her face and saw in her eyes the fatigue that went too deep to cover, the exhaustion that made dealing with decisions so difficult you reached the point it didn't matter anymore. She may have slept in, but stopping had just let the fatigue crash down on her. She ought to be back in bed, sleeping away the entire day.

He hated this disease. She needed someone taking care of her, not the other way around.

His mom brought coffee and the cinnamon rolls, then left them to talk. A few minutes later, James heard vacuuming upstairs.

Rae ate the cinnamon roll slowly, trying to get a conversation started, trying to inject some emotion into her voice, but the exhaustion was too heavy. She would lose her train of thought and go quiet for increasing amounts of time. Just sitting down had made her body long to sleep.

James pushed himself carefully to his feet, his ankles flaring with pain at the movement. He clenched his jaw and ignored the pain. "Rae, come on. The living room couch beckons."

She moved with him to the other room. He lowered himself down on the couch, using the armrest to keep the movement slow.

Rae moved toward the chair and James stopped her. "Sit beside me Rae, please."

She was reluctant to do so, but he didn't release her hand and didn't give her much choice. She sat down on the couch beside him. He wanted her to rest, put her head against his shoulder and close her eyes, but she protested she was fine, just a little tired. He looked at her skeptically.

She reached for the television remote. "Which college teams are playing today?"

Discussions of a serious nature were not going to happen today. James reluctantly let the conversation change to basketball.

His ribs hurt where her weight leaned against him. She had been farther away on the couch and he had intentionally maneuvered her closer so she leaned against him and he could put his arm around her. It took twenty minutes, but the pain won the contest of wills. He was at the point of having to ask her to shift away from him when he saw her try to unsuccessfully stifle a yawn. He pulled a couple of throw pillows over. "Rae, stretch out on the couch and get comfortable. I won't mind if you catnap for a while."

She turned to look up at him. He could see the fatigue shadowing her eyes. "You don't mind?"

He tenderly brushed her cheek with his hand. "I don't mind," he reassured softly. "Come on, stretch out."

She moved away from him and the pain in his ribs began to ease. Her shoes landed on top of each other on the floor and she stretched out, using the pillows he offered to rest comfortably against the other end of the sofa. "Thank you, James."

"Close your eyes and try to get some more sleep," he whispered.

Within ten minutes he could hear her breathing become steady and low as she slept.

It felt good, it felt right, to have her relaxed with him. He muted the basketball game, then leaned his head back against the cushions, and watched her sleep.

They had to do something about the hours she was working. She couldn't keep up the pace, not when she was this exhausted.

"Rae, I understand. Don't worry about it. Go meet with the clients then call me when you get home."

He was going to miss not having dinner with her, but it was probably best today that her work had intruded. He was stretched out in the recliner, looking at the bird that had come to check out the bird feeder, waiting for the medication to temper the ache in his body. It had been fourteen days since the relapse began, and even the careful exercises in the pool each day were agonizing. The doctors had come up with nothing that could even check the damage. His joints were inflamed, his muscles burning. He lost more and more mobility each day.

Dave knew, but with Rae it was a carefully laid out cover-up. She was worried enough about him that it was important to try to hide the worst from her.

He had watched her over the past two weeks, moving toward the point of being close to collapse herself. She was not getting the sleep she needed. She was worried about him, trying to make time in her schedule to come over and help him, doing it at the expense of her sleep.

He hated the situation. He hated it with a passion.

He wanted to be well. He wanted to be able to be the one to go to her place, fix dinner for her, take care of errands for her, help ease the pressure on her. Instead, this disease was ensuring he was adding to the stress she was feeling.

He spent the evening reading a book, often pausing to set the book aside, to lean his head back, think, pray.

If he didn't begin to recover soon, he wasn't sure what he was going to do. But he couldn't do this to Rae. He couldn't let this disease end up affecting her health, as well. He refused to let that happen.

It was a quarter to eleven at night when Rae rang Dave's doorbell. He came down the steps from his studio office, flipped on the porch light. He saw her and flipped the locks open. He was still in sweats from an evening playing basketball at the gym.

She didn't apologize for the hour. Their history went back many years. He knew, without being told. He took her jacket and draped it over the stair railing, then put his arm around her as he walked her to the kitchen.

"You look…tired, my friend."

She took the soda he offered. "You understate things very well." She took a long drink. "Can you get me tickets to San Diego for tomorrow morning, return flight Sunday night? Lunch and dinner reservations at a quiet, elegant place conducive to talking serious business?"

He looked at her and she let him see the truth, let her mask slip to show the reality going on.

"I'll be glad to Rae. Find a comfortable spot on the couch, relax. I'll make a few calls."

He joined her in the living room twenty minutes later, handed her a piece of paper from his desk stationery.

Rae glanced at it wearily, knowing it would be complete, finding it was. A limo to pick her up from the office, first-class seats there and back, restaurant reservations, hotel accommodations, Dave had arranged it all, or rather one of his contacts had. "Thank you," she said softly.

He handed her two business cards. "They are good. Use them if you need them."

Two attorneys, both top names in the business. Men you didn't just make appointments with; they picked their clients.

"The numbers are their direct lines. They will make themselves available."

Rae nodded, knowing it would be true. "Thanks, friend."

"You're going to sell."

She leaned her head back against the cushion, looked at the ceiling. "I'm going to…consider the possibilities. The Hamilton trusts are not definite, but the indications from dinner tonight are positive. I've got to have help, Dave. Good help. Since I can't find the right partner with the business at twenty-six million, I'm going to do my best to make it a business of seventy million and see if I can get either Richardson in Texas or Walters in New York to move. They are the only two men whose track records and style fit what I really need. But if neither one of them works out—" she sighed as she looked at the page of notes "—then yes, I'm seriously considering selling the business."

Dave rubbed her hand which was clenching and unclenching around the throw pillow she had picked up. "Rae, Gary is a good guy. He'll make you a fair offer, he'll keep your employees, he'll do good for your clients. There could be worse solutions."

She heard the reluctance in his voice. "You don't think I should sell."

"I think you're going to really miss the work."

She sighed and looked at the page of notes again.

"I know. I've told myself for months that I would do it only as my literal last resort. But I'm close to being there, friend."

"You're tired."

She laughed. "I can barely remember the last day I felt rested. I don't want this anymore, Dave. I don't want the responsibility and the fatigue and the hours. I'll find a partner, or I'll face the reality and sell."

James touched the tile wall of the pool, let himself finally stop. Five laps. It wasn't great, it was a long, long way from fifty laps, but it meant he was finally back to a four on his scale of pain. He let the water float his body as he tried to catch his breath. A month. It felt like an eternity.

He had begun to privately wonder if the recovery was ever going to come. It was a battle to keep hope alive and at the same time try to accept and live with reality.

He would take Rae to dinner tonight to celebrate.

The idea brought a smile. She had been traveling on weekends this past month—San Diego, Texas, New York—business meetings with outcomes she remained noncommittal about. He had missed her, missed the Saturday afternoons spent together, the rare chance to see her without the burden of work pressing on her.

The past month had simply reinforced how important she had become in his life. It was one of the reasons he had struggled so hard to keep hope alive. If he didn't recover, they didn't have a future together. That reality had made him willing to push through the pain and endure the toll the exercises took. There was finally a glimmer of hope, and it was time to celebrate.

Rae's office was less than twenty minutes away. He felt like making the request in person.

Janet pointed him toward the trading room with a smile.

"Hey, lady," he called softly, pausing at the door to watch Rae. Her attention was so focused on the information in front of her, his words startled her.

"James!"

He loved the sight of the smile that lit her face. She was glad to see him and it made him very glad he had come.

She crossed the room to join him at the door. "What are you doing here?"

He leaned forward and softly kissed her, watched the blush spread across her cheeks. "Want to go out to dinner?"

"I would love to."

"When should I come back and pick you up?"

She looked back at the screen she had been studying, bit her bottom lip. "Give me twenty minutes and I can wrap this up for the night."

"You're sure? Don't hurry on my account."

She grinned. "Twenty minutes. Can we do Chinese?"

He laughed. "Yes."

They ate at the restaurant across from the office complex, a leisurely dinner, the conversation moving from Dave and Lace, to church, to her work.

She was close to signing a major new client and as he listened to her he heard the excitement, but inside he wondered if it was a good decision for her to make. A new client would increase her workload, increase the demands. He didn't understand entirely why the idea appealed so much to her. But it did, and he was not one to limit anyone's dreams—certainly not Rae's. It mattered to her, so it mattered to him.

He had been about a week premature in his decision to celebrate. By the end of the dinner, he was reluctantly ready to admit it was time to go home and rest. The pain was back, strong and fierce, ugly.

"Come on in, Rae. The door is open."

It was easier to call than to walk. His ankles were protesting even this journey to the kitchen. The hint of a recovery had been more of a wisp of hope then reality. Six weeks, and the pain in his joints was still severe.

The room vibrated to life with her entrance. Her eyes were sparkling and her cheeks were pink. "James, I got the contract. I'm going to be managing the Hamilton estate, and all its various trust funds."

"Rae, that's great," James said, pleased for her. He handed her one of the sodas he had retrieved. She accepted it from him with a thank-you and spontaneously reached forward to hug him.

She pulled back. "What kind of pizza...?"

He hadn't been able to mask the pain in time.

She took a hesitant step back and her eyes suddenly widened.

"It hurts when I hug you," she said, the appalling realization shaking her voice. "Oh, James. I'm sorry. I didn't think..."

He saw the look of horror fill her face, and then she turned abruptly and hurried from the room. He didn't have the luxury of being able to hurry after her. By the time he reached the door she had fled through, her car was already pulling from the drive.

* * *

Rae opened the door for him, her eyes red, her face pale. She looked at him and he looked just as seriously back at her. "Can we talk?" he finally asked.

She swung open the door and walked toward the living room.

James set his wallet and car keys down on the end table. She had moved to stand by the window, her arms wrapped around her middle. He stopped by the end of the couch and looked at her. It was better if she spoke first. It was a long wait.

"I wish you would just say when something causes you pain."

She was trying so hard not to cry....

With a deep sigh, James crossed over to her side. He had never intended this.

She didn't want to look at him.

He tipped her chin up. "It hurts when you hug me, but I'm not going to let a little pain rob me of the pleasure. I love it when you hug me. I don't want you stopping to think before you hug me. That's why I didn't tell you."

He wiped away her tears. "Rae, I like your hugs."

It took several moments before she replied. "You're sure?"

"Absolutely."

She carefully wrapped her arms around him. "It feels so awful to realize I was hurting you."

He gently brushed her hair back from her face, settled his arms firmly around her waist. "Rae, it would hurt me worse to have you stop."

He held her for a long time, relieved to have her back.

He leaned down and gently kissed her. "Are we okay now?"

She sniffed a final time and nodded.

"Good. Then how about going out for that pizza?"

It made her laugh.

"Uncle James, I helped make the rolls. They are really good." His niece met him at the door, sliding her hand in his, smiling. James propped the cane in the umbrella stand. He thought he could get by without it today.

"That's great, Emily. You're going to become a great cook like your grandmother."

"She made clam chowder. Do you like it?"

"Love it."

Emily's grin widened. "So do I. We've got turkey and dressing, and my rolls, scalloped potatoes—my mom made those—that green stuff I like, homemade noodles, and for dessert there's pumpkin pie, apple pie and chocolate pudding. I can't wait for lunch."

James laughed and tickled her tummy. "Where are you going to put all that food?" He wished he could pick her up. He knew better than to try.

"In my hollow leg," Emily replied, giggling.

James loved Thanksgiving Day. It was something they didn't celebrate in Africa.

"Where's your dad?"

"Getting the card tables from the basement."

The kitchen was busy, both his mom and sister fixing snack and relish trays. "Do you think we have enough to eat?" James asked, looking over the loaded counters.

His mom grinned and gently hugged him. "Even with nine people at the table, we're going to be sending lots of leftovers home with people. It's one of the things that makes it a good day. Are Dave and Lace with you?"

"They're on the way," James assured her. "They were going to go spring Rae from her office."

"She's working? Today?"

James grimaced. That was what he thought, as well. "A couple of hours. Need any help?"

"We're close to being done."

James nodded. "Patricia, how's my future niece or nephew doing?" She was due in another eight weeks. His sister was loving being pregnant.

"Having a wonderful time kicking the inside of my ribs. He's an active little guy."

"Think it's a boy?"

Patricia grinned. "I've got a fifty-fifty chance of being right."

James affectionately squeezed her shoulder. "I pick New Years Day as the estimated time of arrival. I think you're going to be early."

Patricia laughed. "That would be fine with me."

James accepted a drink and went to see if he could help Paul. He couldn't carry much, but there should be something he could do. Find out what football games were on that afternoon if nothing else.

He was looking forward to seeing Rae. Dave and Lace, too.

He was having a moderately good day. A four on his scale of ten. He could walk without much pain today. It was probably a short reprieve, but he would take it while it lasted.

Dave, Lace and Rae arrived, amidst a lot of laughter. James met them at the door, grinned at Rae who was wearing a feather tucked in her hair.

"James, they are calling me a turkey."

"Gee, I wonder why."

She swatted his arm. "I have to show some Thanksgiving Day spirit. They wouldn't let me bring any food."

"Thank you both," James gratefully told Dave and Lace, then double-checked to make sure Rae knew he was teasing. He would hate to hurt her feelings. She wasn't *that* bad of a cook.

She tucked her hand under his arm. "One of these days, you are all going to regret these comments." She was grinning.

"Sure, sure. That's what you always say," Dave replied, grinning back.

"What did you bring?" James asked Lace, looking at the foil-covered tray she was carrying.

"Homemade candy. Fudge, chocolate-covered cherries, caramels."

"You've been hiding this talent all these months?"

Rae laughed. "Dave made them, James. Lace just sat on the stool and kept him company."

"I'm impressed," James told Dave.

"You should be. Caramels take forever to make."

They already knew everyone in his family, but Dave and Lace had not seen the house before, so James gave them a guided tour, not letting Rae get far from his side. She didn't seem to be in any hurry to move away either. His arm around her shoulders, he hugged her gently. He was very glad to have her here.

The kitchen timer went off, and Emily announced her rolls were done. It was time to eat.

Dave and Lace were flirting with each other. James watched the two of them as they moved around the buffet table filling their plates. Dave would lean over occasionally and make a soft comment; Lace would blush and whisper something back that would make Dave chuckle.

Rae nudged his arm. "They went to some comedy club downtown last night. I think Lace had a good time," she whispered.

"I think you're right."

James held out the chair beside him at the table for Rae.

"Thanks."

"My pleasure."

Rae leaned against him as she asked if he would pass the butter.

James reached around her to pass the basket of rolls to Dave, let his arm linger around her shoulders.

"Would you two quit flirting and eat?" Patricia finally asked, laughing.

James and Rae looked over, caught, only to find that Patricia was looking at Dave and Lace.

"It goes for you, too, James," his mom said, seeing his look of relief.

"Me? I'm the innocent party in all this," James protested. Rae reached over and ruffled his hair.

He caught her hand, leaned over. He kissed her to the delight of those at the table. "If I'm going to get caught, it should be worth it," he told Rae softly, watching her blush.

She leaned forward until they were touching noses. "You just used up your one kiss for this date," she reminded him.

James blinked. She was right.

She laughed at his expression.

James took Rae home shortly after 9:00 p.m. His mom had sent a sack of leftovers home with her—soup, sandwiches, noodles, pie. James reached for the sack on the back seat only to have Rae stop him. "Let me carry it."

"Rae..."

"I know it's a good day, I know it's not heavy. Humor me."

James was in too good a mood to argue the point. They walked up the drive together.

"What would you like to do tomorrow?"

"Sleep in till eight, have a leisurely breakfast, shop, go see a movie."

"Sounds perfect. I'll pick you up at eight-thirty?"

"That was only a suggestion, James. Are you sure you want to go shopping? It will be crazy tomorrow with the Thanksgiving Day sales and the start of the Christmas shopping."

"Shopping will be fun," he replied. "We've never done it together before."

Rae grinned. "There is a reason for that, you know."

James grinned back. "I'll take my chances. Eight-thirty?"

"Fine."

James leaned forward. "Can we make it a two-kiss date?"

Rae moved the sack to her far arm. "I think that can be arranged," she replied with a smile. He leaned down to kiss her and Rae closed her eyes.

A groan of pain broke apart the kiss.

She had stepped forward. His left ankle refused to take his shifted weight. His reflex to keep from falling put his hand heavily on her shoulder.

"What...?"

"I'm okay." He gingerly tried to put weight on the ankle. The tendons and joint flared with pain.

"I did it again." Rae was angry with herself, her arm going around his waist, the sack she still held tipping precariously. "James, I am so *sorry*."

"It's not your fault." He took several deep breaths, fighting back the pain. "It's why I carry the cane." The cane was, of course, still propped in the back seat of the car.

"I'll get it."

He stopped her movement. "No. Walk me back to the car. I've been on my feet too long today."

It was a painfully ugly way to end the evening.

Rae walked with him back to the car, James clenching his teeth at the pain in his left ankle. If it had been his right, Rae would have been driving him home. "We'll have to play tomorrow by ear," he said, admitting the obvious.

"No problem, it's not important. Call me when you get up."

It *was* important and it *was* a big deal. But he didn't have a lot of options.

"I'll call you," he agreed, resigned. The pain had managed to ruin a good evening.

The phone rang at eight-thirty the next morning.

"Did I wake you up?"

Rae smiled. "No. Though I am still in bed. I'm editing the last couple chapters I wrote for my book. How are you, James?"

"We can scratch off today. I'm sorry, Rae. I was looking forward to it."

"The pain is bad?"

Rae heard the broken sigh. "It's bad."

She felt terrible for him. "Is there anything I can do?"

"I wish there was. I really wish there was."

The situation was wearing him down and it showed in his voice. "I don't mind a lazy day watching movies. What interests you? I'll bring a few over," she offered, trying to lift his spirits.

"Rae, you don't need to do that. Go shopping. Enjoy the rare day off."

"I would rather spend it with you."

"I'll be selfish and say I would like that, too. But I'm lousy company at the moment, Rae."

"You've got cause." Rae worried her bottom lip, trying to decide what would be best. "Why don't I come over about two o'clock with a puppy and a movie."

"A puppy?" Rae could hear his smile.

"One of Margo's litter. You said yourself puppies were good medicine."

"You will be chasing it all over the house."

"Probably. Say yes."

James chuckled. "Sure, why not? I'll leave the door unlocked. Let yourself in."

The puppy that had been named Justin adored riding in the car. He sat on the passenger seat with his nose stuck out the slightly opened window, loving the motion.

Rae had done her shopping, two hours in the crowds convincing her there were better places to be on the day after Thanksgiving. She had chosen three movies at the video store, then stopped by the kennel to pick up Justin.

Last night had been yet another realization of what kind of obstacles they continued to face. James wanted to view his health as his problem, but he was wrong. It was their problem. She loved him. They were headed for a future together. The reality of the pain he faced every day was part of that future. She had seen it go into remission twice. Eventually, this episode had to go into remission, as well. He was getting better, even he would admit that, even if it was occurring at a snail's pace.

She hated to see him in pain. Hated to know something she had done had contributed to that pain. The day she had realized hugging him hurt him... She still winced when she thought of that day. She had inadvertently done something similar again last night. He was a rugged, masculine, strong guy. Looking at him, it was hard to fathom that at times the simple actions of carrying something, shaking hands, walking, were physically painful for him to do.

God, why? I'm in love with him. I hate to see him in pain. I hate the fact there is so little I can do to help.

Thankfully, she had a leash and collar for Justin or the puppy would have wiggled himself out of her arms as she walked up the driveway to James's home. She loved this house. She loved the structural changes he had made. She would love to live in this house. She pushed open the front door, calling James's name.

"Back here, Rae."

She found him in his office working on a sketch at the drafting table. He got up from the stool, moving very stiffly.

Rae didn't comment on his pain. She squeezed his hand gently and looked at the drawing. "This is for the Grants?" They were adding another bedroom and a family room onto their ranch-style home.

"Yes." James reached over to pet a squirming Justin. "You can let him down in the house."

Rae slipped the puppy off the leash. He started exploring the room. "The sketch is very good."

"I had a few minutes to kill," James replied.

Rae could tell he wasn't satisfied with the drawing yet. "I brought three movies for you to choose from."

James motioned toward the living room, walked with her, leaning heavily on the cane to favor his left ankle. "Good choices?"

Rae smiled and told him the names of the films.

"You honestly expect me to choose?"

"Prioritize," Rae conceded. "I really want to see them all."

James laughed. "I can do seven hours of movies if you can."

"Watch me."

They ended up on the couch, Justin alternating between sitting in one or the other's lap and playing on the floor with James's rolled-up socks.

They started with John Wayne. They laughed together through most of the movie as any loud sound effect in the movie made Justin scamper for cover. He preferred burying his head under James's arm. They took a couple intermissions in the movie, Rae knowing James needed to move around frequently to keep his joints from stiffening too much.

"James, where do you keep the plastic wrap?" Rae opened yet another kitchen cabinet drawer. James had agreed to let her fix dinner as long as she simply reheated leftovers from the Thanksgiving Day meal.

"Try the second drawer to the right of the dishwasher."

"Thanks."

She came back with thick turkey sandwiches, scalloped potatoes, and two large slices of pumpkin pie.

James took the plate she offered. "I could get used to this."

Rae grinned. "Of course. Everyone likes to be waited on."

"I was referring to the food, but the service is not bad either."

Rae considered batting him with a pillow, but refrained due to the fact it might actually hurt him. "Just be glad I'm here. Without me—no movies, no puppy, no pie."

James leaned over and kissed her. "Forgiven?"

"For a kiss, I would forgive almost anything," Rae replied, grinning, at the same time, serious. She meant it.

James pointed to her plate. "Eat. I can't afford to kiss you again."

James selected the action-adventure film as the next movie. Rae was glad. She didn't need to be watching a romance at the moment.

They both laughed at the same places in the movie. Rae had seen it numerous times and still liked the way it had been plotted. It was a long movie. The ending felt good. The good guys had won.

"Are you sure you want to see all three in one day?" James asked.

It was dark outside, the credits for the movie were rolling by. Rae was tired, the puppy was asleep in her lap. But it wasn't that late.... "I'm game. It's one of my favorite movies."

James changed the movies.

"Come here, stretch out and get comfortable," he encouraged when he was seated again. Rae didn't need to hear the suggestion twice. She carefully settled the puppy, and stretched out on the couch, using James's lap as a pillow.

It felt good having his hand resting against her waist, occasionally brushing through her hair. It felt good to be close to him.

"Whoever thought of this script came up with a wonderful storyline," Rae said.

"Your book will make a good movie someday."

Rae looked up, surprised. "You think so? At the rate I'm going, it will never get finished, let alone find a publisher and interest a movie studio."

"You should have reserved a few hours today to work on the book."

Rae shook her head. "No. The book and the business can fight for the same time. I'm not letting the book compete with time I can spend with you."

"Rae..."

She cut him off. "I want to watch the movie."

She felt him sigh, but he dropped the subject. She knew it bothered him, the fact she was getting only fragments of time to work on her book. But she didn't view taking time away from their relationship to be worth the price. The book had been part of her life for three years; if it took another two years, that was the unfortunate reality. She loved days spent with James too much to want to create a tug-of-war between spending time with him and working on the book. James came first. It was that simple.

It was late when Rae reluctantly moved to go home. The puppy was coming home with her for the night.

James made sure she had her jacket on.

James rubbed the sleepy puppy under the chin.

"He's going to wake you up very early in the morning."

Rae smiled. "That would be okay."

She wanted to hug him good-night, but her hands were full holding the puppy and carrying the videotapes. He had been unusually quiet for the last hour; she wished she knew what he was thinking about. It was something serious, that was obvious.

He leaned down and kissed her very gently. "Drive careful, Rae."

"Good night, James."

Chapter Ten

She had carried in his groceries.

James lowered his head, his hands resting against the counter. This was not right!

The anger inside—at God, at the pain, at the unfairness of what was happening, at the lack of sleep—roiled through him.

"I don't need another mother," he snapped at Rae, taking the last sack from her as she came in from the garage. "I can put away my own groceries."

She pulled back, her eyes going wide. He watched as the light of animation gave way to confusion and deep hurt. She started to say something, stopped, then left the kitchen.

"Rae…"

He'd been to the doctor and then to the store and she'd been waiting for him when he got home. He was tired, in pain and frustrated with what he couldn't do. He didn't need her doing one of the few things he could do.

She didn't deserve having her head bit off because he was in a foul mood.

"Rae." He found her sitting on the couch in the living room. He lowered himself into the chair opposite her, setting the cane down. "I'm sorry. That was uncalled for."

"If I help you, you get mad. If I don't, I feel horrible."

He leaned his head back, hating the situation. He wanted her help, but resented it, too. "I know. I've been a bear with a sore head lately. I didn't mean to snap."

"Can I at least fix dinner?"

It pulled a half smile from him. "Would you settle for helping me fix it?"

She bit her lip as she sighed. "Sure. The doctor's news was bad?"

"Nothing different than last time. Wait it out." It was impossible to make light of how desperate he was to get some sustained improvement. There were few if any glimmers of hope.

Kevin was right. He had to accept the limitations and learn to live with them. But he hated it, hated the implications of a life with this pain. Hated the cost he was going to have to pay.

If he didn't recover, they didn't have a future together.

She didn't want to talk about the possibility of this pain being a permanent reality. She still believed it would fade with time. He was no longer sure.

The only thing he was certain of was that he could not burden her with it.

It was dawn. Rae looked out her office window to see the clouds turn pink on the horizon, slowly glow as the sun touched them.

She looked down at the list of her day's priorities and slowly curled her hand around the pen she held. Had it been a pencil, it would have cracked under the pressure.

There was too much to do and not enough time to do it.

It was no longer a matter of delegation, of prioritization, of managing her time better, of controlling interruptions. She was in over her head, and she had two options. She could throw away everything outside of work that was important in her life to deal exclusively with delivering the kind of investment returns her clients had the right to expect, or she could sell the business. A partnership was not going to happen. Richardson had regretfully declined last week, Walters had called her last night.

Rae looked at the list of items to be done, looked around her office, quietly closed the schedule book.

God, I've been thinking about Psalm 37 for months now. Verse 23 says the steps of a man are from the Lord. We've been talking about this decision for a long time. It's time, isn't it?

Rae was surprised at the peace she felt.

She was selling the business.

The demons liked to come in the middle of the night. His personal ones. Doubt. Anger. Frustration. The clock beside his bed showed 2:00 a.m. The pain had ensured he had yet to fall asleep.

God, I am so angry at this pain! Why, God? Why me? Why show me a future I would love to have and then cripple me so I can't have it?

It's not fair.

I love Rae. I can't do this to her. I can't so limit her life to this level.

I know what marriage demands of people. Why put love in my heart and deny me the health I need to enjoy it? For years I have accepted being single as one of the costs to pay for serving on the mission field. Is this how You reward that sacrifice? Why, God? I don't understand.

How do I explain this to Rae? She's not going to understand and I don't have the words. She's going to see the things I can't do—mow the yard, take out the trash, carry a sack of groceries, that long list of daily obstacles I am dealing with—as minor things. But they are not. They are the tip of that iceberg of energy and responsibility necessary for a marriage to work. It can't be such a one-sided equation that she is put in a position of constantly having to give. The marriage would never survive.

Oh, God, why does the pain not leave? What caused this relapse to be stronger and more persistent than the others? Is there anything else I can do that will help? Anything else the doctors have not tried? Just lying here in bed is making my muscles burn. I can feel the joints stiffening. I know morning is going to be another adventure in agony. I am so tired of it, Lord. There is no relief. I am dreading where this is heading.

How do I tell the lady I love that I can't marry her?

Chapter Eleven

"Because I've got energy and you don't, you're dumping me."

He couldn't let this disease end up affecting her health, as well. And it was. Rae was burning out trying to manage the new account and make time to help him. He refused to let it happen. Today, hearing yet another cautious verdict from his doctor, he had finally realized he no longer had the luxury of assuming his health was going to improve.

James was exhausted, in more pain than he could ever remember, and she had left work to come help him do laundry. She reluctantly admitted when directly asked that she was going to have to go back to work for a few more hours when they were done. He could see the fatigue etched in her face. He knew she had her own long list of errands and tasks to do; he knew she had ceased to work on a book that was very important to her in order to be there to help him. He wanted her in his life, but he was no longer willing to have her life limited by his. It wasn't fair to her, and it was not something he could accept. It was too high a price.

"Rae, I thought I would be getting better. I'm not. It's crazy to go on with a relationship that can't go any further."

"Did you ever think I might simply like you? That I might like being with you? James, I could care less what we actually do."

"Rae, it's hard to accept help."

"Well, it's hard to see you in pain, too." She paced, frustrated. "If I help you, you get mad, and if I don't, I feel horrible. It's a no-win situation."

"Which is exactly my point. Rae, we tried. It just won't work. You've got your job and the time demands of it, I've got this disease and the implications of it. You don't have time for a relationship and I don't have the energy for one. Let's face the facts and let it go. We'll still be friends."

She was crying. "James, I don't want us to just be friends."

He closed his eyes at the plea in her voice. "Rae, I'm sorry, but that is all we can be."

She didn't know where to direct the anger. At James? At God? At herself?

Rae drove, not caring where she went. Her heart was too broken to know how to process the hurt.

The napkin from the morning's fast-food restaurant coffee was tucked in her hand, wadded up, too wet to absorb any more tears. She let the rest run unchecked down her face as she drove.

Friends.

She didn't want to be just friends.

Lord, why? Why tonight of all nights?

The paperwork was beside her, the contracts to sell the business. She and James had been planning to go to dinner and she had planned to tell him about the deal after dinner. She had known he would be against the idea, would feel as if she were sacrificing her business on his account. She had known they would need time to talk it through.

It was a good offer.

For the good of their future, it had been the right decision for her to make.

They didn't have a future anymore.

Her home was up ahead, dark, quiet. Rae pulled the car into the drive, wiping away the tears. Already her eyes were burning from the salt, feeling gritty and swollen. Her headache was intense. She left the car, feeling the cold strike her wet face.

Lace was in New York. Dave was in Dallas. She wanted her friends—needed them. Knew even if they were here, they couldn't fix the problem.

A scampering puppy met her at the door. Justin had become a permanent resident. Normally she would have scooped him up and spent thirty minutes playing with him, but tonight she greeted him, rubbed his coat and put him back down.

She went outside to the deck and tossed the contract pages onto the grill.

One strike of a match and the contract flared into a bright ball of heat, curled black and turned to ash.

She had her work and her book. She didn't have what she really wanted.

She watched the flames burn until the contract was entirely ash.

God, I let him get close, and I got hurt.

I'm tired of getting hurt.

Next time, remind me to say no when I get asked for a date.

Rae went downstairs at 1:00 a.m. to answer the doorbell. Tired of lying in bed fighting the tears, she had finally gotten up and settled in the recliner with one of her mom's books, trying to bury the pain in the old familiar words of a children's fantasy.

It was hard to read when you were crying.

Dave. He had been in Dallas. He had called her from there expecting to hear she had told James about the deal. Instead, he had heard a carefully edited explanation of the evening. He must have chartered a flight. Rae blinked against the tears.

He stepped inside.

She had never been so glad to see someone.

"You look like you could use a hug," her friend said quietly, opening his arms.

She buried herself in his strong protective arms, letting the pain finally come out. Her dreams had died tonight. It was a pain that went deeper than any loss she had ever felt before. Leo had not made a choice to leave her. James had. It stung. Deep inside her soul, it stung.

Dave held her for a very, very long time.

"He's a jerk."

"No, he's not, Lace. He did what he thought was best."

Rae didn't feel the forgiveness she expressed, but said the words again anyway. She had said them a lot in the past week, Lace was like a lioness ready to take James apart. Rae was no longer angry. She was sad, tired, licking her wounds in private. Anger was a luxury of energy she didn't have to spend.

The funny thing was, she honestly did understand his actions. His back against the wall, not able to deal with the demands the relationship required while in such physical pain, he had ended it as gently as he could. She had been ready to do the exact same thing with her business, admit she couldn't carry the weight, sell out. Thank God she had not actually signed the pages.

"Lace, I love your company, I appreciate the lunch, but..."

"...let me get back to work," Lace finished for her, getting to her feet.

"Yeah. Sorry."

Lace leaned her hands on the desk. "It's okay. As long as you come over tonight, watch a movie, eat popcorn, forget about work for at least three hours."

Rae grimaced. "Can I call you?"

Lace shook her head. "Come. That's an order from your friend. You haven't left this office for the past week."

"I'll try to be there by eight."

"If you're not, I'll kidnap you."

It was the first smile Rae had felt and meant in days. "I'll be there, Lace."

James had expected a reaction from Dave and Lace. He hadn't expected the ice.

It began to thaw slightly as they watched him carefully set down his coffee mug, before he dropped it. The pain was intense tonight. Had it not been for the slight chance he'd see Rae, he would have passed on the get-together.

Rae hadn't come.

Lace, across from him, asked about his family. She didn't approve of what he had done, that was obvious, but she was at least being polite.

It seemed that Dave had not taken sides.

James wanted to ask how Rae was doing, wanted to hear anything about her, but neither Dave nor Lace were willing to mention her name. During the past week, James had picked up the phone several times to call her, but always reluctantly replaced it. He hoped she would eventually forgive him.

Chapter Twelve

"James, she's taking it pretty hard. She doesn't let many people inside her shell and she did you," Lace told him. "She doesn't understand."

Lace, knowing how bad he missed her, had finally relented, begun to call him, tell him what she knew.

Almost two weeks without seeing Rae. It was crushing him. James felt as if he had lost his right arm, so deep was the void where their friendship had been.

Christmas was drawing near and Rae was pleading the pressure of end of year work to avoid him. She had skipped the party tonight, and he had come for only one reason, to see how she was doing, to give her an early Christmas gift. He had never meant to hurt her, not this way.

They couldn't have a future together; it was for her own good that he had pulled back. But he was miserable and it didn't help to know she was also as miserable. This was for the best. It had to be. No matter how many times he stopped to consider the options, it always came down to a simple fact that he didn't have the energy for a marriage, to provide for a wife, let alone the energy to raise a family. He couldn't do it. He couldn't take away her dreams of a family, her dreams of writing, just to make his life easier. She would wear out caring for him.

He was no longer a nice, patient, optimistic man to be around. The pain had removed that pair of rose-colored glasses. The pain had taught him that he wouldn't be able to have everything he wanted. It felt like a cruel lesson, and he hated the reality, but he couldn't change it. He couldn't make the pain go away.

He wanted so badly to be well, to be fit enough to ask Rae to marry him, to build a home with her, to raise a family with her. But reality and what he wanted were a long way apart. It took energy to be in a relationship. It meant being able to at least take walks with her, carry out the trash, repair things that broke, mow the lawn, be there to take care of her when she got a cold. In the shape he was in, she would be constantly having to take care of him. He hated that reality.

But he had never meant for her to get hurt.

He needed to see her, to explain again as best he could why it had to be this way. She was still at the office, Dave had told him that. Since she was avoiding him, he would need to go to her.

He looked at the clock. There was no better time than tonight.

Dave had given him the key to the office suite, and for the first time he walked through the rooms to find them quiet, dark, silent. Her office door was open, the light spilling out into the research room.

She sat at her desk, her head in her hand, the droop of her shoulders weary, as if she felt the weight of the world pressing her down. She was walking a pen down a spreadsheet of numbers, deep in thought. Two weeks. He looked at her and wanted so badly for things to be different. He loved her so much.

"Hey, lady," he said softly, "it's awful late."

She looked up.

Her face lit up momentarily when she saw him, then clouded again. "James. What are you doing here?"

"May I come in?"

She nodded to the chairs in front of her desk, then out of consideration, moved from the chair behind the desk to one of the group in front of the desk. Not the one beside his.

"How are you?" she asked quietly.

"Four out of ten," he replied in the shorthand they had used for a long time. He studied her face, missing her, hoping something could be done to restore at least their friendship. "You look tired." It was an understatement. He hated what he saw, but knew he had contributed to it.

She grimaced. "There's been a lot of work to do," she replied.

He reached in his pocket and retrieved the gift he had hoped to give her tonight at the party. "I brought you something."

She hesitated before accepting the envelope, opening it.

He loved the smile he saw for he had the feeling she had not smiled in the past two weeks.

"Tickets to the Bulls game?"

"You need an evening away. If it turns out to be a bad day for me, Dave volunteered to take you," James said with a slight smile.

"Dave will help you have a bad day so he can go in your place," Rae replied, amused.

"Will you come?"

James watched her bite her bottom lip.

"Rae, it's a simple question."

She shook her head and handed back the tickets. "Thank you, James, but no."

He felt the rejection cut deep into his heart. He did his best not to show it. He deserved it. "What if Dave is the one who takes you?" he asked quietly.

She shook her head.

"Rae, you need a break."

"I've got one. I've been working on the book in the evenings."

"When are you sleeping?"

She didn't like him pushing; he could see it so clearly in her expression. It was buried alongside an enormous pool of hurt. He had never meant to leave her with that.

She got to her feet. "James, I'm okay. Honestly. But I've got a lot of work to do."

He could hear the unsaid goodbye in her actions.

He hated this, hated this death of a friendship. "I'm sorry, Rae. I don't want it to end this way."

"Neither do I. But it has to be this way." There were tears in her eyes as she moved back to her desk.

James had never felt more helpless. "Will you call me if you change your mind about the game?"

She nodded. "Take care of yourself, James," she whispered.

"You too, Rae."

He left, feeling his heart break. He walked to his car, the tears flowing down his face, hating the disease which had cost him what he most wanted in life.

* * *

Rae tried to concentrate on her book, tried to pick up where she had left off in the story, but the page blurred and the words ran together. She wasn't going to cry anymore. She wasn't!

The tears slipped down onto the page anyway.

James had looked so tired tonight, in so much pain. She desperately wanted the right to be with him on nights like this; to be his wife, have the right to hold him, help him, be with him. Instead, she sat alone in her home, trying to distract herself with a story that would probably never be finished, let alone be published.

God, why?

It was a prayer whispered around choking sobs. She hurt so badly.

He was the man she loved, the man she so hoped would become her husband, and he had instead simply said, "I can't." Nothing in her life had ever hurt this bad. Not the death of her parents, not the death of her grandmother, not even the death of Leo.

God, why?

"James, are you sure I can't get you something?"

James reached up and softly squeezed the hand that rested on his shoulder. "Thank you, Patricia. But I'm okay."

His sister didn't believe him. James couldn't blame her. He looked and felt like something that had been flattened by a semi. "You ought to be off your feet," he cautioned.

"I'm fine."

James tugged her to a chair with a smile. "Sit."

She reluctantly did as ordered. "I feel like a beached whale."

"You look beautiful pregnant. Enjoy it."

"You're not the one who gets to feel Junior kick for the fun of it."

James laughed. The sound was rusty; he hadn't had reason to laugh for a while. "Still sure it's a boy?"

"I don't know. Emily was like this, too, active. I guess I'm willing to wait for the surprise." His sister rubbed her aching back. "You saw the doctor this morning?"

James rubbed his aching wrist. "Same old, same old. Another anti-inflammatory medication to try. They don't have many suggestions."

"I'm sorry, James."

"I know." He wished he could stay even slightly optimistic that the pain would fade like it had done before. "It's the breaks."

"How's Rae?" Patricia asked softly.

James felt his face grow taut. "Angry. Hurt. About what I expected."

"She'll forgive you, James."

James sighed, feeling so old. "Someday."

The office was silent. Rae rubbed her burning eyes, trying to restore her concentration. She had added the numbers three times and come up with different answers each time. She had work to do. She couldn't afford to be calling it a night at 9:00 p.m.

Her body had other plans. Wearily, she conceded the choice was no longer hers.

She closed the folders and added them to the stack at the side of her desk. Tomorrow morning. She could finish them then.

Her life was entirely this job. She had chosen to

make it that. No use having a pity party over her own choices.

Her car was in the first spot in the parking lot, since she was normally one of the first people to arrive at the building in the morning. Tonight, her car was also one of only three cars left in the parking lot. She got in, tossed her briefcase and purse onto the passenger seat, flipped on her car lights.

Her body reminded her that she had not eaten since ten that morning, and she wearily gave in to the insistent demand. There wasn't much at home. She needed milk. Some ice cream wouldn't be bad, either.

Traffic was sparse.

Rae drove home, trying to pull her mind off work and think about her book, what she would write that night. Some nights it was only a page or two, but it was better to be working than to be thinking about James.

She wasn't angry at him anymore. She knew how hard the decision had to have been for him to make. She didn't necessarily want to see him again, either. Lace was upset with her because she had canceled joining them tonight. She didn't want to see James, didn't want to feel the hurt, didn't want to be reminded of what she wouldn't have. Marriage. Children.

At first, the hope had been strong that he would recover and change his mind. As the weeks were passing and reports from Lace and Dave were of no change, her hope had dwindled. She was down to Psalm 37, verse 30. God was her refuge in time of trouble. The verse fit; it helped. She had never needed a place of refuge more deeply than she did now.

"Is Rae coming?" Dave asked.

"She pleaded work when I called," Lace replied.

Dave's mouth tightened. "This is getting ridiculous. She takes on new clients and refuses to hire more help."

James, seated on the couch, knew what Rae was doing but also felt a need to defend her. "She'll eventually pull back again, Dave. She's hurt and work is her first defense."

Dave sighed. "Any suggestions?"

"No. I wish I had one. Would you stop by her office, offer to take her to dinner? Lace says she's losing weight again."

"I'll do that. Why don't you two just get back together?"

James shifted the cane he was now forced to use all the time. "She doesn't need another burden, Dave."

"Really? Was that her decision or yours?"

Rae chose the corner store near her home to pick up milk, was disappointed with the ice cream options and ended up choosing plain vanilla.

A light freezing drizzle had begun to fall. Rae shivered as she slipped back inside the car, was grateful for the warmth. She pulled to the corner and waited for the red light to turn.

Her car was hit in the driver's door as she pulled out with a green light.

When Lace returned to the living room after answering the phone, her face was white. James felt himself bracing even before he heard her words.

"Rae's been in an accident."

Chapter Thirteen

It was an indication of how badly Rae was hurt that there were two surgeons who joined them in the waiting room, both men still in surgical greens.

James watched them from his seat, his hands tightly held together, his elbows braced on his knees. He leaned forward, searching their faces for the truth. He looked at them and knew it was going to be bad.

Fear gripped his body as he read the news in the men's faces.

Dave wrapped his arm around Lace's shoulders.

"The worst injury is a fracture in the back of her neck, just above the fourth vertebra. She's in very critical condition. We've got her stabilized, but it's going to be a long night. As the swelling around her spine goes down, we'll know how much movement and sensation she'll get back. When she was brought into the emergency room, she had no sensation or movement of any kind below her neck and she was having severe trouble breathing."

"She's going to live?" Dave demanded.

The doctor hesitated.

"She's also got broken ribs, a collapsed lung, a dislocated shoulder. She's started to run a temperature. None of those injuries is life threatening, but the shock is a problem. We will know a lot more in twenty-four hours."

"She'll be out of recovery and moved to ICU in another hour," the other surgeon said. "We'll take it day by day. Don't assume the worst or the best. Reality is likely going to lie somewhere between the two."

The intensive care unit had a waiting room with couches as well as chairs, a coffee stand in the corner of the room. Dave paced, and Lace used the phone, calling friends to let them know what had happened. James sat on the couch fighting the pain and fighting the panic.

She had to be okay. She just had to be.

Rae had worked herself to the point of exhaustion, having been at the office by 5:00 a.m., not leaving until 9:00 p.m. She had stopped to buy a gallon of milk at the store on the way home. The accident had happened at a busy intersection less than four blocks from her house, her car hit on the driver's side by another vehicle. No one was quite sure what had caused the accident.

James felt like it was his fault.

She was paralyzed, she had broken ribs, a collapsed lung, a dislocated shoulder. It should have been him, not her.

His mom, Patricia, Kevin, all came to join the silent vigil. Patricia came over and hugged him. It hurt his ribs and helped his heart.

"She'll be okay, James."

James nodded, wishing he could share his sister's optimism.

It was almost two hours before Rae was moved to the ICU and they had the first chance to see her, only five minutes each hour, only one of them at a time. James didn't ask to be the first. He wanted to, but the situation was complex at best, for he carried the guilt of knowing his actions had contributed to her fatigue. Lace and Dave looked at each other and took pity on him, sending him with the nurse.

James stepped into the quiet room, afraid of the worst. Rae was in a steel brace to keep her neck still, a respirator breathing for her. They hadn't mentioned how badly her face had been bruised.

"Hey, lady," he whispered softly, fighting the tears.

He eased her lax hand into his, very gently stroked her hair. "I hear you're having a rough night, so I came to keep you company," he said softly. "Lace and Dave are here to see you, too."

He kept stroking her hair, talking softly, fighting the tears that wanted to fall. She was a mess.

He didn't care.

He didn't care if she could walk or move. He loved her. He didn't care what stuff she could no longer do.

He realized in that instant what she had meant when she said she didn't care how much energy he had. Love really did make the limitations irrelevant.

A few of the tears slipped across his smile. "Rae, I love you. Everything is going to be all right. Just keep fighting, okay?"

He tenderly brushed back the hair from her forehead, uncovering yet another ugly bruise. He tried to stop the smile that refused to be contained; it was smile or cry. "Honey, you really did do a good job this time. I don't think black and blue are your best colors," he quipped gently. "Can you open your eyes for me?"

It took her a few moments, but her eyelashes fluttered open.

He tightened his hold on her hand but realized with a sinking tightness in his chest that she could not feel it.

He touched her cheek. She could not speak with the respirator, but he could see the emotion in her eyes; the fear, the pain, the confusion. "You're going to be all right, honey. I love you and everything is going to be okay," he said softly.

Her face stiffened at the respirator and he carefully soothed out the tension. "Don't fight it, honey, your body just needs time to heal. Let it."

Slowly he saw her relax.

"That's better. Lace and Dave are here, too. We're going to keep you company tonight."

Her eyes blinked. They suddenly welled with tears and he shifted, ignoring the burning pain in his back, reaching forward with both hands to gently touch her bruised cheeks, wipe away the tears, careful to avoid the bandage on her neck. "You're going to be okay, Rae. Please, don't cry. I know it's scary, but we're here, we're not going to leave you."

The panic in her eyes… It scared him, because she was so desperately frightened. She had realized she couldn't move. "Rae, you've got a small fracture just above the fourth vertebra in your neck. It's the swelling that is causing the paralysis."

Her eyes went dark.

"It's temporary, Rae. The swelling will go down. All your injuries will heal."

He held her face, held her eyes with his, until she

accepted the hope he offered, until she finally released the panic and trusted him. She blinked and he very gently wiped away the tears.

"Try to sleep, Rae. I promise, we'll be here through the night. I love you."

Her eyes drifted closed, the tears still slowly trickling down her face.

Dawn came slowly, tingeing the sky with a brush of pink. James eased the coffeepot back onto the warmer plate. One of the hospital volunteers had brought in muffins and bagels. James looked at the platter. He should eat, but there was no way he could.

He carried the coffee cup with him back to the couch.

Lace was asleep.

It had been a difficult night, the waiting, the lack of news. Rae was getting worse, that was apparent. Each visit saw the temperature higher, her eyes more clouded, the distress more apparent.

He was afraid. Afraid like he had never been before in his life.

The doctors were coming in more often—a bad sign.

"Did you reach Jack?" James asked as Dave came back into the waiting room.

"Yes. The business is taken care of, at least for the next few days."

Dave looked as burned out as James felt. A night without sleep was taking its toll. He had sent his mom and sister home shortly after 1:00 a.m., asked Kevin to drive them. Patricia especially needed to sleep.

James looked at the clock. Another ten minutes before they could see Rae again.

* * *

Dave went in to see her first, they had been rotating each hour. James could see the distress on his face when he returned. He was obviously shaken.

"James, she's not doing well. I'm going to wake up Lace."

James's hand involuntarily clenched around the cane his weight rested on. Waking up Lace... He moved through the doorway to the ICU, needing desperately to see Rae.

He knew. As soon as he saw her, he knew.

The nurse with her finished her task, touched his arm. "Talk to her. It will help," she said softly.

Her temperature had shot up.

She no longer opened her eyes. It wasn't because she was sleeping.

He stroked her cheek, feeling the heat radiating off her body. They were using ice to try to give her some relief.

"Rae, I know it has got to be so hard right now, to breathe, to want to fight. Rae, you need to fight. Don't let this injury win."

What did she have to fight for? A job that wore her out? A man who had walked away from her, not understanding the truth?

"Rae, I love you. Please, fight off this shock. I know you can do it."

She looked so fragile, so broken.

He was afraid that it was not only her body that was broken, but also her spirit.

James napped awkwardly in a chair throughout the morning, catching ten minutes here, twenty minutes there, enough to keep him going.

He had aged ten years in one night.

There was no improvement in her condition.

The hardest thing to accept was the fact that Rae was holding on only by a thread.

There was a flutter developing in her heart rate, a wandering missing beat. James had seen it occur, watching the monitors, and the sight of that momentary flat line had been horrifying.

Her temperature was holding at 103 degrees.

God, I've been trying to pray for the last several hours and I simply don't have the words. My heart is breaking. She's so badly hurt. Don't take her away, God. Give me another chance. Please.

He came awake with a start, someone lightly shaking his shoulder.

It was Lace.

"Sorry, James, but I thought you would want to see her."

Through the exhaustion, James saw the smile. "She's awake."

The smile widened as Lace nodded. "She's awake. The fever is down to a hundred and one."

James struggled to get up. His body rebelled at the movement, threatening to send him crashing to floor. Lace steadied him.

"Thanks," he said, grateful for the help.

"Go see her. She's still got that look of panic in her eyes. I don't think she remembers much of what's been going on around her."

He entered her room and walked to the side of her bed. "Hey, lady. How are you doing?"

He moved into her line of sight and saw the tension in her face start to relax.

"I'm glad to see you awake," he whispered, gently stroking her cheek. She was still flushed, her body hot, but not as dangerous as it had been an hour ago.

With the paralysis and the brace holding her head, she had no movement of any kind. The respirator breathed for her, steady, constant, no variation. He could see the fear in her eyes, and the pain.

"Do you remember me saying I love you?"

Her eyes looked troubled. She had not remembered.

He smiled softly. "I love you, Rae." He brushed the hair back from her forehead, leaned forward to gently kiss her. "Keep fighting to heal. I'm not going anywhere."

"I know what you meant about pain being a malicious enemy." Her lips were white with the agony of having the dressing of the burn on her neck changed.

They had removed the respirator that morning.

James tightened his hold on her hand, wishing she could feel it. He carefully wiped away the tears on her face. "Hang in there, the pain will ease off."

She couldn't feel ninety percent of her body and where did she get burned? Someplace she *could* feel. He hated the maliciousness of this accident.

She had slept most of the day.

He had tried to rest, trading places with Lace and Dave regularly, but it had not happened. His own body ached. He didn't care. He wasn't leaving.

"They said seventy-two hours?"

"Rae, you've got a long way to go before the swelling comes down and you know something definite. Don't borrow trouble."

"It's been almost three days, James."

"And the scans this morning showed little reduction in the swelling. Wait it out."

She tried to laugh. "I wasn't praying for patience."

He gently wiped the tears away from her eyes. She had cried more in the last three days than he had seen her do in their entire relationship. She had cause. He eased forward to kiss her forehead, wishing so hard for God to answer his prayer. "I know it's hard," he whispered. "You can make it."

"Tell me again."

"I love you. I'm always going to love you."

She was biting her bottom lip. He gently stopped her. "What do you need to ask?" He hated the pain he saw in her eyes, the uncertainty.

"Even if there is no change?" she whispered.

She had risked her heart to ask that question. James felt a tear slide down his own cheek. His finger rubbed her chin. "Even if there is no change."

Chapter Fourteen

They put the Christmas tree on the table where she could see it. It had been the nurse's suggestion—something for Rae to look at as she fought to keep her spirits up. It was porcelain, the lights blinking different colors.

Four days, and no change.

Rae was desperately afraid. They all were.

Christmas Eve last night had been a time to pray for her and hope for the best.

"I'm sorry I didn't get you anything," Rae said, breaking the tension and making the group of them laugh.

"You always were a Christmas Eve shopper," Lace replied. "Would you like me to be your hands?" she offered softly. They had brought in Rae's stocking. It was filled with little gifts. Most of them made her laugh, for they had been bought with that in mind.

The little white dog like Justin with a red heart for a tag made her cry.

"We couldn't smuggle in the puppy, so we had to improvise," James told her, brushing away the tears.

"It's very nice. Thank you," she whispered, choking on the words. "How is he?"

"Staying with Emily and Tom. Missing you."

"She moved her toes!"

James felt his heart lurch as Lace stopped in front of him. He was sitting in the ICU waiting room, weary beyond belief, fighting the grief, trying to pray. He looked at Lace and it took a moment for her words and grin to sink in. "She moved."

"She moved. Both feet. You should have seen her smile. Come on, you need to see her." Lace offered a hand and James took it, his wrist flaring in pain, his joints fighting the movement.

His smile began slowly, cautiously. He had been at the hospital for six days, had left only to change, take a shower, catch a few moments of sleep. He had never felt such a deep loss of hope. The obstacles they faced were so deep; if she didn't improve, she would need so much help that would be beyond him to provide.

She had moved.

The nurses let them enter the ICU together.

James stopped by the door, for Rae had two doctors with her. He stayed and listened as the doctors reviewed how much improvement had occurred. It was slight; she could move her toes and she had feeling in her hands. The paralysis had a long way to go before it faded, but both doctors were smiling.

James crossed over to the bedside when the doctors finished, moving into Rae's line of sight. "I hear you've got news." He slipped her hand carefully into his and squeezed it.

Her smile was wide, and there were tears in her eyes—finally tears of joy. "I can feel your hand, I can move, just a little. I was so afraid none of it would come back."

James pulled a chair over, sitting down to take the strain off his ankles.

"I was so scared."

"I know you were, Rae." He gently brushed her hair back from her face.

"You look awfully tired, James."

He smiled. "I've got a lifetime to sleep. I love you, Rae."

"I love you, too," she whispered back.

"What else do you think she will want?" It felt uncomfortable walking through Rae's home, packing for her.

"I'll get her book. See if you can find her Bible. It's normally on her bedside table," Dave replied.

James nodded and walked upstairs, keeping a firm grip on the staircase railing. The house was exactly how Rae had left it the morning she left for work and didn't return. Dishes from dinner the night before had been left in the sink, the bathroom counter was still cluttered, and bills she had planned to mail were sitting on her desk. He had a disquieting thought; it would be like this if she had died; walking into her life as she had left it.

She had made her bed. Clothes she had considered and chosen not to wear still lay across the chair arm.

James found her Bible and her diary resting on the pillow of her bed. She must have had devotions that morning and dropped the books there. He picked up the Bible, its leather cover cool and worn. He had seen her with this Bible in her hand on so many occasions. He could see the shadow of her handprint worn into the leather from the oil of her skin. Her grip was smaller than his.

The Bible fell open to Psalm 37 showing how frequently she smoothed this spot in the spine. Rae was one to highlight and underline and make notes.

It was comforting to get a glimpse into her real life. She could never have known someone would see her home as she left it that morning. She had devotions because she had chosen to; in the normal course of events, no one would have ever seen the evidence.

He picked up her diary, figuring she would appreciate having it, as well.

The picture of Leo was gone.

James felt his hand tighten around the books he held.

The picture of Leo and the engagement ring were gone. She had done it sometime in the past, before this accident and his words "I love you."

When had she done it? When they'd started to date? In the weeks that followed?

It had to have been before he broke up the relationship—before he announced they could just be friends.

He looked at the empty spot on the bedside table and finally felt hope.

He knew how badly he had damaged their relationship. He had backed away because his health was not improving. He could feel the sinking fear in his gut that Rae might decide to do the same thing. Even though she said "I love you," it was far different from saying she would accept a relationship again, consider marrying him. She could move her toes slightly, could feel someone holding her hand. It was still a formidably long way from being totally recovered.

The doctors were being cautiously optimistic. The

swelling was still there, lessening a little more each day. What they didn't know was how far the recovery would go.

He was afraid of what Rae might decide to do.

What if the accident left her in a wheelchair? What if she got mobility back in her right hand but not her left? Her spine had taken a severe blow—the fracture had cut into the nerves. What they didn't know was what would heal and what was permanently damaged. It was an ugly circumstance to consider.

He was ready to deal with it; he knew he could adapt to whatever the final outcome was. The question was, could Rae? If she remained partially paralyzed, would it be her choice this time to leave the relationship just friends?

It was difficult, watching physical therapy. She was out of intensive care, in a private room in the rehabilitation wing of the hospital. The paralysis persisted. The swelling still lingered. There was no determining which muscles in her back, arms and legs obeyed her wishes and which ones still did not get the message to move.

The broken ribs hurt. She was constantly fighting a headache. Because she wasn't able to move easily, her body throbbed with pain from lying in one position for too long.

James felt for her and wished there was something he could do.

He sat on the far side of the room and watched as the physical therapist worked on helping her get motion in her arms. He could see the strain on Rae's face as she tried to coordinate the muscles in her shoulders and upper arms to get the movement she wanted. It was difficult—lying flat on your back, head in a brace to prevent your neck moving, knowing you had to battle to raise your arms.

After fifteen minutes the therapist declared the day a success and spent several minutes talking with a discouraged Rae to explain the improvements that were occurring.

James could see the improvement, too. Rae was getting better. It was slow, but it was definitely there.

After the therapist left, James moved back to Rae's bedside. "You are getting better," he confirmed.

She wanted to reply with something sharp, but bit back her words. James couldn't blame her for the bad mood.

"Would you like to get some sleep, talk for a while, have me pick up reading where I left off?" he asked, keeping his voice neutral.

She sighed. "Finish the book."

James studied her face, finally nodded. He picked up the suspense novel he had been reading to her, pulled the chair back to her bedside. "Is the mirror angle okay?"

"Yes."

She hated the mirror. Positioned over her, it let her see the room while she was flat on her back. She really hated it. James reached over and gently squeezed her hand, didn't let go of it as he used one hand to find the page they were on in the book. He began reading.

It took her several minutes, but she turned her hand over to grip his.

Rae was able to move now, but only with great care. The physical therapist had had her on her feet yesterday, a reality that had caused her an immense amount of vertigo. The exhaustion after therapy had caused her to sleep through the afternoon. James had sat with her, reading a book, watching for any signs of the nightmare returning.

She had been dreaming about the accident recently, waking terrified, reliving the moment she had turned her head and seen the headlights right there, the instant before the car had slammed into her driver-side door. She had no memory of the accident past that point; didn't remember the emergency room, nor much from the first couple days in the ICU. James wished her memory had erased those first few moments before the accident, as well.

The first time the dream had happened, her heart rate had jumped to almost one hundred sixty beats per minute in only a few seconds. The nurse had seen it happen and shaken her awake. The doctors told her the dream would fade in intensity with time. James preferred to be there to shake her awake rather than let her complete the dream.

"She's bored."

James laughed at Lace's conclusion, joining her at the hospital cafeteria table for a cup of coffee. "I brought the reference books she asked for with me. That should help serve as a distraction."

Rae was healing, feeling better, fighting to regain motion, mobility, strength. She was fighting her way back to health.

"I hear she goes down to the physical therapy room today," Lace commented.

James carefully picked up his coffee mug, knowing his hands might drop it if he didn't concentrate. He nodded. "They want to get her relearning to walk."

"Did the doctors say what yesterday's MRI results were?"

"The swelling below the fracture point is down but it's not gone. At least that implies more improvement is still likely."

The sunlight woke her up. Rae lifted her right hand into her line of sight, flexed the fingers into a fist, pleased to simply watch the movement.

She had grown accustomed to these quiet moments. It was early. Soon the nurse and physical therapist would be in, the steel locking pins would be turned and she would be mobile again, her neck held straight by a smaller brace.

She breathed in deeply, let it out slowly.

There were a few benefits to a severe accident. She got to lie in bed for a good portion of the day, nap, read, talk to friends. She had the strength and energy of a newborn kitten.

She knew what James felt like now.

Concern for how the business was doing tensed her body and she forced the thought away. She wasn't going to worry about something she had little control over. Jack was there. Her staff were good. Dave was going in each day for a couple of hours.

She touched her hand to her face, exploring how far the swelling had come down. She had nearly broken her jaw. It still ached.

"Good morning, Rae."

She smiled at the voice of her favorite nurse. "Good morning."

A few seconds later, the face connected with the voice appeared in her line of sight.

"Breakfast is coming."

"I'm hungry," Rae remarked, surprised.

Her new friend laughed. "Your body is letting you know it's tired of IVs."

Rae held her breath as the pins were released and she was once again mobile. It felt great to be free of the large brace, but also scary. Her neck was still fragile; a fall could paralyze her for life.

The nurse helped her dress in sweats, ease back onto the bed. She was grateful physical therapy was not for another hour and a half. It was hard, knowing she should be able to do so much more, to accept the fact that her body could not do it yet.

God, I understand so much better the frustration James must feel. It's the frustration of all the little things. The fact I have to concentrate to be able to take even a single step. The fact I can't put on a pair of shoes. The fact I can't reach the book I want to read without first carefully maneuvering to get in position. The fact I get tired so easily.

"Hey, lady. Like some company?" It was a soft question from her left.

Rae turned carefully, smiled. "I was just thinking about you."

James crossed the room. "Good thoughts, I hope."

"Hmm." She watched carefully as he moved, was grateful that his pain appeared to be under control this morning. He looked like he had finally had a decent night of sleep. She had been worried about him.

He kissed her good-morning. She was reluctant to end the kiss, a fact that made him laugh. "You taste minty," he remarked, reluctantly easing away. He sat down in the chair beside her bed.

She wrinkled her nose. "Toothpaste."

He grinned. "Whatever."

She loved his smile. She loved the fact he chose to spend his days with her.

"What, no James?"

Rae had gotten adept at using the mirror above her bed, finally accepting its reality. "Hi, Lace. I sent him home." It was late and she was flat on her back, not going to be moving again until morning.

Her friend appeared in her line of vision. "I know, I'm just teasing. I saw him in the lobby."

Rae smiled. She loved James and Dave, but there were times when a girlfriend was the one who really mattered. "He looks good, doesn't he?"

"Dave or James?"

Rae chuckled. "Yes, I noticed the change in Dave, too. James."

"I think the new medication is helping. He's in less pain."

"I think so, too. Have you and Dave been dating?"

"Do you expect me to kiss and tell?"

Rae grinned. "Absolutely."

"He brought lunch over yesterday. Yeah. I think we're really dating."

"This is good."

"This is murder. I can never tell when he's pulling my leg and when he's serious."

Lace pulled a chair over, settled into it, adjusted the mirror for Rae. "I bought the baby gift you wanted for Patricia. I had it wrapped for you. I'll leave it in the second drawer of the chest, with your purse."

"Thank you, Lace."

"No problem. It was fun to wander through the baby clothes. They've got some cute fashions."

Rae groaned.

"What?"

"I just had a vision of your children, Lace. Remember kids like to play in the dirt."

"I'm not planning to have children."

Rae looked at her; her friend smiled. "Okay, so the thought has crossed my mind a few times. Anything else you need? I'll swing by on my lunch hour tomorrow."

"Thanks, Lace. I can't think of anything else."

"Then I'll see you tomorrow," her friend promised.

"All right, Rae!"

Sweat was dripping from her body. She stood at the far end of the walkway, gripping the handbars to keep herself upright. James could see the muscles in her arms quiver with the excursion.

Her smile told its own story.

The physical therapist helped her turn and carefully sit down in the wheelchair he brought over.

Dave handed her a towel.

"You made it the distance, Rae."

James pushed himself to his feet, using the cane to steady his weight, relieve the pain in his ankles. "Another couple of days and you'll be doing stairs."

Rae grinned. "Of course."

The session over for the day, Dave pushed her wheelchair back to her room where the nurse kicked them out so Rae could have a shower and change clothes.

James took advantage of the time for a little physical therapy of his own, a walk around the hospital floor. It was hard to walk any distance, and the improvements he could see were scarce—a little less pain, a little more flexibility, but he kept to the daily routine. He was determined to be able to do ten laps in the pool this month.

"How is Rae's business doing, Dave?"

Dave grimaced. "Not good. I've been dreading her questions. Jack can manage for a few more days, maybe a few weeks, but it is becoming apparent how badly Rae needs to be back setting the direction."

"She can't."

Dave looked annoyed. "I know that. I also know she will kill me if the business loses too much ground."

The question was raised by Rae an hour later, as she sat in the hospital bed, the end raised to let her sit up. She wanted to know how Jack was doing.

Dave told her the truth.

James, sitting on the other side of the bed, reached forward and captured one of her hands, held it, stroked the back, tried to distract her. She stayed focused on Dave.

"Call Gary and ask if he'll loan us York for four weeks," she finally requested. "York reviewed our books when we wrote the contract to sell the business. He's Gary's right-hand man."

James froze. She had a contract written to sell the business?

"I'll call him when I get home," Dave promised.

James looked at the profusion of flowers sitting on the windowsill, his thoughts in turmoil. She had gotten as far as a contract to sell the business? When had this happened? The thought made him sick. She loved her work. It was followed by a worse thought. Had she done it because of him?

He eased her hand from his. "I'm going to get a soda. Would you two like anything?" He needed to get out of this room.

They both declined.

She had been planning to sell the business. James tried to absorb that fact as he walked the halls to the vending machine.

Her business was more than a career for Rae. It was part of who she was, just as being a builder was an intrinsic part of who he was. She had been planning to walk away from it?

He had come to the point where he was willing to accept that they could have a future together even with the limitations he faced. But he had been thinking about practical sacrifices that could make it possible. A live-in housekeeper. Limiting the type of activities they planned. He had never envisioned the sacrifice of her career.

Everything in him rebelled at the thought of her sacrificing her career, selling the business, for him.

He slammed his fist against the pop machine when the can refused to drop all the way to the slot. He gasped at the pain that coursed through his wrist, elbow and shoulder.

Reality.

He *hated* this disease.

She was working on her book.

James paused in the doorway to her room, watching her. She was able to be out of bed for longer and longer periods of time now. Sitting in the chair by the window, using the bed as a table to spread out her materials, she was writing on a legal pad of paper, her concentration intense.

He loved her.

He loved seeing her like this, absorbed in her work.

The latest MRI had shown the swelling was gone.

The paralysis that had been lingering in some of her muscles had finally faded. She had to move slowly, she had to concentrate on her actions, her strength and stamina had a long way to go, but the doctors were now talking about a full recovery being probable. Lace had brought in a cake so they could celebrate the news.

James quietly came into the room, set down the newspaper he had brought in for her.

Rae looked up, smiled. "How's Patricia doing?"

James took a seat, grateful to get off his feet. "Contractions are now every four minutes."

Rae set aside the pad of paper and glanced at the clock. "Six hours. But she's having a wonderful time."

"She kicked me out of the room," James replied, ruefully.

Rae laughed. "Poor boy."

"Emily and Tom are pleading for a chance to see you. Care to take a stroll downstairs?"

"Sure."

She looked at him, helpless. "Can you do my shoes?" With the brace, shoes were still impossible to do on her own.

James found the tennis shoes, knelt down, smiled at her as he tweaked her socks. "I think I kind of like you just a little bit helpless."

She swatted his shoulder. "Don't get used to it. It's temporary." She giggled as he tickled her left foot, tried to pull it back. "Behave, James."

He put on her shoes, tied the laces. He got up, braced his arms on her chair, leaned forward and kissed her. He loved her blush. "Come on, lady. Time to go get smothered by the family."

Emily and Tom had drawn pictures for her of Justin so that she could see they were taking good care of her dog. Rae gratefully sat down on the sofa James led her to, then turned her attention to the children. Excited about a new baby, they gave Rae a blow-by-blow account of how their mom had gone into labor while making breakfast.

His new niece was born at seven-thirty that evening. James stood beside Rae at the glass to the nursery, his arm around her waist, looking with her at the sleeping infant.

"She's beautiful."

James turned and leaned around the brace, softly kissed Rae's forehead, comforted by the fact she was with him. "Yes." They would have children of their own someday. He looked back at the sleeping infant. He wanted to be a dad. He wanted to be Rae's husband.

Rae settled carefully down on the couch, her muscles trembling at the expense of energy it had cost her to reach this point. Dave had a careful grip on her arm to make sure she didn't stumble.

She was home.

They had decorated. There were streamers, a cake, a big Welcome Home sign stretched across her entertainment center. Rae had never felt more cherished.

"Okay?"

Rae nodded in reply to the concerned query from James. She was exhausted, but that was to be expected. It was her first substantial trip since the accident. She was still trying to relax muscles that had tensed at the experience of riding in a car again.

James helped Rae off with her jacket. It caught on the neck collar she now wore and he carefully eased her forward, sliding his hands around to free the jacket.

Rae wanted to bury her face against his chest and just be held for a very long time. She missed being in his arms. It was the fatigue as well as the reality that she was finally home that was bringing the tears.

"Hey, what's wrong, honey?" The soft endearment made her catch back a sob. His hands gently gripped hers.

"I'm okay."

"Sure you are," Dave said lightly, tucking a handkerchief in her hands. "We're glad to have you home."

She sniffed back the tears. "I'm so glad to be here."

Lace was the practical one. "Here, this should help. One homemade, chocolate fudge shake."

Rae laughed and accepted the tall shake Lace had prepared. "Thank you, Lace."

"Dave, make yourself useful, go rescue the luggage," Lace told him.

Dave tweaked her hair, but did as she asked.

James settled down on a sofa beside Rae, very conscious of the fact he didn't want her trying to turn her head and strain her neck. "Come here," he urged softly, guiding her down to rest against his side. His ribs ached at the pressure and he didn't care. She was home and she was mobile and he loved her. The limitations they both faced were going to be overcome, somehow, someway.

"James?"

"Hmm?"

"I'm going to fall asleep on you."

His smile was gentle. "Go right ahead, Rae. I'll just drink your shake."

He felt her laughter.

* * *

"Rae, what was it like when your parents died?" James asked.

The question surprised Rae and she turned slightly. They were sitting on the couch in her living room watching the credits of a movie go by. She was almost asleep, resting comfortably against his shoulder, his arm around her waist, an afghan thrown across her legs. "Scary. Why do you want to know?"

"Curious, I guess. You never talk about them."

Rae let her eyes close again, too tired to fight the pull of sleep. "I remember my mom's friend Gloria came and got me from school. I remember wanting to go to my bedroom and find my doll, the one Mom had made for me. It's kind of a blur."

"What do you remember about them?"

"I remember them as being nice, loving, fun. When I got home from school, Mom would take a break from working on her book to join me in the kitchen and share a snack, normally cookies she had baked that morning. She wore perfume I really liked and used to braid my hair for me. Dad I remember as this big guy who used to pick me up and make me laugh. He liked to play checkers and read me stories."

James squeezed her hand. "Thanks."

She reluctantly pushed herself up, her hand going to protect her ribs.

"I'm sorry the ribs still hurt so bad," James said, his hands helping support her movements.

"So am I. I miss getting a hug," Rae said ruefully.

Justin was asleep on the floor in front of the couch. Rae eased over so she could get up without disturbing him. "Thanks for coming over tonight."

She sensed rather than saw James's disappointment

with her remark. He didn't say anything. She knew her decision to keep some distance between them was bothering him. She didn't have the luxury right now of giving him the commitment he wanted.

"Lace said she was bringing you over dinner tomorrow night?"

Rae nodded.

"Then I guess I'll see you Thursday to give you a ride to the hospital. Noon okay?"

"I can call a cab, James."

"Physical therapy is tough enough without worrying about transportation, too. I can work at a table there just as well as I can at home."

There was no way she was going to win the discussion. Rae nodded. "Noon will be fine. Thank you."

He kissed her at the door, a lingering kiss that was touched with regret. "Sleep well tonight, Rae."

"You too," she said softly.

She turned off the porch light after his car pulled out of the driveway, walked carefully upstairs. Her muscles still quivered when the fatigue was bad, threatening her balance.

God, please help James understand. I don't want to get hurt again. I'm too beat up to be able to handle a marriage. I don't know what I'm going to do about work. Please, help James understand. I can't be what he wants, not right now. I regret that, but it is the reality.

"Rae, you're keeping your distance and you really don't need to. James isn't looking for a hostess, housekeeper and cook."

Lace was over, helping Rae clean house.

Rae could do some of the picking up, load the dishwasher, but doing the laundry, mopping the floor, cleaning the bathroom, vacuuming—they were all still beyond her stamina.

They were working together on the kitchen, having finished the upstairs earlier. Rae lifted the corner of a Tupperwear lid, suspicious of what might be lurking inside. She was cleaning out the refrigerator. "Lace, I know that. But just the logistics of planning a wedding, setting up house together, creating a workable routine are beyond me right now."

"So have a long engagement. Rae, he's miserable."

Rae set yet another container of spoiled food to discard in the sink. She had to lean heavily against the counter to wait for the pain in her back to subside. The accident had left her with a whole new appreciation for how much she had taken her body for granted. "He wants me at his place so he can take care of me." She breathed out in relief as the pain subsided, carefully reached for the next item on the refrigerator shelf.

"Is that so bad?"

Rae wrinkled her nose at something that was now green. "Yeah."

Kevin hesitated, holding the sledgehammer. "James, are you sure you want to do this?"

James closed his eyes, pinched the bridge of his nose, thought about it, reconsidered for about the ninth time. He nodded. "I'm sure."

Rae was going to need a walk-in closet. It was a minor detail, but it was important. He wanted her to feel at home here...if, no, *when* they had a future together.

He had to keep that hope alive.

He was incredibly worried that she was going to

continue to keep her distance, not allow the relationship to go forward. She was not willing to let him get close while she was less than fully recovered. She fought the muscles that refused to do her bidding. She fought a body that ached with pain. How well he understood her motivations—a misplaced belief that love would not knowingly place her burden on him. It was the same thing he had done to her.

They were both wrong.

He just had to convince her of that.

Somehow he had to find a way to get her to trust him again, risk a relationship, despite her limitations, despite his.

It took all the faith he had to hold on to that hope.

Kevin knocked out the wall.

"Rae, can I come in?"

James saw her move to rise from where she lay on the couch. "No, don't get up."

He joined her in her living room, took a seat across from her, lowered his cane to the floor. Rae did not look pleased to see him. James chose to ignore it. Justin came over to greet him. He reached down to gently tug the puppy's ears. "Hard day?"

She ran her hand through her hair. "Lace and I went grocery shopping. I don't think I'll do that again soon."

James could see the tremor in her hand from the fatigue. "Some days you will have more energy than others. It will improve with time."

"I called it quits before we got to the ice cream. Now I wish we had started at the frozen foods and worked toward the vegetables, rather than the other way around."

James understood exactly what she meant. "I was going to see if you wanted to go out this evening, but I'll ask that another night. I'll fix us dinner here."

"You don't need to do that."

Interesting tone. He hadn't heard this one before. "I'm going to anyway," he replied, his voice neutral but determined. "Would it help to nap for a couple hours, shake the fatigue?"

"Probably. I don't want to."

James grinned, he couldn't help it. "Rebellion. This is good."

Rae laughed against her will.

James walked into her kitchen only to find it was a mess. It made him stop, rather stunned; he turned and looked back to the other room, frowning heavily. She was hurting a lot more than she was willing to let on. The rebellion must have begun earlier in the day. Lace would have instinctively moved to clean the kitchen for her. It was not like Rae to toss her best friend out of the house and it would have taken that to get Lace to leave.

James poured her a glass of juice and brought it to her. "Want me to dial Lace so you can apologize?"

She looked rather mutinous as she took the glass. "It's a private fight."

He didn't move from his position standing beside the couch. She felt miserable, it didn't take a rocket scientist to see that; miserable and close to tears, and angry at the entire world. "Her work, home or cell phone number?"

"Home," Rae finally said softly.

James found the cordless phone on the third step of the staircase, and also brought her a box of tissues.

"Lace? It's James. Rae would like to talk to you."

Lace sounded as if she had been crying, a fact that made James all the more troubled. James handed Rae the phone, set the tissue box within her reach, and left the room to give her some privacy.

It took about twenty minutes to get the kitchen back in shape. After an inspection of the refrigerator contents, he settled on broiled fish for dinner.

He heard her come to the doorway and quietly set the phone down on the counter. He gave her a moment before he looked up from the asparagus he was cutting. She looked awful after she had been crying. "Everything okay now?" he asked softly, hurting for her.

She nodded. Sniffed. "What did you find?" Her voice was husky.

"Broiled trout, baked potato, asparagus. Sound okay?"

"Yes."

She sounded so incredibly…sad. Everything wasn't okay, she was just stuffing the pain. He set down the knife and dried his hands. She was resting against the doorjamb, her hand cradling her ribs, her energy spent. He tipped her chin up, studied her face, saw so much pain in her eyes. He put his arms around her and pulled her gently against him, taking her weight, easing her head down against his chest. He held her stiff frame and gently rubbed her back. Her body finally softened against him.

He felt the first sob ripple through her. "You must hate me!"

The emotion coming from her made him flinch even though he had known it was likely. "I don't hate you. I love you," he said calmly. "You're just tired, honey, that's all," he reassured quietly, threading his fingers through her hair. She was exhausted way past the point she could function.

It took a focused effort of all his own reserves, but he leaned down and picked her up. Upstairs was out of his possibility, so he carried her into the living room. He held her through the bout of tears, until the emotion ran its course and she finally cried herself to sleep.

He made her as comfortable on the couch as he could, quietly reassured Justin, and went to fix himself a sandwich. He wasn't going anywhere.

The phone rang. James caught it before the second ring, checking carefully to see if it had woken Rae. It was Dave. James carried the phone with him to the kitchen. "What's up?"

"I'm at Lace's place. How's Rae doing, James?"

"She'll be fine," James assured him with a confidence he didn't totally feel. "She just got overtired and her ribs are really hurting."

"Lace said Rae tripped on the stairs when she was carrying in the groceries. That was what triggered the argument, apparently. I gather she's still refusing to see the doctor?"

James's hand tightened on the phone. "Rae didn't mention she fell," he replied. His voice was level, but he could feel the anger building inside him. That lovable, crazy, irresponsible lady. She could be really hurt and she hadn't said anything.

He left the phone on the counter after saying goodbye to Dave and strode with purpose back into the living room.

"Rae, there are times I really regret you are so stubborn," he whispered softly, tucking the afghan around her. He sighed and debated what he should do.

Let it go. It wasn't worth a fight.

She stirred shortly after 10:00 p.m. Without being asked, he handed her two aspirin.

"Thank you."

He sat down beside her on the couch and gently brushed her hair back from her face. "You need to eat something, Rae. Feel up to it?"

She seemed surprised when she nodded. "I'm hungry."

He smiled. "Good."

She moved to get up, winced.

"Ribs hurt?" he asked.

She looked up at him sharply and reluctantly nodded. She wanted to know if he knew about her fall but she wasn't going to ask him. He slid a hand under her elbow and carefully helped her sit up.

"I'm sorry it's so late."

"Don't worry about it. I've been reading a good book."

She looked over to the chair he had been sitting in, looked back at him. He had been reading her recently written chapters of the manuscript.

"Are they any good?"

He smiled. "Yes."

He resumed fixing the dinner that had been interrupted hours before. He soon heard her move through the house, and then he heard water running in the bathroom.

She came back with her face washed, her hair brushed. She helped him set the table.

He broiled the trout to the point it flaked apart,

found sour cream and chives for the baked potatoes. It was a quiet meal, Rae asking only a few questions about his day. James was content to sit and watch her when he finished his dinner before her. He was glad to see she had meant it when she said she was hungry, and especially glad to see she ate a decent amount.

She helped him carry dishes from the dining room back to the kitchen when they were done eating.

He was reaching for the dish soap to clean the broiler when she paused his movements, resting her hand against his forearm. "Thank you, James."

He studied the serious expression in her eyes, then he smiled. The mood needed to be lightened around here. He ruffled her hair. "You're welcome."

He hummed softly as he washed the pans and she cleared the rest of the table.

"I didn't crack a rib, I'm sure of it."

He looked up from the pan he was rinsing off. "An X-ray could tell you that for certain." He didn't know what he wanted to do, accept her opinion or push the matter.

She shrugged. "I'm clumsy these days, I pick up bruises."

He understood instantly, the moment he saw that shrug.

She was embarrassed.

She was embarrassed about the fact she was not as steady on her feet as she had been before.

"I'll buy you a cane," he replied lightly. "What's your favorite color?"

She wrinkled her nose at him. "Remind me not to come to you for sympathy."

He tugged her over with one hand. "You'll get sym-

pathy, even empathy. Just not pity." He kissed the tip
of her nose. "Deal?"

She kissed him back, her arm sliding around his
waist. "Deal."

She adapted to limitations better than he did.

James watched Rae carry in her briefcase from the
car, noticed the way she moved, using the cane he had
bought her to keep her balance as she came up the
steps. The unsteadiness was not improving with time,
was still made worse with fatigue. James was worried
about her going back to work, but also dreading the
options she was considering.

They had spent the morning installing a second
handrail for her staircase, then she had gone to meet
Gary, Dave and York for lunch, while he painted the
trim.

He held open the front door for her.

She smiled as she got to the top of the stairs,
slightly out of breath. "Thanks."

"You're welcome."

She paused at the bottom of the stairs. "This looks
nice, James."

James agreed. The fresh coat of paint looked
good. "I was just cleaning the brushes," he remarked,
moving back to the kitchen. Rae joined him. "How did
the lunch go?" he asked, turning back on the water.

Rae found a cold soda on the bottom shelf of the
fridge and offered him one also. When he nodded,
she opened it for him, then set it down on the counter beside him. She leaned against the cabinets beside
him. "Will you really be upset with me if I sell the
business?"

James didn't know how to answer that question. He

hated the idea, but he certainly understood why she was considering it. "I wouldn't want you to do it because of me, Rae," he finally said.

She nodded, staring at the soda can for a long time. "The business doesn't leave time for a relationship, James. That's the bottom line of it. I have seen you more since the accident than I did for all the months before it."

She sighed and turned so she could touch his arm. "You still want to be a builder, but the illness says you can't right now. For the first time, I'm facing a limitation that says the business may not be the best thing for me to do. I want to sell the business so I can avoid the fatigue, so I can continue to have time to write. But I have to be honest, our relationship is also one of the reasons I want to sell. I don't want to give up my time with you."

James dried his hands, reached over and pulled her into a hug, careful of her healing ribs. "Rae, forget what I said in the past about your schedule and my energy. I'm not going anywhere. I love you. Do you really want to sell the business? Are you going to regret it in six months?"

Her hands slipped up to his shoulders. "I really want to sell the business."

"Then sell it." He leaned down and kissed her. "It *will* make a honeymoon easier to schedule," he offered. James watched her blush and found it endearing. He tipped her chin up with one finger, unable to contain his soft laughter. "Rae, I've just been waiting for you to recover before I hit you with my timetable. Marry me. I've got the chapel reserved for the twenty-fifth."

She pushed away from him. "Four weeks?"

"See any reason to wait?"

"Besides a dress, invitations, flowers and the rest... no."

He leaned down and kissed her again, felt her hands curl into his shirt as she leaned into him. He reluctantly broke the kiss so they could breathe. "Good. Lace, Patricia and my mom will help with the arrangements."

Her arms slid around his waist so she could carefully hug him. "I can't believe you already reserved the chapel."

He chuckled. "I reserved it for the last Saturday of every month for the rest of the year," he assured her. "You're going to marry me."

He felt her laughter. "Were you nervous I would say no?"

"With Lace and Dave around? It was never a possibility." He smiled as he brushed her hair back from her face. "But Dave figured you might play hard to get."

She leaned back. "Did he?"

"Now Rae, go gentle with him. I figure his turn is coming with Lace."

"Absolutely."

"I love you, Rae. I'm sorry it took an accident to make me realize what I was walking away from."

She gently traced his face with her hand, her expression serious. "It's okay. I understand better what it is like to have good days and bad days. If you can put up with my cooking, I can adapt to a slower pace of life and quiet evenings."

"You're being kind."

"No, I'm not. I love you."

James kissed her. "Not as much as I love you."

Rae grinned and rested her hands on his chest. "How much do you love me, on a scale of one to a hundred?"

James considered the question, smiling at her. "Maybe…about ninety-nine."

"What?"

She giggled as he teased her with another kiss.

"I still love Africa," he replied, being fair.

"Would you show it to me someday? Your clinics and your kids?"

James took his time with the next kiss. "It would be my pleasure."

* * * * *

Dear Reader,

Thank you for reading *God's Gift*. It holds a special place in my heart as my second book published. This was a good story to write, for it reaffirmed hope that love can overcome any challenge. Everyone faces unexpected troubles in life, and how we respond and cope is one way we show our faith. God is still in control.

I would love to hear from you. You can find me online at www.deehenderson.com, email me at dee@deehenderson.com or write me c/o Love Inspired Books, 233 Broadway, Ste. 1001, New York, NY 10279.

Sincerely,

Dee Henderson

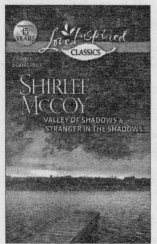

REQUEST YOUR FREE BOOKS!

2 FREE INSPIRATIONAL NOVELS
PLUS 2
FREE
MYSTERY GIFTS

Louisa Morgan loves being around children.
So when she has the opportunity to tutor bedridden Ellie,
she's determined to bring joy back into the motherless
girl's world. Can she also help Ellie's father open his
heart again? Read on for a sneak peek of

THE COWBOY FATHER

by Linda Ford,
available February 2012 from Love Inspired Historical.

Why had Louisa thought she could do this job? A bubble of self-pity whispered she was totally useless, but Louisa ignored it. She wasn't useless. She could help Ellie if the child allowed it.

Emmet walked her out, waiting until they were out of earshot to speak. "I sense you and Ellie are not getting along."

"Ellie has lost her freedom. On top of that, everything is new. Familiar things are gone. Her only defense is to exert what little independence she has left. I believe she will soon tire of it and find there are more enjoyable ways to pass the time."

He looked doubtful. Louisa feared he would tell her not to return. But after several seconds' consideration, he sighed heavily. "You're right about one thing. She's lost everything. She can hardly be blamed for feeling out of sorts."

"She hasn't lost everything, though." Her words were quiet, coming from a place full of certainty that Emmet was more than enough for this child. "She has you."

"She'll always have me. As long as I live." He clenched his fists. "And I fully intend to raise her in such a way that even if something happened to me, she would never feel like I was gone. I'd be in her thoughts and in her actions every day."

Peace filled Louisa. "Exactly what my father did."

Their gazes connected, forged a single thought about fathers and daughters…how each needed the other. How sweet the relationship was.

Louisa tipped her head away first. "I'll see you tomorrow."

Emmet nodded. "Until tomorrow then."

She climbed behind the wheel of their automobile and turned toward home. She admired Emmet's devotion to his child. It reminded her of the love her own father had lavished on Louisa and her sisters. Louisa smiled as fond memories of her father filled her thoughts. Ellie was a fortunate child to know such love.

Louisa understands what both father and daughter are going through. Will her compassion help them heal—and form a new family? Find out in
THE COWBOY FATHER
by Linda Ford, available February 14, 2012.

Love Inspired Books celebrates 15 years of inspirational romance in 2012! February puts the spotlight on Love Inspired Historical, with each book celebrating family and the special place it has in our hearts. Be sure to pick up all four Love Inspired Historical stories, available February 14, wherever books are sold.